PRAISE 1

"With *Seven Summers*, Paige Toon breaks your heart then stitches it back together with expert hands. An emotional roller coaster about second chances, grief, and everlasting love, this book wrecked me in the best possible way."

—Carley Fortune, #1 *New York Times* bestselling author

"Nobody writes angst and joy and hope like Paige Toon."

—Christina Lauren, #1 *New York Times* bestselling author

"Paige Toon's romances are powerful and poignant and never fail to leave me clutching her book to my chest."

—Mia Sheridan, bestselling author of *Archer's Voice*

"Paige Toon writes the ultimate love stories: beautifully written, complex, and filled with longing."

—Annabel Monaghan, *USA Today* bestselling author of *Summer Romance*

"Paige Toon is the queen of heartrending love stories."

—Sophie Cousens, *New York Times* bestselling author of *This Time Next Year*

"Every Paige Toon romance is five stars. Her beautiful, emotional love stories sweep me away."   —Beth O'Leary, author of *The Flatshare*

"Toon urges us to risk everything, to never play it safe when it comes to the heart, and to know that caring is always, always, worth the cost."

—Caroline Leavitt, author of *Pictures of You* and *With or Without You*

"Toon's writing is emotional and riveting."

—Jill Santopolo, *New York Times* bestselling author of *The Light We Lost*

"Unique and moving."   —Josie Silver, author of *One Day in December*

WHAT IF I NEVER GET OVER YOU

Paige Toon

G. P. PUTNAM'S SONS
New York

PUTNAM
— EST. 1838 —

G. P. PUTNAM'S SONS

Publishers Since 1838

An imprint of Penguin Random House LLC

1745 Broadway, New York, NY 10019

penguinrandomhouse.com

Book design by Angie Boutin

Library of Congress Cataloging-in-Publication Data

Names: Toon, Paige, author.

Title: What if I never get over you / Paige Toon.

Description: New York: G. P. Putnam's Sons, 2025.

Identifiers: LCCN 2024029457 (print) | LCCN 2024029458 (ebook) |
ISBN 9780593718735 (trade paperback) | ISBN 9780593718742 (epub)

Subjects: LCGFT: Romance fiction. | Novels.

Classification: LCC PR6120.O58 W53 2025 (print) |
LCC PR6120.O58 (ebook) | DDC 823/.92—dc23/eng/20240202

LC record available at https://lccn.loc.gov/2024029457

LC ebook record available at https://lccn.loc.gov/2024029458

p.   cm.

Printed in the United States of America

1st Printing

The authorized representative in the EU for product safety and compliance is
Penguin Random House Ireland, Morrison Chambers, 32 Nassau Street,
Dublin D02 YH68, Ireland, https://eu-contact.penguin.ie.

For Hannah, my lovely friend. Thank you for always being there.

WHAT IF I
NEVER
GET OVER
YOU

PART ONE

1

"IS THIS SEAT TAKEN?"

I'm so caught up in the action on the page that it's an effort to drag my eyes from my book to the face of the guy in front of me. His hair falls in shaggy, dark gold waves to a defined jawline that hasn't seen a razor in days, but it's his warm, clear, light brown eyes that make my heart trip and stumble. I have no idea what he just read in my expression, but he does a small double take as our gazes collide.

"Go for it," I say, returning my eyes to the novel, though at the edge of my vision I watch him shrug a big army-green rucksack off his broad shoulders and drop it to the ground with a thud.

"Nice view from up here," he comments casually as he folds his tall frame into the seat.

We're on the crowded rooftop of a hostel in Lisbon, Portugal, under the shade of a bamboo canopy that's creating a barcode of light and dark stripes over the table. Across the adjacent terra-cotta-tiled rooftops looms a red suspension bridge carrying a steady hum of traffic from one side of the wide green river to the other, where a towering monument of Jesus Christ stands with his arms outstretched in the hazy late-afternoon sunshine. The bridge has Golden Gate vibes while the monument is directly inspired by Rio de Janeiro's Christ the Redeemer, as my earlier Google search revealed.

"I don't know if I'm in San Francisco or Brazil," I respond, reaching for my peach iced tea and taking a sip.

His small huff of laughter and lovely smile cause my glass to hitch against my bottom lip.

"I'm Ash," he says with the ease of someone who has had no trouble making friends on his travels.

"Ellie," I reply.

"Are you staying here too?" he asks.

"Yep." I give up on finishing the chapter and fold over the corner of my page.

"Sorry, I'm interrupting," he realizes as I close the book.

"It's fine."

"But you're right near the end," he notices.

"Two chapters and one page left," I confirm.

"I can just sit here while you finish."

The thought of this is so ludicrous that I laugh. His corresponding grin makes me feel giddy.

"Actually, I'm gonna grab a beer." He flattens his palms on the table. "Can I get you something? It's happy hour," he adds temptingly.

I hesitate for all of two seconds. "Go on, then, I'll have a rosé. Thanks. I owe you one."

I try to read while I'm waiting, but where minutes ago I was riveted, now I can't seem to digest the words. I glance over to Ash at the bar, standing with his back to me as the barman takes his order. My eyes skate over the breadth of his shoulders and along the length of his arms, lean and golden. He must be six foot three or four.

The irony of it hasn't escaped my notice: the fact that some-one is being nice to me right after I decided to quit interrailing. And not just any someone: *him*.

I grab my phone and tap out a quick text to Stella: I think I might have been thrown a curveball.

Ash returns to the table with our drinks. "Is it hard going?" he asks as I fold over the exact same corner as earlier and close my book.

"No, I'm just trying to stretch it out."

He reads the title aloud: "*A Court of Thorns and Roses*. What's it about?"

"It's about a girl who basically gets kidnapped by a sexy fa-erie," I reply with a grin. "My best friend recommended it."

"Sounds like the sort of thing *my* best friend used to read," he says fondly, taking a sip of his beer.

"Where are you from?" I ask as he brushes away the foam on his upper lip.

"Wales."

I'd guessed as much from his accent and the way he rolls his *r*'s. "Which part?"

"North Wales, near Wrexham. You?"

"North London."

"How long have you been in Lisbon?" The tip of his nose is sunburnt, which is oddly endearing.

"I've only just arrived."

"Same. Are you interrailing?"

"Yep."

"Where have you traveled from?"

"Coimbra, and before that, Porto," I tell him.

"You came across the north of Spain?"

"Yeah." I reach up to lift my hair from where it's clinging to my neck. It's after five, but the air is close and sticky.

"I came along the south," he replies, tracking the movement of my hand with his eyes. "I'm heading to Porto next."

"It's great—you'll love it. I'm off to the Algarve."

My parents are meeting me there, and a week later, I'll be flying home. The thought of this filled me with relief earlier, but now the reality is setting in and suddenly I feel flat.

"What's your favorite thing you've done so far?" Ash interrupts my thoughts.

"Um . . . Probably visiting my great-grandfather's war grave at Bayeux. It was surprisingly emotional."

"I'm pretty sure I've got a great-uncle who's buried there. Why was it *surprisingly* emotional?"

"I didn't think I'd be affected by it, I just thought I'd see a whole bunch of graves and feel, I don't know, *good* that I'd gone. But actually, the enormity of so many people losing their lives and one of those people being an ancestor of mine . . . My granddad was only a year old when his dad died. He came so close to not even existing, and if he hadn't, well, where would I be?" I shrug self-consciously, but he's staring at me with a small, steady smile on his face, seeming genuinely interested in what I have to say. This conversation is already so different to every other casual chat I've had while traveling.

"I wasn't even planning on going there," I admit, our intense eye contact making me feel edgy. "But it's definitely one of my highlights."

"What are your other highlights?" he asks.

I like the way he's looking at me and it's on the tip of my tongue to tell him about the château I visited in the Loire Valley, with its stunning formal gardens and the nearby zoo built out of a quarry where you could hand-feed giraffes. Or the bike ride I took on the Île de Ré near La Rochelle, or the bar I sat at, drinking sangria, overlooking San Sebastián's sparkling La Concha Bay. But the truth is that I was lonely as hell doing those things on my own and I can't quite bring myself to lie to him about how awesome it was.

"We should just exchange Instagram details," I reply lightly. "All my highlights are on there."

"*Great* idea. I'd *much* rather stare at a screen than speak to a fellow human." I laugh at his gentle sarcasm and his eyes crinkle at the corners as he says, "Alas, I don't have a phone. Or Instagram."

I give him a baffled look. "You don't have a phone? Have you lost it?"

He shakes his head and takes another sip of his beer, a smile playing about his lips. "No, it was a conscious decision to come away without one."

My jaw drops. "You've been traveling around Europe without a phone?"

He nods. "It's nice being off-grid."

"What about maps? And music? And calling home?" I ask with astonishment.

"I have paper maps," he replies, leaning back in his chair so his tanned face is out of the shade of the canopy. "And I use hostel phones to call home. I do miss music, though."

His eyes are the same color as the peach iced tea I've been drinking: they catch the sunlight too, and sparkle with it.

"Do you fancy getting something to eat?" he asks out of the blue.

Definitely been thrown a curveball . . .

———

"**I REALLY NEED** to go to a launderette tomorrow. This is my last clean dress," I say to Ash about my little black number as we wander along the cobbled streets of the LX Factory, between buildings plastered with posters and street art.

Our hostel is about three kilometers from the city center in an area that used to house a thriving textiles industry, but now the old warehouses have been converted into artsy shops, cafés, bars, galleries, and hip restaurants filled with beautiful people.

"Yeah, this is my last clean T-shirt," Ash replies.

And what a T-shirt it is. The apricot color brings out the golden tones of his skin.

"I think there's one around the corner from the hostel. Maybe we could go in the morning."

"Are you asking me on a *date*?" He slides me a sideways smile.

"You can come if you want." I'm trying to come off as flippant, but goddammit, I blush.

"I accept," he replies with amusement.

As we sit down at a restaurant with tables spilling out onto the pavement, it occurs to me that this is likely just another night to Ash; he will have connected with loads of people on his travels. He has good energy and a warm, easygoing nature. Tomorrow he'll probably meet someone else he'll want to spend the day with. The thought is sobering, but I steel myself against overthinking, not wanting to ruin tonight. I've spent so many evenings wandering vibrant cities alone, only to return to my hostel to listen to other backpackers talk and laugh with their friends. The loneliness has been crippling, yet I've missed Stella so viscerally that I haven't been able to find it in me to be sociable with strangers. Until tonight.

Now that I've called time on my travels, a weight has lifted. I feel happier and more relaxed knowing that I only have two more days to get through.

Lisbon is the perfect place to end my adventures. It's the city Stella most wanted to visit and I plan to tick off every item on her bucket list. She'll be with me in spirit, even if she can't be here in person.

"Have you got any other plans for tomorrow?" Ash asks after the waiter has taken our drinks order.

"Yeah, I pretty much have the next couple of days mapped out," I reply, pulling *A Court of Thorns and Roses* out of my bag.

"You brought your book out with you?" he asks with surprise.

He dropped his rucksack in his dorm room before we left the hostel and I had time to stash away my book too, but I don't like letting it out of my sight.

"It's kind of become my Lisbon travel guide," I explain. "My best friend, Stella, wrote a bunch of things to do here on the inside cover."

"Can I see?"

I turn the book round to face him, smiling as I remember how hectic Stella was when she wrote the list, scrambling around for a piece of paper for all of three seconds before writing on the first thing she could lay her hands on—the book she'd just lent me. It was so typical of her: never enough patience, never enough time.

Ash squints as he deciphers Stella's messy scrawl.

"The Initiation Well?" He looks up at me, hair falling into his eyes.

"It's in Sintra, at the Quinta da Regaleira."

"Oh, I've heard about that place. Doesn't it have an amazing Gothic spiral staircase?"

"Yes, that's the Initiation Well. It's not actually a well. It's the thing my friend was most excited about—it looks like something out of a fairy tale—but I've heard the gardens are beautiful too."

"I'd planned to check out Sintra. When are you going?" he asks.

"I thought the day after tomorrow."

He shoves his hair back. "Do you fancy going together?"

It's an effort to mask how pleased I am. "Sure."

He returns his attention to Stella's list. "The TimeOut Market . . . Castle of São Jorge . . . Yep, yep. What's Pavilhão Chinês?" he asks with a frown.

"It's a bar. It used to be an old grocery store, but now it's like a museum with a bunch of old toys and memorabilia that the owner collected. The waiters dress in fancy waistcoats and they play mostly eighties music." Stella's *favorite*. "I might go there to-morrow night." I lift a shoulder. "You're welcome to come."

"Thanks. Sounds fun." He smiles at me. "So did your friend—Stella?—not want to go interrailing with you?"

I shake my head and reach across the table for her book. "She couldn't," I murmur as I slip it back into my bag. "What about you? You didn't want to go traveling with friends?"

"That was the plan, but it didn't work out," he replies, scratch-ing his eyebrow and averting his gaze.

I have a feeling I'm not the only one who's being cagey here.

WE GO TO another rooftop bar after dinner that is even closer to the bridge, but the traffic noise is drowned out by loud music and the chatter of people.

When I return from the bathroom, Ash is standing with his elbows propped on the bar top, waiting to be served.

"I'll get these," I say. "You got the ones at the hostel."

"Yeah, but they were cheap as chips."

I jolt at the warm press of his fingers on my wrist as I attempt to retrieve my purse. He lets go to pull a wad of notes out of the pocket of his gray shorts.

"How much cash do you carry around?" I ask with alarm, distracted from the touch of his hand on my skin.

"I do have a bank card," he replies with a smile as he turns toward me, leaving one elbow resting on the bar top. "But it's become a bit of a challenge to see how far I can go without using it."

"So when that runs out . . ." I nod at his cash.

He shrugs. "I've been doing odd jobs where I can find them, sleeping on a few beaches to save money."

"What sort of jobs?" I'm intrigued at the thought of him working his way round Europe.

Part of what I like about interrailing, despite the loneliness, is that there are no airs and graces—everyone's in it together, pinching pennies, staying in youth hostels, and doing laundry in crappy launderettes. Ash is clearly at ease with this lifestyle and yet there's something about him that sets him apart from the crowd.

"Washing dishes, cleaning boats. I helped one guy fix his roof—saw him working on it as I was walking by and asked if he could use a hand. It's surprising how much work is out there if you look for it."

The bartender is ignoring us, but I don't mind. I love the gentle rise and fall of Ash's Welsh accent—I could listen to him talk for hours.

"That sounds stressful."

"It's actually been quite liberating."

I shake my head at him, smiling. I'm tall at five foot nine, but he still has a good half a foot on me. His extra height means that his eyes are downcast as they rest on mine. They seem a darker brown under the shade of his eyelashes.

The moment stretches on.

"What are you thinking right now?" I ask, surprising even myself as I let the question slip out.

He laughs and looks away before meeting my eyes again, an abashed tilt to his lips.

"You remind me of someone," he admits.

"Oh! Who?"

"She's not real," he replies. "I'm just trying to explain why I can't stop looking at you."

Butterflies burst into life inside me. "Okay, now I'm *really* intrigued."

His eyes dance under the glow of the festoon lights hanging above our heads. "She's a manga character."

"You think I look like a *cartoon* character?" I ask with faux outrage.

"Well, no." He frowns, but his lips continue to curve upward at the corners. "More like a comic-book character."

"Is there a difference?"

"Yeah. My friend Taran used to be into manga. He could have talked your ear off about it."

"Is this the same friend who likes fantasy?"

"The very same," he confirms with a nod and a small smile.

"You know you're going to have to show me this character you're talking about, don't you?"

I'm trying to sound flippant, but I'm still feeling a bit jittery about his earlier comment: *he can't stop looking at me!*

He shrugs. "I don't have a phone, so I can't look her up."

"Ah, but *I* do." I get it out and unlock it before passing it to him.

He smirks as he taps something into the search engine and scrolls for a moment before handing it back.

I stare at the character on the screen. She has flame-red hair with golden highlights, huge blue eyes framed by long dark lashes, and a pointed chin that is almost pixie-like. She's stunning.

I glance up at him. *Is this how he sees me?*

"*Okaaay*," I say with a laugh, screenshotting the image.

We meet each other's eyes again, just as the bartender finally materializes to take our order. My every nerve ending is on alert.

As Ash turns toward the bar, I become aware of just how hemmed in we are, how many people suddenly seem to be clamoring for space. A trickle of panic starts below my rib cage as someone presses against me from behind. I go rigid. I can't see his face, but I know it's a man.

Ash looks over his shoulder at me and freezes. "What's wrong? Hey, can you back up?" he asks sharply, looking over the top of my head at whoever is crowding me.

"Where am I supposed to go?" I hear a deep voice retort.

I come to life, making a break for it. There's a group of potted palms and tree ferns by the railings and I head straight for them through the crowd.

"Sorry," I gasp as Ash joins me.

"Are you all right?" he asks, touching his hand to my lower back.

I flinch and he immediately retreats, which makes me feel even more wretched.

"I just got a bit claustrophobic," I try to explain, struggling to catch my breath.

"Do you want to leave?" he asks.

I nod. "But we need to pay for our drinks," I say weakly.

"I'm sure they'll give them to someone else."

"I'm going to head back to the hostel, but you don't have to come."

He scoffs. "Fuck that. I'm walking you back."

My stomach warms at his protectiveness, but I point out: "I've been backpacking around Europe on my own for almost three weeks."

"That's your choice. This is mine." He nods toward the exit.

But it wasn't my choice, I think. I'm not interrailing on my own because I wanted to feel free and independent—although I had hoped I *would* feel those things when I finally made the decision to go. I'm alone because my best friend couldn't stick to the deal we made when we were seventeen.

My heart aches later as I text her: I miss you so much.

It's just another in a long line of messages that have gone unanswered.

2

ASH AND I AGREED TO MEET AT NINE FOR OUR LAUN-
derette run, but at nine thirty the next morning I'm still at
reception, with no sign of him. I'm more gutted than I thought I
would be, given that I'd prepared myself for disappointment. I
knew he'd have no trouble finding someone else to hang out with.

I stare down at my book, feeling miserable. It's taking monu-
mental willpower not to open it. I want to read the last chapter of
the last book Stella lent me tomorrow evening, on my final train
journey to the Algarve to meet up with my parents. I thought it
would be a symbolic way of rounding off the trip I'd looked forward to with my best friend for years.

Bracing myself against the sudden tightness in my chest, I
check my watch. I feel weirdly sick at the thought of not seeing
Ash again, but I'm just wasting time now. Doing laundry is already going to eat into too much of my day.

I really don't want to deal with the shitty comments that I
know will come if I meet up with my parents with a bag full of

dirty clothes, but am I being stupid? Is it worth sacrificing some of my last hours in Lisbon?

To hell with it. I get to my feet just as Ash tears into the lobby.

"You're still here," he gasps, staring at me with wide, panicked eyes.

My heart flips at the sight of him. He's clean-shaven, but his hair is a hot mess.

"I'm so sorry, I don't have an alarm," he quickly explains. "I've been waking up early, but I couldn't sleep last night and—fuck, I'm sorry I'm late."

"It's okay," I reply with a grin. "I was just about to leave. I've decided not to bother with laundry."

He nods. "Can you give me a sec to brush my teeth? I've literally just rolled out of bed. I showered last night, so I'll be fast. If . . . I mean, only if you don't mind me coming with you . . ."

I shake my head, the knots in my stomach loosening at the sound of his sweet hesitancy.

"I'll see you out front."

"I FEEL SO guilty about this," I admit with a laugh after the waiter has delivered our drinks and left us to it.

"I know, but sometimes a person just really needs a spaghetti carbonara," Ash replies with a grin, referencing the sudden craving I experienced when we walked past this place.

We're having lunch at an Italian restaurant on the outer perimeter of the TimeOut Market, under big umbrellas in the sunshine.

"Anyway, we've got Portuguese cuisine covered with the *pastéis de nata*," Ash points out, nodding at the paper bag full of custard tarts that's sitting on the table between us before staring at the colorful outdoor market across the road.

"See anything you like?" I ask after a moment.

"I should probably get a new shirt," he replies dryly, giving the armpit of yesterday's apricot T-shirt a quick sniff.

"I dare you to go Hawaiian."

He flashes me a grin.

"Maybe I should buy a new dress," I muse aloud as I feel sweat trickle down my back.

"I really am sorry for oversleeping," Ash apologizes again as he sits forward and props his elbows on the table. "Thanks for waiting for me."

"It's okay," I brush him off.

Two guys dressed in bright red-green-yellow-and-black-striped tracksuits bound by outside the restaurant, banging tambourines and shouting. We watch as one starts playing music from a portable stereo before stepping off the pavement to hold back the steady stream of foot traffic while the other backflips along the road.

"Whoa!" Ash says as I sit up straighter, clapping along with the bystanders who've gathered.

"Brazilians. Capoeira," explains our server as he places bowls of pasta in front of us.

"They're amazing," I say as the street performer walks past on his hands, kicking his legs over his head in a fluid movement.

We all go wild at the finale, which sees the same guy taking a running jump and backflipping right over his companion's head.

As an upturned cap makes the rounds, I empty my purse of coins while Ash digs into the pocket of his shorts, pulling out a five-euro note. The street performers move on and we get started on our food, but a couple of minutes later, an old lady shuffles by on the pavement. She comes to a stop at our table and holds out her hand to me.

"I'm so sorry." My face warms as I shake my head, realizing I have no more change.

She stares at me, her weathered face blank. Ash pulls out another fiver and she takes it from him without a word and hobbles away.

"I feel terrible, but I only have twenty-euro notes left," I explain awkwardly as Ash picks up his Coke and takes a sip. Before I can think better of it, I quip, "For that money, I'd want to see a backflip."

Ash splutters his drink while I clap my hand over my mouth. Then he cracks up, laughing at my horror.

"I can't believe I said that," I squeak through my fingers. "It's the sort of thing my mum would say and mean it."

He chuckles, then sees my face. "Wait, really?" he asks with surprise.

"She's a bit of a snob," I reply, twirling my spaghetti carbonara around my fork.

"A bit" is putting it mildly.

"Do you get on?" he asks as he pushes his bowl aside. He's made short work of his cacio e pepe.

I shrug. "As long as I do what I'm told."

His eyes are hidden behind square aviators, so I have no idea what he's thinking as he cocks his head to one side. "How old are you?"

"Twenty-one, but I'll probably still be like this when I'm thirty. I'm the ultimate people pleaser when it comes to my parents."

"Maybe a couple of months away from them will help."

"I'm seeing them tomorrow evening."

His eyebrows jump up above the rim of his sunglasses. "Where?"

"In the Algarve, near Albufeira. They've rented a villa for the week."

"And then you'll be on your way again?"

I shake my head, my lips downturned. "I'm flying home with them." I force another forkful of spaghetti into my mouth, but suddenly I've lost my appetite.

"Haven't you only been away for, like, three weeks?"

"Less than. I'm supposed to have another month or so, but . . . I don't know. I don't think I'm cut out for interrailing." I push my bowl away.

He reclines in his chair, regarding me for a long moment, and then turns to look at the market. His jaw is even sharper without his stubble. My eyes track the line of his profile, drifting down his tanned neck to the muscled curve of his shoulder.

He returns his gaze to me and I try to regain my train of thought.

"That surprises me a little," he admits.

"What?"

"That you're not cut out for interrailing."

"Why does that surprise you?"

"You've seemed to love exploring today."

"It's not that. I've just found it to be a bit isolating."

"Isolating?"

"Lonely."

It's embarrassing, but I'd rather he know the truth. I tuck my hair behind my ears and stare at the market as my cheeks heat.

"Which color?" he asks.

I glance at him and realize that he's looking at the rail of Hawaiian shirts.

"Green," I reply, grateful for the change of topic.

"I think you'd rock a crocheted top."

I laugh. "What, the tiny little triangles of see-through fabric?"

"Why not?" he asks mildly.

"I'm not sure I could pull that look off."

"I don't think you give yourself enough credit."

I snort and he grins.

"Come on, let's go have a look," he prompts, signaling for the bill.

It's only a small market—a row of white gazebos with each vendor selling a selection of clothes, jewelry, bags, or souvenirs.

"It's a little lurid, don't you think?" Ash asks dubiously as I hold the green Hawaiian shirt against his chest to determine the fit.

He's so tall.

I stretch the fabric sideways to see if there's enough of it.

And broad.

The warmth of his skin soaks right through the cotton. It's an effort to stay focused.

"It is a little lurid," I agree with a smile, eyeing the clusters of bright orange flowers overlying dark green palm leaves on a lime background. "But I like it." I grin up at him and he smiles down at me, my blood fizzing as he picks up a dove-gray baseball hat and pops it on top of my head.

"*You* should get the cap." I blush as I take it off, docking it on his head instead. "Your nose is sunburnt."

He touches his fingers to the tip. "Is it?"

"Yes. Have you got any sunscreen on?"

"No."

I tut and shake my head at him, slapping the Hawaiian shirt against his chest. He laughs and catches it, accidentally brushing his hand against my thumb and making my breath hitch.

Ash buys the shirt and cap, then steps from the shade into the sunshine and casually strips off his T-shirt. The sleek muscles on his back ripple as he slides one arm into the sleeve of his new shirt, followed by the other. He turns around and slowly walks back toward me, his gaze downcast as he concentrates on fastening the buttons. The taut ridges of his abdomen disappear, and then the line of dark blond hair traveling from his belly button down his flat stomach.

He's right in front of me before I realize I've been staring.

"Your turn," he says in a deep, low voice that steals the remaining air from my lungs.

We move to the neighboring stall. Ash slings his T-shirt over his shoulder so he has both hands free to riffle through the racks. He's wearing the cap.

"What about this?" he asks, pulling out a horrible Aztec-print pink-and-purple vest.

"I don't think so."

"But it would please me to see you in this and you're a people pleaser, so . . ."

"Fuck off," I mutter with a laugh.

He chuckles and slides it back onto the rail.

"I actually do quite like the crocheted tops," I muse, fingering an emerald-green one. "But I can't very well go around Lisbon dressed in a holey top and knickers."

"Oh, but that would be so fun to see," he says playfully, hooking his arm over the end of a rail and smiling at me.

I shove his arm and wish I could let my hand linger. My urge to touch him is strong.

"No, it has to be a dress to replace the one I have on," I state adamantly.

"What about this?" He pulls out a lightweight summer dress that is a classic red and dotted all over with tiny white flowers.

"Ooh," I coo appreciatively, my heart rate spiking when our hands brush again. "Have you been shopping with girls before?"

"One of my best friends is a girl," he reveals with a shrug.

Interesting. I return my attention to the dress. It's pretty.

"Red always makes me think of *Annie*. You know, the musical? The dressmaker says that blue is her best color, then she changes her mind and says, 'No, red, I think.' But as a kid I didn't get the subtlety of the pause. I just heard 'No red' and then couldn't figure out why they put red-haired Annie in a red dress. I avoided red for years, not sure what to believe."

I look up at Ash, note his sweet smile, and suddenly I want to be inside his head again, reading his thoughts.

"Is there anywhere to try it on?" I catch the stallholder's eye and ask the question.

"You pay for it, take it to the restrooms at the market to try on, and if you don't like it, I will give you a refund," she assures me.

I'm grateful that so many people here speak English.

Ash waits outside the restrooms while I change. I come out to find him by a flower stall, his lime-green shirt standing out against the dark wall he's leaning against. He looks stupidly cool with his tousled dark gold hair and strong jaw. He's staring off to the side, but when he turns his head and sees me, he does a tiny double take, like the one he did the first time we met.

"Whoa. Okay," he says, pushing off from the wall and taking a few steps toward me before halting. He has his T-shirt clutched in his hand.

"Whoa, okay, what?" I ask self-consciously.

"I think we can safely say that red *is* your color," he says slowly.

He lifts his eyes, which have swept the length of my body.

"Yeah?" I ask nervously.

"Mm-hmm." He rakes his hand through his hair, and to my

surprise, I see that his cheeks have taken on the same hue as the tip of his nose. He pulls his gaze away to stare out of the wide market doors. "Where to next?" he asks weakly.

"Castle of São Jorge?"

He nods. "Sounds good."

3

DON'T WANT TO GET AHEAD OF MYSELF, BUT I THINK ASH might quite fancy me in this dress. Out of the corner of my eye, I keep catching him looking at me and it's making me feel as though the electrical cables intersecting the cornflower-blue sky are charging my bloodstream as well as the trams. We wander the streets between attractive tiled buildings with wrought-iron balconies and occasionally a tram trundles along, canary yellow against the urban backdrop.

There's a lot of interesting street art and at one point I pause in front of a black-and-white painting of a weary-looking man with the words DREAMS ARE FOR THOSE WHO SLEEP IN BEDS sketched onto his sweater.

"That's heartbreaking," Ash murmurs as he comes to a stop beside me.

I was about to get out my phone and take a picture, but his comment stays my hand. I find myself just standing there quietly beside him, appreciating the art, before moving on.

"Do you regret not having a camera?" I ask curiously as we wander through a massive plaza.

The sparkling harbor is on one side and the others are bordered by grand ocher-colored buildings above arched sandstone walkways.

"Sometimes," he admits.

"I bet you feel more connected to your experiences without one, though."

"Definitely. Although that sounds a bit pretentious, so I tend to keep it to myself." He throws me a grin before returning his gaze to the stone archway looming ahead of us.

"Did you go to university?" I ask, keen to get to know him better.

He nods. "Cardiff."

"How old are you?"

"Same as you: twenty-one. I've just graduated."

"Me too."

He moves closer to me to avoid a group of tourists and his arm presses against mine. All the blood in my body rushes to our point of contact and my skin still feels warm as we come out onto a black-and-white cobblestone backstreet and he makes room between us again.

"What did you do?" I ask.

"Physics and astronomy."

"Oh, wow." I love the thought of him studying the stars.

"What about you?"

"Furniture design."

"Really?" he asks with interest. "My family has a furniture workshop."

"No way. Mine too."

"Ours is only small," he says hastily, which makes me think that we're talking about very different family businesses. Knap Sofas is already pretty big, but my parents are intent on building an empire.

"Where did you go to uni?" he asks.

"Central Saint Martins."

"Whoa, seriously?"

I glance at him to see that his eyebrows are raised.

"Yes, why?"

"My friend was desperate to go there, but she couldn't even get an interview. She's bright as fuck, so you must be really talented."

"Is this the same friend you go shopping with?" I ask curiously.

"Yeah, Beca. I've only been shopping with her once," he clarifies. "Never again."

I smile at the look on his face. "Have you known each other long?"

"All our lives. Our parents are friends," he explains.

"Have you ever gone out?"

"Dated?" He shakes his head. "No. Much to our mothers' dismay," he adds aridly. "Hey, this is the design museum," he realizes, glancing at the building we're about to walk past. "Do you want to go?"

"Not really. Not unless you do?"

"No, I was thinking about you."

"Let's stick to the plan."

It's kind of him to offer, but traipsing around a design museum—even a blissfully air-conditioned one—is the last thing I want to do. It feels like a small rebellion against my parents to walk straight past it.

IT'S NOT EVERY day that you get to see an eleventh-century Moorish castle in the middle of a big city, but it's too hot to properly enjoy it as we walk from tower to tower along the castle walls. Eventually I take my crumpled black dress out of my bag and drape it around my shoulders, an action that prompts Ash to place his new cap on top of my head with an amiable, "You need it more than I do."

"You have to put some of this on, though," I insist, handing him my SPF 50 before adjusting the size of his cap to fit. We've paused under an umbrella pine. "I love these trees," I say. "I'd kill to have one in a garden someday. Or maybe a few. I adore pine nuts," I add with a smile, glancing at him to see that he's put his sunglasses on top of his head while he applies sunscreen to his face.

I get a small shock at seeing his light brown eyes again after so long. They're incredibly clear.

"Is this where pine nuts come from?" he asks with interest, staring up at the branches.

"All pine trees produce pine nuts. But only around twenty species grow them big enough to bother with harvesting."

"How the fuck do you know that?" he asks with a baffled laugh.

"I googled it once. I don't know why."

"Where are you planning to live when you go back home?" he asks.

"Where I've always lived—with my parents."

"You didn't move out when you went to university?"

I shake my head, noticing a small spot of sunscreen that he hasn't rubbed in properly. "It was easier to commute."

I act on impulse as I reach up and smooth my thumb over his

brow. His eyes flare wide as he stares down at me. His hair is falling forward, caressing his high cheekbones. He's *so* good-looking.

"I'm starting to regret not going to the air-conditioned museum," I say awkwardly as I back up and fan my face.

"We could go there now?"

"I'd rather head to a park," I reply hopefully.

"Happy to follow your lead."

THE BOTANICAL GARDEN is closer, but as soon as I see the name Jardim da Estrela on my phone map, I'm sold. *Estrela* means "star," *Stella* does too, and Ash studied astronomy, so it feels like fate.

The garden is a green oasis in the middle of the city, countless trees and beds bursting with flowers. We wander past fountains and statues and a pond full of carp before settling on the grass in the shade of a jacaranda tree.

"This is the most walking I've done in a single day," I say as I take off Ash's cap and my white trainers, desperate to let my skin breathe.

"Yeah, I reckon we've earned a few drinks tonight," Ash replies.

"Are you still up for the Chinese bar?"

"Absolutely. I'm intrigued."

He's wearing his shirt with the top two buttons undone and the hot breeze is causing the fabric around his neck to flap, revealing occasional glimpses of golden collarbone.

I shiver and pull a spare hair tie off my wrist. I feel the weight of his eyes on me as I fashion my hair up into a high ponytail.

"Ooh, I know what we need." I remember the *pastéis de nata*.

"Fuck yeah," Ash says when I get them out of my bag and offer him one.

I moan as my teeth sink into the flaky pastry and vanilla custard dusted with cinnamon.

Ash's eyes dart away, pink high on his cheeks.

"Christ, that's good," he says when he takes a bite of his own.

"Unbelievable," I agree with my mouth full.

He laughs and it's catching. If I don't swallow, I might choke.

"So, furniture design, hey? You're going into the family business?" he asks warmly.

My smile drops right off my face. "Yep."

He frowns. "You don't seem that thrilled about it."

"I'm not," I confess, then shake my head. "No, that's unfair. It's a really good job and I know it's a cool career, but—"

"Your heart's not in it." He's hit the nail on the head.

"I take it there's no pressure on *you* to join the family business?" I assume not, going by his course choice.

"Nah. But I have an older brother who's taking the heat off." He clears his throat. "So what would you rather be doing instead?"

I let out a brittle laugh and give him my honest answer. "Gardening."

"Why is that funny?" He sounds confused.

"It's not," I reply seriously. "I just grew up knowing that my parents would never allow it. My career path has been set in stone ever since I can remember."

He looks alarmed. "But it's *your* life."

I shrug and dust pastry off my hands. He leans forward and plucks my sunglasses right off my face.

"What the hell?" I blink at the sunlight as he sits them on top of my head.

"I need to see your eyes for this conversation," he says, taking his off too and throwing them to one side. "That's taking parent-pleasing too far, Ellie."

I experience a fierce thrill at hearing him say my name while looking at me directly.

"You don't know my parents," I murmur, holding eye contact.

His pupils dilate as he stares back at me. Then his expression softens. "What do you like about gardening?"

Some of the tension eases from my shoulders. "Everything. I love being outdoors, surrounded by nature. The smells, the sounds. I feel so at peace." I drink in our surroundings as I say this. "And I love the cyclical nature of gardening, watching plants you've tended come back year after year. I'd give anything to work for the National Trust or English Heritage," I add wistfully.

"What about a private estate?"

I wrinkle my nose. "I don't really agree with all that."

"All what?"

"All these massive mansions being passed down from eldest son to eldest son for hundreds of years. Those places should be opened up for everyone to enjoy."

"But plenty of private estates *are* open to the public," he points out, pulling up a blade of grass.

"Yeah, only to line some posh twat's pockets, though. They're not doing it out of the kindness of their heart."

"Those old properties cost a bomb to maintain. It's still in the public's best interest to preserve them for future generations."

"If the owners cared about the public interest, they'd donate them to charity. Sorry, but you won't convince me on this. This sort of thing is a hangover from a class system which does more harm than good."

"Fair enough, but I don't think you should cut off your nose to spite your face. I know someone who's a head gardener at a private estate and he loves his job."

"Why are we talking about this as though there's any chance of it happening? I'm going to be designing sofas for a living." His brow creases with sympathy as I slip my sunglasses back on. "Now I *really* need a drink," I say significantly.

"OOH, I WANT one of those!" I cry like a small child, pointing at a wooden stall selling real pineapples filled with piña colada. "I'll get it," I say as Ash digs into his pocket. "Do you want one too? Go on, it would look perfect with your Hawaiian shirt!"

He laughs and shakes his head. "I'll get a beer."

"Spoilsport!" I call after him as he breaks off toward the beer hut.

We're in the Bairro Alto district, at the top of one of Lisbon's famous seven hills. It's cooler than earlier and this street market looked lively as we were passing on our way to the Chinese bar, so we thought we'd have a drink in the sunshine.

The air is filled with the sound of trickling water from a fountain and guitar music from a fado musician playing nearby as Ash and I go to check out the view.

I make a big show of knocking my giant spiky fruit cup against his small beer glass before taking a sip of my piña colada through the straw. He laughs as my eyes widen.

"Your eyes are ridiculous," he says with amusement. "They're *so* big and blue. How can anyone ever say no to you when you look at them like that?"

This drink isn't carbonated, but it may as well be from the way my stomach has just exploded with tiny bubbles.

"Stella used to call them my superpower," I confide. "When we were at sixth-form college, she'd dare me to stare at random guys in bars and would count aloud to see how long I could last before chickening out," I recall fondly.

The nights we had . . . The nights we'll never have again.

My eyes weren't my superpower. Stella was.

I take another sip of my drink, trying to swallow the lump in my throat. Ash is still smiling at me, which is a good distraction.

He shakes his head, neither of us severing the connection.

"I don't understand how you've been lonely," he says out of the blue, and all the bubbles in my stomach go flat. "Sorry," he says quickly, seeing the look on my face. "It's just that you're so funny and warm."

Well, that's nice. "Before I met you, I was kind of withdrawn," I admit. "I didn't really feel like being friendly to strangers."

"What changed?" he asks.

Apart from you being so lovely? "I made the decision to quit traveling. Knowing I only had two more days to get through lightened me up."

His brow furrows. "Are you dead set on going home?" he asks. "I mean, could you still change your mind?"

I shrug. "I guess I still could, yeah. I only told my parents I was considering it, so nothing's set in stone. But I'd have to seriously psyche myself up to be more sociable."

"I can't imagine you being antisocial. I could talk to you for hours."

My insides light up. I realize we *have* been talking for hours. In a way, being with him has felt as natural as being with Stella. I'm taken aback as that sinks in.

Breaking eye contact, I tuck my prickly pineapple under my arm, then wince, thinking better of it.

"Do you want another one?" he asks, chuckling as I place it at my feet.

"Nah, I'll save it for the Chinese bar." I prop my elbows on the railing beside him, our arms just touching as we take in the view of the colorful buildings and the glinting ocean in the distance. I feel like I'm floating, here with him, above the city.

A LITTLE WHILE later, we're staring across the road at the tiny bar Stella recommended, which is sandwiched between Barbour International and a high-end antiques shop. Embroidered net curtains hang at the two windows, the paintwork is peeling and patchy, and the canopy stretching across the front is sagging in the middle. Whether by design or unintentional, it lends it the architectural flavor of a traditional Chinese pavilion, which is apt for the name of the bar: Pavilhão Chinês.

"Um," I say.

Ash casts me a grin, totally unfazed by the shabby outward appearance of the place.

Inside my bag, my phone begins to buzz. I pull it out and my stomach drops at the sight of the caller ID: **Dad**.

"It's my dad," I murmur. "I have to take this."

"Shall I see you inside?"

I nod. "I won't be long."

He sets off across the road and I answer the call, trying to inject cheerfulness into my voice.

"Hi, Dad."

He doesn't answer, but I can hear him talking to someone. "It's fine."

"No. Send it back," I hear my mum retort.

They sound like they're in a busy restaurant.

"Excuse me!" Dad calls.

"Dad!" I say into the receiver.

"Eleanor?" Dad booms in my ear, making me wince.

"Hi."

"Ah, you're there."

"The wine is not chilled," I hear my mum saying haughtily, probably to some poor waiter.

"All set for tomorrow?" Dad asks me.

"Yes. What time's your flight again?"

"Around ten, I think."

"Ten fifteen," I hear Mum correct him.

"I'm not getting there until the evening, so will you text me the address?"

"What time's your train coming in?" he asks.

"Six thirty or something like that. I'll jump in a cab."

"No, Alison will arrange a car for you." That's my parents' no-nonsense PA. "Text her your details."

He never lowers his voice when he's speaking on the phone in public—it's mortifying when you're with him, and even now I'm embarrassed about what the other diners must be thinking.

"Tell her about the flight," Mum prompts.

"Oh, she's booked your return flight too," Dad says.

My face heats. "But I told you I hadn't made up my mind."

For several long moments, as dread envelops my insides, all I can hear is the restaurant noise.

"Has she got a problem with it? I knew she would," my mum comments saltily.

"Well, it's done now," Dad snaps, his hackles rising. He gets defensive when anyone points out anything close to resembling a mistake. "Check your email for confirmation. Alison managed to get you on the same flight as us, so make sure you thank her."

My skin feels hot and prickly. "I will," I force myself to say.

"You're welcome," Dad replies acerbically. "See you tomorrow." The line goes dead.

I stand there on the pavement for a minute, some of the last words Stella said to me ringing in my ears. *Stop being such a people pleaser—it's frustrating!*

My fingers shake as I type out a text to her, fighting back tears: I really wish you were here right now.

It doesn't come close to saying all the things I want to say, but there's no time to get caught up in another monologue. I force myself to take a couple of calming breaths before setting off toward the bar on the other side of the road.

4

"SMALLTOWN BOY" BY BRONSKI BEAT IS PLAYING OVER the sound system when I enter the dimly lit venue. I have this song on a playlist Stella and I made together and it does a good job of brightening my mood as I round the corner and take in the peculiarity of the interior. Glass cabinets, lit from within, line the walls and contain an array of memorabilia: plastic vintage Disney characters, old-fashioned board games, model train sets, folding paper fans, and so much more. The carpet is dark red, the ceiling is rose pink with gilded detailing on the plasterwork, and the polished wooden tables and sagging chintz-covered bench seats look as though they've been in use for decades.

There are a few groups of people dotted about, but it's not that busy and there's no sign of Ash, so I make my way toward another room at the back. A smartly dressed waiter in a blue waistcoat and bow tie comes through the doorway carrying a tray of colorful cocktails, just as the instantly recognizable piano melody of Bonnie Tyler's "Total Eclipse of the Heart" begins to play.

I step out of the way, feeling as though I've been winded. This was our song—Stella's and mine—the first song that came on the radio after she picked me up, having just passed her driving test. We sang along to it at the tops of our voices, completely out of tune, and she had to pull over because we were laughing so hard.

I can picture her vividly, her mouth stretched ludicrously wide, her chin-length dark hair straightened to within an inch of its life, her heavily mascaraed eyelashes clumped together with tears of hysteria. Black winged eyeliner, hot-pink lipstick. Trademark Stella.

The backs of my eyes sting as I stand in front of a vintage map of the Portuguese Empire, trying to compose myself until I'm ready to carry on into the next room.

I spot Ash in his Hawaiian shirt immediately. His forearms are propped on the ornate wooden bar top running along the left-hand wall and he's resting his weight on his right leg, his narrow hips jutting slightly to the side as he flips through a cocktail menu. As I stare at his tall, broad frame, my heart begins to beat a tiny bit faster.

The second verse is almost at an end and, as the song changes key with the lyrics *Turn around, bright eyes*, Ash looks over his shoulder and clocks me.

It is a moment of such perfect, silly coincidence that a giggle erupts from my throat.

And then the refrain repeats and Ash turns fully around, resting his back against the bar and giving me his biggest, sweetest grin as he folds his arms across his chest and watches me walk toward him.

The drums have kicked in and Bonnie is belting out the uplifting, heart-soaring chorus, and it's all so dramatic and funny and so fucking tragic that I begin to laugh properly.

Maybe it's because we've both had a drink and our defenses

are down, but the next thing I know, I'm in Ash's arms and his whole body is shaking with hysteria as the chorus builds to a crescendo. But when the song dies down again, a stillness settles over us. I rest my forehead on his shoulder and he moves his hands to my upper arms and just holds me as tears stream down my face.

I become aware of his warmth, of the steady, centering strength of his palms, and the oddest thought strikes me that it will be Ash I think of first the next time I hear this song.

"Are you okay?" he asks in a low, deep voice near my ear.

"I don't know why I'm so upset," I reply, sounding choked.

But I do. I'm upset because I've just allowed my parents to railroad me again. I'm upset because I can never stand up to them—or anyone. I'm upset because I'm giving up on my dream of seeing Europe. And I'm upset because I would give anything to be here in this bar with Stella, drunkenly singing along to eighties classics and laughing until we cry.

But the only explanation I give to Ash is: "This song reminds me of Stella and I miss her."

I feel his sharp intake of breath, and then he cups the back of my neck and draws me to his chest. The fabric of our market-bought clothes is thin and there's barely a millimeter separating our skin as we stand there, connected all the way down to our knees. I'm conscious of my pulse skipping and skittering, and then I also become aware of his heart thudding against mine.

I've never properly listened to this song before, not even when I've caterwauled it at full volume, but the lyrics begin to register, sentiments like forever and love. On a wave of embarrassment, I pull away, suddenly overcome with shyness.

"I'm going to nip to the toilet to sort myself out," I say with an awkward laugh, feeling Ash's eyes on me as I brush away my tears.

"Drink?" he offers gently.

"Yes, please. Can you choose me something? I'm not fussy. I promise I'll get the next ones."

In the bathroom, I splash my face with cold water and stare at myself in the mirror. I feel a little shaky as I retouch my makeup with the bare essentials I carry with me, and then I spy the red lipstick that Stella made me buy when she wanted me to feel bold and brave. I could use a little help with that right now, so I slick some on.

Ash has moved from the bar to a table in an adjoining room. "When You Were Mine" by Cyndi Lauper is playing.

Stella loved Cyndi Lauper, but at least I don't have strong memories attached to this one.

"This place is so crazy," I say with a forced laugh as I sit down opposite him. I don't want to dwell on what's just happened.

"Isn't it?" he says, following my cue. "It looks tiny from the outside, but it's like the TARDIS crossed with Aladdin's cave in here."

The cabinets in this room are filled with vintage war toys and there are model airplanes and miniature die-cast soldiers hanging from old-fashioned parachutes attached to the ceiling.

"There are pool tables here too!" I realize with astonishment, peering over his shoulder at yet *another* room beyond this one, which looks huge in comparison.

"I know! Fancy a game in a bit?"

"Sure."

He slides two cocktail glasses on cardboard coasters toward me. One is a tulip glass filled with a garish green concoction. The other is a martini glass containing red liquid.

"What are these?"

"I actually can't remember," he replies sheepishly, then, nodding at the green drink, "That one's the house cocktail, but choose whichever you prefer."

The green drink has a stirrer with ribbons of gold foil spilling from the top, and the red has a cherry and orange garnish that makes me think of Christmases at my grandparents'.

I try the red. It's fizzy and tastes of strawberries. My decision is made.

"You have the green one—it matches your shirt."

He smirks as he picks up the glass. "You do realize that the red one is the same color as your dress."

I look down and laugh.

"And your lipstick," he adds in a low murmur, ducking his head to take a sip through the straw.

"How is it?" I ask, my blood humming as his eyes rest on mine. They're glinting under the light of the opulent cut-glass lampshade fixed above our heads.

"Drinkable," he replies, straightening up. "Are you all right?" He's clearly still concerned.

"Yeah, I'm fine."

"Want to talk about it?"

"No, I'll only get upset again."

He nods slowly. I try to think of something to say, some question that will direct attention away from me.

"So why physics and astronomy?"

His smile instantly becomes relaxed and easy. "My answer is going to make me sound like I'm a five-year-old boy," he warns, before adding, "I *love* space."

God, he's cute. "What do you love about it?"

"There's literally nothing that I don't love," he replies, swirling his elaborate gold stirrer around his drink. "It's the only thing I've ever really been interested in. My friend Taran had a telescope and I used to hang out at his house a lot when we were growing up. Things could be a little hectic at home, but when I looked at the night sky, everything else just sort of faded away. It all seemed so still and peaceful, but later I learned that it wasn't still or peaceful, that there are whole other worlds up there raging with storms and being blasted apart by volcanoes, and all of it made *me* feel small, as though anything I was dealing with was inconsequential in the grand scheme of things. Space has always taken me outside of myself."

I've been watching, rapt, as he's spoken about something he clearly loves with a passion. I have so many questions, but when he meets my eyes, I forget them all.

"What sort of job are you hoping to do?" I ask, wrestling my concentration back under control.

"Well, I'm going back to uni at the end of September to do a master's in astrophysics, but after that, I'm not sure. I'm interested in the research that's being done into space weather."

"I didn't even know there *was* such a thing."

"There are these large explosions on the sun known as coronal mass ejections and they can spew out billions of tons of charged particles and magnetic field into space. When these disturbances reach Earth, they can trigger geomagnetic storms and increase particle radiation levels, which causes all sorts of disruptions to power grids and satellites. More research is needed to work out how it affects the weather and climate. Sorry, I'm going off on one."

"No, you're not."

He sounds really fucking smart.

He wraps his hand around his ice-cold glass and draws it closer. I'm staring as his lips quirk slightly at the corners, and when I lift my gaze, his eyes are already on mine.

"Pool?" he asks.

"Is there a table free?"

"Those people have just finished." He lifts his chin in the direction of a couple on their way to the bar.

"Okay."

I haven't played pool in years. Not since Stella and I hung out at the pub where her older brother worked—he used to give us free games when we popped in to see him.

"Do you want to break?" Ash asks as he racks up.

"No, go for it."

The balls scatter as he takes his shot, then he turns to me and holds out the cue. Our fingers brush as I go to take it and, for a beat, our eyes lock and hold. He releases it with a small smile and my belly does a slow somersault.

I want him.

But I can't have him, I remind myself. We're going our separate ways tomorrow.

There's always tonight, the voice in my head whispers.

No. No casual flings. I know my triggers and I can't handle that.

I try to focus on my shot, but I slip and put barely any power behind the white ball.

"Competitive?" Ash asks, eyes sparkling as I let out an annoyed yelp.

"Yes!" I snap jokily, reaching out to give his shoulder a small push, but he's too quick for me and he catches my wrist. "But only when it comes to games," I clarify as my heart hiccups inside my chest.

We're standing inches apart, my wrist in his firm grip, and I wish he'd use it to pull me even closer.

"I'm not competitive anywhere else in life," I add, sounding a bit breathless.

"I'm the same," he replies, his voice low.

We're still waiting for my ball to come to a stop, and he's yet to release me. I feel edgy with awareness of his body, the air between us sparking as we watch the ball creep forward. It looks as though it will land a mile off the pocket, but then it slowly turns and begins to veer left. My eyes widen with delight.

"Oh my God!" Ash exclaims with outrage as it drops neatly into the pocket I was aiming for. "This table has got such a lean on it!"

"Ooh, you *are* competitive," I tease as his grip on my wrist tightens momentarily before he lets me go.

I *really* like the feeling of his hands on my skin.

He's right, though, the table *does* have a lean on it. Every time either one of us shoots the ball toward that same end, it rolls into the corner pocket. To begin with, it causes cries of indignation from one of us and glee from the other, but pretty soon we're both just laughing.

"I know a poor workman blames his tools, but this is ridiculous," Ash says, taking the cue out of my hands and simultaneously reaching for the chalk behind me.

My breath catches as his arm brushes against mine and then it becomes shallow as he chalks up the cue, standing deliciously close. His gaze roves from my lips to my eyes and back again before dropping to the pool cue.

As soon as he moves away, I nervily knock back my drink and walk over to place my empty glass on a nearby table, but when I turn around, I feel as though I've stepped onto a merry-go-round.

"What's wrong?" he asks as I hastily place both hands on the table to steady myself.

"I think I probably need to line my stomach before drinking any more."

"Shall we go get something to eat?" he asks.

"I noticed an Indian restaurant across the road and a Mexican a couple of doors down?" I'm cutting my trip short, so I have money to blow. But does Ash? "Or we could go somewhere cheaper—"

"I'd murder a Mexican," he interrupts me.

"Let's hurry up and finish this game then."

He turns around and pots the black ball. "You win," he says flippantly.

"I can't believe you just lost on purpose!"

"I'm sure you would have beaten me anyway."

Generous *and* unlikely, given he's already four balls down.

"What do you feel like eating?" he asks over his shoulder as we walk out through the bar.

"I thought we were murdering a Mexican?"

"Shh!" he hisses, shooting an alarmed look at the other punters. "People might think we're homicidal."

I'm still laughing as we set off along the pavement.

5

A TABLE COMES FREE JUST AS WE ARRIVE AT THE MEXI-
can restaurant a few doors along. The interior is long and
narrow with a back wall lined almost entirely with brightly lit tequila bottles. Tables and chairs run the length of the left-hand
wall and on the right is a long counter, behind which four chefs
are busy preparing food. It's buzzy.

We order nachos, which are brought to the table right away,
and we've already demolished most of them when our drinks appear a few minutes later. I went for lemonade, but Ash chose a
pineapple margarita and my eyes must go round at the sight of the
pineapple-and-lime popsicle poking out the top because he plucks
it out by the stick and offers it to me.

"Are you sure?" I ask, my fingers itching to take it.

"I wouldn't have offered if I wasn't."

I accept the gift and lick the remnants of his drink off the
end. "Oh, wow. You have to try."

I casually brandish the popsicle in his face and then go completely still when he catches my hand in his to hold it steady. His

lips part and his tongue sneaks out to take a lick, and the bolt of attraction I feel almost knocks me sideways.

"You all right?" Ash asks with a frown, releasing me.

I have no idea what my face just did.

"I'm fine." I pick up my lemonade and take a gulp, acutely aware of the phantom impression his touch has left behind. It's like he's still holding my hand.

"Really?" he presses.

"I'm fine," I repeat, avoiding looking at him.

"Please don't tell me what you think I want to hear. If you don't feel well and you want to go back to the hostel, just say. I don't mind."

I drop the popsicle back into his drink and bury my face in my hands.

A moment passes. "Um. I'm at a bit of a loss now." His lovely lilting voice is laced with worry.

I laugh into my palms and wearily lift my head. "You're so nice."

"I'm too nice?" he asks with confusion.

"Not *too* nice. You *are* nice. I'm not used to it."

"Not used to *what*?" Now he looks alarmed.

"People caring about what I want."

He stares at me. His expression is disconcertingly grave.

I sigh and reach over to pluck the popsicle out of his drink again. I've sobered up enough to know that I'll be ordering one of these for myself before long, but I'm tipsy enough to still have my guard down.

"Part of the reason I was upset earlier was because my parents have booked a flight home for me before I'd decided I was definitely giving up on interrailing," I explain. "They only knew I was considering it. I know I should be grateful. I *am* grateful—"

"No," he interrupts, shaking his head. "They should have checked with you first."

I'm taken aback by how serious he looks.

"It's just that . . . What if I'd changed my mind?"

"You still can," he states.

I laugh at him. "You *really* don't know my parents." I said the same thing earlier, but I can't stress it enough.

The server brings over our tacos. We thank him in Portuguese. Neither of us makes a start on eating.

"Do you get along with *your* parents?" I ask.

He rubs his jaw. "My mother more than my father. He's always so busy at work, he doesn't have a lot of time."

"Does he make time for your brother, seeing as he's going into the family business?"

"Yeah, he does," he confirms wryly, reaching for a taco. "I don't really care, though, because at least I get to have a career in the space sector. My dad used to say, 'There's speculation, *wild* speculation, and astronomy,' and then I went to uni and did a degree in it."

"Physics too, though, right?"

"That's the part he tells his friends."

"Sounds like we both have complicated relationships with our parents."

He lets out a caustic laugh and takes a ferocious bite of his taco.

"I think I take after my grandparents more than my parents," I muse, retrieving a taco for myself. "They were salt of the earth—Londoners born and bred. My grandfather was a carpenter and my grandmother was a seamstress."

Ash regards me with interest, warmth returning to his expression as I tell him about how they built the family business from scratch, designing and making quality sofas and coffee tables that they sold out of a little shop in North London.

They taught my dad the family trade, but my father had bigger ambitions, and after meeting my mother at business school, the two of them scaled up the business and took it online.

It's hard to explain how I can be impressed by my parents' achievements and yet also deeply resent them for the way they went about growing their business. I don't tell Ash that they remortgaged the house to send me to an elite private school so they could make more connections. When I think about how much of my happiness they were willing to sacrifice in order to social-climb their way to success, I could cry.

I still remember the misery of my fourteenth birthday. I'd wanted to go to the cinema with Stella—*just* Stella, the one person I felt truly comfortable around—but my parents insisted on throwing me an excruciating whole-year party. I'd only started at my new school six months earlier, after they pulled me out of the other school I'd been attending with Stella, and I had *no* friends. Kids still came anyway—nowhere near as many as we'd catered for, but it was a free party and I think some of their parents were curious to see what my mum and dad could pull off after schmoozing their way through various social events.

I know Dad finds it draining to suck up to the people he rubs shoulders with—he was raised with no airs and graces, so he's had to adopt them. These days he sounds nothing like the dad I grew up with.

Charming the upper class comes more naturally to my mother, and you'd think she's having the time of her life when she's in the midst of it, but I'm pretty sure fawning over them makes her bitter too.

I wonder what my parents would think of Ash, and then I stop wondering because I know. He's salt of the earth, like my grandparents. My mum has always been snobby about my dad's family and even Dad turned up his nose at his parents toward the end of their lives.

But I loved them to bits. They died a few years ago, two months apart, and their loss still feels like a punch in the gut.

They would have liked Ash. That matters to me more than anything.

"So what are you going to do?" Ash asks. "Will you catch that flight home?"

"There's no way I can't now. My parents would kill me if I wasted their money." They have plenty to spare, but they count every penny. "And anyway, I'd decided to quit for a reason. I'm not even sure I could psych myself up to travel on my own again," I add flatly, getting my lipstick out of my bag; red takes some serious upkeep.

Ash's attention is fixed on my mouth as I reapply.

"Where else were you planning to go?" he asks.

"I was thinking about Seville, Madrid, and Barcelona, and then along the coast of the South of France before heading to Italy."

"What if we made a plan to meet up in Madrid?"

I hesitate. And then I feel as though someone has lit a sparkler inside my stomach.

"Are you serious?" I ask as he leans in closer, his eyes shining.

"Completely. We get on, don't we?"

"I thought you liked traveling on your own."

"I'd rather travel with you."

I cannot contain myself as I break out into my biggest, brightest smile.

"Can I think about it?" I ask, not wanting to make promises I might not be able to keep.

"Of course," he replies with a grin, knocking back the remainder of his margarita.

LATER THAT NIGHT, after we've been to another bar that sells dangerously cheap beer, we head back to the hostel in a tuk-tuk decorated with plastic yellow flowers.

I squeal as we turn a corner at speed.

Ash laughs across at me. "Give me your phone," he says as the wind blows my hair into a tangled mess.

I do and he opens up my camera app and aims the lens at me, clicking off a few shots.

"Your turn." I waggle my hand at him.

Our fingers overlap as we exchange the device, and once more the tiny touch feels impactful in a way that is entirely unbalanced.

He leans against the side bars, his elbow propped on top of the bench seat, his upper body twisted toward mine. His shirt is flapping against his collarbone even more violently than earlier and he's holding back his shaggy hair with his free hand, giving me a small smile that feels as though he's bringing me in on all his secrets.

"What time do you want to set off for Sintra in the morning?" he asks when we arrive at the hostel.

"Eightish, maybe?" I follow him into the lobby, staring at his broad shoulders. "I need time to stash my rucksack in a locker."

"I'm leaving mine at the train station in Sintra so I have it handy for tomorrow night."

"What's happening tomorrow night?" I ask with confusion.

"I'm sleeping on a beach west of Sintra."

"You're not coming back to Lisbon?"

"Only to catch my train up to Porto the next day."

I hate that we're going our separate ways.

But what if it's only for a week? Could I find the strength to stand up to my mum and dad and continue interrailing with him instead of flying home? My insides vibrate with a strange kind of effervescence at the thought.

"Do you want to head straight to the Quinta da Regaleira?" he asks, still talking about Sintra.

"Yeah, I'd love to go first thing, before the queues get too long."

"You might have to wake me up so I don't oversleep again," he says as we climb the internal staircase.

"I can if you like, but how will I know where to find you?"

"My dorm is on this floor." He nods ahead to a door off the first-floor landing. "I'm in number—"

His voice breaks off.

"Number what?" I ask.

"I actually can't remember." He looks endearingly unsure of himself. "It's the fourth bed along, I think, top bunk. I'll have to give you my key so you can let yourself in, but let me check the number."

He unlocks the dorm room and pushes open the door with a heavy whoosh. I follow him inside.

As with my girls-only dorm upstairs, it's a long, dimly lit space. Stylish red numbers are painted on the white wall to our right, running from one to twelve, with a row of offset top bunks accessed by ladders. Gray curtains have been drawn across each of the bedroom spaces and it's quiet—people are either sleeping or they're all still out on the town.

"It's this one." He drags back a curtain that has the number nine painted on the wall above it.

"Let me see what you've done with the place," I joke, climbing up the ladder and peering in at the single bed with its clean white duvet. "Ooh, very minimalistic."

I vaguely wonder if it's appropriate as I climb the rest of the rungs, but I know instinctively that Ash won't mind. There are metal shelves holding personal items at the back and there's a phone-charging station, although it's empty. Ash's rucksack is stashed in the corner. His bed suddenly looks irresistibly inviting and when I flop down, I discover that his pillow smells of coconut. It reminds me of something and as he face-plants on the pillow next to me, I remember what.

"Body Shop!" I exclaim in a tipsy whisper.

"Body Shop?" he mumbles, turning his face toward mine.

"You use coconut wax from the Body Shop," I state with the confidence of Sherlock Holmes.

"How did you know?" He looks perplexed.

"I can smell it on your pillow. I used to use it myself."

His face breaks into a delightful smile. "I love your hair," he says, and his eyes flare momentarily, as though he's surprised that just slipped out.

"I like yours too," I reply with a grin, reaching out to finger one of his locks and drunkenly marveling at how soft it is. "It's not frizzy at all."

He sniggers and I suddenly realize how ridiculous this conversation is.

"Shh!" someone hisses from an adjoining bed.

We freeze and stare at each other like rabbits caught in the headlights and then crack up, trying to stifle the sound in his pillow.

We're not successful because the next shush is even louder and angrier. I press my face against Ash's shoulder and he wriggles and lets out a high-pitched squeal. I'm silenced for all of the two seconds it takes for him to tell me "I'm ticklish!" and then we're both done for.

We're crying with laughter, clutching his pillow to our faces, trying to get our hysteria under control. I have no idea how we manage it, but eventually we do, much to the relief of whoever we're annoying, I'm sure.

Ash rolls onto his side, propping his head on his hand as he smiles at me. I mirror his body language. His eyelashes are wet with tears, his nose is pinker than ever, and his hair is back to being a hot mess. I must look a state and I don't care.

"I love your laugh, so much," he whispers. My insides light up. "I *really* love it," he says, and it's adorable, the way he's looking at me. "The way you do that little giggle or snigger—I don't know what to call it—that little noise you make, right at the end of a laugh . . . It's like a . . . a . . . a *sniggle*," he decides.

I crease up with silent laughter before asking, "A *sniggle*?"

"Yeah, a sniggle."

We're both still laughing at each other, only a little, but his eyes are full of an affection that I can't believe I've earned in only twenty-four hours. The way he's looking at me . . . He *likes* me.

And I like him. So, so, so, so much.

I scan the shape of his face, the sharp line of his jaw that I have a sudden urge to trace with my fingertip. He still looks clean-shaven. I wonder when his stubble will grow back and how many days he'll leave it before he has another shave. I won't be around to see.

It's only when his eyes meet mine that I realize they were fixed on my lips a second ago. I am suddenly acutely aware of every millimeter of space he's taking up.

I'd advise against getting intimate with anyone who you're not in a serious relationship with. Trust takes time to build.

I startle as the all-too-recent words of my counselor come back to me.

"Right, then," I say abruptly, sitting up. "I'd better get to bed. What time do you want me to wake you?"

Ash blinks slowly at me as I look over my shoulder at him. I have to press my lips together to keep from smiling at how sleepy he looks right now.

"Er, seven forty-five?" he says uncertainly, passing me his key card.

"You only need fifteen minutes?" I ask with surprise.

He lifts a shoulder.

"Okay, seven forty-five it is." I shuffle down to the end of his bed and turn around to climb down the ladder.

My gaze travels back along the length of his long, tanned legs, past his broad chest to his face. His head is propped up on one hand, his carelessly disheveled hair falling into his beautiful eyes as he watches me leave.

I force myself down the last remaining rungs before I do something I might regret.

6

WE'RE ON A CANARY-YELLOW TRAIN HEADING FOR Sintra and I should be excited, but my chest feels heavy. I don't want to see my parents this evening, and I don't want to leave Ash. We only have a few more hours together before we'll need to say goodbye. I feel miserable at the thought. I've felt such a lightness in his presence. Laughter is never far from his lips, or mine.

He's subdued too as he stares out the window, and I wonder what he's thinking. I don't have the energy to strike up a conversation, but an idea comes to me and I get out my phone and headphones. He jolts out of his daze as I nudge his knee.

"What sort of music do you like?" I ask.

"Indie, rock, alternative," he replies with a lazy shrug.

"What was the last album you listened to?"

"Er . . ." He rakes his hand through his hair as he thinks. "*The Ride* by Catfish and the Bottlemen, I reckon."

"Oh, that's their new one, right? I like them. Aren't they from North Wales too?"

"Yeah, Llandudno."

How I love his Welsh accent.

"I remember you saying that you missed music." I pass him one of my earphones.

He slides me a sideways smile as he docks it in his ear.

Neither of us says another word as the album begins to play, and after a while the warmth of his arm against mine and the gentle rocking of the train make my eyelids droop. Without thinking, I rest my head on his shoulder.

In my semiconscious state, my mind drifts back to my last visit to Nottingham to see Stella on Valentine's Day. To her prickish boyfriend, Julian, and the drugs I didn't say anything about. Stella sensed that I was upset about something and she was frustrated with me for not being straight with her.

But my patience for her has always been immeasurable—she is my rock, my champion, my home—so I didn't lay into her about the company she was keeping. And look how that turned out.

"ARE YOU ALL right?" Ash asks as we arrive at the Quinta da Regaleira.

"I'm a little hungover," I say to explain my quiet mood.

"Yeah, I'm feeling it too," he replies.

I wonder if he's using that as an excuse, like I am. I've been so caught up in my own thoughts that I haven't considered where his head might be at. We said a lot of vulnerable things to each other last night. Did he mean it when he asked me to go traveling with him? Does he have regrets?

I don't want to overthink—I want to be present for our last few hours together—but it's a tall order.

It takes us half an hour to walk up to the Quinta da Regaleira via Sintra's pretty town center and the place is already swarming with people. Through the wrought-iron gates, we can see gleaming white spires and ornate chimneys rising out of a sea of greenery. We're keen to check out the palace later, but we agree to go straight to the Initiation Well.

It turns out that everyone else has had the same idea. The line of people snaking away from the cave-like entrance goes on and on, up a dusty curved path edged with ferns and boulders. The farther uphill we climb, the more hopeless I begin to feel.

This well was Stella's main reason for wanting to come to Portugal. She saw it on Instagram that last time I visited her and she thought it looked like something out of *A Court of Thorns and Roses*, the book she'd just finished reading. She'd already insisted I borrow it, but when she started researching other cool things to do in Lisbon, she grabbed it back and scribbled her list on the inside cover.

That book links me to Stella, to this place, and I needed to come today to feel closer to her.

But this queue is too much.

"I don't know what to do," I say desperately, slowing to a stop.

"Why don't we come back later?" Ash suggests. "What time's your train?"

"Four o'clock," I reply dully.

"It's okay, we've got hours. Maybe the queue will die down."

"I really don't want to miss out on seeing it."

He places his hand on my shoulder. "I promise that you won't."

When I meet his eyes, I believe him. I release a long breath and nod and then we turn to head back down the hill.

Off in the distance are the yellow dome and red tower of the famous Pena Palace, and in the foreground, on the lower part of the property, mist rises up over towering palms, leafy tree ferns, and primeval-looking cycads.

"Check that out!" Ash exclaims, coming to a stop by a white stone wall.

"It must be water vapor from the fountains," I say as I join him. "Real mist would have burned off in this heat."

"Let's pretend. It makes this place seem more mystical."

I give him a small smile. My mind is still in overdrive about whether he feels awkward about last night, but the smile he mirrors back at me allows me to relax a little.

"Do you want to sit down a sec? Take a breather?" He nods past me at a stone bench seat that has been carved out of a boulder.

I nod.

The temperature is brutal, but it's relatively cool once we take a seat in the shade of the giant oak branching out over our heads.

"What do you know about this place?" Ash asks as he gets a packet of spearmints out of his pocket and offers me one.

"Only that it was built on the whim of a very rich man and by an Italian architect who used to design opera sets. Oh, and that it has approximately five hundred different species of trees from all around the world."

"But of *course* you remember *that* fact," Ash says teasingly, bumping my arm.

I let out a small laugh as my gaze wanders. There's a stone tower nearby with a small balcony looking out over the lower terraces.

"I kind of like that there are no manicured beds here, at least from what I can see. It all looks so wild and lush and overgrown."

"Which do you prefer?" Ash asks. "Formal gardens or wild ones?"

"I like both," I reply. "But when it comes to flowers, cottage-garden plants are my favorites—irises and peonies, rambling roses, drifts of foxgloves and big clouds of purple *Nepeta*," I say with a smile. "My nan had the most incredible collection of lupins in just about every color under the sun. She only had a garden the size of a postage stamp, but boy, did she make the most of it. She planted them all out in a floral rainbow."

"Is that where you got your passion for gardening from? Your nan?" Ash asks, his expression full of warmth.

"Yeah," I reply sadly. "I used to go over to my grandparents' house after school and help Nan with weeding and clearing. I felt so at home with my hands several inches deep in the soil."

"When did you lose them?" he asks, his tone gentle, compassionate.

"When I was sixteen. They passed away two months apart. I wanted to dig up some of Nan's lupins before we sold the house, but my mum wouldn't let me."

"Why not?"

"They were just about to flower and she thought they'd help to attract a buyer. I asked if I could take some once the sale was going through, but she insisted the new owners had to get the garden they'd paid for. I wish I'd done it anyway. There were so many, no one would have noticed a few missing."

He looks crushed on my behalf.

"Shall we go for a wander?" I ask.

Sunlight streams through the leafy cover of magnolia, chestnut, cedar, and cypress trees as we make our way along the meandering paths. A hot wind flattens the long grass growing in some of the beds, and the clink of cutlery at the café carries on the breeze, along with the indistinguishable chatter of tourists.

Ash and I are both wearing the same outfits as yesterday and the wind is wreaking havoc on my red dress. As we walk up a spectacular staircase carved out of giant boulders, I have to hold it down so it doesn't blow upward.

"I like your hair like that," he says with a smile as I secure it with a butterfly clip—the wind tore it loose.

We've come to a stop by a stone tower with a narrow spiral staircase winding up the inside.

"You liked it last night too," I tease.

He laughs and his cheeks grow pink. "Last night was fun. The most fun I've had in a long time."

"Me too," I admit.

His expression grows serious as he stares down at me. I can't drag my eyes away and jitters start up in my stomach as we stand for a minute, unmoving.

"I guess we should go get in line for the Initiation Well," he murmurs, breaking the spell.

The queue is still long, but it's nowhere near as bad as earlier.

I pull my water bottle out of my bag and take a few mouthfuls before offering it to Ash. He gratefully accepts. My eyes catch on his lips, pressed to the rim, then on a drop of water tracing its way down his neck. I try to distract myself from the lust rampaging through my body by firing off a quick text to Stella: I'm finally going to see the spiral staircase that you wouldn't stop bleating on about!

I throw my phone back into my bag and we shuffle forward a pathetic couple of feet. We're going to be here a good half hour at least.

My phone buzzes.

My first thought is: *Stella*. And even though I know it's wishful thinking, I get my phone back out and check the display.

And there—in bold text—is her name.

My head spins as I open the message.

Don't think you meant to send this to me. This is my new
number.

I immediately feel shaky. The phone slips from my grasp, and
in my haste to catch it, I somehow knock it flying into a boulder.
It makes a cracking sound as it tumbles over the rocky surface before falling to the ground a few meters away.

"Whoa," Ash says, hurrying over to pick it up.

When he returns to my side, I'm horrified to see that the
screen is shattered and the display is dark.

"Is it broken?" I can hardly bear to ask.

He presses at it, his expression tense. "Looks like it. I'm sorry.
Are you okay?" He touches his hand to my shoulder. "You've gone
white as a sheet."

I swallow rapidly and nod, unable to speak. And then my vision goes blurry and a moment later two tears break free from my
eyes and slip down my cheeks. I hastily brush them away before
they can reach my chin.

"Ellie, is this just about your phone?" Ash whispers. "You still
have your SIM, so you should be able to replace it pretty easily. Or
is something else wrong?"

"Stella died five and a half months ago," I reply in a choked
voice, unable to keep it in a second longer.

Ash bristles with shock.

"I still text her, but her parents must have given up her mobile
phone contract, because her number has been assigned to someone else. A stranger just replied to my message."

"I'm so sorry," he murmurs, placing his hand on my lower
back as my chest begins to shake with silent sobs.

Everyone around us is distracted. The boys from the family in front of us are scrapping, and behind us a group of tourists are talking loudly among themselves.

Miraculously I manage to wrestle my emotions under control, but Ash rubs my back for a minute before asking, "Can you tell me what happened?"

"She took MDMA at university." I breathe in unsteadily. "And then she danced so hard that her heart stopped."

Stella was my sunshine, my breath of fresh air. She was the daughter of the high-street greengrocer, and she was down to earth and funny, never giving a shit what anyone thought of her. For the first eleven years of our lives, we grew up in terraced houses right next door to each other and we would scrape our knees daily climbing over the fence to play. We were joined at the hip all through primary school, and I'd assumed we'd stick together at secondary school too, so I was devastated when my parents pulled me out after two years.

I felt like a fish out of water at my new school, which was one of the most elite in London. Without Stella at my side, I lost confidence. I was tall for my age, and curvy too, and some of the kids took to calling me the "lumbering ginger giant," but their taunts weren't the lone reason I loathed my new classmates. I was only there because my mum and dad wanted to rub shoulders with their wealthy, well-connected parents. I was so angry at them.

All I wanted was to go back to riding the bus with my best friend, to passing secret notes to each other in class. But while I became a shadow of my former self, Stella continued to thrive, strengthening friendships that in the past had only ever been peripheral. I envied her, but she thought *I* was the lucky one—her parents would have killed to send her to private school. They'd been saving up her entire life for her to go to university.

We drifted apart but came back together at sixth-form college and we intended to go to the same university too. Nottingham Trent had great courses in both media studies—her choice—and furniture design, but my getting a place at Central Saint Martins scuppered our plans. My parents wanted the prestigious college to be featured in my bio on their website for the business and they refused to pay for me to go anywhere else. Stella was frustrated with me for not trying harder to convince them. If I had, would things have turned out differently?

"We almost went to the same university," I tell Ash miserably. "I keep thinking that maybe if I'd been there, I could have steered her away from the arsehole she was dating." I would have eventually been honest with Stella about what I thought of Julian, if only we'd had more time. "He was a posh, entitled twat who flashed his cash around," I say bitterly. "The last time I saw Stella, he was snorting coke, so I'm sure he gave her the Ecstasy. We'd never done drugs before."

At least, I hadn't. There was a chance Stella had been keeping secrets from me. I hated that losing her cast doubt over how well I'd known her. Grieving has been a complicated process.

"I was so furious at her," I say hoarsely. "But I miss her so much. Being able to text her has helped."

The first time I texted Stella, I laid into her about what she'd done, telling her that she was stupid, full-on raging. I got all my anger off my chest while ugly-crying my heart out, but afterward I was horrified at the thought of her parents reading what I'd written.

I remember how nervous I was, going to see them at the shop. When I confessed to what I'd done, her mum told me in a voice racked with emotion that Stella's phone was turned off and she was unlikely to ever turn it back on again. She promised that she'd never read my message and that if it helped, I could text her again. I felt so relieved.

Later, I felt compelled to apologize to Stella for all the mean things I'd said. I tried to explain why I was so angry and that helped too: I was sorting through my feelings as I wrote them down and it felt like a form of therapy before I actually *did* do therapy—something my tutor recommended to help me through my final months at university. I was in serious danger of stumbling at the last hurdle.

But recently I've begun to text her about more general things— my plans for interrailing, gossip about old friends, gripes about my parents. It's been comforting.

"I naively thought I'd be able to carry on texting her forever," I say to Ash.

He makes a noise of compassion and slides his arm around my shoulders, pulling me close as more tears spill down my cheeks. His strong embrace and the steady beat of his heart slowly soothe me.

"Thank you," I mumble. "I wanted to tell you before, but it's hard to talk about her without getting upset."

A moment passes before he speaks. "I know exactly what you mean."

Something in his tone causes me to turn and look at him properly.

He lets me go and shoves his hands into his pockets, then he blinks and I'm taken aback to see that there are tears in his eyes. He swallows, his gaze fixed on the ground, but then he throws me a heavy look.

"I lost my best friend too," he confesses in a husky voice. "Taran."

"Oh, Ash, I'm so sorry," I murmur, distraught. "What happened to him?"

"Leukemia." I inhale quickly as he continues. "We used to

talk about going interrailing too. I don't think he ever really believed he was going to die until days before he did."

He looks at the ground again as we shuffle forward in the queue. I loop my arm through his—he still has his hands in his pockets.

"When did you lose him?"

"It will be two years next month." It's the middle of August. "He passed away a week before I was due to start my second year."

"That must have been so hard."

"It was," he agrees.

"Taran had a telescope, right? He got you into space?"

He nods. "It was technically his dad's," he says softly. "I'm still close to his family."

"You said that you spent a lot of time at his house, growing up?"

He nods again but doesn't elaborate.

He had mentioned that his home life could be hectic. He also said something about space making anything he was experiencing down on Earth feel inconsequential. Did he have a difficult upbringing? I so want to get to know him better.

"Anyway, he's been on my mind a bit," he says.

"I understand."

"And the weird thing is, you do."

The look we share carries so much weight.

It's probably another quarter of an hour before the entrance to the Initiation Well comes into view and during that time Ash and I stay close but don't speak. I can't explain how it feels, the silence. It's more than comfortable—it's profound.

Just before we reach the entrance, he casts me one of his small, steady smiles and takes his hands out of his pockets. I let go of his arm and he reaches down to interlace our fingers. My heart flutters at the press of his palm against mine as he leads me through the rocky doorway.

We come out at the top of a beautiful spiral staircase, and I know that I'm wearing the same look of wonder that's etched on his face.

The wide staircase curves round a hollow space in the center that is completely open to the elements, and the rough stone walls are alive with green moss. When the people in front of us pause to take photos, Ash squeezes my hand in sympathy. It pains me to realize that I've probably lost all my pictures of Lisbon, but I focus on soaking up every detail and committing them to memory in the same way that Ash has been doing for weeks without a phone.

Down below is a patterned floor, and above is a disk of daylight encircled by jagged stones that look like trolls' teeth. This circle of light shrinks as we walk round and round, descending several stories underground.

The farther we go, the cooler and damper the air gets, and I become increasingly aware of the heat of Ash's body whenever we come to a stop. There are people ahead of and behind us, but they're all so consumed with taking videos and photographs that I feel as if we're on another plane altogether.

Eventually we reach the bottom and find ourselves in a man-made tunnel lit by a warm glow. The rocky walls and ceiling curve over our heads, and stalactite-like pillars that look as though they're made of candle wax come down from the ceiling to perch on the ground. We head toward a pocket of sunlight and discover a waterfall trickling down the rocks into a pond dotted with a confetti layer of green algae. A mossy bridge made of rough stone spans the water.

"Everything looks so natural, it's hard to believe it's a construct of some rich guy's imagination," I say.

It's the first time either of us has spoken in almost half an hour.

Ash looks at me, his gaze piercing, and then he tugs me into the relative darkness of the tunnel, letting me go as we turn to face each other.

"What is this?" he asks quietly as he motions between us.

My scalp prickles at the intensity in his expression. It's a few seconds before I'm able to reply.

"I don't know." It's the truth. "What do you think it is?"

I sound nervous, but his eye contact is unwavering.

"It feels like something."

Goose bumps race down my arms as I nod at him. "It feels like something to me too."

He's studying me, his eyes glinting.

"Come to the beach with me," he murmurs.

"To swim?"

"No, to sleep. Don't catch your train this afternoon."

My eyes widen. "But my parents are expecting me."

"Can't they expect you tomorrow?"

Ash is asking me to sleep under the stars with him. The thought of it is tantalizing, dizzying.

"But I can't even call them," I point out.

"We'll find a phone."

Another idea occurs to me. "If we could get to an internet café, I could email their PA." Then I wouldn't even have to speak to them. Do I dare?

"Come on," Ash encourages. "You can do it."

I let out a giddy laugh and he closes his eyes and lets his head fall back momentarily before looking at me again through lowered lashes.

"What's that look for?" I ask, baffled.

"I really, *really* love your laugh," he says slowly, candidly, placing his hand over his heart.

Snakes could come slithering down these walls and they wouldn't wipe the smile from my face.

I nod at him. "Yes. Yeah, let's do it. Let's go."

7

ADRENALINE IS PUMPING THROUGH MY BODY AS WE
collect our rucksacks from lockers at the train station—I'm
so glad I followed Ash's lead and brought mine with me to Sintra
instead of leaving it back in Lisbon; I'd be gutted if I didn't have
my things.

Climbing into a waiting taxi, Ash pulls out a map and shows
the driver, pointing at a beach.

"Retro," I tease after he's leaned back in his seat.

He shoots me a smile that livens up the butterflies that have
been residing in my stomach since the cave. "Get on board, Ellie.
You're off-grid now."

I love it when he says my name.

Our rucksacks are on the seat between us and I'm glad of the
separation. I need a minute.

Turns out I need half an hour, which is about how long the
journey takes.

When I started seeing a counselor in the wake of Stella's
death, it brought up other things I'd never dealt with, and my

counselor recommended that I wait until I'm in a proper relationship before getting intimate again. But what I'm feeling for Ash—it *does* feel like the start of something real, something permanent. The thought of it makes me breathless with hope.

We're high up on a cliff when we catch our first glimpse of the ocean through the taxi windows, and then we wind our way down a dirt track, between tall wild grasses blowing in the wind, and come to a stop at the edge of the sand. On our left is a café and surf school that have already closed for the evening, and way over on the right is a wooden walkway and steps up to a restaurant and other buildings.

I climb out of the cab and stand for a moment, breathing in the fresh, salty air and watching clear green waves crash onto the white sand in the not-too-far distance. Suddenly I can't wait to get in the water and wash off the dust and sweat from the day.

Behind me, I hear Ash arranging a return journey for nine o'clock in the morning. I feel a flurry of nerves at the thought of the driver not showing and stranding us here, but then I think, what's the worst that could happen? If I miss my train, I'll find another internet café and email Alison to let her know that I'm on a different one.

The sense of freedom I'd felt at letting my parents' PA know that I was delayed by twenty-four hours was addictive. It's so rare for me to choose to follow my heart, to do what *I* want to do rather than what's expected of me. I could get used to this feeling.

Ash slings his rucksack over his shoulder and saunters over to me. He nods toward an outdoor shower near the wooden walkway. "En suite."

I laugh and he smiles at me.

"There are toilets there too." He points them out behind the café.

It's almost six o'clock and the beach is emptying, but it still feels weird to be the only two fully dressed people walking out onto the sand. We head left, away from civilization. On our right is the shoreline and on our other side are jagged cliffs the color of peaches and cream.

"Are you allowed to sleep on the beaches in Portugal?" I ask Ash as we pass the last couple of people on this stretch of sand.

"Um, it's not *strictly* legal," he says.

"What?!"

"But I've had no trouble so far," he claims. "It's not like we're putting up tents or making a fire, and we'll clean up after ourselves. It'll be fine, I promise. We're heading for those rocks." He lifts his chin to indicate a crop of boulders. "We need to stay away from the cliffs in case of rockfall, but we should be quite sheltered from the wind."

"What about high tide?"

"The tide's going out." He points at a line on the sand. "It won't come back up past this line tonight—it's a waxing crescent moon."

"What does that even *mean*?"

He nods at the pale white C in the clear blue sky. "Yesterday that was a new moon—it rises and sets with the sun, so you don't see it at all. When the earth, the moon, and the sun line up like that, the pull of gravity is at its strongest, so the tides are more extreme. You get the same effect when it's a full moon too, but for the next week or so, the tide line will continue to recede."

"I'm so clueless, it's embarrassing. I used to think that the earth's shadow caused the different phases of the moon. I still don't really understand how it works."

"Do you want to know?" he asks tentatively.

"Sure."

We've reached the rocky outcrop, so he drops his rucksack onto a boulder and gets down on his knees, drawing two circles a few inches apart in the sand to represent the earth and the sun. "Now, imagine this is the moon." He draws a circle to the left of the earth, but a little higher. "Half of the moon is almost always lit by the sun." He draws a dotted line straight from the moon to the sun, then picks up a stone from the sand and moves it in a flat circle through the air. "As the moon orbits Earth, our perspective of it changes, so the only time we see the whole half that's lit up is when it's a full moon."

He's so cute right now.

"I'd love to know more about the stars," I say with a smile.

"How much time do you have?" he asks with a grin, discarding the stone.

"I've got all night." Did that sound flirty? "What about you?" That definitely did.

"I guess I've got all night too," he replies in a similar tone, his eyes glittering.

Heat flickers over my skin and the hairs on the back of my neck stand up as his gaze darkens. He makes a low noise at the back of his throat and tugs his eyes away as he gets to his feet. "I don't know about you, but I'm up for a swim before dinner."

I suspect it's taken some effort to sound casual.

"Definitely." I sure as hell need to cool down.

I face the other way while Ash gets changed into his swimming trunks and then I spend the next twenty seconds half-heartedly hunting out my bathing suit while watching him walk, half naked, toward the water. I'm unbuttoning my dress when he dives straight into the waves, and when he surfaces and flicks his hair out of his eyes, I let out an audible sigh.

I need to get a grip.

"What's the water like?" I shout as I drag my bikini bottom on under my dress.

"Beautiful," he shouts back.

He's still facing away from me, as that was our deal, but I don't tell him when I'm ready, as I'd rather be fully immersed in the water before he sees me. That plan goes out the window as soon as a wave crashes over my legs and I let out an earsplitting scream.

"It's freezing!"

He looks over his shoulder, laughing. "You should try wild swimming in Wales. This is balmy in comparison."

He turns around and sinks beneath the water, eyeing me as I wade in deeper.

I flinch as waves crash over my thighs, too consumed with how cold it is to worry about what I look like. He's out past breaking point, so his body is rising and falling with the swell.

Taking a deep breath, I slip under an incoming wave, forcing myself to stay in up to my neck. My teeth are chattering as I swim out to Ash, glad to find that my feet can still touch the sand.

He's been watching me, a small smile on his face. I'm waving my hands and arms rapidly under the water, trying to warm myself up, while his movements are languid and unhurried. We're both moving in a slow circle, facing each other. Right now, the sun is at my back and shining on his skin. He's golden in this light. My eyes trace the contours of his broad shoulders, the shadows under his collarbone. Even if I wasn't gasping at the cold water, I suspect he'd take my breath away.

"Now you're reminding me of Ariel from *The Little Mermaid*," he says in a low voice as I take my turn facing the sun.

"Oh, I'm a cartoon character now, am I?" I ask with a laugh.

Before, it was a comic-book character.

I let my hair down before I came in and I can feel it floating around my body, caressing my chest, back, and upper arms. My bikini is a dark forest green and there's not an awful lot of it. I was feeling brave when I packed it.

Ash smiles and shrugs and sinks farther beneath the water so his mouth and nose are submerged. We've changed positions again and the sunlight is bouncing off the dazzling water onto his eyes, making them seem an even clearer, lighter brown than ever.

I mimic him. We're a few feet apart and we're still looking at each other, rising and falling with the waves. My body has grown used to the temperature now.

Ash comes up to breathe, but he's still staring at me.

"I can't work you out," he says out of the blue.

"In what way?" I ask as I also surface for air.

"You come across as superconfident sometimes, but . . ."

"The rest of the time I'm a needy people pleaser," I finish for him.

He frowns. "I'm not sure I'd put it that way."

I like that he wants to make sense of me. "As you've probably gathered, my parents are kind of domineering. They don't let a lot stand in their way if they want something, not even me. I'm different when I'm around them. More insecure, I guess. With Stella and my grandparents, I could be myself. They brought out the best in me."

"Would you say that this is the real you?" Ash asks, lifting his chin at me.

"This is the me I wish I was all the time."

"I like that," he says with a smile.

"I guess you bring out the best in me too."

We keep our eyes on each other as we start another slow circle.

"Taran brought out the best in me," he admits. "I used to wish I'd grown up at his place, with his family. I felt so at home there."

"What was Taran like?"

"*So* weird," he says with a grin, making me laugh. "Seriously, he was quirky and funny, and he didn't give a shit what anyone thought of him."

"He sounds like Stella."

He smiles. "I wish we could all have hung out. Fuck, I miss him so much." The sight of his sudden agony and his eyes filling with tears has me moving toward him.

I'm not thinking as I wrap my arms around his neck, and he doesn't hesitate to draw me close. It's only when our bodies align under the water that I remember just how barely dressed we are. My heart is bouncing off my rib cage as I feel his sleekly muscled body flex and clench against the goose bumps shivering over my skin.

Blood rushes through my ears as he lifts his head to gaze at me, his pupils darkly dilated. One second passes, two, and then three, before his mouth slowly comes down to mine in a brief, gentle kiss.

The heat left in the wake of his lips as he pulls back to study me sears through my body. And then I'm very quickly lost to sensation as our mouths reconnect, our tongues gliding together and his grip on me tightening. My legs encircle his waist and his hands hold me in place, warm and strong. He tastes of salt and spearmint and summertime. There's not a millimeter of space between us and yet it doesn't feel close enough. Then suddenly he breaks away.

I register the hard press of his erection only after the cold water has flooded the space between my legs.

"Gah, sorry," he mutters.

My ankles are still hooked together around the backs of his thighs and his hands are on my hips, holding me inches away from him. I can feel the tension in his muscles, the restraint.

"I thought it was too cold for that, but I underestimated my attraction to you," he says against my neck.

The sound of his lovely, lilting accent, his rough voice bashfully admitting that he wants me, unleashes something in me.

I strengthen my grip, using my heels to close the space between us, and as our hips reconnect, he loses whatever control he had. Our tongues lock and tangle and I realize that we've been moving into shallower waters as waves crash over our legs. Then he's lowering me onto the sandy shore, and his hard body is coming down over me. We're a tangle of limbs and lips and grinding hips and, oh shit, there are people on this beach!

Ash seems to remember this at the same time I do, because suddenly he's lifting himself into a press-up position, bracing himself above me, his biceps bulging. We stare at each other, chests heaving, shell-shocked. His irises are almost entirely black, and I'm guessing my lips look as bee-stung as his do. He rolls away onto the sand beside me, adjusting himself beneath his swimming trunks.

"*Fuuuuccckk*," he says in a low groan, dragging his hand across his face. His other hand is still trying to hide his considerable length without much success. He casts me a sheepish look. "Sorry. It's been a while."

I lean in and give him a quick kiss before saying, through a smile, "I might go and take a shower."

"Okay." He sits up. "I'll get dinner sorted."

There's hardly anyone left on the beach now and no one is using the showers. I rinse myself off before walking back along the shoreline, trying to collect my scattered thoughts. Going by what's just happened, I'm not confident I'll be able to follow my counselor's advice about waiting until I'm in a proper relationship before taking things to the next level.

Would it really be so bad if we had sex? Our connection feels different to anything I've experienced before. There have been occasions in the past when I've clammed up or frozen around guys, but Ash makes me feel safe.

And if we got even closer, maybe I'd have the conviction to stand up to my parents, to keep traveling through Europe. With him.

It occurs to me that I'm depending heavily on someone I've only just met to help me rebuild the sense of self I lost after Stella died. I'd hoped traveling on my own would do that, allow me to know my own mind and grow my confidence, but it's had the opposite effect. I'm disappointed in myself, knowing that without Ash there's no way I'd even consider defying my mum and dad.

There's a cool breeze blowing in off the ocean, but there's still heat to the sun, so my skin dries as I walk back to Ash. He's laid his sleeping bag out on the sand, unzipped like a blanket, and the picnic he's prepared looks incredible. He went to grab some bits from a delicatessen in Sintra while I was at the internet café.

I get dressed again and comb out my hair, my thoughts still swirling.

"Where did you go?" Ash asks as I sit down.

From the look of apprehension on his face, I realize that he doesn't mean geographically.

"It bothers me that, without you, I wouldn't feel strong enough to carry on interrailing, or go against my mum and dad," I admit quietly.

"Ellie," he murmurs sympathetically, reaching out to take my hand. "It's okay to draw strength from a friend, you know. I used to do it with Taran. I still do it with Beca. Our parents might have raised us and put a roof over our heads, but mine didn't always make me feel that safe and secure growing up, and it sounds as though yours didn't either?" He waits for me to nod in agreement before continuing. "It helped getting some independence when I went to uni, but you didn't have that, still living at home."

"I feel so trapped at times," I admit, and suddenly it's all spilling out. "I want to please them. I want to impress them and make them proud. I went to the school they wanted me to go to, I studied furniture design at the university they wanted me to attend, and soon I'll take up my place full-time in a business I've been involved with part-time for years. And I'm okay with that. It might not be my first choice of career, but I'm a decent designer. I know I'll make them money. But I just don't think that anything I do will ever be good enough. They're always going to want more from me."

My eyes prick with tears and he lets go of my hand and slides both of his around my waist. I'm pulled into his lap and he wraps his arms around me, holding me close and allowing me to soak up his warmth and the feeling of someone caring enough to try to understand me.

"I'm sorry it hasn't been easy for you either," I say.

"My mother's fine, but my father is complicated. It's a double-edged sword with him, though, because on the one hand I'm glad he leaves me alone in favor of my brother, but on the other it hurts that he doesn't even seem to like me."

I squeeze him hard. "*I* like you," I whisper against his skin, my lips pressed to his neck. "I really, *really* like you."

"You have no fucking idea how much I like *you*," he replies.

I close my eyes and let that sink in for a moment before saying, "I'm going to come traveling with you."

He pulls away to look at me.

"I mean it," I say firmly. "I'll do whatever it takes. I'll meet you in Madrid next week."

The sudden joy on his face makes my heart cartwheel. He curves his hand around the back of my neck and draws me in for a kiss, our teeth knocking together because we can't stop smiling.

We eat and drink and kiss and talk and when we've finished eating and drinking we kiss and talk some more.

He tells me about Taran and how they used to camp out under the stars in a clearing in the woods near their homes, how they started when they were boys and continued right up until a couple of months before Taran's body succumbed to his illness.

Ash was there with Taran's parents and brother when Taran died and he watched as the last breath left his friend's chest. He still has nightmares about it and wishes he could wipe the memory from his mind.

I kiss away his tears and assure him that one day it won't hurt so much and he'll be glad of the comfort he brought Taran and his family when they needed it the most.

I confess that I wish I'd been with Stella when she died, but instead she was with her boyfriend and uni friends, whom I hadn't much cared for when I'd gone to visit. The thought of them all freaking out and not staying strong for her as she fell unconscious keeps me awake at night.

And he holds me when *I* cry, and kisses away my tears too.

We speak more about our parents and how when mine drink, my mum gets meaner and my dad gets louder. His parents drink on their own and socially, but rarely together.

He tells me more about Beca and how there was a weird moment just before he came away when she looked at him and he thought he saw more than friendship in her eyes. And it worried him, because he doesn't feel that way about her. I feel both jealous of her and sorry for her at the same time, because who wouldn't fall in love with Ash if they'd known him all their life? He's been in my life for less than three days and I can already feel my heart loosening its grip.

As the sun dips toward the horizon, lighting up the ocean with a blazing glow, we get dressed in warmer clothing and snuggle in close, staring out over the water. I sit with my back flush to his chest, his arms wrapped around me, and he presses kisses to my cheek as we watch the color show in the sky.

We speak about our past relationships and how neither of us has ever been in love, and when the sun disappears from sight, we use the cover of my thin sleeping bag and each other's body heat to keep ourselves warm.

When the night sky darkens, I ask him to tell me about the stars and the planets, and I have a surreal feeling that I could listen to his voice for the rest of my life and it still wouldn't be long enough.

Hours after the earth has rotated away from the moon and our faces are lit only by the light of distant suns, we stare at each other, finally lost for words.

He reaches for me at the same moment I reach for him, but this time our kiss is slower and more intimate. I feel as though I'm pouring myself into it. I want him to take my heart, my soul, *all* of me. I want to give myself to him, emotionally *and* physically.

I know that I tend toward overthinking, but when the voice inside my head cautions against rushing into things, I shut it down. I *trust* Ash, and I want this.

As I move on top of him, I make my intentions clear. His hands cut a slow path down my waist, hips, and thighs, tucking me against him. We're still fully clothed, but I can feel that he's already exactly where I wanted him and the low moan that emits from his throat is the biggest turn-on of my life. We begin to rock together, the need, the desire growing in intensity. Our kisses have become deeper and more demanding and I am so ready for him, so close to exploding, that I can barely find the words to ask if he has any protection.

"Are you sure?" he whispers once he's hunted out a little foil packet from an inside pocket of his rucksack.

"So sure," I whisper back.

He unzips my hoodie and slides it off my shoulders while I unbutton his shirt. He moves to tackle the much smaller buttons on my dress, and as our hands clash and get in the way of each other, we laugh and see to ourselves.

All our amusement dies once we're fully undressed. His eyes are glinting in the starlight and goose bumps chase the path of his hands over my skin as he pulls me onto him. I feel weightless and grounded at the same time, like I'm floating in the ether and yet connected to the earth and to Ash in a way that feels deeply profound.

Neither of us lasts long, and as the sound of our breathy moans pierces the darkness, I know with acute certainty that I'll remember this night forever.

8

WE FALL ASLEEP IN EACH OTHER'S ARMS AND I WAKE with the sunrise only a few hours later. Ash has one arm behind his head, propping it up so he can stare at the ocean, but he glances down at me when he feels me stirring.

"Good morning," he says huskily, pressing a kiss onto the tip of my nose.

"Morning," I whisper, not chancing my voice at full volume.

He hasn't put his shirt back on and his chest is bare and lovely. I trace my fingers over his stomach and he strokes my arm. I put my hoodie and underwear back on after we had sex, but I didn't bother with my dress.

"I wish I had some clean clothes to wear for seeing my parents," I murmur. "It's going to be hard enough as it is without giving them any more ammunition."

"We might be able to squeeze in a trip to the launderette before your train," Ash muses. "I built in extra time and I still need to do my clothes too."

"Our first date at last," I say with a grin.

"I feel like the last two and a half days have been our first date," he replies with amusement.

"If Lisbon was our first date, I can't wait for our second." I raise an eyebrow at him. "So . . . Madrid?"

He gives me his sweetest smile, the one that makes my heart sing.

"Shall we come up with a plan?" he asks.

I nod and he reaches for his rucksack, dragging it over. He gets out a map and flips onto his stomach, spreading it out. We both lean in close to study the city center.

"How about Plaza de España—" he says at the exact same moment that I suggest "Plaza Mayor?"

We smile at each other and take a closer look at the two options.

"This one has a monument," Ash points out.

"This one has a statue. I wonder if one of them has a café so we'd have somewhere to wait if we're early."

"Or late," he says. "Let's go with your suggestion, it's a bit smaller. Less chance of our not being able to spot each other."

We agree to meet at three o'clock in exactly one week's time.

"I'll give you my number too, just in case anything goes wrong." Before I can overthink it, I pull *A Court of Thorns and Roses* and a pen out of my bag.

"Are you sure about this?" Ash asks uncertainly as I write my mobile number on the inside cover. "I know it belonged to Stella."

I meet his eyes. "I trust you."

"I'll guard it with my life," he replies seriously.

"Okay." I smile at him and hand it over. "It has the contact for my parents' PA in there too, so if for any reason I can't get the same number for my mobile, at least we have a backup plan. Her name is Alison."

He studies the front cover for a moment, then says, "I think I'll get a phone when I'm in Porto. That way I can text you and we can stay in touch this week."

"You're coming back on-grid?" I ask with amazement.

He laughs at the look on my face and it makes me laugh too.

"I'm going to really miss your sniggle," he says fondly. "It's ridiculously cute."

I feel as though I'm evaporating with the way he's looking at me right now.

The sun has not yet risen behind the cliffs, but the sky is a wash of neon apricot.

"You're so fucking pretty," he murmurs. "Your hair is the same color as the sky right now, it's insane. I seriously regret not having a camera."

"How don't you have a girlfriend?"

He laughs and kisses me again, this time with more intent, and before I know it, I'm beneath him, feeling completely lit up.

Sex is so much more intense in the daylight. We don't break eye contact, not once, not even when we're in the process of falling and I'm clutching on to him, feeling his muscles tighten beneath my fingers.

When it's over, I try to commit every second to memory, knowing I'll relive them in the days to come.

LATER, WE STAND on the platform at Lisbon station, in each other's arms. Everything has gone to plan—we've been to the launderette and we even managed a final lunch at the TimeOut Market before arriving in good time for our trains. He's catching one to Porto in half an hour.

"Stay strong with your parents, Ellie," Ash urges fervently, cradling my head in the gap between his jaw and his collarbone.

I press my lips to his neck and feel the echo of his heart leaping against my mouth before looking up at his face, my resolve strengthening.

"I will."

He meets my eyes. "Just before Taran died, he said something to me that's stuck." He swallows and I wait for him to go on. "He said that if he'd known how little time he had, he would have swum in more rivers and stayed up late more often to watch the stars. He wished he'd cherished the sound of the rain on the roof and the birdsong in the woods. But the thing is, Taran did appreciate all of those things. He just knew what he loved and regretted not doing more of it." His expression is grave as he stares down at me. "Seeing you in the gardens, hearing you talk about trees and your favorite flowers and your nan's lupins . . . Gardening is your passion, Ellie."

His eyes shine with emotion and I bury my face against him, fighting back tears as I hold on tightly, but he hasn't finished.

"Please don't let your parents bully you," he implores in a low, urgent voice in my ear. "Follow your own path. Life is too short not to do what you love. You and I know that better than most."

The whistle blows and we jolt, breaking apart. I brush away my tears and pull him in for one last hard hug before wrenching myself away to step onto the train.

I want to do as he urges, but I just don't know if I can.

He's standing outside the open doorway when I turn around to face him.

"I'll see you in Madrid," he says seriously.

I nod quickly, unable to speak past the lump in my throat. My tears won't let up.

Suddenly, leaving him feels like madness. What am I doing? I could stay with him, not go to the Algarve. I've already been to Porto and the other places he wants to visit, but it would be completely different with him at my side.

The doors whoosh shut on my racing thoughts and on impulse I slap my palm against the glass, panicked.

His eyes meet mine through the window, his expression worried, but beneath that is a steadiness that centers me.

I trust him. We'll be together again in a week.

It'll be okay, he mouths, his brows knitted together.

I nod quickly, wanting to believe him, as the train slowly pulls away, leaving behind the one person I want in my future.

9

TEARS STREAM DOWN MY FACE AS I SIT AND STARE OUT
the window, trying to soothe the ache in my chest by reflecting
on my time with Ash. I can't help but smile at some of the memories we created—even going to the launderette felt special, sitting
close with his arm hooked around my neck, my leg dangling over
his, not caring about PDAs as we kissed and talked and laughed.

But now it's six days later and Ash still hasn't called. I managed to get the same number on my second day here after finding
a phone shop that sold fully unlocked devices, but it hasn't made
a difference. I haven't heard from him. I'm staying strong with my
parents regardless, though the atmosphere at their villa has been
thick with tension. When I arrived, my dad was okay—he was in
full holiday swing—but Mum was infuriated by my insolence at
being twenty-four hours late. Her icy reception was tame compared to how she took the news that I planned to continue interrailing. She had already told people that I'd start working at Knap
three weeks earlier than expected, so the delay would cause her to
look as though she'd lost control—her kryptonite.

Eventually I cracked under the weight of her declarations of how selfish and ungrateful I was, and admitted that I'd met someone and wanted to continue traveling with him.

I regretted it as soon as I said it, and she didn't disappoint, shaking her head at me pityingly as she said, "I should have known you were following a man. You've always been a sheep."

It didn't help that I had to admit I didn't know Ash's surname. How could we have left so much unsaid? We talked about everything that mattered and yet it never occurred to me to ask for his last name. We don't know each other's addresses or social media handles—I'm not even sure if he's *on* social media; he didn't have Instagram. If he'd come to the internet café with me instead of going to get picnic supplies, he would have seen the name of my family business on the website, but he didn't.

I know there will be an explanation for why he couldn't contact me. I remember the tightness of his arms around me as we hugged goodbye, and the intense look in his eyes as he told me he'd see me in Madrid. I just have to make it to him.

Now it's one week since I left Ash and it's imperative that I get to Madrid on time. But to my sheer and absolute horror, the bus from Albufeira breaks down on the way to Seville. My heart is thumping so hard as we're told to disembark and wait at the side of the road.

What follows is the longest hour and a half of my life—I'm shaking with panic by the time I see our replacement bus coming along and the relief literally makes me feel so weak at the knees that I have to sit down. As long as the trains from Seville to Madrid are running on time, I should be okay.

But when I race into the hot, stuffy station and see the hordes of people waiting, I know something is wrong. It turns out a train broke down earlier and it's taking time to clear the backlog.

When a train to Madrid eventually comes, it's carnage with all the people trying to board. I push my way onto a carriage with a ferocity that only my determination to see Ash could conjure. For two and a half hours, I stand in the aisle of the crowded train car, rucksack between my legs, bouncing on my feet and muttering under my breath. With every glance at my watch, my heart rate ratchets up and my sense of helplessness and loss of control increases.

Please wait, Ash. I'm coming.

What if he thinks that I couldn't stand up to my parents and didn't keep my promise to him? What if he gives up on me?

I'd built in enough time to be an hour early, but I'm forty-five minutes late as I shove my way off the train and run toward the taxi rank. Plaza Mayor, where we've agreed to meet, is a half-hour walk from here, but if I can just jump in a cab . . .

I almost scream with frustration at the massive queue, but I hold it together and begin to run. I'm racked with anxiety, sweat breaking out over my skin as I pound the pavements under the ferocious glare of the sun. I'm so hot and breathless by the time I reach the square that I feel sick. And when there's no sign of Ash by the statue, I almost do throw up. What if he's already left?

There is a café, as I'd hoped, but he's not inside, so I search the shops around the perimeter, returning to the center of the square after every visit. When there's nowhere else for me to look, I sit down at the base of the statue, trying to keep my stinging arms in the shade as tears stream down my cheeks.

Maybe he's late too. Surely he hasn't given up on me—I never would have given up on him so soon.

I wait for two more hours in the blazing Madrid heat.

My mother's laughter when I revealed I didn't know Ash's last name rings in my ears, as well as her snide comment: *That's a red flag, if ever I saw one. What's he hiding?*

What if she was right? What if he didn't come? What if he's never coming? Did I read too much into those three days? Ash could have had anyone—what makes me think I'm special? Maybe I wasn't. Was I just a hook-up to him?

Fuck, it's messing with my mind. My heart feels like it's in a vise. Am I being ghosted?

No. No. It was real, what we had. It was *something*. He said he'd be here, and he will be, even if he's late. And if he was early or on time, he would have waited for me like I'm waiting for him. He would have given me the benefit of the doubt, at least for a couple of hours.

But why didn't he call? Surely he wouldn't have lost Stella's book—he knew how important it was to me. Doubts continue to crowd in as I spiral.

I decide to wait in the café, but another hour passes and I grow desperate.

He couldn't have faked the way he looked at me, I try to reassure myself, replaying our time together on the beach. I think of how we lay side by side on the sand, studying his map and trying to decide where to meet, and suddenly a thought occurs to me.

Oh my God. Have I got the wrong square?

I leap to my feet, my heart racing as I check Maps on my phone. I almost run out of the café without paying and have to quickly backtrack to settle up.

The walk to Plaza de España is seventeen minutes. I'm almost certain we agreed on Plaza Mayor, but I go to the other square anyway. My skin is burned to a crisp, the soles of my feet sting, my throat is parched, and my heart feels cauterized. Every inch of my body is stretched to breaking point, but I keep searching. I look under every tree, behind every statue and monument, inside every shop, bar, restaurant, and café I can find. I do this until the light fades from the sky and I'm forced to find somewhere to stay for the night.

The next day I do it all over again. And the next day. And the next.

I can't bear to leave Madrid, can't face the fact that Ash will be lost to me forever if I do. I can't accept that he didn't come, that I wasn't worth showing up for. So I stay there as the days roll into one another, my heart broken, an empty vessel wandering the streets, searching but never finding.

After calling my parents' PA for the eighth day running to check whether Ash has been in touch, she tells me that she's booked a flight home for me the following day. I don't argue. I have no strength left.

Even my mother holds her tongue when she sees me, but I can tell that she's shocked. I start work the next day; I need something to take my mind off Ash.

AFTER A WHILE, the pain begins to recede. I'm not sure I'll ever escape the dull ache, but the crippling agony of betrayal, of not being enough, grows muted with time. I spend most of my waking hours at the office, and six months after leaving Madrid, I find myself at my desk late on a Friday night, the technical drawings for my new Stella range laid out before me. It's just sold into John Lewis. I wish it made me happy.

My parents quite like this new me, the emotionless, hard-working daughter my mother always wanted me to be.

———

A FEW MORE months pass and the office lifestyle is getting to me—the traffic on my way to work, the fluorescent lighting, the sound of ringing phones and irate voices. I frequently find myself staring out of the window, thoughts of Ash coming unbidden. I suppressed so many of my memories after Madrid and it still hurts to think about him, but for some reason, now I can't stop.

A YEAR AFTER we parted ways, I'm studying a fabric sample for my new Lisbon range—the same color as the peach iced tea I was drinking when we met, the color I recall Ash's eyes being. Everyone else went home hours ago, but I can't bring myself to get up from my chair.

What happened to you?

A rush of emotion overcomes me and I go with the tidal wave. I get through almost a whole box of tissues that night.

ANOTHER YEAR PASSES and I'm going through life on autopilot, but no one notices, or if they do, they don't care. I push out range after range after range, and my career goes from strength to strength. I have never felt more alone.

MY CONFIDENCE GROWS and my heart begins to harden. My parents congratulate me when my ranges are featured in the press, but their compliments bounce off me, just as their occasional insults do. I no longer care about people-pleasing.

I tell myself that I don't need anyone. I don't need my parents,

I don't need my grandparents, I don't need Stella, I don't need Ash. The only person I can depend on is myself and it's time to take back some control.

EXACTLY THREE YEARS after leaving Ash in Lisbon, I walk into the boardroom for a meeting that I've called with my parents and hand them a check for £30,000.

"That's for my university tuition," I say leadenly, laying it on the table along with my letter of resignation and an agreement from my lawyer that signs over my shares and revokes all future profits from my designs.

I don't want to owe them anything. It's the only way I'll be free to live my life the way I choose to live it.

Whatever happened to Ash, I still believe in the words he spoke to me on the train platform. *Life is too short not to do what you love.* And I'm tired of living to please my parents.

Mum and Dad leave work soon after I do, arriving home in time to see me carrying my bags to the front door. The shock on their faces makes me feel oddly numb.

"If you walk out that door, you're gone for good," Mum warns.

"Marian," my dad interjects.

"If that's what you want, that's what you'll get," I reply, avoiding my dad's gaze.

I can't deal with the thought of him being hurt. I have to keep my eyes set on my goal. It's time to follow my own path.

PART
TWO

10

"YOU'RE FULL OF SHIT," I SAY TO EVAN. "IT'S WARMER here than in Surrey. Where's all this rain you keep bleating on about?"

"You'll get it soon enough." He throws me a lazy grin from the driver's seat.

I think that was an unintentional double entendre, but I can never be sure with Evan. There's always been an underlying tension between us, the kind that a tussle between the sheets would probably cure, but that sort of thing would have been inappropriate before.

I doubt it would be a good idea now either, seeing as we're about to start working together, but at least I'm fully qualified. When I was doing my training, the balance of power was far too heavily weighted in his favor.

We met while I was doing a horticultural operative apprenticeship at RHS Garden Wisley in Surrey. I'd secretly been looking into doing a Level 2 qualification with the Royal Horticultural Society when I saw that applications for their apprenticeship program were open. On a whim, I applied, but I didn't think any-thing would come of it. I couldn't believe it when I landed a place.

The lady who interviewed me said that my design training was an asset and easily transferable, but I think she was touched on a personal level by the stories I shared about Nan.

Accepting the apprenticeship required a leap of faith, a full-on jump into a new career. It was a two-year fully paid posi-tion, but the salary was a pittance compared to what I'd been earning at Knap. I can't deny it—I was terrified to walk away.

My dad and I speak every couple of months or so, but our conversations are strained. He texted me the same night I left home, asking me to keep him abreast of what I was doing.

It took several months for me to pluck up the courage and con-fess that I'd left Knap in pursuit of gardening. He was shocked. I can't imagine what my mum thinks: that I've lost my mind, that I'm having a breakdown, that I'm breathtakingly stupid . . . Prob-ably all those things and more.

She and I haven't spoken since the day I walked out. She's es-tranged from her own mother, so I shouldn't be surprised that she has it in her to cut me out of her life. My chest feels tight when I think of her, so I try not to do it often.

Christmases are the worst. I may have hated living with my parents at times, and often I felt desperately lonely, but only now do I appreciate what it means to be truly alone.

Sometimes the weight on my shoulders feels so heavy, but not when I'm gardening. When I'm surrounded by nature, I am happy and light.

Evan was one of the staff members who trained me, a down-to-earth Aussie with a cheeky sense of humor—he was only three years my senior and we hit it off immediately. He used to work at the Royal Botanic Garden in Sydney, but had been living in the UK for a few years—his mother is Welsh.

I was gutted to see him go toward the end of my apprenticeship when he accepted a job at Berkeley Hall, a privately owned estate on the Welsh side of the border with England, but we stayed in touch.

Once I'd qualified, I managed to secure part-time work staying on at Wisley, filling my free hours working as a gardener for private clients. But it's been tough financially, and my living arrangements have also been a challenge. For the last three years, I've been a lodger in a family home, living with a couple in their late thirties who have two small children. They're nice enough to me, but I've always felt like I'm encroaching on their space. It has never felt like home.

"Almost there," Evan says.

He collected me from Wrexham train station in a big black estate-owned Range Rover and is wearing his uniform of a dark green polo shirt with black shorts and brown boots. I've seen him donning the Berkeley Hall getup on his #hotgardener profile on Instagram. His handle is his name, Evan Kite, but his friends and colleagues have taken to using the hashtag in the comments to tease him because he occasionally posts bare-chested pictures of himself.

I'm a little mortified that he puts himself out there in this way—you'd never catch me posting half-naked pics of myself for likes—but there's no denying that the sight of him shirtless does get me a bit hot under the collar.

He's gorgeous—tall at just over six foot, well-built with a head of thick, short, scruffy hair—and so likable and easygoing that I'm surprised he hasn't been snapped up. He was dating someone in the early days of my apprenticeship, but that ended and to my knowledge he hasn't been serious with anyone since.

I drag my eyes away from his toned forearms and tanned hands gripping the steering wheel and feel kind of edgy.

Now thirty to my twenty-seven, Evan is still senior to me, but he's not my direct boss. I'm one of three gardeners and he's assistant head gardener. We both answer to the head gardener, Owain, who interviewed me over the telephone a few weeks ago. It made my heart pinch to hear his warm Welsh accent—the way he rolled his *r*'s was exactly the same way Ash had—but he was a lot older, in his early sixties from what Evan has told me. I sensed he had already made up his mind about hiring me on Evan's recommendation. Jobs rarely come up at Berkeley Hall, so I'm lucky.

"I reckon," Evan says thoughtfully as we drive along a narrow country road lined with leafy beech trees, "I might be able to show you the gatehouse before it shuts up shop."

"What time does the house close to the public?" I ask, checking my watch. It's four thirty.

"Usually five o'clock, but last entry is at four unless there's a private function. They don't do many of those, though," Evan says as we pass by a group of modest 1970s houses. The land opens back up again onto fields on our right, while on our left is a redbrick wall, too high to see over. He slows to a snail's speed and turns left, passing through tall wrought-iron gates.

"This is the family's private drive. The public entry runs parallel to this road, just a bit farther on, but you need to see the hall from this perspective for your first time."

My eyes widen with wonder. Up ahead, at the end of a long, narrow stretch of asphalt flanked by green fields, is the house.

I've seen it in pictures, of course, but nothing compares to seeing it in real life. The sunlight is hitting the cream stone, making it look golden, and the crenelated facade is so wide that if it were set down parallel to one of the ordinary London streets where I grew up, it would be the length of ten terraced houses.

"The bays on the left and right were added in the late 1700s, but the Tudor gatehouse in the middle was built in the early sixteenth century, although it's had a few alterations over the years," Evan tells me of the central, more decorative section of the building. It has hexagonal turrets and curved bay windows with long, thin panels of glass that reflect the sunlight. "It was gifted to the family by Henry VIII," he adds, throwing me a significant look.

I'll admit I'm fascinated by the history, even if I don't agree with the principle of wealthy white men handing down property to wealthy white men for hundreds of years.

"Has the same family owned it all this time?" I ask curiously.

"Yep. Five hundred years and twenty-one generations."

"Holy shit," I murmur.

He grins at me. "Once upon a time, people on horses and carts used to ride straight through the gatehouse to a courtyard at the back." He points to enormous arched doors at the base of the gatehouse, which are wide open. "But when the bays on either side were built, the owners sealed it up and incorporated it into the rest of the house."

"It's beautiful."

"Wait until you see the gardens." He pulls to a stop in front of the house.

"Can you just park here like this?" I ask with surprise. There are no other cars in sight.

"Yeah, the main car park's down the hill, but staff use this door for deliveries."

"We don't have any deliveries."

"You're a delivery," he says flippantly, reaching for the door

handle. "I'm delivering our lovely new gardener to her new home."
He winks at me as he climbs out of the car.

"Where *are* the workers' cottages?" I ask, because I know that
I'm not living *here*.

"On the other side of the walled garden, so not far at all."

I would have jumped at the chance of a full-time gardening
job anywhere, but the fact that this position came with accommo-
dation was a *massive* bonus.

Evan was the person I most connected with at Wisley, so I'm
thrilled to be working with him again and I'm excited to meet
some new people—apparently there's a whole social aspect to living in the workers' cottages. There's a sawmill and a workshop on
the estate that employ a team of cool young guys, some of whom
also live at the cottages, and Evan thinks I'll really get on with
Siân, my new housemate, and Bethan, who I'll be working alongside in the gardens.

I had no problem about leaving the South of England to relo-
cate to Wales, even with all the teasing about the weather. But I
still can't think of Wales without remembering Ash. It's been almost six years, but I'm not over him and I'm not sure I ever will be.
He was at the forefront of my mind when Evan told me he was
moving here, and when a gardening position came up, I thought
of Ash again.

It can still keep me awake at night, wondering what happened
to him. It's a mystery that I've had to accept I will never solve.

I've tried to let him go, but being here in his home country is
probably going to set me back.

It's not that I haven't been on other dates, because I have in
the last couple of years, and I even had a short-term relationship,
though it didn't last more than a few weeks. The chemistry I felt

with Ash was so electric, nobody else has come close to lighting me up the way he did.

Evan is the only person I've felt might have potential.

It's getting late in the day, but it's a Sunday and the weather is so temperate that I'm surprised this whole place is not teeming with visitors.

"Is it usually this quiet?" I ask as we enter the gatehouse, our footsteps reverberating off the thick stone slabs of the floor.

"No, but most people will be outside in the gardens on a day like this," Evan replies.

Above our heads is a gorgeous vaulted ceiling and there's a large faded tapestry hanging on a wall. A suit of polished steel armor stands in one of the bay windows. Double doors lead off to the left and right, where a couple of people are loitering, but my attention is drawn by what's beyond the big arched doors straight ahead.

We step outside into a courtyard garden with low hedges and flower beds bursting with miniature pink roses, set around a beautiful central fountain. On the left is what looks like a very old section of the house. It has a pitched roof and is part timber-framed and part redbrick, with lead-paneled lattices on the windows holding tiny glass panes.

"There used to be two other wings just like that one," Evan says, pointing at the old section.

"Tudor?" I ask.

"Yep, built not long after the gatehouse. The Great Hall is Regency." He nods to our right at a second, more modern but still very old wing made of cream stone with tall windows and glass doors that open directly onto the garden. Looking through a window, I can see a bunch of round tables dressed with white tablecloths. "This courtyard used to be fully enclosed," Evan says. "But the north and east wings burned down in the early nineteenth century. Whoever was custodian of the place at the time decided not to rebuild the north wing, and why would you?"

He nods ahead at the view. It's breathtaking, a gently undulating hill that dips and then rises into woodland in the distance.

There's a clanking sound to my right and a large window in the Regency wing flies open. An attractive older woman with windswept chin-length blond hair leans out.

"Evan, darling, can we borrow you a minute?" she calls in a cut-glass accent. "We need a nice big pair of strong male hands."

"Sure, Mrs. B.," Evan replies amiably, turning to me and saying: "If you want to head that way and hang a right, you'll come to the rose gardens and a view of the orangery. I'll see you there in a minute?"

"Okay."

"Oh, is that Eleanor Knapley?" the woman calls out eagerly as I begin to walk away.

"Fresh off the train," Evan replies.

I glance over my shoulder to see him genially beckoning me back.

"It's wonderful to meet you," she gushes. "And we *must* have a proper chat soon, but right now I've a small emergency with a fridge-freezer. Come, come!" she urges Evan.

He gives me an amused look as he sets off toward a pair of double doors farther along the building.

I come out of the courtyard garden onto a wide gravel path that's lined with towering topiary columns. To the left, a couple of hundred meters away, is an old church sitting in a field of long grass accessed by a winding path. My eyes sweep right over the far sunlit trees climbing the hill in the distance and pause on a stretch of water at the edge of the woods. The estate certainly seems vast. Luckily, we're only responsible for the formal gardens.

A neatly mowed lawn slopes down from this top terrace to a lower level where a young family is playing with oversized Jenga blocks. As I wander right, along the path, I notice giant chess pieces and other garden games too, and there are a couple of people lying on the steep slope, soaking up the last of the day's sunshine. There are a few other visitors about and it occurs to me that this might be my one and only chance to enjoy the gardens just like them—from tomorrow, I'll be an employee here, wearing a gardener's uniform.

Today I'm dressed in jeans and a lightweight sweater, with my long hair piled up on my head in a messy bun. I breathe in deeply, my gaze roaming over the cottage-garden plants in the beds by the house: spicy orange roses climbing the old stone walls, clusters of blousy pink peonies, and tall vibrant purple irises swaying in the late-spring breeze. The perfume from the rose gardens up ahead hits my nose.

Everyone who heard I was moving to Wales warned me to:

"Pack your wet-weather gear!"

"Don't forget your raincoat!"

"Make sure you've got a good umbrella!"

Or some variation on the same theme.

Even Evan told me to "Say goodbye to sunshine!"

But according to the weather forecast, it's supposed to be sunny all week. It's only the middle of May—I can't believe my luck.

I head in the direction of the formal rose garden, which is laid out in a traditional design around a central gray stone fountain, and then I take a left past a tall hedge. The orangery comes into view at the end of a long sloping lawn and it's stunning: Georgian, I assume, with tall double doors and a pitched glass roof that I can just make out from this higher perspective. At the bottom of the hill behind the orangery is a glittering lake—the stretch of water I saw from the house—and beyond it, the woods climb back uphill in the distance.

My attention is caught by a vibrant block of red in the wide garden beds butting up against the lawn that leads down to the orangery. My breath catches: lupins. Masses of them. And not just in red, but all colors.

My heart lifts as I walk down a few steps and come to a stop, drinking in the sight. It's like Nan's rainbow garden scaled up to the power of fifty, beginning with reds and oranges, morphing into pinks and purples, and ending with blues, yellows, and whites.

Nan would have given her right arm to come and see me working in a garden like this.

For a moment, I imagine her standing there beside me, her face lit up with wonder and pride. Tears prick my eyes at the thought.

I have come a long way.

11

EVAN COMES TO FIND ME AFTER A FEW MINUTES.

"What do you think?" he asks with a smile.

"Amazing. I can't wait to start work."

"You haven't seen the half of it yet. We should probably move the car, though. I can give you the rest of the tour tomorrow."

"Sure thing."

We make our way back out through the courtyard. There are still a few visitors around, but I'm guessing they'll soon be ushered toward the exit.

"Who was that lady who needed your help?" I ask of the woman who interrupted us.

"Oh, sorry, I should have introduced you properly," he says as our feet crunch over the gravel at the front of the house. "That was Philippa Berkeley."

"You're shitting me!" I exclaim in a hushed voice. "*That* was the lady of the house?"

She looked so ordinary in her dark green zip-up vest and

unbrushed hair. Her accent was superposh, but I just assumed she worked here.

"Yep." He sounds amused. "She's a character all right."

"I can't believe you call her Mrs. B.," I say as we climb into the car.

"She loves it," he replies with a grin. "I'm the only one who dares, though."

That's because he's a cheeky flirt and can get away with it.

"Harri, Bethan, and Siân call her Lady Berkeley," he adds as he starts the ignition.

Harri and Bethan are gardeners at my level, although they're both a couple of years younger than I am. Siân, my new housemate, works in the kitchens.

"What's Peter Berkeley like?" I ask about the viscount of the house as Evan does a U-turn.

"Haven't seen too much of the guy, to be honest. *Lord Berkeley* doesn't involve himself with staff," he adds, affecting a Queen's English accent and grinning.

"But Lady Berkeley does?" I ask with amusement at his teasing. She knew who *I* was.

"She involves herself with *everything*," he says meaningfully.

We head along another track leading off the private drive. Up ahead is a high redbrick wall—the walled garden, I suspect. Evan turns down the right-hand side of it and drives along a narrow dirt track, coming to a stop at the end. Running parallel to the rear of the wall, set well back, is a row of five tiny Victorian terraced cottages.

Yellow climbing roses crawl up the gray stone walls and each of the front doors is painted a different color: green, purple, pink, blue, and yellow.

Evan tells me that they were built to house estate workers in the late 1800s and they're still used for the same purpose today.

"Owain and his wife, Gwen, live at number one—on the right," Evan tells me of the cottage with the yellow door. "Gwen heads up the kitchen."

And Owain, of course, is our boss.

"Harri and I live next door in number two, you and Siân are right by us in three, and those last two cottages are occupied by rangers and workshop crew. The workshop is over there, the saw-mill behind it." He nods at the Victorian outbuildings beyond the cottages.

"How many rangers are there?" I ask.

The rangers handle everything past the formal-garden boundaries: the woodland, parkland, and everything in between, including the lake.

"Two. You'll meet them later. I've invited everyone for a few beers and a barbie. A little party to welcome our new arrival."

"Aw." I smile at him, feeling both touched and slightly nervous at the prospect of getting to know so many new people.

Bethan and Siân are who I most want to meet, but Siân is away on holiday until the end of the month. In some ways it's not a bad thing: I'll have almost two weeks to settle in and make the cottage my home before she returns.

I'm a bit apprehensive about living with someone I've never met, but at least I'm used to sharing other people's spaces—I've done it my whole life.

"Does Bethan live on-site?" I ask.

"Nope, she commutes in from Wrexham." That's where we've just come from, about half an hour away. "But she's been staying here a lot lately, as she and Harri recently started seeing each other."

He gives me a knowing look and gets out of the car, walking around to the boot.

"Leave them," he says when I try to help with one of my suitcases.

He carries them both to the middle cottage with the baby-pink door and sets them down by the porch. There are so many bees buzzing around the climbing roses.

"Right, here are your keys." He pulls a set of keys on a black leather key ring out of his pocket and hands it over. "The square one's for the front door, round one's for the back, and the skeleton key accesses the walled garden. Use it anytime."

"Seriously?"

"It's the one place staff have unrestricted access to," he says, gripping the posts on either side of the porch, his posture casual and easy as he rests his body weight against the frame. "We tend to avoid the formal gardens outside working hours, but no one will mind if you go for a wander farther afield. I'll be amazed if you have the stamina for it, though. We're going to work you hard."

Did he mean that to sound sexy? It gives me a thrill anyway.

He grins and rakes his hand through his dark hair, ruffling it up a little as he backs away.

"I'll let you settle in. Gwen has stocked up the fridge to get you started, and she's also left some shirts and fleeces for you to try on for size. You have black shorts?"

"Yep." He sent me the uniform requirements a couple of weeks ago, so I'm all sorted.

"Great. Come over at around six thirty? Use the back door, as we'll be outside."

"Thanks so much for collecting me from the station."

"No worries. See you later," he replies with a grin.

The cottage is small and cozy with a living room off the front door and a kitchen at the back. The living room has matching faded blue two-seater sofas that have seen better days, a rectangular white coffee table, and a TV. In the kitchen there's a small round dining table with a yellow tablecloth and four wooden chairs. Fresh flowers sit in a vase on the top, a mixture of irises: violet, mauve, and butter yellow. I wonder, warmly, if my new boss's wife, Gwen, put them there.

It takes some maneuvering to get my bulky suitcases up the narrow staircase, but finally I make it into my bedroom. There's a neat pile of dark green polo shirts, long-sleeved shirts, and fleeces on the bed, which is a small double with a Cath Kidston–style bedspread: white with tiny red roses.

I pick up a polo shirt and study the Berkeley family crest embroidered in white in the top right corner. It looks like a shield with feathers spilling out the top. I noticed the same crest printed on the black leather key ring Evan gave me.

I don't love that I couldn't stick to my principles when it came to working here. But the pay is decent and hopefully I'll get the experience to one day work for an organization I believe in, like the National Trust. That's the plan, anyway. For now, I'm doing what's necessary.

Throwing the polo shirt back on the bed, I walk to the window. It faces onto the walled garden and the house beyond, so I'm guessing Siân's view is of the Victorian outbuildings and fields at the back. A shared bathroom divides our bedrooms.

Pulling up the sash window, I prop my elbows on the windowsill, unable to keep from smiling. The walled garden is by far the largest I've seen and it's bursting with life and color. Victorian lean-to greenhouses line the south-facing wall on the right, and parallel to them is a large vegetable patch and rows of espalier fruit trees, trained against horizontal wires. The middle of the garden comprises mostly round and crescent-shaped beds set among lawn, and on the far left is an arch of laburnums in full bloom, yellow flowers raining down. Beyond the stretch of wall closest to the cottages is an orchard of apple trees, but there must be other beds at the base of the wall that I can't see—an abundance of purple wisteria spills over the top.

Gardening is everything I dreamed it would be and so much more. I love what I do now and I have never felt more comfortable in my own skin.

I breathe in deeply and want to pinch myself. I can't believe I get to live and work here.

MUSIC STARTS PLAYING through the walls of the neighboring cottage a good twenty minutes before Evan said to come over, but I wait until just after six thirty before venturing outside, opening the back door to the smell of barbecue coals.

The five dwellings share a communal garden: a long stretch of lawn bordered by lavender that hasn't yet come into bloom. A patchwork of farmers' fields lead to hilly woodland on the far left, and the land is basking in a warm glow from the early-evening sunshine.

A group of men are hovering around a barbecue farther along the garden, cans of beer in their hands. They're all dressed casually—most will have had the weekend off—and Evan is among them. He looks over and clocks me as I pull the door closed.

"Ellie!" he shouts with a grin, setting down a pair of tongs and stepping out from behind the grill.

He's changed into light blue shorts and a white T-shirt and he looks relaxed and casual as he approaches. The other men stop talking and turn to watch me. Evan's introductions mostly go in one ear and out the other, but I do meet the two rangers and a couple of workshop employees, plus fellow gardener Harri, a tall, ruddy-cheeked lad with sloping shoulders and a mop of bright blond hair.

An older man emerges from the last cottage, shouting over his shoulder, "Come on, Gwen, the party's already started!" before making a beeline for me with a crooked smile on his face. "You must be Ellie," he says in a voice I'm already familiar with.

"Owain?" I guess, taking his hand.

"That's me."

He's a touch shorter than me and stocky in build, with thinning gray hair.

"And this is my wife, Gwen." He waves over a curly-haired woman who has just come out of the cottage.

Her face lights up with a smile as she opens her arms to me.

"Welcome!" she says, enclosing me in the sort of several-seconds hug that would normally be reserved for people who know each other well. "Is it Ellie or Eleanor?" she asks as she withdraws, keeping her hands on my upper arms.

"Ellie."

"I heard Philly call you Eleanor earlier, so I wasn't sure."

"Philly?"

"Well, probably Lady Berkeley to you. Some of us have worked here a long time, so we're on more familiar terms," she adds with a twinkle in her eye.

A moment later, a tall brunette in frayed denim shorts and a sunshine-yellow sweater bounds out of Evan and Harri's cottage.

"I'm so glad to have another girl on the team!" she exclaims, swooping in for a hard hug before releasing me and beaming. "I'm Bethan."

I like her immediately.

In fact, I like them all.

My feelings only grow stronger as the evening wears on. These people act like a family and in many cases, they are. Owain's brother Edmund heads up the sawmill and workshop, and their other brother, Gareth, used to be head ranger here, but now Gareth's son Celyn is. Bethan's aunt works in the kitchens, and the person whose position I'm filling is assistant ranger Dylan's cousin.

It's a little overwhelming being surrounded by so many people who sound just like Ash, and when Catfish and the Bottlemen—a band we listened to on our way to Sintra—come over the sound system, he's *all* I can think about.

"Where are these guys from again?" I ask Celyn.

His name is pronounced KEL-in.

"Llandudno."

My heart hurts—he sounds so much like Ash.

Is there a chance, any chance at all, that I might be in Ash's old stamping ground? It's hard to believe that we could bump into each other, but I'm imagining it nonetheless.

When the temperature drops and people begin to call it a night, Evan invites me into the cottage he shares with Harri.

Bethan lets out a squeal of excitement as she sits on the sofa beside me, squeezing my arm. I look at her face and laugh. She is so friendly, I love it.

"What's Siân like?" I ask as Evan and Harri bring over drinks and snacks from the kitchen.

"Oh, she's *great*," Bethan enthuses. "When Eleri left, I thought about moving into your room just so I could live with Siân."

"Why didn't you?" I ask with a smile. "And who's Eleri?"

"Eleri worked in the kitchen with Siân, and I didn't because I love living at home. My mam and I are very close."

I smile through a pang of envy. She's lucky.

"She also does the best lamb cawl I've ever tasted," Harri chips in.

"What's lamb cawl?" I ask.

"It's like a lamb-and-vegetable stew."

"It's more of a soup," Bethan argues.

"Whatever, I *love* it," Harri says dramatically.

Bethan grins at him. They're a cute couple.

"How long have you guys been seeing each other?" I ask.

"Too long!" Evan says, at the same time that Bethan and Harri reply simultaneously, "Two months."

Harri whacks Evan's arm and Evan chuckles, turning to me. We smile at each other and then he drops his gaze and takes a swig of his beer.

No one looks at me like Ash did.

But I'm tired of being on my own. I'm sick of feeling desperately lonely. I want to fall in love. I want to get married and have a family of my own one day, bring children into the world who will never for a second doubt my love for them.

I used to wish with all my heart that Ash and I would find our way back to each other, that he might be my person, the person I would spend the rest of my life with. But I've spent a lot of time wondering if I built those three days into a bigger deal than they were. That connection felt *so* strong . . . But I think it might be time to lower my expectations and start being a bit more realistic.

I look down to where Harri's ankle is hooked around Bethan's and feel another twinge of envy.

I'm attracted to Evan. I like flirting with him and we have good banter. If he made a move on me, I'd welcome it. But could I fall in love with him? Is it worth the risk? What if it gets messy?

Argh, I'm overthinking again. I should probably call it a night.

"Right, bed is calling," I say as I stand up. "Ready tomorrow morning by eight?"

"Yep," Evan replies, getting to his feet. "I can knock for you or you can meet us in the walled garden. It's where the volunteers congregate and where we kick off each day."

"Cool. I don't know whether to go home through the front door or the back."

"We need a hatch in the wall," Bethan says. "Or a secret doorway hidden behind wallpaper like the ones in the house!"

It hits me, once again, that I've landed a job at a five-hundred-year-old historic home. I have a roof over my head in a gorgeous cottage, a steady, reasonable-sized salary, colleagues I like and who may even come to feel like family, and a job I *know* I'm going to adore with all my heart. I've done it. I'm proud of myself.

That night, I go to bed feeling so happy I could cry.

12

WAKE AT DAWN TO THE SOUND OF BIRDSONG AND DON'T even bother trying to doze back off. I could barely sleep last night with the excitement. There's a chill in the air as I climb out of bed and go to the window, drawing back the curtains. A thin layer of mist hovers over the garden within the walls, and I can see it drifting in long swathes across the fields at the front of the house. It creeps into the woodland in the north and sits on the hills in the west like a blanket—a bit farther on are the Berwyn Mountains. Farther still is Snowdonia National Park. Evan said I can borrow the staff Range Rover on days off and explore. I have so much to look forward to this summer.

I'M READY TO go long before eight, champing at the bit to get started.

Evan laughs when I exuberantly open the door to him. "All set?" he asks with a smile.

"All set," I confirm.

"Good morning!" Bethan calls as I walk down the garden path.

I turn around to see her exiting number two with Harri hot on her heels.

"Ah, the whole team's here!" Owain says as he comes out of the end cottage, reaching back to pull his yellow door closed.

"Wait!" I hear Gwen call from behind him.

He quickly opens the door again and she bustles out, shooing him from under the porch so she can get on her way. "Morning all!" she calls curtly as she stomps off along the dirt path in the direction of the house.

Owain casts his eyes at the heavens. "She'll be glad when today's over," he says ominously.

"What's happening today?" I ask.

"Lord and Lady Berkeley's fortieth-wedding-anniversary party. They've got about two hundred people coming to the Great Hall later. Gwen is stressed about a Women's Institute afternoon tea she has to get out of the way before they can start clearing tables."

I hate the thought of Gwen being stressed.

"I forgot we were closing early today," Harri says.

He and Bethan turn to each other and start making plans for that afternoon—a friend of Bethan's has just had a baby and she wants Harri to go with her to visit. I'm only half concentrating. Evan has just unlocked the big arched door to the walled garden. It's made of thick, heavily weathered wood and is hung on big hinges that groan as he pushes the door open. He stands back and waves me through.

I smile at him and lead the way, looking around reverentially.

Garden beds that I couldn't see from my bedroom window line this side of the wall. They're heavily populated with ferns, and rising out of the feathery fronds are thick ropes of tangled wisteria exploding with long trailing purple blooms. We head out through an apple orchard of old trees with gnarled trunks and come to the center of the garden.

It's set to be another nice day, weather-wise, and even though it's a Monday and unlikely to be as busy as it was on the weekend, we'll try to tackle the most invasive gardening work before the hall is opened to the public in a couple of hours.

While Owain mows the terraces, Harri and Bethan take two volunteers each to do some weeding and deadheading in the courtyard and East Court. Meanwhile, Evan and I get to work on the tall topiary columns on the upper terrace. We're trimming them a little earlier than usual, but the Berkeleys want the grounds around the Great Hall to look shipshape for the party tonight.

My stomach feels as though it's full of tiny bubbles of joy that don't fade, even as the morning wears on. I'll never take this job for granted—I feel like the luckiest person in the world right now and I don't think that will get old.

After breaking for tea in the Mess Room, a converted Victorian garden shed that's hidden from view of the house by an old yew hedge, Evan takes me for a proper tour of the grounds, teaching me the names of the garden "rooms" I haven't yet come into contact with. The formal gardens are all sensational, but my favorite bed is the one heading down toward the orangery. Every time I catch sight of the lupins, I think of Nan.

By three o'clock, I'm aching all over and ready for a hot bath, but I go with Evan to do a final check of the courtyard. The Regency wing opens right onto it.

The Great Hall has already been closed to the public, so it seems Gwen got her afternoon teas away on time. A hive of activity can be seen through the tall windows and double doors: people folding up tablecloths and moving tables and chairs.

"Hmm," Evan says, frowning at the path where patches of

dirt are spilling from some of the beds. A couple of the volunteers were here earlier, doing some weeding. "I'd better grab a broom and sort that out."

"I'll help you." Together, we'll make short work of it.

"I'm so ready for a nice cold beer," he says when we're almost done.

"It's only three twenty," I chide.

"Perfect. You want to join me? Sit out in the back garden, put your feet up?" He props his hands against the end of his broom and smiles at me.

"Sure, but you'd better find me a patch of shade. I got a little sunburnt today."

"Ellie!" he exclaims, half amused, half chastising.

"I know, I wasn't expecting it in Wales," I reply with a laugh, showing him one of my arms. "Usually I'm all SPF 50'd up."

"I can't believe someone with your complexion chooses to work outside all day." He shakes his head at me as he gets back to sweeping, the muscles in his tanned arms rippling. "*And* you get hay fever," he points out, teasing.

It's true, I do. I'm laughing as a window in the Great Hall opens, and it's like déjà vu when Lady Berkeley leans out, looking all panicky.

"Evan!" she shouts with relief.

"Oh, hey, Mrs. B. Happy anniversary," Evan replies.

"Eleanor, you're here too! Darlings, we're having a nightmare!" she exclaims, and I get the feeling she tends toward melodrama. "The catering staff are dropping like flies—two more have just canceled and another has gastric flu. Would any of you be available to help out?"

Evan glances over his shoulder at me, his brow furrowed, be-

WHAT IF I NEVER GET OVER YOU · 121

fore returning his attention to Philippa Berkeley. "I'm afraid we're the only two here. Harri and Bethan have made other plans."

"Would you be so kind?" she implores, pressing her palms together in a prayerlike plea and giving us full-on puppy-dog eyes.

"What would we have to do?" I ask reluctantly, noticing that I subconsciously adjusted my accent to sound a bit more "proper."

"Just serve champagne, the caterers will do the rest. We would be so grateful."

I really don't fancy serving champagne to a bunch of toffs, but she's asking nicely and is clearly stressed. Plus, she seems decent and the job sounds easy enough.

"Okay," I agree just as Evan says, "No worries, Mrs. B. What time do you need us?"

"Could you come back at four?" she asks hopefully.

Evan checks his watch as my eyes widen with alarm.

"Or four thirty?" she amends.

That's still no time at all.

"Do you need us to wear a uniform?" Evan asks.

What have I let myself in for?

"Yes, black. You can help yourselves to a polo shirt from the storeroom if you need to."

"All good, see you in a bit," Evan says.

She turns around and shouts jubilantly across the room: "All sorted, Gwen! Our glorious gardeners are stepping in!"

I SHOWER, DO my hair and makeup, and change into a knee-length black dress before grabbing a quick bite to eat. I don't know how long I'll be expected to help out, but hopefully it won't be all night.

Evan knocks on the cottage door at 4:20.

"Is this okay?" I ask when I answer, waving my hands at my dress. "Or do I need to wear a polo shirt too?" The black one he has on must normally be used by catering staff, but it's the same design as our gardening uniform with a white embroidered crest.

"No, you look great." His gaze catches on my lips.

I'm not sure he's ever seen me wear red lipstick before. I wanted to feel bold and brave.

"The only black shoes I have are heels." They're the only pair of heels I have, period—I gave so much away when I left home and these have still barely been worn. "I'm going to regret this, aren't I?"

"I'm not sure we had much choice," he replies with a grin.

"No," I agree wryly, following him out the door and locking it behind me. I slip my key into a pocket, along with my lipstick. I'm traveling light tonight.

The Great Hall is beautifully bright and airy, with white-washed walls, a cream stone floor, and sunlight pouring in through a multitude of windows on three aspects. The garden views are stunning.

I had assumed Gwen would be overseeing tonight, as she was here earlier, but I soon learn that the outside caterers are in charge. Their boss is a total dragon lady.

"Can you put that ponytail into a bun?" she barks at me as she proffers a frilly white apron, hustling me into it. "And your lipstick is too bright. Please remove it."

"I don't have any bobby pins," I reply irritably, at which she huffs with annoyance and instructs another girl to go and get some for me.

Who's doing who the favor here? Am I even being paid for this?

Once I've grudgingly removed my lipstick and styled my hair

to the dragon lady's approval, I'm shooed into the kitchen, a 1970s modern addition that is in dire need of updating. Guests are due to arrive from five thirty and there are still a lot of champagne glasses that need polishing. Evan is already hard at work at one of the pockmarked gray laminate counters. I'm in a foul mood as I grab a tea towel and join him, but when the string band starts warming up, I pause. What the hell? Is that "Creep" by Radiohead?

Indie rock songs must be their thing, because "Bitter Sweet Symphony" by the Verve is next. I wonder who booked the band.

Evan nudges my arm. "You've perked up."

"I like this music."

I'm in a much better mood by 5:25 when the resident viscountess pokes her head around the door. We're in the process of filling champagne flutes, a mass of bottles laid out on the counter beside us.

"Hello, darlings. All okay?"

I nod and Evan gives her a perky "Yep!"

Her hair has been blow-dried into a neat bob and she's wearing a long mauve slip dress with a blinging necklace. Are those real diamonds?

"We're all set. I imagine we'll be outside until speeches, as it's such a fine day. Do keep the champagne flowing!"

"We will!" Evan chirps.

"And please make sure it's extra chilled!" she calls as she leaves. "In fact," she says, turning back and nodding at the trays we've already filled, "can you leave those now and top up as you go along?"

"No worries," Evan agrees.

"Wonderful." She swans out of the room.

Fuck this, I'm putting my red lipstick back on.

———

BY SIX O'CLOCK, the courtyard and upper terrace are swarming with people. The catering staff are outside, circulating with canapés and trays of drinks. Evan has just taken a bottle of champagne to top up glasses and I'm in the kitchen filling fresh flutes, trying to make sure they're as close to ice-cold as possible.

Evan comes to grab another bottle and asks me to go and collect empty glasses from the windowsills outside, a directive from our dragon boss. I grab a tray and get to work.

As predicted, my feet are killing me, but I'm glad to be outside in the fresh air. I'm tempted to knock back a couple of half-empty glasses of fizz just to take the edge off my pain, but I resist, even if it is a crying shame to waste good champagne.

A strings rendition of "Common People" by Pulp is spilling out of the open windows and I smirk, wondering if this was on a predetermined playlist or if the band are taking the piss.

"I hear congratulations are in order!" a Hooray Henry booms from right beside me.

For a split second, I wonder if he's talking to me, but then I see a twenty-something brunette coyly flashing a diamond solitaire the size of a rock at him. Someone get me my sunglasses.

"Oh, that's smashing," he effuses as I reach for an empty glass behind him. "Have you set a date?"

He's completely oblivious to the fact that I'm trying to get past.

"No, not yet," the woman replies.

"You'd better get in quick before Berkeley and Bex," he says conspiratorially as I irritably snatch the glass.

"Yes, Berkeley and Bex will be next," she concurs.

"I heard there might be an announcement tonight," Hooray Henry adds, brushing up against me.

I freeze so abruptly that I almost lose the contents of my tray, but he doesn't even seem to notice. It's as though I've tumbled back in time to my school days and I both hate and resent being made to feel invisible.

I take a breath to steady my racing heart and regain my composure, then move on.

My mum would be in her element here, swanning around, trying to charm everyone. And perhaps some of the people here *would* be interested in what she had to say. Maybe she'd make a connection that would bring in business. Or maybe they'd just indulge her and as soon as she had her back turned they'd raise their eyebrows at each other, faintly amused by her gall.

My dad would also be sucking up, but far less gracefully, and he'd know deep down that he wasn't cut out for it. He'd feel defensive and resentful if someone didn't pay him enough respect and later there would be a dark cloud hanging over the house.

I used to try to cheer him up when this sort of thing happened, and my mum would make cutting comments about how I'm such a daddy's girl, a people pleaser.

Flinching from the memories, I make my way out onto the upper terrace and pause for a moment to stare at the woodland in the distance, bathed in golden light. In the courtyard, the sun has sunk below the roof, but out here it's perfect. I wish I could just keep walking and get away from these people. It's triggering being here among them, *serving* them.

Ringing sounds out from behind me and the chatter dies down. I turn around with a sigh, intending to make my way back to the kitchen before the speeches kick off, but I see that my entrance is blocked by Lady Berkeley and a man I assume must be her husband, Viscount Peter Berkeley. They're standing at the top of the steps to the Great Hall and Philippa is knocking two champagne flutes together to command everyone's attention.

"Thank you all for coming," Lord Berkeley says loudly. He's wearing a sharp navy suit with a white handkerchief poking out of its breast pocket. His hair is more salt than pepper, but he's quite handsome. "Might I just say a few words . . ."

I back up into the warm sunshine and try to ignore the stinging in the balls of my feet as Lord Berkeley addresses the crowd. Could I take off my shoes for a minute while everyone is distracted? I move closer to one of the topiary columns I was trimming earlier and try to balance my tray of empty glasses on one hand as I bend down to slip off my shoes. I almost groan out loud as my bare feet sink into the grass. Christ, that's heaven.

"Rebecca, come here," Lady Berkeley calls, and I straighten up in time to see her urging one of the guests to join her on the steps.

A sleek light blond bun rises up out of the sea of heads, and Philippa Berkeley smiles warmly as the woman, who looks to be about my age, takes her place on her left. Her eyes are dancing and she seems amused, as though she's trying not to lose it laughing. Despite how I feel about this crowd, I like the look of her. Is she Philippa and Peter's daughter?

I still know very little about the family I'm working for, and don't really care too much; I'm here for the garden, not the people.

Lord Berkeley beckons to another guest. "You too, son."

"Put a ring on it, Berkeley!" a posh twat heckles as a man with dark blond hair climbs the steps.

"I think we can all agree that my parents are an inspiration," the man replies.

Why do all these people have cut-glass English accents when they live in Wales?

"But I'll put a ring on it when I'm good and ready," he adds, and my breath catches at his playful tone, even before he's glanced over his shoulder at the heckler in the crowd.

I catch a glimpse of his profile and stop breathing.

No. It can't be.

"Come on, Ashton," Philippa Berkeley prompts merrily, opening her other arm to bring him into the gap between her husband and herself.

My heart pounds in my ears as Ashton Berkeley turns around and faces the dozens of guests standing before him.

Holy Mother of fucking God, it's Ash.

13

IT'S LIKE WATCHING AN EARTHQUAKE PLAY OUT ON-screen: the empty champagne glasses on my tray begin to shiver and shake so violently, it's as though the ground is moving. The glasses knock together, making a tinkling sound, and a few people in front of me turn around to look at what's causing the commotion. And then it's like a ripple effect, a wave of attention, which all too quickly reaches the people on the steps.

I see him glance my way briefly, and in the split second before he does a double take, I wonder if I'm mistaken, if he might be a look-alike or a long-lost twin. But then his eyes clash with mine, and his face freezes with shock.

I stare back at him, a mirror image of disbelief. His hair is shorter, not as shaggy or wild, but a few strands still fall carelessly into his eyes. He's wearing a fitted white shirt, the top two buttons undone to reveal the edges of his collarbone, and his skin is golden, his cheekbones high, his jawline sharp.

It's Ash. It's Ash. But how can it be? How can *that* man up on *those* steps be *my* Ash, my easygoing, salt-of-the-earth Ash? What's happened to his accent, his attractive Welsh lilt? Who *is* that posh impostor?

The statue comes to life just as I back away, trembling, glasses chiming. Peter Berkeley has begun talking again and people have faced forward to listen, paying no more heed to the incompetent waitress at the back. As carefully as I can, I set the tray on the ground before I drop it. My hands have turned to jelly, but it's my heart I fear for the most, it's beating so hard and fast. I look back over at the steps in time to see Ash break free of his parents, the crowd surging as he pushes his way into the throng, but I don't wait to see what happens next.

I make it to the rose garden before I hear his voice.

"ELLIE!" he shouts.

It almost brings me to my knees. I feel as though I'm having an out-of-body experience as I slowly turn around and see him striding toward me in a panic, his hand held up, begging me to wait.

"Ellie," he says, coming to a stop a couple of meters away. "It's you! It's really you."

"Who are you?" I ask in an appalled whisper, shaking my head. I can't comprehend his upper-class accent. I'm vibrating with shock. What's going on?

"Ellie, it's me. It's Ash. Lisbon. Six years ago," he says desperately, misunderstanding my horrified bewilderment.

"I know who you are," I reply unsteadily. "But I don't know *who* you are. You live here? This is your home? Your name is Ashton *Berkeley*? Those are your parents?"

He looks tormented as he gives me a single measured nod.

"You sound different," I say hoarsely.

"I'm still the same person."

I shake my head. "No, you're not."

Heat hits the backs of my eyes.

"Ellie," he murmurs, reaching out to me as my vision goes blurry.

"No," I say quickly, backing up. "Was that *Beca*?"

I'm almost too scared to ask.

He halts where he's standing. He looks the same, a bit broader, perhaps, but his eyes are still peach-iced-tea brown, clear, flawless, and gleaming with what now looks like regret as he nods.

"Is she your girlfriend now? Was she *always* your girlfriend?" My heart jolts at the thought.

"No!" he exclaims.

"She's *not* your girlfriend?" Which question is he saying no to?

"No, she is, but—"

"Or is she your fiancée?"

He seems to shrink a little, wilting. "Not yet." He sounds strained. He starts toward me and stops. "I *am* the same person, I swear."

I shake my head. "Your voice. Your accent." I can't get over it.

He hesitates. And then he says, in the exact same Welsh lilt I remember from my dreams, "Would it help if I spoke like this?"

I'm so taken aback at hearing him switch seamlessly from one persona to another that I reel backward, staggering into a rose-bush. And it hits me like a slap in the face that *this* is the reason why he didn't turn up in Madrid, why he left me heartsick and broken. Because everything about him was a lie. We're from two completely different worlds, and he knew it, even if I didn't.

He lurches forward, trying to help me, but I'm so freaked out that I don't want him anywhere near me. His strong hands circle my forearms and he pulls me out of the thorns.

"Get off me!" I shriek, but it's too late, because he's already setting me back on my feet. And now he's *right there*.

I shove his chest to create more distance between us and he stumbles, his expression crestfallen.

"ASH!"

We both look over to see Beca—Rebecca? Bex?—standing twenty meters or so away. Her expression is a picture of apprehension.

"What's going on?" she demands to know.

Ash holds his palm up to her, a silent request for patience, but it's all too much for me. I hurry away through the formal garden.

"Ellie, wait!"

And now I'm running, instinct screaming at me to get away.

"*Ash!*" Beca calls, sounding hurt and incredulous.

"I'll be right back!" I hear him shout at her.

He catches up with me on the dirt track leading to the walled garden. I left my shoes where they lay and I can't run now on these stones.

"Ellie, wait!" he gasps as I gingerly but determinedly try to make my way home. "I can't let you leave, not again."

"You don't have a choice!" I need space to get my head around this.

"Ellie, please," he begs, and something in his tone has me looking over my shoulder at him.

I've never seen anyone look so frantic, so distressed. It stays me momentarily.

"I *cannot* let you walk out of my life again," he says.

"I'm not," I reply, my head buzzing, my thoughts scattered.

"Not?"

"Not walking out of your life." I nod down the track before meeting his eyes. "I live here."

A flicker of confusion crosses his features, followed by hope.

"You live here?" he repeats.

"In the workers' cottages," I confirm.

"Wait." He shifts his weight from one leg to another, still staring at me, still uncomprehending. "You *work* here?"

"In the gardens."

His expression morphs into wonder, and then a few seconds pass and his eyes soften, the tension in his shoulders loosening.

"You did it," he whispers.

The look on his face unravels something in me. He's proud, I realize.

My body begins to turn toward him.

But I don't even know who this man is. He has no right to feel proud of me or my achievements.

"Go back to your girlfriend, *Ashton*," I say bitterly.

This time he lets me go.

14

ONLY REALIZE HOW MUCH I'M STILL TREMBLING WHEN I
can't get the key into the lock. It takes several attempts, but once
the door is open, I rush inside, beyond thankful that Siân is away.

I can't believe it. How is Ash a *Berkeley*? He's the son of a *viscount*, for fuck's sake!

I sink down on the sofa, shaking from head to toe. I feel as
though all the blood has drained from my body.

How can I have found Ash and lost him in the same moment?

But then it hits me like a ton of bricks.

That *was* Ash. And I *have* found him, even if he's not who I
thought he was.

I've replayed our time together over and over in my mind. I
opened up my heart to him in a way that I'd never opened up my
heart to anyone, before or since. We confided in each other. Was
any of it real? It was for me. But what else did he lie about?

We shared stories about our parents, talked about our hopes
and dreams—was it all just bullshit? Did he even study astronomy
and physics at university?

We laughed so much together, but was he laughing *at* me?

I remember every single minute of our time together on that beach, and every single second of what it felt like when his lips were on mine. I remember the feeling of his body beneath and on top of me.

And I remember his small, steady smile, the way he looked at me like he adored me.

I.

Remember.

Everything.

But that Ash didn't exist. *That* Ash was a down-to-earth guy who used to camp out in the woods with his friend. He came from a normal household and had a difficult upbringing. He struggled with his dad, who had no time for him because he was so busy toiling away in a fucking furniture workshop.

He sure as hell wasn't born into nobility, and he sure as fuck didn't grow up living in a five-hundred-year-old mansion with all the wealth and privilege that entails.

A well of emotion bubbles up inside me. I've found Ash, but he's not *my* Ash. I thought my heart had broken when he didn't show up in Madrid, but this might even be worse. Why did he pretend to be someone he wasn't?

My throat swells and the pressure behind my eyes builds and then my body begins to shake with sobs.

I give up and let myself grieve.

I DON'T KNOW how long I cry for, but when I finally stop, I feel completely shattered. I don't even have the energy to drag myself upstairs to bed, and I must fall asleep on the sofa because knocking on my front door jolts me awake. Evan calls my name.

"Ellie? Are you in there?"

He sounds worried, and I realize, of course, that I just disappeared. A wave of shame crashes over me. I dumped him in it—and all the other serving staff. Jesus, my shoes are still back there on the grass.

"Ellie?" he calls again. He's still knocking gently, obviously wondering if I've gone to sleep, but the light by the door is on.

I don't want him to see me like this. I don't want *anyone* to see me like this. But he's clearly troubled and my conscience gets the better of me.

Swallowing my pride, I peel myself off the sofa. "I'm here," I call through the door. I have to clear my throat and repeat myself because my voice sounds so weak and croaky.

"Are you okay?" he asks.

"I'm sorry, I wasn't feeling well."

He falls silent and my face warms. I'm so embarrassed.

"I'm sorry," I say again. "I'm already ready for bed, but I'm sure I'll feel better in the morning."

A few seconds pass. "Okay," he says uncertainly. "Let me know if you need anything. I found your shoes on the lawn. I'll leave them here."

"Thank you."

I place my hand on the door, fresh tears breaking out at his concern. I wait until I hear his own front door closing before switching off the light, grabbing my shoes from the doorstep, and dragging myself up to bed.

I'M THE FIRST one outside the next morning, but I don't go into the walled garden. I wait until Evan sees me so he knows that he doesn't have to knock.

"Hey, how are you feeling?" he asks carefully.

"Much better, thank you," I lie, forcing a tight smile. I'm wearing sunglasses to disguise the shadows beneath my eyes. "I'm sorry again about last night."

"No worries at all. Are you sure you're okay to work today?"

"Absolutely. It's another beautiful day," I add, trying to sound cheerful.

"It is."

He doesn't pry further and I'm relieved. I just want to lose myself in work.

I spend the morning staking delphiniums and other perennials in Maple Garden, down past the orangery. The tall plants haven't yet come into bloom, but I can already imagine the drifts of brilliant purples and blues, soft pinks and whites. Ducks quack on the nearby lake and birds sing in the woods. I'm about as far from the house as it's possible to get and I'm glad of the solitude as I tie string around each individual hollow-stemmed plant, attaching them to bamboo stakes to ensure they stay upright once their flowers threaten to weigh them down.

Usually I'd find this repetitive work soothing. It's mind-numbing, but never boring, allowing room in my head for thoughts to wander. Sun, wind, or rain could be hitting my skin and I'd still be at peace spending my hours in the open air.

But today my thoughts are not calm. Fury has sprouted up overnight, consuming the barren wasteland of shock and devastation.

I keep flashing back to Madrid, to searching those squares in the searing sun, heartsick and desperate, day after day after day. I'm remembering the anxiety I endured with my parents just to get there, and underneath it the sweet, budding optimism for the future.

Ash obliterated that hope when he didn't show up. He reduced me to a shivering wreck who ran home with my tail between my legs, and I will *never* forgive him for that.

I will never forgive him for lying about who he was, for speaking to me with an entirely different fucking accent. Was there any part of him that believed what he was saying to me? Or did he know all along that he was out of my league, that I was just a bit of fun, a plaything to entertain him?

A little voice inside my head whispers that this doesn't ring true, but I shut it down. He's a sick bastard and now he's ruining *this* for me too.

Cold dread engulfs me as I realize just how much he really *could* ruin for me—not only my enjoyment of this ordinary gardening task, but my whole employment here. His parents are my bosses. I can't go around laying into their son, however much I want to.

I hope he stays away from me.

I end up working right through my tea break, and my wheelbarrow, which was previously full of bamboo canes, is empty when I return to the cottage for lunch.

So far today, I've managed to avoid exchanging many words with my colleagues. I feel bad about it, but I've been too messed up to be sociable. I'll make more of an effort this afternoon.

When I open the cottage door, I see that a white envelope has been pushed through the letter box.

At the sight of my name scrawled across the front in sloping cursive, I feel physically sick.

Breaking the seal, I pull out a note.

Ellie,

Can we talk? Please. I'll come by tonight at seven.

Ash

No, you won't, I think to myself darkly as I shakily stuff the note back into the envelope. *No, you fucking won't.* What excuse could he possibly give me that will make all this okay?

The three days we spent together felt like the start of something. And when he didn't call or turn up, when he left me stranded and alone, it *destroyed* me. I had the biggest high followed by the lowest low and I *still* haven't recovered.

I can't believe I've wasted almost six years of my life pining over a man who didn't even exist. I have never felt more hurt or betrayed.

"**I WAS JUST** coming to find you," Bethan says brightly as I exit the cottage, having forced some tea and toast down my throat. "I'll help you stake the perennials in Maple Garden."

"I've done them," I reply.

She jolts. "You've done them?"

"Yes, I did them this morning."

She gawps at me. "But there are loads!"

I shrug. "I work fast."

"Well, you'd better slow down," she says with alarm. "You'll make the rest of us look bad."

I purse my lips at her, contrite, and she laughs.

"I don't usually work that quickly," I admit as we wander through the walled garden, nodding at the visitors we pass. "I guess I was just superkeen to get started."

"The novelty will wear off," she assures me.

I feel a bit better as we work side by side in the White Garden beyond the lower terrace, chatting as we lift and clear the spring bedding: a combination of wallflowers, hyacinths, and daffodils, plus the tulips that the squirrels haven't eaten. Soon I can feel my-self beginning to relax again.

"Are you up to anything tonight?" I ask as we're finishing for the day and wandering back to the workers' cottages.

My mood has improved from this morning, but my blood still simmers and I know that if I think about Ash too hard, it'll be back at boiling point.

"Nope," she replies.

"Is there a local pub somewhere? I quite fancy a pint in a beer garden. Would you be up for that?"

There's no way I can handle seeing Ash yet. I'll lose it. I want to be anywhere but the cottage come seven o'clock.

"Absolutely, and there's one in the village," she replies.

"Where's the village?"

"Down the farm track behind the workshops. It's about a twenty-minute walk."

Perfect.

Evan and Harri are keen too, and when the four of us are showered and dressed in casual clothes, we set off out the back, but not before I've scribbled my own note to Ash and stuck it on my front door.

A couple of the guys I met at Evan's barbecue are sitting on deck chairs, farther along the lawn. They live together in the second-to-last cottage—Dylan is a ranger and Jac is employed by the workshop.

"Where are you lot off to?" Dylan calls.

"Pub," Harri calls back.

"The more the merrier?" I say it as if it's a question.

They glance at each other and nod, and then Celyn comes out of the fifth and final cottage in the row with his girlfriend, Catrin, and they decide to join us too.

I'm on a bit of a high as the eight of us traipse down the country lane in the early-evening sunshine. Catrin is warm and friendly and Bethan is funny, a total goofball.

Just as we're arriving at the pub, Harri remembers that it's fish-and-chip Tuesday and I actually laugh at how happy everyone is.

We stay out until closing time and then wander back along the pitch-black lane, stumbling over holes made by tractor treads.

I've had a surprisingly good time, even if Ash has been on my mind. How long did he stick around when he realized I wasn't at the cottage? I suddenly have a vivid mental image of him still waiting and a thrill rips through my body.

We all go into our respective cottages through the back doors, but as soon as I'm inside, I hurry to the front door and nervously crack it open.

"Hello?" I call quietly into the darkness.

Silence.

My note is exactly where I pinned it earlier and my chest constricts at the sight.

Did he even come by?

I pull out the tack and take the envelope back inside, opening it.

My heart jumps at the sight of fresh handwriting.

I'd drawn a line through his plea to talk and underneath I'd scrawled: *FUCK OFF.*

But below this, he's written: *Not happening.*

I can hear the way he's said it and I can picture him staring at me, determined, and also a little bit playful.

I could kick myself as I walk upstairs, because I'm trying not to smile.

15

AT SOME POINT IN THE MIDDLE OF THE NIGHT, THE TONE of Ash's note begins to take on a sinister edge. While I was drunk, I thought that he'd written *Not happening* with kind of a cute, flippant air.

But once the high of alcohol wears off, paranoia sets in and I begin to wonder if he meant *Not happening* in a meaner way, as in: *This is my home and I'm not going anywhere. If you've got a problem with that, you fuck off.*

I don't know him, not the way I thought I did. He's got a girl-friend, a soon-to-be fiancée. If I cause trouble for him, he could have me fired. He holds all the power. I'm just a nobody gardener, easily replaceable.

But I can*not* lose this job.

I'm still on edge later that morning when I'm with Evan in West Court, making a start on the summer bedding. We're plant-ing an annual mix of *Verbena hastata*, *Salvia* "Love and Wishes," and *Ageratum houstonianum* and it's the sort of work I normally adore, pushing my hands into freshly prepared soil, feeling a connection to the earth, imagining how these tiny plants will grow into huge clouds of purple, pink, and blue in the coming months.

But today my mind is all over the place.

I don't like being this close to the house. West Court backs right up against the Tudor wing, behind the west bay of the eighteenth-century section of the house, which is where the family's living quarters are.

Ash could be looking down from any window. He could be around any corner.

"How are you feeling today?" Evan asks.

"Hungover," I reply, an easy answer after last night's sesh. "What about you?"

"I feel fine, actually," he replies with a grin, glancing at my arms. "Still suffering?"

For a second, I wonder if he's talking about the scratches I sustained when I fell into the rosebush, but then I realize he's referring to my sunburn.

"Better. Just being careful."

I've kept my arms covered since Monday evening, but my long-sleeve shirt is as much to hide my injuries as it is to protect my skin.

Evan looks past me. "Oh, hey, Mrs. B."

I instantly go tense.

"Hello, darlings! Evan, Eleanor," she says.

I don't know why she insists on saying our names every time she sees us, or why she calls me Eleanor instead of Ellie, although Eleanor *is* my proper name.

Maybe that's why: because it sounds more "proper."

I force myself to look over my shoulder at her. "Good morning."

I haven't seen her since I ran out of her anniversary party. Does she know I did that? She doesn't appear to be regarding me any differently, but I'm seeing her through new eyes. That's Ash's *mother*.

"Those peonies are marvelous," she says, admiring the blousy tree peonies growing at the corner of West Court.

"It's a good year for them," Evan agrees. "Want me to cut some for you to put in a vase?"

Her face lights up as though this is the best idea anyone has ever had.

"Would you? That would be wonderful!"

I can't help but smile at how accommodating he is as he carefully steps back out of the garden bed and grabs his pruning shears from his trug. The wooden baskets they use here are even fancier than the ones we used at Wisley.

I'm about to carry on with what I'm doing when Ash walks round the corner. My stomach drops off a cliff. And then my heart begins to *pound*.

"Ashton!" his mother calls with delight. "What are you doing here? Have you met our new gardener?"

In the moment it takes Ash's eyes to find mine, his mother is already introducing us.

"This is Eleanor Knapley. She's come all the way from RHS Garden Wisley," she adds proudly. "Eleanor, this is my son, Ashton. Evan is just cutting me some peonies," she carries on happily.

"That's nice," Ash says mildly, nodding a greeting at Evan.

"What are you doing here, darling?" his mother asks. "You're not normally outside at this time of day."

What is he, a vampire? Nothing would surprise me.

Ash looks over at me again, his gaze catching and holding. I don't feel angry now—I feel like I'm standing on a knife-edge. And maybe he sees that vulnerability in my expression because something keeps him from elaborating.

"I'm just on my way out," I hear him say as I drop my gaze.

My hands are quivering as I continue with what I'm doing, but out of the corner of my eye I can see that Ash has not left.

A familiar tickling sensation hits the back of my nose, and before I know it I'm engaged in a sneezing fit.

"Bless you, Eleanor!" Lady Berkeley exclaims.

But, oh, I haven't finished.

Evan chuckles. "She's the only gardener I know who suffers from hay fever."

Still sneezing, I hastily dig around in my pocket for a tissue, but before I can hunt one out, Ash is already stepping forward with his hand outstretched.

His lips are curved up at the corners as I snatch the tissue from him and blow my nose.

"Bless you, Eleanor," Lady Berkeley calls over again.

"Thank you," I reply, avoiding Ash's gaze.

"Will these do?" Evan asks Philippa Berkeley. "Or would you like something else to go with them?"

"Ellie," Ash whispers.

I shoot my eyes toward his, panicked, and give him a tiny shake of my head.

He looks pained for a second and then nods pointedly toward the western bay of the house. *Meet me there.*

I shake my head more fervently. *Please. I can't.*

He cocks his head to one side. *Yes, you can.*

Evan and his mother have disappeared around the corner of the Tudor wing.

Ash nods emphatically toward the end of the house again and gives me a meaningful look. "See you later," he calls to his mother and Evan.

"Yes, bye, darling!" I hear his mother reply from what sounds like a fair distance away.

I try to get back to work, but I'm distracted by Ash's retreating frame. He's wearing a white shirt tucked into mid-gray trousers with a black belt. He looks smart, as though he might be going out for a fancy lunch or something. He looks good, actually, though that's not something I want to notice. But it's impossible not to: his shoulders are so broad and his hips so slim, and those trousers really do fit him very well . . .

He turns around and looks back at me. I've got my hands five inches into the soil, tentatively carrying on with what I was doing. I try to ignore the way he's staring me down, but my heart is stuttering, and a moment later, he throws his arms up in the air and I can't be sure he won't catch the attention of his mother or Evan if one of them suddenly reappears.

My temper spikes, quashing some of the fear I felt a moment ago.

Fuck's sake, fine. You win.

I climb out of the garden bed and walk toward him, dusting off my hands without a word. He disappears around the corner of the house.

"What?" I snap as soon as I'm sure we'll be out of the eyesight of Evan and his mother, should they return. I can say I went to get more tissues.

"Eleanor Knapley," Ash says significantly.

"Yes, well done, now you know my last name," I reply caustically, giving him a round of applause.

My hands are filthy. I try to brush off some more dirt after I've finished my sarcastic clapping.

"Well, it would have helped." There's a bite to his tone. "If you'd told me that you were Eleanor Knapley of Knap Sofas, I would have found you sooner," he has the gall to add.

Wait a sec. "How did you know about Knap?"

"I googled you yesterday. What, you thought I learned your surname just now?" He shakes his head and frowns. "No. *Obviously* I looked you up on the payroll system as soon as I could. I'm a big fan of your Lisbon range."

His tone is difficult to work out. I can't tell if he's toying with me or being genuine. There's an edge there, as though he's a little pissed off with me. But what the hell have I done wrong? Diddly-squat, that's what.

"I like the canary yellow," he says, still talking about sofas. "Inspired by the trams, I presume? But I couldn't work out why you went for light brown."

I'm damned if I'm going to tell him that the range was half inspired by his eyes.

Suddenly he looks baffled. "Why *did* you downplay your family's business?" Ah, so that's why he's put out. "Knap is huge. My mother has a copy of the *Sunday Times* Home section inside with a huge advert on the back cover."

"Let's not get into how little we told each other about our families' businesses," I reply darkly.

I only downplayed Knap because I didn't want to rub his nose in it after he told me that his family only had a small workshop.

"Why did *you* tell me that your family had a furniture business?" I ask. "What was the point in that?" I'm *furious* at the lie.

"They *do* have a furniture business," he replies calmly, unashamed, walking a bit farther on until he comes out at the front of the house. "There."

I glare at him, but go to see where he's pointing.

"You've got to be kidding me," I mutter resentfully when I realize that he's got the Victorian outbuildings in his sight.

There is no way he can claim that *that* is his family business! *This* is his family business! *This* right *here*, this *house*!

"That is a furniture workshop, Ellie," he states. "In front of the sawmill." I can't believe he has the nerve to sound annoyed. "I used to hang out there all the time with Taran. He used to work there. *I* worked there too once. His uncle still runs it."

I'm caught off guard. "Edmund is Taran's uncle?" I ask with surprise of the man in his late fifties with the warm handshake and kind smile. I met him at the barbecue on Sunday and have seen him around since.

"Yes. Owain is too. Taran's father, Gareth, used to be head ranger here. He's retired now, but he and his wife, Carys, used to live here on the estate with Taran and Celyn."

I shake my head, confused. "Celyn?"

"Celyn is Taran's older brother. He's head ranger now."

My head spins as all these threads connect. I can barely believe that I've ended up right here on Ash's home turf. On *Taran's*.

"We have so much to talk about," he states heavily.

"I need to get back to work."

"Not yet. Wait."

I meet his eyes. "Don't wreck this for me."

He recoils, shocked at my plea, and shakes his head quickly, as though denying that he ever could.

I don't trust him as far as I could throw him.

"I don't want anyone to know about us."

As soon as the words are out of my mouth, I feel stupid. As if *he'd* want anyone to know about us! I'm just his bit of rough from the old days.

"And I don't want you to be seen near my cottage," I spit, my temper spiking again as humiliation swallows me up.

If my new colleagues had any idea that I once thought I had a future with him . . . It would be beyond embarrassing.

And not just because I'd appear delusional—where, outside of a fairy tale, does a gardener snap up the son of a viscount?—but because I hate the idea of them thinking that I'd even *want* this life.

"Then let me give you my number so we can arrange a time and a place to meet," Ash says.

"I don't have my phone on me," I snap. "But wait, I've got an idea," I add mockingly. "Why don't you write it down on your dead best friend's book and shove it through my letter box?"

He flinches.

"Where is it?" I demand to know. "Stella's book?"

He shakes his head miserably.

"What did you do with it?" I ask, my voice rising.

"I lost it," he admits in a whisper.

"You *lost* it?" I feel hot and prickly.

"I'm so sorry."

He does look genuinely remorseful, but I can't contain the fiery-hot fury that bursts from me.

"Reading that book was like having a conversation with her, the last conversation we could ever have! How could you *lose* it? You knew how important it was to me!"

He shakes his head, stricken. "I'm so sorry." He reaches out to me, but I slap his hand away, and then suddenly it dawns on me.

"Is *that* why you didn't call?" I ask in a small voice, breathless with hurt and yet somehow hopeful.

I've been so convinced that he didn't call or turn up in Madrid because of all *this*, because of this *lie*, but if it was because he lost Stella's book . . .

His eyes widen with surprise. "Of *course* it's why I didn't call. I mean, there's more to it than that, but . . ." He sighs. "We have so much to talk about."

I stare at him, wanting to believe there was a real reason he never called, never showed up.

But then I remember the days I spent searching Madrid, bereft and alone. I remember that he lied about who he was and where he came from—even putting on a fake accent.

And he's got a girlfriend now, a soon-to-be fiancée. It would be in everyone's best interests if we just pretended we'd never met.

My throat begins to thicken, but I'm damned if I'm going to shed another tear over this man.

"Please just . . . Just let me do my job," I say dully.

His jaw clenches as I turn and walk away.

16

THE THING IS, IT STILL DOESN'T MAKE SENSE. ASH MIGHT have lost Stella's book—and damn him to hell for that—but what's his excuse for not meeting me in Madrid? He must have had a change of heart. Even if some of his feelings for me were genuine, he knew that we couldn't go anywhere, that he needed to cut his losses and move on.

And he has moved on. He's with Beca now. He said he didn't have feelings for her then, yet clearly they've developed from friends to lovers. The thought of him with her, or with any other woman, makes me feel as though I've swallowed glass, which is disturbing. My heart and head are so confused. I can't reconcile *my* Ash with *that* Ashton. I don't want to have feelings for either of them. I want to be over him so he doesn't have the power to wound me again.

When I come home from work that day, there's a package on my doorstep. I take it inside to the kitchen table and open it, pulling out five books by Sarah J. Maas: *A Court of Thorns and Roses, A*

Court of Mist and Fury, A Court of Wings and Ruin, A Court of Frost and Starlight, A Court of Silver Flames.

My heart feels like it's trying to escape from my rib cage as I open up the accompanying note.

Just in case you never read the last chapter. I'm so sorry I lost Stella's book. I know I'll never be able to make up for it, but I thought these might still help you feel close to her. It sounds as though she would have enjoyed the other books in the series if she was into sexy faeries.

He signs off the note *Ash* and his number, adding: *Please call me when you're ready.*

I burst into tears.

I should have let him go years ago, and I certainly need to let him go now—so why is he making it harder for me?

I work straight through Thursday without texting him, and I'm relieved when Friday afternoon comes and I still haven't cracked. We finish early on Fridays and the other cottage-dwellers are having another barbecue, so I go with Evan to the local supermarket to pick up a few bits and pieces.

"How's your first week been?" he asks conversationally as we wander the aisles.

"Good."

"Think you'll be happy here in Wales?"

"Absolutely." I'm trying to sound definitive. I want to get back to the joy I felt on Sunday when I first arrived. I was so happy going to work that first morning. I can't let Ash sour this for me.

"Got any plans for tomorrow?"

"No." I glance at him out of the corner of my eye.

"I wondered if you might fancy going to Chirk Castle with me. I haven't been yet."

"I'd love that."

"Love" is a slight exaggeration. I'm far too unsettled about Ash to think about anything happening with Evan, but I could do with a break from Berkeley Hall, that's for sure.

When we return, we go straight to his cottage to unpack the shopping. The back door is wide open.

"Hey!" Harri says, coming inside with four empty beer cans. "We're all down at Celyn's."

I still can't get my head around the fact that Celyn is Taran's older brother. I wonder if they look alike. Celyn is built like an oak tree and has a big black beard. I always imagined Taran to look a bit like Ash.

"Cool," Evan says. "We'll be with you shortly."

Harri grabs a few more cans and disappears back through the door. Evan sorts us out for drinks, but I have a sneezing fit as we walk outside and accidentally throw some of my wine. He chuckles and determinedly extracts the glass from my hand before I can waste any more alcohol. As soon as I've stopped sneezing, I start laughing.

"You're a liability," Evan says warmly.

"Yep."

And then I see that Ash is sitting on a deck chair farther along the lawn in full sunshine, watching us. I jolt violently.

What the hell is he doing here?

He puts a bright blue craft beer can to his mouth and tilts it, looking casual as anything in gray shorts and a grass-green T-shirt, his long legs stretched out in front of him.

"Just going to put my bag inside," I tell Evan, pausing outside my cottage to unlock the back door.

As soon as I'm out of sight, I grab the note with Ash's number and type out a new text message.

What are you doing here?

I peer out of the window in time to see him pull his phone from his pocket. He frowns at the message and then lifts his chin and stares toward my cottage.

I watch, confident that he can't see me from this angle, as he taps out a reply.

Having a drink with my friends.

I read it and snort derisively. Is he taking the piss?
Another message comes in: Have you got a problem with that?
Yes! I type back furiously.

Why?

I'm not coming out if you're there!

I watch his jaw clench and realize that he's annoyed. Good. He's typing something back to me.

What are you doing tomorrow?

The cheek of him!

Going to Chirk Castle with Evan.

He's still staring down at his phone screen, his mouth pressed into a straight line. Does the thought of that bother him? I don't know why, but I want it to.

Saturday night? he types back.
Out. I haven't got plans yet, but I'll make them.

Sunday.

I hesitate. That one wasn't a question.
I just need a little of your time, he adds.

Why?

Because I can't imagine what's going through your mind right
now. Give me a chance to explain.

Out of the blue, I feel devastated. I can't keep him at arm's
length forever. Not when I work at his home. If he wants to see
me, he can see me. If he wants to tell me his side of the story, he
can do that too. And then he'll leave me alone.

I'm frustrated at myself for how crushed I feel at the thought
of Ash leaving me alone.

Where can we meet where no one
will see us?

Down the farm track behind the sawmill, at the first bend in
the road. 10:30 a.m.

OK.

I watch him drain the rest of his beer, stand up, and say his
goodbyes.

AT 10:20 ON Sunday morning, I let myself out the back door of the cottage and walk down the farm track behind the outbuildings. They're all locked up for the weekend, but I did talk to Jac, one of the workshop employees, on Friday night. He explained that the sawmill has ten members of staff and the workshop employs an additional four. He's one of the four skilled woodworkers who make chairs and tables, so the Berkeleys do have a furniture workshop. Jac still had remnants of sawdust on his arms after the day's work.

I feel as though ivy has taken root within me, coiling its vines around my insides as I walk around the bend in the road to see Ash, wearing a black leather jacket and denim jeans, sitting astride a retro-looking motorcycle. The word TRIUMPH is written on the olive-green tank, a yellow line striking through it, and much of the bike's silver machinery is naked and exposed.

Ash watches every second of my approach.

"We going somewhere?" I ask with a frown.

"Yep." He passes me a matte-black helmet that's hanging from the handlebars.

"Where's yours?" I ask as I take it.

He nods at the helmet in my hands and shrugs off his battered leather jacket, waiting until I've pulled his helmet over my head and fastened it before handing me that too.

"It's a bit loose," I say of the helmet.

"We're not going far."

"Why aren't we walking then?" I ask as I slip my arms into his jacket. It's still warm.

"Because this is more fun."

I feel a tingle beneath my rib cage at his playful tone.

It's a pretty bold move to expect me to go along with this. What if I'd said no?

There was never any danger of that, though. I've always wanted to ride on the back of a hot guy's motorbike.

I chastise myself for putting Ash in that category.

He pats the back of his seat. "Watch your leg on the exhaust. There's a heat guard, but be careful."

I'm wearing a navy dress and there's every chance I'll flash my knickers as I throw my leg over, but Ash faces forward to protect my modesty as I step up onto a small silver flip-down footrest. As soon as I'm seated, I feel myself slipping toward him, pressing snugly against the outer edges of his legs. His jeans feel rough against the delicate skin of my inner thighs.

"Don't you have a spare helmet?" I ask over his shoulder. I don't like that he's not wearing one himself.

"No." He pauses. "I've never had anyone ride pillion before."

What, not even Beca?

He starts the engine before I can consider asking that question and it roars into life, then he places his hand on my knee.

He's not wearing gloves and my heart jolts violently at the skin-to-skin contact, but it's over within a second—he just gave me what I suspect was supposed to be a reassuring pat, because he raises his voice over the sound of the engine to say, "I won't crash. We're just using the forest track into the woods. I'd never take you on the road without proper protection."

I tentatively slide my hands around his waist, my breath growing shallow at the feeling of his warm, hard body beneath my palms. He's wearing a faded yellow T-shirt and I feel his stomach muscles tense under the worn-thin material.

He sets off and I clutch him tighter as we jerk forward, but then he turns off the dirt track onto an even narrower one—the width of a car—and takes off at a smooth, comfortable pace. High hedgerows line the track on either side, so I can't see the surrounding fields, only the sky.

His dark blond hair is blowing wildly in the wind and if I tilt my head to look past him, I can see the sharpness of his jaw as it curves up toward his earlobe.

A shiver runs down my spine as a memory comes back to me of pressing my lips to that very spot.

I don't realize I've adjusted my hold on him until I feel his stomach muscles contract again.

I'm hit with more flashbacks of our time on the beach, and emotion begins to gather like a storm inside my chest.

What's the point of any of this? Why is he so desperate to explain? What if he has a reason for not meeting me that has nothing to do with the lies he told? I couldn't bear to understand him only to lose him again.

But it's too late to turn back.

The track climbs uphill and leads right into the woods, the leafy cover of oak, beech, and maple snuffing out much of the light of the sun. The sound of the engine seems extra loud in our peaceful surroundings.

As we crest the brow of the hill, a two-story log cabin with a pitched roof comes into view. It's all on its own, encircled by tall trees.

Ash pulls to a stop and waits for me to get off before kicking his footrest down and swinging his long leg off the back.

He turns to face me. I'm already unclipping the helmet, but he takes it from me and it's hard to gauge the look in his eyes.

Then he drops his gaze and hangs the helmet on the handlebars, seemingly avoiding watching me as I slip off the jacket. He takes that too, laying it over the seat before leading the way to the front door and opening it. It's unlocked.

"Was this Taran's house?" I ask, holding my breath as I wait for his answer.

He told me that his best friend had a house in the woods.

"Yeah." His voice sounds rough.

So he didn't lie to me about that.

It's cold inside—colder than outside—but Ash goes straight into a small living room off the hallway and passes me a thick blanket hanging over the back of the sofa. It's knitted from gray wool and is so soft—warm, too, as I discover within seconds of sitting down and snuggling under it.

He gets to work building a fire in the fireplace.

"How was Chirk Castle yesterday?" he asks over his shoulder.

"Good," I reply. We're doing small talk now? "It's beautiful around here," I add.

"It is," he agrees, hesitating before asking, "So you went with Evan?"

"Yep."

"You know him from Wisley?"

I nod. "He trained me."

I sense he wants to know more about the nature of our relationship, but I don't enlighten him.

I'm not entirely sure how to explain it myself. Yesterday was nice, and the grounds of Chirk Castle were stunning—the topiary there is even more impressive than ours. It's just hard to feel anything right now. I'm far too on edge.

"Tea?" Ash asks, straightening up.

"Have you got any milk?"

He nods.

In his ordinary T-shirt and jeans, he looks more or less the same as he did in Lisbon. But he still sounds like Ashton Berkeley with his posh English accent. It's more than a little disconcerting.

"Thanks. No sugar," I add, steeling myself against him.

He walks out of the room, seeming oddly rattled himself.

I sit there, taking in my surroundings as I listen to the sounds coming from the adjoining kitchen: the kettle filling, cupboards opening, the clink of cutlery and crockery.

There are bookshelves built into the wall cavities on either side of the fireplace and they're full of books, from fat, tattered paperbacks to tall hardbacks. I squint, trying to read the spines, and then I get up to take a closer look.

There are a lot of books about space here, and in front of the window is a brass telescope sitting on a wooden stand. It looks vintage.

I turn around to face Ash as he returns, drawing the blanket tighter around my shoulders. He meets my eyes briefly and sets down two mugs onto coasters on the low wooden coffee table.

"Did you really study astronomy and physics at university?" I ask, sounding wary.

He recoils. "Of course I did."

"So the stuff about Taran having a telescope and getting you into the stars . . . ?"

He stares at me, alarmed. "Everything I told you was true."

I scoff at that and he winces.

"Who lives here now?" I ask, returning to the sagging, faded sofa.

He sits down on a threadbare red armchair. All the furniture in here looks antique.

"I do," he says to my surprise, clarifying it with, "Most of the time."

"With Beca?"

He shakes his head quickly, seeming almost perturbed at the idea. "She hates it up here," he explains in response to the confused look on my face.

Why would he choose to live in the damp, dark woods instead of in a grand mansion in the sun?

Things could be a little hectic at home . . .

Just because the ordinary house I'd pictured in my mind is different to the mansion he grew up in doesn't mean the statement itself can't still be true, I realize.

"You told me you used to hang out at Taran's house a lot, that things could be a little hectic at home. Did you mean it?"

"I meant everything I said to you," he replies seriously, picking up a mug and passing it to me. "I struggled, growing up there."

A shimmer of heat licks over my skin as our fingers brush and I stiffen.

He looks pretty tense himself as he picks up his own mug and settles back in his chair. The fire is blazing away in the fireplace, but I keep the blanket around my shoulders, needing the extra comfort.

"Why did you struggle?" I prompt.

"That house has been open to visitors my entire life."

I let out a small snort and he frowns, shifting on his seat.

"Yeah, okay, I know how privileged that sounds," he says gruffly. "But can you please just try to imagine it? I'm not an extrovert like my mother. I've never felt comfortable walking around the grounds like she does."

I'm conflicted. I don't want to feel sorry for the son of a viscount.

"My bedroom used to be in the Tudor wing of the house," he continues. "The building overlooking the courtyard?"

"I know where the Tudor wing is, Ash."

He has the grace to look self-conscious. And then he says, "Never mind." And I hate that he's given up on trying to get me to understand.

He rakes his hand through his hair. It still looks windswept. A couple of strands fall forward into his eyes. He stares toward the window, his jaw clenched.

"Tell me about your bedroom," I say, softening my tone. Silence. "Ash," I prompt.

"Never mind," he says again, his Adam's apple bobbing up and down.

I wish I hadn't shut him down.

"I know how you feel about posh twats," he mutters, taking a sip of his tea.

"Is that why you didn't tell me?" I ask. "About all this?"

"I would have told you eventually."

My heart squeezes. *When?*

"I understand how much it must have freaked you out to hear me switching between accents, but it's something I've done all my life," he says. "I spent just as much time in this house as I did in that one." He nods in the direction of Berkeley Hall. "Gareth and Carys were like second parents to me. Taran and Celyn were like brothers. Taran, especially, as we were the same age. I used to hang out at the workshop all the time. I felt comfortable there. I didn't like to sound different, though, and at some point I just started speaking like the people around me. But then I'd go home, and my parents would freak out. They sent me off to boarding school, which I hated, but it's *what we do* in our circles," he finishes sardonically.

I frown at the fire, taking a moment to process all that he's said.

He sighs. "Haven't you ever adopted a different accent to fit in?" he asks.

I have done that. I did it when I went to private school, but I still made a conscious effort to sound like myself around Stella and my grandparents. Now, though, I simply sound like one person, not two.

Or do I? I put on a more proper-sounding voice to speak to his mother, but it's only a mild adjustment, nowhere near as extreme as what he did.

"It's like someone who grows up to be bilingual," Ash continues. "They can switch between languages seamlessly."

"It's not the same."

"Maybe not, but it's not something sinister. When I was younger, it came so naturally. I was Ash here and at the workshop and Ashton back at the house and at school."

"You just wanted to fit in."

"What kid doesn't?"

I'm beginning to get it. "And interrailing? You wanted to fit in there too?"

"That wasn't so much about me trying to fit in as me doing what felt most natural. I wanted to be off-grid, away from all that." Once more, he nods toward the house.

"So you're like two different people," I muse contemplatively.

"Not two people. One. This is me, Ellie." He indicates his chest with one hand. "You met *me*. You know *me*." His eyes are gleaming, pleading with me to understand.

I drop my head, overwhelmed.

"Like I said, I would have explained all this to you eventually," he reiterates. "It was only a matter of time."

My heart feels heavy. "You're speaking like you were intending to come to Madrid."

"I was." He sounds surprised.

I lift my head to look at him. "What happened then?"

He hesitates, breathing in deeply. "I don't know if you had it in the Algarve, but there was a big storm the night after I left you. I managed to get a room in a shitty hostel and I slept with Stella's book next to my pillow because I didn't want to lose it." He seems distressed as he's telling me this and my chest feels tight. "But I was out cold after barely sleeping on the beach and it must have fallen onto the floor and someone picked it up, because it wasn't there in the morning. I was in such a panic, asking everyone I could see if they'd taken it, but whoever had it must have already checked out. Of course, we still had our Madrid plan, and I was determined to get there the day before so nothing could go wrong. I bought a new phone for when we met up so I'd never be without a way to reach you again. And then, two days before we were supposed to meet, my mother called me about Hugo's accident."

"Who's Hugo?" I ask.

He stares at me, dazed. "My brother?"

"Oh. You never told me his name, only that he was stepping into your parents' shoes, running the family furniture business," I remember with a flare of irritation.

"No. I said my older brother was stepping into my parents' shoes, taking on the family business. You assumed I was talking about furniture."

"You let me assume it," I respond sharply.

He sighs and concedes with a nod.

"So what about Hugo?" I prompt, realizing that we've gone off track.

"He jumped off a bridge to go swimming in a lake and broke his spine."

I gasp. "Oh my God."

"You really didn't know?" he asks. "It's all over the internet."

I shake my head, stunned. "It didn't even occur to me to look up the family who owned this place before I took the job here. It was all about the garden for me."

He releases a small, sad puff of air, his eyes fixed gently on mine. It's a few seconds before he continues.

"Well, he was in intensive care and my parents wanted me home straightaway. For a fleeting moment I thought about going to Madrid first to tell you what was happening, but I had to get home in case we lost him. And then we did."

"He died?" I'm shocked.

He nods miserably. "The day after I was supposed to meet you."

"Oh, Ash, I'm so sorry."

He shakes his head. "I was in such a state. I found out that there was a café on the square and I called to ask if anyone would go out at three o'clock and look for a girl with red hair. There was hardly any phone reception at the hospital, but I managed to get through again to ask if they'd seen you. They said they hadn't. I called again, asked if they could take another look. I offered to send money to cover the inconvenience, but they said it wasn't necessary. I don't know if it was the language barrier or whether they were fobbing me off, but they claimed they never saw you."

"I was late," I reveal, as the agonizing memories flood back.

Eight days of stress and panic in the blistering heat, looking and never finding.

"Did you ever go back to interrailing?" I ask.

"No, that was the end of it for me. It was kind of the end of everything." His voice sounds strained as he explains. "Hugo was seven years older than me. We weren't close. He was the heir and he grew up knowing he had responsibilities, which he took seriously. It was different for me. I was allowed to pretty much do what I wanted, but Hugo always knew what was expected of him. After we lost him, I had to step into his shoes."

He looks downcast, and then he pitches forward and places his hand on the armrest near to where I'm sitting, staring at me intently.

"I would have met you in Madrid. I'm sorry I couldn't."

My eyes fill with tears.

"Ellie," he murmurs, covering my hand with his.

My heart hurts so much at the contact because my body recognizes him. The thought of pulling away is agonizing, but I force myself to slip my hand out from under his grasp, still trying to make sense of everything.

"So what were you planning to do?" I ask melancholically. "Travel together for a few weeks and *then* call it off?"

His brows pull together as he shakes his head. "Why would I call it off? I don't know what would have happened once we'd got back to the UK, but I thought we'd play it by ear."

"How was this *ever* going to work?" I ask, flustered.

He seems lost for words, and a deep weariness comes over me.

"I think you should take me home."

He swallows. And then he nods, averting his gaze.

He drives me back to the cottage on his bike. I tap his stomach as we turn out onto the farm track, reminding him that I don't literally want to be dropped at home.

"You really don't want to be seen with me, huh?" he says dryly as I climb off and remove his helmet, handing it back.

"No." I slide off his jacket.

He frowns. "You know, I grew up with a bunch of those guys. They're friends. None of them are worried about favoritism."

I laugh. "Is that what you think concerns me? That's a little entitled of you," I say acerbically.

"You're bothered about how this looks," he says slowly, and I can practically see the cogs in his brain whirring. His eyes widen. "Are you embarrassed about us?"

"Does that surprise you?"

"To be honest? Yes," he replies, shrugging his jacket back on. "I've never met anyone like you." He looks a little amused.

"I'll take that as a compliment," I respond.

"You should," he says, pulling his helmet over his head and flipping down the visor.

It's the last thing he says before he rides away in the opposite direction.

17

BET ASH BOOKED THE STRING BAND FOR HIS PARENTS'
fortieth. I can just imagine him adding Pulp's "Common People"
to the playlist and having a bit of a laugh about it. Did he go to
boarding school with some of those Hooray Henrys? He said he
hated it there—does he even get along with those people?

There's still so much I want to know about him. I feel as
though we've barely scratched the surface.

It must have been so hard to lose his brother like that, and
then for his role to suddenly change. He's explained why he didn't
turn up in Madrid, and I understand, even if it can't retroactively
erase the hurt. Still, it's not like anything can come of the connection we forged all those years ago. Maybe now that we've had our
talk, he's done, he's said his piece. He's got his closure and her
name is Beca.

I finally cracked and googled him last night. The sight of the
Honorable Ashton Berkeley and the Honorable Rebecca Brampton

looking dolled up to the nines at some society event made me feel seasick. I won't inflict that torture on myself again.

As the week unfolds without Ash reaching out to me again, I become increasingly convinced that he's drawn a line underneath our relationship. It's what he should do, of course—it would be dishonorable to do anything else—but I can't help feeling as though I'm carrying a weight around, even when I'm gardening.

I want to get back to the lightness I felt when I started here, but I suspect it might take some time. I don't feel angry toward Ash anymore, just sad. The anger was easier to handle.

Siân is due back from holiday on Friday, so on Thursday evening I clean the house from top to bottom and pick fresh flowers from the walled garden to welcome her home. I'm determined to be upbeat for my new housemate—I've wallowed behind closed doors for long enough—but I'm not naive; I know it's going to be strange sharing a space again, especially when my head is so full of Ash.

On Friday afternoon, it's drizzling when I finish work for the day, but the weather won't stop us from having what I now know is a regular welcome-the-weekend barbecue. It's been raining steadily for three days, but it's supposed to clear up later.

I'm in the process of towel-drying my hair when there's a knock on the door. Is that Siân already? Evan went to pick her up from the station, but they're not due back for a bit.

I'm not fully dressed yet, so I go and peek out of the window and catch a glimpse of someone's arm beneath the porch roof. I open up the sash window and lean out, keeping the lower half of my body hidden.

"Hello?" I call.

I almost have a fit when Beca steps out from under the porch and looks up at me. She's wearing a light gray shift dress and enormous black sunglasses even though it's overcast.

"Hello," she says unsmilingly.

"Hi." My heart jolts unpleasantly. What's she doing here?

"Do you think I could come in?" she asks, and there's a hostility in her tone that makes my anxiety spike.

"Sure, I'll just finish getting dressed," I reply awkwardly.

She nods and returns under the porch to wait while I quickly pull the sash window back down and drag on a pair of denim shorts to go with my lightweight sweater.

My hair is a wet, tangled mess and I'm wearing no makeup, but I'm quite sure that's the least of my problems. The thought occurs that she's here to warn me off Ash, but that's the most ridiculous notion. What if she's here to threaten me? Could she get me fired?

I open the door and step back, my heart thumping.

Her long blond hair is contained in a fishtail braid that drapes across one shoulder and loose tendrils frame her slim oval face. She's about three inches shorter than me, but she's standing tall and proud.

"I'm sorry, but I don't know how long we'll have before my new housemate arrives. We haven't met yet and she's due back from holiday today," I say as I turn and pad across the floor in my bare feet to the kitchen.

"I won't take up much of your time," she replies in a clipped English accent as she follows me inside.

"Can I get you anything?" I ask.

She's still wearing her sunglasses.

"Just a glass of water, please."

I take a deep, steadying breath as I fill a glass.

"I'm Ellie, by the way." I set the glass on the table and pull out a chair.

She lets out a weak laugh as she also sits down. "I know who you are. I knew who you were the second I saw you, standing there with your tray of glasses."

She picks up her drink, but she doesn't take a sip. "I knew who you were the second Ash looked at you," she continues dully. "Even before he left me standing on the steps with his parents."

My chest constricts at the thought of her watching that scene play out. I've tilted my body toward hers, but she's staring down at her water. Her lips are rosebud pink and she has a perfect Cupid's bow.

"Oh God." She takes off her sunglasses just as I notice that her bottom lip has begun to tremble.

At the sight of her puffy eyes, my insides swell with sympathy. She begins rooting around in her handbag, but I hurriedly get up and grab a box of tissues from the counter, placing them on the table.

"Thanks." She blows her nose, but her eyes continue to leak. She pulls out another tissue.

I have no idea what to say or do. I want to comfort her, but how can I? She's a stranger, and presumably she's crying over a man I thought I'd left in my past.

"I've dreaded the day for almost six years," she confides in a thick voice.

My heart clenches as she begins to sob. I reach out and touch her back—how can I *not*?

"You must know that you have nothing to worry about," I say, wanting to reassure her, because this is insane. "We barely know each other. We literally hung out for three days. I'm a gardener, for fuck's sake."

She laughs a genuine laugh and leans back in her chair, looking at me directly. Her eyes are light blue and rimmed with red. She's wearing no makeup, but it's possible she's cried it all off.

"You really have no idea, do you?" I stare at her, bewildered, as she continues. "He was broken when he lost you. While everyone else was grieving for Hugo, Ash was grieving for you. Of course, he was grieving for Hugo too, but that made it so much worse for him. He went to a dark place, and I mean *dark*. I was there. I saw it. I helped him climb out." She heaves out a big, shuddering breath. "I just can't believe you're here. I've loved him for so long and we've barely given ourselves a chance." She starts to cry again as she adds, "At least we weren't engaged. That would have been so much worse." Her eyes go wide at the thought.

This is so surreal.

"I should get out of your way." She grabs another tissue as she gets up from the table.

"I'm still not sure why you came," I reply hesitantly as I rise to my feet.

"I just wanted to meet you. I'm sorry it's not in better circumstances, but I wanted to say hello before I leave for London."

"Wait. You're going?"

She sniffs and nods as she walks toward the door.

"You haven't broken up with Ash?" I ask with astonishment as I follow her.

"Sorry, I thought that was obvious," she replies as my stomach drops off a ledge. "Good luck, Ellie," she says as she opens the door and slips her sunglasses back on. "Ash is at the ranger's cabin in the woods. He's upset right now, but I'm sure you'll console him." She doesn't even sound bitter.

She walks away, leaving me reeling.

18

I NEED TIME TO PROCESS WHAT'S JUST HAPPENED, BUT I don't have it: Siân arrives home from holiday minutes later. It takes every ounce of strength I have to fix on a smile and pretend that nothing's out of the ordinary.

"Hello!" she exclaims, bustling through the front door.

She's about five foot three and curvy, with one of the brightest smiles I've ever seen.

"Come here, roomie," she says warmly, dropping her carry-on bag to the floor with a thump and opening her arms. "Bring it in."

I laugh and step into her arms.

"Jesus, you're tall." She releases me and cranes her neck as I straighten up.

Evan has just come in behind her with her suitcase.

"How was your holiday?" I ask, somehow managing to throw a lasso around the headfuck of thoughts wreaking havoc on my mind.

"Too bloody hot. I'm not built for warm weather."

"We've had a few warm days here too," I tell her.

"Ugh," she groans, pushing her hands into her thick dark curls and giving them a shake as she adds, "I've heard it's going to be a long, hot summer. You'd better get the sprinkler on me, Evan," she calls over her shoulder as she wanders into the kitchen and picks up the kettle.

I like the way she says *Evan*. Bethan speaks so fast, but Owain—and Siân, it seems—have a slower, more melodic way of speaking. Their syllables are more pronounced, more deliberate-sounding: EV-aan.

Siân swirls the water inside the kettle indecisively and then goes to fill it from the tap.

"Are you having a cuppa?" she asks me.

"Sure."

He was broken when he lost you. While everyone else was grieving for Hugo, Ash was grieving for you.

I give my head a small shake and try to concentrate.

Has Beca really left Ash? It can't be over between them. It makes no sense.

"Sorry, what?" I realize Siân has just asked me something.

"You looked to be in your own little world there. Do you take milk and sugar?"

"Just milk."

"Are you having one, Evan?"

"No, I'm holding out for a beer." He leans against the kitchen counter and folds his arms, smiling at me.

There's a jaunty knock on the back door, but Bethan doesn't wait for us to answer it. "Siân!" she cries, swooping in for a hug right past where Evan's standing.

Siân laughs. "All right, all right, get off me, I've only been away two weeks."

"It's been too long. I've missed you."

"You've missed my carrot cake."

"I have *really* missed your carrot cake," Bethan agrees whole-heartedly.

Ash is at the ranger's cabin in the woods. He's upset right now, but I'm sure you'll console him.

I feel as though I've just gone downhill on a roller coaster.

ABOUT HALF AN hour is all I can manage before I crack and text him.

Are you OK?

I keep coming back to the message as the afternoon lengthens into evening, but there's no indication that he's read it.

Everyone who lives at the cottages is here tonight and the camaraderie is in full swing. When I'm three glasses of sangria in—Siân has been in Spain and she was insistent on re-creating her favorite holiday tipple—I text him again. If Ash needs cheering up, this is where he should be.

Siân is back from holiday and we're all having a BBQ, I tap out. You should come.

I hope he'll understand that I still don't want anyone to know about us, but I also hope he'll see that I care.

But this message remains unread too.

I can't do this. I have to see him.

My head is swimming, but alcohol has not deadened my nerves nearly enough as I go back inside. Luckily, I have the presence of mind to make sure my bedroom door is closed so Siân will think

I've slipped away to bed, then I change into my gardening boots and grab my raincoat and a flashlight on my way out the front door.

The sounds of my new friends laughing and talking carry across the fields as I set off along the farm track, and if I look over my shoulder, I can still see light shining from the backs of the cottages. But once I turn off onto the narrower track at the bend in the road, the high hedges on either side block out all artificial light. I reach into my coat pocket for my flashlight and hesitate, noticing that the clouds have broken apart to reveal a starry sky. I decide to give my eyes a chance to adjust to the darkness and they do, surprisingly quickly.

As the damp night folds around me, I leave the noises of the party behind, walking at a swift pace as the road begins to incline uphill. Tall trees loom out of the darkness and an owl hoots as I make my way into the forest. The starlight doesn't stand a hope in hell of filtering down through the thick tree cover, so I have to turn on my flashlight, and weirdly, the artificial light makes my surroundings feel more ominous. I'm a little on edge as I search for the cottage, but when I find it, all is quiet and dark.

My heart sinks. What if Ash is asleep? What if he's not even here? I feel dejected at the thought of turning around and walking the half-hour return journey without seeing him.

Bracing myself for disappointment, and hoping that I'm not going to piss off a very tired man, I walk up to the cabin door and knock.

Silence greets me.

I knock again and back away, looking up at the first-floor windows for any signs of life.

Nada.

Swearing under my breath, I pull out my phone, checking to see if he's responded to my text messages, but I'm not even sure he's read them. Should I call him? No, I can't even do that, I realize: there's no mobile reception.

So maybe he hasn't received my messages. Then I see his motorbike. He must be around somewhere . . .

Skirting the outside of the cottage, I notice something beyond the tree trunks up ahead: long green grass. I realize that the trees stop at the edge of a grassy hilltop.

"Who's there?" I hear someone shout from off in the distance.

"Ash? It's me!" I shout back.

"Ellie?"

I catch him in the beam of my flashlight. He's right at the top of the hill, sitting up, using his hand to shield his eyes from the light.

"Sorry," I say, quickly switching it off as I venture out from under the trees, hoping the stars will light my way again.

"What are you doing here?" he asks as I approach. His voice sounds raw.

"I texted you."

"Did you?"

"Beca told me you were here."

"Beca?" He's taken aback.

"She came to see me."

He's just a silhouette in front of me now, but he's risen to his feet. I can barely distinguish his features in the darkness, but I can see how tall he is, make out the breadth of his shoulders, the shape of his hair.

"What did she say?" he asks edgily.

"That she was going back to London."

"Yeah. She left me." He sounds as though he has the weight of the world on his shoulders.

"I'm sorry."

My eyes have grown used to the darkness enough to see that trees encircle this entire hill. My toes touch the edge of something and I realize that I've stepped onto a blanket.

"Can I sit?" I ask him tentatively.

"Sure," he replies heavily, settling down beside me.

"Is this the clearing where you and Taran used to camp out?"

"You remember?"

"I remember everything."

There's a beat, and then he folds over and begins to sob, and it's utterly heart-wrenching.

"Oh, Ash," I murmur, rubbing his back.

He's wearing a dark-colored hoodie and my hand bounces up and down as his body shakes violently beneath it.

"I'm so sorry."

He's inconsolable. I hadn't prepared myself for this level of grief. I'm out of my depth. He's so in love with her, in so much pain.

"Don't give up on her." My chest contracts even as I say it.

"You don't understand," he chokes out, roughly brushing away his tears with the sleeve of his hoodie. "Once Beca's made up her mind about something, she doesn't change it."

How my heart recoils at hearing him talk like this.

"But you'll still try, right? You love her."

"Of course I love her. After Taran, she was my closest friend. That's why I'm so fucking sad. I've just lost another friend." He buries his head in his hands and lets out an anguished sob.

"Ash," I murmur again.

"Sorry," he gasps. "I shouldn't be crying to you."

"Do you want me to go?"

"No," he replies adamantly. "No. I don't."

I drape my arm around his back, resting my chin on his shoulder, and after a moment he lets his weight fall against me.

We just sit there next to each other, in silence, and eventually his breathing settles into a slow, even pace.

My insides are a mangled, writhing mess, but I'm trying not to think about how much I'm hurting right now.

I lift my head to look at the stars. There's a superbright one, right near the horizon.

"Do you know what that star is called?"

"It's not a star, they're two planets." His voice is still laden with emotion. "There's a close conjunction between Jupiter and Mars tonight."

"What's that?" I ask.

"It's when the planets align. They look like they're practically on top of each other, but they're almost three hundred and fifty million miles apart."

His tone has lifted a little and I realize that my questions might be a welcome distraction.

"Huh. How interesting. I heard there was a lunar eclipse the night I arrived. Something about a rare spectacular blood moon? I saw pictures of it on TV the next morning." I'd woken up early and watched the news. "I was a bit gutted to miss it."

"You didn't miss much. It clouded over in the night."

"Ah, okay." A few seconds pass. "The thing I really want to know," I say slowly. "The thing that has kept me awake at night . . ."

He tilts his head toward me, waiting.

". . . is how can it be called a full moon if it's only half a moon that's lit up?"

He releases a small laugh. "Do you really want an answer to that question?"

"Have you got one?"

"No."

I giggle at him. He flinches and a second later he drags his hand over his face, leaving it buried in his palm. I'm worried that he's going to start crying again, but he doesn't. I can just hear his jagged breathing.

"Another thing I'm curious about . . ." I'm trying to stop him from retreating into his own pain again. "Why is it called moonlight when it's actually sunlight that's reflected back at us? Is there any such thing as moon *light*?"

I'm staring up at the sky, but out of the corner of my eye, I see him turn his face toward me again.

"I missed you," he whispers, and his voice sounds so plaintive, so full of longing.

And maybe I shouldn't, but I can't stop myself from sliding my arms around his neck. His hands come around my back and he pulls me toward him, but I wish we were closer. I give him a small squeeze and let him go before I do something stupid.

"Do you want to tell me what happened?" I ask. "She said she knew who I was when she saw me at the party."

I hear his heavy swallow. "Yeah, I used to talk about you a lot." He releases a long breath. "After Hugo had his accident, I was so fucked up, but I still believed I'd be able to get in touch with you somehow. I don't think it really hit me until after the funeral that I had no way of finding you. I didn't have Stella's book, we hadn't exchanged surnames or addresses. How did we not do that?"

"I've asked myself the same question. *So many times*," I reply disconsolately. "I think that sort of detail felt like small talk, inconsequential. We were in so much deeper than that."

He leans his weight into me a little harder, bringing me closer. I rest my knees against his. My heart is jumpy and light.

"Are you warm enough?" he asks gently.

"I'm okay. Still cooling down after the walk."

"You walked up here?" he asks with surprise.

"Yeah. Why? How did you think I got here?"

"I hadn't actually thought about it, but I would have assumed you'd brought a car."

"No. Walked."

"You just set off, in the dark, and hiked all the way into the woods to a house you've only been to once before?" I can tell that he's smiling.

"Yes. Why are you smiling?"

"I just like that about you. I like your adventurous spirit."

"You think I have an adventurous spirit?"

"You slept on a beach with me."

"Well, we didn't do much sleeping," I quip.

He lets out a laugh, but the sound cuts off abruptly, as though his thoughts have turned to Beca. He must feel like he's being disloyal, thinking about us at our most intimate moments.

"So Beca knew about me," I prompt, putting space between us by wrapping my arms around my knees.

"Yeah. She saw me at my worst after I realized I'd lost you. I was obsessed with finding you. I was like that for years. We only got together at Christmas, so she couldn't believe it when you turned up here."

"You only got together at Christmas?" I ask with surprise, my mind half caught on *obsessed with finding you*.

"Christmas Eve."

"And before that?"

"We were friends. She broke up with her boyfriend just before Christmas and she was seriously pissed off at him. We got hammered on tequila and . . . I don't know how it happened, actually, but . . . Yeah."

I don't want to know the details and yet I'm morbidly curious to find out how their relationship veered into romantic territory.

"I remember you telling me that you thought she might have feelings for you."

"That's right," he replies quietly. "I loved her too, platonically. But I was under pressure from my parents to get married and have kids—"

"And produce the twenty-second Viscount Berkeley," I interrupt him. I don't mean to sound judgy.

"You've been doing your research."

"Evan mentioned that twenty-one generations of Berkeleys have lived here. I'm presuming you're the twenty-first, the next to inherit?"

"Mmm," he replies shortly.

"That's a lot of pressure."

He doesn't say anything in response, but after a moment he rakes his hand through his hair. "Anyway, I thought we owed it to ourselves to give it a shot," he says brusquely.

I frown into the darkness, lost in thought. I'm holding my breath as I ask, "Were you going to propose to her on the steps at your parents' anniversary party?"

"No!" He sounds alarmed.

"It's just that I heard a couple of people talking about it. 'Berkeley and Bex will be next!'"

He groans. "You probably met some of the people I went to school with."

"I didn't meet anyone. I was an invisible waitress."

My words hang heavy in the air.

"I'm sorry," he says.

"Finish telling me about Beca. I'm sorry, we keep getting distracted."

"There's not much more to say. She wanted me to talk to you. I suspect she thought I'd get some sort of closure if I did, but when

I went to see her after you and I spoke last weekend, she was distraught. It was as though I'd failed a test I didn't know she'd set me. Things have been really bad over this last week. She was so convinced I'd leave her to pursue something with you that she decided to get ahead of the curve."

My mind is tripping and stumbling over his words, trying to keep up.

"How could Beca think that you'd leave her for me?" I ask, perplexed. "She's known you all your life. I knew you for three days."

He doesn't answer my question. His face is tilted up toward the stars.

I wonder if Beca let Ash go because she believed that he'd come back to her. Does she think that if she gives him his freedom, he'll realize himself that he and I could never work?

Because we can't work. This isn't a life I was born into, and it isn't a life I would want my children to be born into either. I could never rub shoulders with the upper classes day in, day out. I don't fit into Ash's world and I have no interest in trying to.

Beca, on the other hand, was raised to walk through a life like this. She'd be a perfect Viscountess Berkeley, the sort of wife and mother of his children that Ash needs. And she's his closest friend. He loves her.

They're meant to be together. I'm the one who needs to walk away.

19

WHEN I GO DOWNSTAIRS THE NEXT MORNING, SIÂN IS already up and at the kitchen sink, washing last night's glasses.

"Hey!" I say in greeting.

"*Bore da*," she replies, which means "good morning" in Welsh.

"*Helô*," I respond in turn.

"Ooh, you sounded proper Welsh then."

I smile and grab a tea towel.

"You were very sneaky last night," she says teasingly as I begin to dry up. "Everyone wondered where you disappeared off to."

"Sorry. I popped inside to use the loo and just crashed. I was so tired."

"Hmm."

She can't be on to me already . . .

"Have you got any plans for today?" she asks, and I feel as though I might have dodged a bullet.

"No."

WHAT IF I NEVER GET OVER YOU · 185

"It's Bethan's birthday."

"Is it?"

"I know, she kept it very quiet. But Harri's working and she's at a loose end, so I wondered about doing a pampering afternoon for her."

"That sounds fun."

"Oh, and I'm baking her a carrot cake," she adds. "It's her favorite."

"I heard! What can I do?"

"You can come with me to the shop to get some supplies if you like?"

"Sure."

ASH TEXTS ME at eleven thirty: You invited me over last night.

I did, I reply, smiling.

My text messages must have gotten through at last.

There's no reception at the cabin.

I gathered.

Does this mean you've changed your mind about being seen with me?

No, it means you can carry on as normal with your friends, but you've got to pretend I'm just your gardener.

He doesn't reply.

I text him again. Are you angry?

His answer comes after a few seconds. That's too strong a word.

Upset?

A little.

I bite my lip, staring at my phone. I'm sorry.

It's OK. I get it.

BETHAN, SIÂN, AND I spend the afternoon sitting on the sofas, wearing facial masks, eating carrot cake, and watching *Glee*, Bethan's favorite TV show from when she was a teenager.

Siân keeps pausing the TV to add to a playlist she's making of the original versions of the songs. It's the sort of thing I used to do with Stella, and my happiness is a touch bittersweet. But I do feel optimistic about these new friendships.

Ash texts me at five thirty when we've just cracked open a bottle of prosecco. Celyn's invited me for a beer. I hope that's OK?

Of course it is, I reply, unsettled by the strength of the thrill that has just rocketed through me.

Harri knocks on the back door soon afterward, freshly showered after a day at work. The pots in the greenhouses wouldn't make it through the weekend if they weren't tended to, but only one of us is needed for the Saturday–Sunday shift.

"Are we boys allowed to join you now?" he shouts over Siân's finished playlist, squeezing his girlfriend's shoulders from behind.

"I suppose we can allow it," Bethan replies genially, patting his hand as Lady Gaga's "Bad Romance" fades to an end.

The sound of a distant motorbike makes my ears prick up. Ash wasted no time getting on his way.

Evan appears at the back door. "Is this where the party's at?" he asks.

"I think it's outside," I respond, getting up from the sofa and smiling at him.

"I wondered if you might be up for another day trip with me tomorrow?" he asks, leaning his hip against the counter as I get myself a glass of water.

"Ooh, is this a date?" Siân cheekily calls over from the sofa.

"No!" I respond, a little more vehemently than I meant to. "Never mix business with pleasure," I add playfully to lighten the tone of my rebuttal, picking up a tea towel from the counter and flicking Evan on the hip with it.

"Ow!" he says, laughing as he bats me away.

The others get up and join us in the kitchen.

"Where were you thinking about going?" I ask Evan, trying to sound nonchalant as I hop up onto the counter beside him.

"There's a waterfall not too far from here. I thought maybe we could take a picnic."

"That sounds very date-like," Siân chips in as she tops up her glass with prosecco.

"Keep out of it, you," Evan replies.

Harri and Bethan laugh at him as they sort themselves out for drinks.

"What are you guys up to tomorrow?" I ask edgily.

"I'm working," Harri replies, but Bethan shrugs and says brightly, "No plans."

"Siân?"

"Oh, we don't want to get in the middle of anything," she responds to me.

My God, she is such a stirrer!

"Would you shut up?" I say fondly. "We're just friends." I look at Evan. "Aren't we?"

"We are," he agrees with a smile.

But his eyes aren't sparkling as much as usual.

"Are you having another one?" Siân asks me, holding up the bottle.

The rumble of Ash's motorbike out the back door makes it hard for me to concentrate on holding my glass still while she pours fizz into it.

"Well, wouldn't you know," she says significantly, looking past me out the window. "It's the Honorable Ashton Berkeley."

Harri chuckles at Siân's tone. I'm not sure if she was being sarcastic, and I don't like the thought of her taking the piss out of Ash. I feel quite protective as I glance over my shoulder to see him climbing off his motorbike, but then I realize that Siân is out the door and halfway across the lawn.

"*Helô*, Ash," I hear her call warmly, and his face breaks into a broad grin at the sight of her.

I hop down from the counter and walk outside in time to hear her say, as Ash climbs over the lavender border with his long legs, "I think you might need a *kutch*, from what I've been hearing."

"What's a *kutch*?" I ask Bethan as she joins me.

Siân freezes theatrically and turns around to look at me. "You don't know what a *kutch* is?" she asks. "C-w-t-c-h," she spells out.

"As if that explains it," I reply with a laugh.

I meet Ash's eyes momentarily and quickly look away.

"It's a hug," Evan says.

"Oh, it's so much more than a hug," Siân corrects him. "It's like a proper emotional snuggle, isn't it? There's no word for it in English. Come here, Ash," she says sympathetically, opening her arms.

He has to stoop right down to embrace her. I watch as he closes his eyes, and it feels kind of personal and intimate, the way she's holding him right now. I experience a funny little twinge of envy.

They break away. "Anytime you need a *cwtch*, you let me know," Siân says to me. "Or ask Evan, he'll give you one," she teases.

This time I blush.

Ash steps forward to greet Bethan, Harri, and Evan, finally turning to me with a small smile.

"Hello," he says.

"Hi." I feel so shy all of a sudden.

Thankfully Celyn comes out of his cottage and calls out to him. Ash strides off and they meet in the middle with a brief but warm hug.

Shit, I actually am kind of peeved that these people get to hug him and I can't.

Jac and Dylan emerge from their cottage next door. "Ugh, can you change the music?" Jac moans.

The Supremes' "You Keep Me Hangin' On" is playing now. Stella used to love the Kim Wilde version.

"Be quiet, you! It's Bethan's birthday, she can play what she wants," Catrin, Celyn's girlfriend, chides from behind them.

The boys grin and pick up their chairs, relocating them to behind our cottage. We make a rough circle on the lawn and they crack open a couple of brightly colored beer cans.

Ash sits down two chairs away from me, beside Celyn on my right. Evan is on my left.

"How have you been?" I hear Celyn ask Ash as the others start talking among themselves.

"I'm okay," he replies, taking a sip of his pale ale.

"I heard on the grapevine what happened."

What has he heard? Siân has obviously got wind of it too, if she wanted to give him that long cuddle.

"I don't even know what to say," Ash replies.

I'm pretending to listen to a conversation between Catrin and Siân, but I can't concentrate.

"She'll come back," Celyn says gruffly.

Ash kicks his foot at the grass. "I don't think so," he replies.

"No, she will. You guys are made for each other."

Ash's eyes lock with mine and I experience a full-body jolt. We both look down. I feel edgy and nervous and yes, okay, I'll admit it, sick with jealousy.

Suddenly this whole thing seems insane. There's no way Beca left him because of me. It makes no sense. There must be more to it than that.

I force myself to turn to Evan. "So you're thinking about heading to a waterfall tomorrow?" I ask sunnily.

"Yeah, do you fancy it?"

"Sure," I reply, just as I realize that Ash and Celyn have fallen silent.

"It's about forty minutes away," Evan adds.

"Where are you going?" Ash asks directly, his eyes moving between us. He sounds casually interested.

"Don't ask me to pronounce it," Evan replies, pulling out his phone. I lean over his shoulder and catch sight of the words PISTYLL RHAEADR before he turns the display toward Ash.

The sound that comes out of Ash's mouth sounds so distinctly Welsh that my chest contracts.

"I've only just realized that you've been talking like Ashton Berkeley!" Celyn suddenly exclaims at Ash.

Ash's eyes flit to mine and cut away again. He laughs lightly and takes a swig of his beer, pink tinging his cheeks.

He doesn't dare speak with a Welsh accent in front of me, I realize. Not after the way I reacted when he switched accents so seamlessly on the night of his parents' party. The last of my scratches from stumbling backward into the rosebushes with shock only healed a few days ago.

I jump to my feet and head inside, grabbing my phone from where it's charging on the countertop.

Be yourself, I text him, glancing out the window in time to see him get his phone out of his jeans pocket. He's only sitting a few meters away, so this time when he looks toward my window, he meets my eyes through the glass. I feel jittery as I wait for his reply.

I don't want to freak you out.

You won't.

He meets my eyes again and it hits me how much I want to hear his voice, the voice that I remember.

I walk outside and sit back down.

"What have you done for your birthday today then, Bethan?" Ash asks her, and God, he sounds like him, like *Ash*, like himself.

I feel all skittery beneath my ribs as he and Bethan talk to each other. I can't concentrate on a single other thing, only the sound of his voice, his slow, melodic lilt, the easy, laid-back quality that seems to come over him.

My ears are tuned in to his every word, and my gaze keeps getting drawn back to his body too. I manage to prevent myself from staring too openly at his face, but I'm drinking in the casual way he's leaning back in his deck chair, the length of his legs in those well-worn jeans, the way his chest and shoulders fill his faded green T-shirt.

I'm struck with a vision of him in his Hawaiian shirt, open at the neck, flapping wildly in the wind as he holds his hair back from his face in a tuk-tuk in Lisbon.

The sound of his voice together with the vivid memories takes me back to a time when my attraction to him was all-consuming. My eyes land on his mouth as he puts his beer can to his lips and tilts it.

Time seems to have slowed down. That prosecco has gone straight to my head.

Bonnie Tyler's "Total Eclipse of the Heart" comes pouring out of the stereo and I breathe in sharply as Ash looks straight at me.

The moment has coincided with a pause in his conversation with Bethan, but he doesn't ask another question or turn to anyone else. While the others talk around us, he and I stare at each other. His eyes are glittering with intensity as he holds my gaze, and inside my chest, my heart has begun to beat erratically.

I need to look away, but I can't. *He* needs to look away, but he doesn't.

Goose bumps race up my neck just as he tilts his head toward the outbuildings, giving them a very subtle look over his shoulder before returning his eyes to mine.

Is he asking me to meet him there? But people will see us leaving.

I give a tiny shake of my head and lift my eyes and chin up toward the roof of the cottage.

Meet me out the front.

He smirks and puts his can back to his lips.

The sight of that small, lazy smile makes my stomach do a slow flip.

Head tingling, I get up and go back inside the cottage, walking straight through it to the front door where my keys are dangling from a coat hook. I know I'll regret this if any of that lot finds out about us, but right now I'm past caring. I want him to myself.

Bonnie Tyler is still building to a crescendo in the back garden, so no one will hear the creak of hinges as I push open the door to the walled garden. Footsteps sound out from behind me on the path. Ash is walking over from the direction of the last cottage. He's grinning.

"For a minute, I thought you were suggesting we meet on the roof."

He still sounds like his old self and I love it. I laugh and lead the way into the dark garden, pushing the door closed behind him and locking it again with the skeleton key, just to be on the safe side.

"Did you want to say something?" he asks.

"Did you?" I bat back at him. "You were the one who suggested we sneak off." He'd looked at the outbuildings first.

The wall rises up around us and the light is eerie under the glow of the stars. The air smells damp and earthy, the grass beneath the apple trees sodden with dew.

He grunts with annoyance. "It bugs me that he's taking you to Pistyll Rhaeadr on a Sunday," he says as we duck under a low-hanging branch. "It's going to be so busy. You should go on a weekday at dawn or much later in the day. He's going to wreck it for you."

"Is that the only reason you're pissed off?"

He pauses beneath a gnarly old tree and hooks his hand over a branch that stretches out past the top of his head. "No," he mutters as I go and stand in front of him. "*I* should be showing you Wales, not him."

A shiver runs down my spine at the sound of his petulant voice.

"Don't you like Evan?" I wonder if I'm pushing his buttons by asking.

"He's fine," he replies offhandedly. "I'm more interested in whether *you* like him."

I feel the intensity of his stare, even in the darkness.

"Yes, I do like him," I reply, but it feels wrong to try to deliberately wound him, so I add, "We're friends."

He stares at me a moment longer. I can just see the glint of his eyes. "Have you ever been more?" he asks.

"Would it bother you if we had?"

"Yes."

"Are you jealous?"

"Of course I am."

It gives me such a thrill to hear him confess to it.

"I was jealous when Siân gave you a *cwtch*," I admit.

"Were you?" He sounds pleased.

"Has anything ever happened between you two?" I ask warily.

"Siân and me? No," he replies firmly. "She's like family. I've known her for years."

I'm relieved. "I was worried you might have lost your virginity to her or something."

He laughs. "No, I lost my virginity to Aspen Montgomery when I was sixteen."

"She sounds posh."

"She is."

It's a reminder, as if I need one, that while he might sound like the Ash I remember, he's still Ashton Berkeley, son of a viscount, heir to Berkeley Hall. He's from another world, a different class, and even if I could step into Beca's recently vacated shoes, I wouldn't want to.

The sudden reminder of his all-too-recent ex makes me feel a little ill.

"So why did you agree to sneak off?" he asks, and his tone is lighter than when we first came out here, more playful. "Did *you* have something to say?"

"No, I just hate that everyone else got to give you a hug and I couldn't," I admit sulkily, trying to ignore the voice in my head telling me that he's not for me.

"Aw," he says gently. "Do you want one now?"

When I don't immediately answer, he lets go of the tree and pulls me toward him. My stomach feels as though it's full of daisies lifting their heads to the sun as his arms circle my waist. I loop mine around his neck and he gathers me close until our chests are completely flush to each other.

"How's this?" he whispers as my body melts against his.

"Mmm" is all I manage in reply.

I really don't want him to let me go, but after a few more seconds he releases me, leaving me bereft.

"I always wanted to climb these trees when I was younger," he murmurs, looking up at the branches.

"Why didn't you?"

"I wasn't allowed. Some of them are so old."

"What was it like to have the run of this place once the visitors had left?" I ask as we venture farther into the walled garden.

"It used to frighten me," he admits. "I was scared of the dark."

"But you love space," I say, flummoxed.

"It's weird. I wasn't scared when I was up at the cabin or out in the woods with Taran. Only here. And in the house," he adds, and there's something about his tone that makes me think he's confiding something to me that he doesn't often talk about.

"Why did the house scare you?" I ask tentatively as we come to a stop.

The air is thickly perfumed by the lilac growing in the nearby central circle.

"Have you been inside?" he asks.

"Only in the Great Hall, and Evan took me through the gate-house the day I arrived," I reply.

"I'll take you inside sometime, show you properly."

I don't know when he plans to do that. In the hours when it's not open to visitors, surely his parents will be around, or any number of staff.

I feel a tickle beginning behind my nose. And then I'm off.

One sneeze.

Ash chuckles.

Two sneezes.

"Oh my fucking God," he says.

Three sneezes.

I hold up my palm to fend him off.

Four sneezes.

"Gah!" I think I'm done.

"Your sneezes are as cute as your sniggles," he says with such sweet affection that I feel as though I've ingested warm honey. "If I get you some bike gear, will you come for a ride with me?" he asks suddenly.

"On your motorbike?"

"Yeah." Now he sounds doubtful, where he didn't a moment ago.

"Sure."

He releases a small snort of amusement.

"What's funny?" I ask.

"No hesitation—you just said yes."

I love the way he sounds right now, so *fond* of me.

"When do you want to go?" I ask.

"Next Saturday?"

"I think so. I'll have to work out what to tell the others."

"Tell them you're catching up with an old friend."

He feels like so much more to me than that.

20

I got you some bike gear today. Can you come up to the
cabin to try it on?

It's Wednesday afternoon and this is the first I've heard from
Ash since Saturday night, so the sight of his name on my phone
makes me feel a rush of anticipation.

When? I reply.

Anytime from now.

I'll set off shortly.

You want a ride?

No, I'm happy to walk. It's beautiful today.

Go down past the orangery and skirt round the right-hand side
of the lake. If you head into the woods from there, it's nicer than the
farm track.

OK, I tap back, smiling.

Siân hasn't gotten home from work yet, so I leave a note to tell her I've gone for a wander.

Sunshine hits my back as I walk out from the shade of the walled garden and set off along the road leading to the car park, stepping onto the grassy verge as the last of the day's visitors drive slowly toward the exit.

It's early June and I think Siân might be right about this being the start of a long, hot summer. The watering alone will keep our volunteers occupied.

Cutting through the formal rose gardens, I breathe in deeply as the scents of *Rosa* "Cornelia," "Abraham Darby" and "Gold-finch" fill my nostrils, and then get a tissue out of my pocket in preparation for the approaching sneezing fit.

Ash said that my sneezes sound as cute as my sniggles. I love that he remembers the name he gave my laughter all those years ago.

I have a flashback to the way he covered his face with his palm when we sat up on the hill by his cabin—I'd just laughed at our exchange about the moon and he looked like he was in pain. Shortly afterward he told me that he missed me.

I don't know why I think of this memory now, or why I suddenly know that his pain was related more to me than to Beca in that moment.

Heading past the sundial sculpture that's set into the lawn and down the steps leading to the Georgian garden, I walk past the rainbow of lupins. At the bottom of the hill, the orangery's windows glint in the late-afternoon sunshine. I pass it and Maple Garden, which is the last of the garden rooms that Owain, Evan, Bethan, Harri, and I are responsible for, and carry on into ranger territory. Celyn and Dylan are the bosses out here.

Skirting the glittering lake, I smile as a duck flies out of the reeds, quacking wildly with fright, and then I pause to watch as ten tiny ducklings zoom through the water after their mother.

Up ahead, the woods are bathed in sunlight. A flock of birds fly through the blue sky overhead, and I turn around and look back at the house, sitting pretty on higher ground. Sun shines on the crenelated roofline—the notches look like battlements, but they're more decorative. The simpler arched windows of the eighteenth-century section contrast with the opulence of the cream stone gatehouse in the middle. My eyes are drawn to the Tudor wing. I can't believe it was built at a time when Henry VIII was on the throne.

I'm struck by the realization that Ash's family owns that house, that it's been in his family for five hundred years. The enormity of it still hasn't sunk in. I think of his parents and his grandparents and his great-grandparents and his great-great-grandparents and my head begins to swim at the notion of an incredible twenty-one generations of his family living there one after the other. And *he* will inherit it one day, and *he'll* have to keep it safe for future generations of Berkeleys. That responsibility must feel huge.

I think back to how Ash said the house had frightened him when he was little. He never elaborated, but my heartstrings twang at the thought of a young Ash feeling scared as he walked down long corridors and turned into old rooms, fearful of what might lie around the corner. I can imagine it, and I know that I'd hate it too. It *would* feel scary, being in a big old house like that.

My mood dips as I carry on past the lake and into the woods, but then the sounds of the forest pull me out of my slump. Birdsong rings out from high branches as I walk over the spongy earth, the crackle of twigs filling my ears.

"Hello."

The sound of Ash's voice doesn't startle me. It's almost as though I knew he would be here.

"Hello," I reply, smiling at him as I approach.

He's leaning against the wide trunk of a giant oak tree, his mouth curved up at the corners. He's wearing khaki shorts and a gray T-shirt with a pair of green Vans that have seen better days.

"Thought I'd walk with you the rest of the way," he says.

"You look as though you've been waiting for me."

"I have. I saw you coming down through the Georgian garden."

"You were watching me?"

"Yes. And that sounds very, very creepy," he adds impishly. "But your hair was glinting in the sunlight and you just looked so . . ."

So fucking pretty.

His compliment from almost six years ago zips through my mind, but whatever words he was going to say hang in the air unsaid.

I look back toward the house. "I can't believe you own that."

"I don't."

I glance over my shoulder at him. "No, I mean your parents."

"They don't really own it either," he says seriously, pushing off from the tree trunk and coming to stand beside me. "We're just custodians."

"Yeah, but if you sold it, you'd get the money from it."

He huffs out a laugh at my bluntness. "Technically, yes. But who's going to sell it? Every parent has a responsibility to pass it on to their children. Imagine being the arsehole to take it away from future generations."

"What if you ran into financial difficulties, though? Don't these old properties cost a bomb to maintain?" A memory slams into my mind. "Oh my God!" I exclaim before he can answer me. "We had a whole conversation about this at the park in Lisbon! I've just remembered!" I sound accusatory, but I'm only a bit piqued. I've given up holding his caginess against him.

"I thought you remembered everything," he says dryly, looking down at me.

I remember the details of our time on the beach with breathtaking clarity, but I admit this particular conversation didn't have a lasting impact.

"I take it *you* remember," I say.

"I do," he confirms. "You think we should donate it to charity, but it's not that simple when you have the weight of your forebears pressing down on you." He nods pointedly into the woods. "We have run into financial difficulties, plenty of times," he confides as we continue walking. "We've had to sell off parcels of land to farmers and developers. My grandfather drove himself into the ground with the stress of it. I sometimes think my father will do the same."

I'm glad that he's opening up to me, but it's hard to hear.

"I don't want that for you, Ash," I can't stop myself from saying.

He sighs. "The pressure of keeping this place up and running already feels immense. My father sometimes talks about selling off the woodland, cottages, and sawmill to developers. I've had so many sleepless nights thinking about my friends losing their homes and jobs and all this being razed to the ground." He looks around at the trees and shudders. "I'll do everything I can to ensure that doesn't happen. We don't only have a duty to future generations, we have a duty to everyone who lives and works here. One day that responsibility will be mine to shoulder and I just have to hope that I'll be up to the job. I couldn't live with myself if I screwed it up. Hugo was so much better at the business side of things than I am—my father thinks I'm out of my depth, but my mother seems to believe in me. I hope I don't let her down."

It hurts to hear him speaking about himself like this. "I'm sure Beca believed in you too, right?" I glance at him.

He looks pained and it's a moment before he nods. "Yeah. She did."

"Did she ever feel daunted by it all?"

He slides his gaze toward me before averting it and shaking his head.

We walk on in silence for a while before I ask something I've been wondering.

"How did you and she come to be such good friends? Before you got together, I mean."

"Her parents are my parents' closest friends. Our fathers go way back—they went to school together—and our mothers fell pregnant with us at the same time. I've literally known her since the day she was born. I'm only three weeks older."

"And it was genuinely platonic between you until last Christmas?" I'm so curious as to how two such stunning humans could be friends with each other and nothing more.

"Completely. I mean, okay, not for her. Things started to change when we went to university. That separation enabled her to think of me differently, she said. But she always felt like a sister to me. We grew up seeing each other warts and all. Snotty noses, grazed knees. Fuck, the tantrums she used to throw . . ." He shakes his head with amusement and then his expression sobers, probably as he remembers the current state of their relationship.

"Does she know Celyn and Siân very well, and all the other workers?" I ask.

"No, not really." He frowns. "It's not that she doesn't *want* to get to know them, I just think she doesn't feel like she fits in."

He's defending her and it's with love.

I come to a stop.

Ash hesitates and looks back at me, puzzled. "Are you okay?"

"No," I confess.

"What's wrong?"

"What are we doing?" I ask.

He turns around to face me properly. "I just want to spend some time with you."

"Why?" I stare up at him. "So you can be crystal clear about how unsuited we are?"

He recoils. "No."

"So *I* can be crystal clear about how unsuited we are? I already know it."

"How can you say that?"

"I'm just an ordinary girl, Ash!" I exclaim. "You and Beca were brought up the same way. She gets all this. She wants it. I don't know why you're not down in London right now, trying to win her back."

He sighs and meets my eyes. "It's hard for me to talk about her to you. I feel disloyal."

"I need to understand, though, Ash."

He looks resigned. "She and I are not that well suited, not really."

"That's not true. She's *so* well suited to this life."

"That life maybe," he says, pointing back at the house. "Not this one."

He looks around the woods and meets my eyes again.

"But *that's* your life, Ash," I say meaningfully, nodding at the house. "That's the life you were born into. That's the life your children will be born into. That's the life you need your partner to want. Beca's perfect for you."

"Technically, I *wasn't* born into that life," he says jadedly. "Hugo was. I grew up thinking I could pretty much make my own choices, live where I liked, do what I wanted, but then we lost him. It took me a long time to get my head around everything that had changed. Beca helped with that—she's been so supportive—but even though I've accepted that my future looks different to how I imagined it, I'm not totally okay with it." His voice sounds labored. "I have no intention of shirking my responsibilities. I *will* do what's expected of me. But I at least want to be with someone who understands."

"Do you think you'll ever find that person?"

There's a gravity in the look he gives me.

"You know I could never live this life," I say seriously.

He breathes in sharply, staring at me. "You are so much more straight-talking than you were when I last knew you."

"Yeah, when I say something now, I tend to mean it."

Six years ago, I was still insecure and dependent on my parents. But in the wake of Lisbon and Madrid, I had to develop a thick skin—I was suffering and I had no one to lean on—and the inner strength I found eventually helped me to break free of my parents. Doing well at Knap, designing ranges that got featured in style magazines, making money for the business and earning myself a degree of respect from both my parents and my colleagues, that helped too. Now I'm standing on my own two feet, doing what I love, and I never want to feel dependent on or beholden to anyone ever again.

"Well, that's good," Ash says sardonically. "I hated having to second-guess you."

I scoff. "When did you have to do that?"

"The whole time we were in Lisbon and for a long time afterward. I really had no idea if you'd turned up in Madrid or not. The not knowing was probably the hardest part about it."

"Why wouldn't *I* have turned up?"

"You were so worried about telling your parents you were going to continue interrailing. How could I know for sure that you'd follow through with it?"

"I told you that I'd meet you in Madrid."

"Yeah, but you might have changed your mind. You'd only known me for three days. I knew what a hold your mum and dad had over you. I wasn't sure any feelings you had for me could compete."

"Come on. It was obvious how into you I was," I snap, stalking off.

The cabin appears among the trees, a wisp of smoke trailing from the chimney.

He jogs to catch up with me and when he's at my side he slows to match my pace, throwing me a grin. He looks pleased with himself.

I roll my eyes.

He reaches over and gives my shoulder a little push, hard enough to make me stagger one step to my left. I laugh and go to push him back, but he hooks his arm around my neck and presses a quick kiss to my temple before letting me go and opening the door.

My heart skips and skitters. This is such a bad idea.

"Why don't Celyn and Catrin live up here?" I ask as he steps back to allow me to walk inside.

"They prefer it at the cottages. It was offered to Celyn when his dad retired, but he didn't want it. Too many memories, I think."

"Does the estate own it?"

There's a fire in the grate, but it's burned down to embers. I don't think there's any central heating, so I imagine it's necessary to take the chill off, even in summer.

"Yeah. Dylan was also given the option of living out here, but he finds it too isolating," he says as he closes the door.

"But you don't?"

"Are you kidding? I'd give anything to be able to camp out in the woods forever, stay off-grid, like a hermit."

"Rubbish. You'd get lonely."

He grins at me as he walks into the kitchen and switches on the light. "Yeah, I probably would. But it's what I dream about sometimes. Do you want a drink? Wine? Beer? Soft drink?"

"Something soft would be good. How many bedrooms does this place have?" I ask, looking around the kitchen. It looks clean, but it hasn't been updated in years—it's probably about as old as the 1970s kitchen in the Great Hall.

"Three bedrooms, one bathroom. The bedrooms are upstairs, bathroom's just through there."

"Ooh, I wouldn't like that," I say as he grabs a couple of cans of lemonade from the fridge.

"Why not?"

"Getting up in the middle of the night to go downstairs to the loo?" I take a can from him before he can decant it into a glass. "No, I'd want an en suite."

"If I ever build you a cabin in the woods, I'll take that into account."

"I'll have a hot tub too, please."

He chuckles and cracks open his can.

"So is this place yours now? Permanently?"

"I wish. I wanted my father to sign it over to me after I agreed not to do my master's—"

"Wait. You didn't do your master's?" I ask with surprise.

He was set to study astrophysics that September.

He shakes his head and nods toward the living room. "There wasn't much point. I'd already delayed a year at my father's request after we lost Hugo. Running the estate is a full-time job, and he wanted me to be prepared to take over if anything happened to him. I had to learn everything he'd been teaching my brother for years."

"So you never went to work in the space sector?"

"No."

I'm taken aback by how much it pains me to hear that.

"Oh, Ash."

He looks at me, regret in his eyes. "It's okay. I'm just doing what I have to." He sounds accepting. He takes a sip of his lemonade before saying, "Anyway, the cabin was a consolation prize, although my father could still sell it out from under my feet if he wanted to. I'd love to own it outright—along with the cottages, sawmill, and workshop—but he likes to hold them over me in case I go off the rails again."

"What do you mean, go off the rails?"

He sighs. "This conversation is taking a dark turn."

"Ash," I implore.

"A couple of years after Hugo died, I took my bike and just left. I had to get away."

"Where did you go?"

"Back to Europe. Spent some time in Romania. Camped out under the stars in the Carpathian Mountains and had a couple of close calls with brown bears." His gaze looks faraway as he remembers. "I just needed a break from it all, some space to get my head around everything. And then my father started talking about selling off the cottages and the sawmill and suggested I come home to take up my place at his side so we could work out a solution."

My stomach drops. "He emotionally blackmailed you?"

He huffs out a dark laugh. "That's one way of putting it." He shakes his head and asks, "Where did you go after Madrid?" I feel as though he wants to move away from the topic of his father.

"Home. Well, I stayed there for over a week, first, trying to find you. But then I went back to start work at Knap."

"I'm so sorry," he whispers, his eyes beginning to shine.

"It's not your fault."

"If it makes you feel better, I was a total wreck myself."

"I felt like I'd been smashed into a million little pieces."

He drags his hand over his face, suddenly seeming devastated.

"It was only three days," I say in a small voice as he turns to stare starkly out the window. "Are we looking back at that time through rose-tinted glasses? Was any of it real?"

He meets my eyes and then says, with absolute conviction: "It was real."

21

I DON'T LIKE LYING TO MY NEW HOUSEMATE, SO GUILT takes the edge off my anticipation at seeing Ash on Saturday morning. Siân invited me to go shopping with her today and I used the excuse Ash suggested about catching up with an old friend.

But that opened up other questions.

"Ooh, who are you seeing?"

"An old friend from work."

"Boy or girl?"

"Girl. Chloe." I did work with a Chloe, but we weren't close.

"Will she come here?"

"No, we're heading out for the day."

"Where are you meeting? Do you need a lift?"

"No, thanks. She's got a car."

"So she *is* coming here?"

"We're meeting at the pub in the village for lunch."

"Bit early for lunch, isn't it?"

Aaargh!

I ended up telling her that I planned to go for a walk first, which was actually true. I can't be seen in my biker gear, so I had to head up to Ash's place to get changed.

The gear he bought for me earlier in the week fit perfectly, which was just as well, because even though the jacket and trousers were exchangeable, the helmet wasn't.

"I still can't believe you risked buying this," I say when I'm standing by his bike, fully kitted up and in the process of trying to tighten the chinstrap of my new olive-green helmet.

My jacket is also dark green and the trousers are black, and they both have body armor sewn in, but they look like ordinary clothes from the outside. I like the utilitarian styling of them. Ash point-blank refused to let me pay for any of it.

"Well, I kind of already knew the circumference of your head," Ash admits, coming over to help me.

"How?" I ask, jerking as his fingertips brush my neck.

"That cap I lent you, the one we bought at the market in Lisbon."

I know the cap he's talking about—I borrowed it from him at the Castelo de São Jorge when he was more concerned about my sunburn than his.

"I never adjusted it back to my size afterward," he murmurs, and I have a very close-up view of his peach-iced-tea eyes looking intense with concentration as he fiddles with my strap.

"You still have it?"

"Mm-hmm." He meets my eyes briefly and then picks up his rucksack and helps me to put that on too.

I'm still feeling kind of flip-floppy once we're seated and ready to go. With my body armor and his, there's a level of separation between us that we didn't have on the other short journeys we've taken. I loved the feeling of his stomach muscles contracting beneath the fabric of his T-shirt, and I liked the warmth of his leather jacket on my skin, but I'm glad we're wearing full protective clothing now that we're going faster. I felt a little short of breath when he first took off along the open road, but I've gotten used to the speed now, the rush of air, the roar of the engine, and the way my body aligns with his as he leans into bends in the road.

I've relaxed enough to take in the scenery too: the wide-open fields and rolling green hills dotted with sheep, the bubbling water racing over rocks in the rivers beside us, the way the light changes when we zoom beneath the dense overhang of trees.

When we've been driving for forty minutes or so, Ash slows down at the entrance of a wide bridge spanning a large lake. It's made out of gray stone that looks almost marbled with the amount of aged lichen clinging to it. He creeps to a stop to show me that the water on one side is lower than the other. The bridge's arches perch on top of a thick stone wall that sinks deep beneath the dark surface.

"It's a dam?"

"Yep."

He drives slowly across to the other side while I look at the boats on the water, and after a couple more minutes he pulls up at the side of the lake and puts his foot down, turning off the ignition.

"We'll stop here for a while," he says, taking off his black motorcycle gloves and helmet.

I climb off behind him and remove mine too, shaking out my hair.

"Okay?" he asks, watching me for my reaction.

I nod, smiling. "That was so much fun."

It warms my heart, how happy he looks.

"Where are we?" I ask.

The water glints between the tree trunks of a narrow stretch of woodland.

"Lake Vyrnwy," he replies, taking my helmet and gloves and leading me between the trees. "This reservoir supplies Liverpool."

"Isn't that quite a long way away?"

"Yeah. The water travels along a seventy-mile aqueduct to get there," he tells me as we make our way toward the shoreline, stepping over dead tree trunks covered with furry green moss.

"Evan's asked me to go to some aqueduct with him tomorrow," I say casually.

"You've got to be kidding me," Ash replies bluntly, coming to a stop so suddenly I almost crash into him.

"What?" I ask as he turns around to stare down at me.

"He's taking you to the Pontcysyllte Aqueduct?" he asks with annoyance, pronouncing it Pont-ker-sulth-tay.

"I don't know what it's called."

"It'll definitely be that one. That bloke is showing you everywhere in the guidebook. It'll be Portmeirion next, or Powis Castle or Anglesey . . ."

"I thought you didn't mind Evan?"

"I'm minding him more." Two seconds pass before he screws up his nose at me cutely and says, in a much more reasonable tone, "I know you're free to do whatever you want with whoever you want, but I really wanted to show you the Pontcysyllte Aqueduct. He's Australian, for fuck's sake. I'm Welsh. I still can't believe he took you to Pistyll Rhaeadr on Sunday," he mutters irritably as he carries on toward the water.

Is it wrong to find his outburst amusing?

I put him out of his misery. "We haven't been to the waterfall yet."

He shoots his head round to look at me and he's so upbeat and hopeful that I can't help but laugh.

"Why not?"

"I don't know, I just didn't really feel like going out after all."

I was a bit freaked out by Siân's teasing that it was a date, so I made excuses about needing a chilled one.

"In that case, we've got a lot to pack in today," he says with a grin, half jumping and half striding off a ledge onto the stony shore.

"You can't show me all of Wales in a day."

"No, but I can show you a chunk of Mid and North Wales. We'll go farther afield next time." He places our helmets on the ground. "If that's okay with you," he adds with a bashful smile, coming back to help me.

"I suppose it could be," I tease as he clasps my forearms with his strong hands and steadies me while I climb down.

On the other side of the lake is a tower that looks like it's part of an old castle, with tall, round, gray stone walls and a conical green roof. A forest rises up behind it, and the water is so still, it reflects a mirror image of the trees, tower, and sky.

As he unzips his black jacket, Ash tells me that it's a straining tower, built at the turn of the twentieth century to extract water from the lake. He's wearing a dark gray long-sleeve T-shirt underneath, with chunky black boots and black trousers. He's definitely giving hot biker.

"So how have you been this week?" I ask as I remove his rucksack.

"All right," he replies.

"Have you spoken to Beca?"

He shakes his head as he takes the rucksack from me and

starts getting out the picnic supplies. "She's not answering my calls." He sounds down.

"What have you told your parents about your breakup?"

"My father? Nothing. He hasn't asked and we don't talk about *feelings*. My mother, only that it's over."

"Bet she was disappointed."

I remember him saying that she wanted him to get together with Beca when he was younger.

"Sometimes we have to disappoint our parents," he says wryly. "Speaking of disappointing our parents, how did yours cope when you broke away from the family business? I still don't know anything about that."

"Yeah, I don't really like to talk about it," I reply morosely.

He looks concerned. "They took it badly, huh?"

"That's an understatement. My mum basically disowned me."

His eyes widen. "Holy shit. I'm so sorry."

"My dad and I speak and text occasionally, but I don't think my mum will ever get over it. I'm still standing, though."

"Yes, you are," he agrees tenderly.

"Can we change the subject? I try not to think about them if I can help it."

He's still looking concerned, but he obliges me. "Tell me about your apprenticeship. What was it like, working at Wisley?"

We chat about me for a while and then move on to talk about his motorbike travels around Europe, and it's nice—it really is like catching up with an old friend.

"I told Siân I'm seeing a girl from my old work, by the way," I say as we pack away the remnants of our lunch.

He looks troubled. "She's going to be upset with you when she finds out you've lied."

"Then she'd better not find out."

"Why can't we just tell people the truth?"

"What, so everyone can look at me differently? No thanks."

"Why would people look at you differently?"

"They might think I'm trying to social climb." I couldn't bear for anyone to put me in the same league as my parents.

He lets out a laugh. "Are you serious?"

"Deadly. You might think you're their friend, but there's a balance of power there that puts you on a different level. Like it or not, you're not equal to them, not in the way I am. Right now, they respect me for being a worker just like they are. I hate the thought of them knowing that I'm your bit of rough from the old days."

His mouth drops open. "Excuse me?" He's staring at me disbelievingly.

"Well, I am, aren't I?"

"Are you fucking kidding me?"

He's outraged, bordering on furious.

"Don't tell me that they'd understand," I say crossly, feeling chastised by the look on his face and becoming defensive instead of backtracking—I am my father's child. "They wouldn't! They'd think that I'm getting ideas above my station. I'm your gardener—an employee. Beca's on your level—they all think you two are a match made in heaven."

"That's *bullshit*," he snaps, aggressively zipping up his rucksack.

"No, *you're* talking bullshit. You *are* a match made in heaven."

He scowls at me and then rakes his hand through his hair and stares across the lake, his back and shoulders tense. I don't know why I'm pushing his buttons like this, but I can't seem to help it.

He sighs and turns to look at me. "Beca would *never* do this. She would never get on the back of my bike and go for a ride. She would never camp out under the stars. She avoids the workshop, she hates the cabin, she doesn't like it when I talk with a Welsh accent. She never gets her hands dirty. She would never go swimming in cold water. She doesn't like picnics—she doesn't see the point. She would never *in a million years* go interrailing and slum it in youth hostels."

He's already said that he feels disloyal talking about Beca to me, so I know that he doesn't want to lay it all out on the line like this. It feels as if he's committing to something by doing so.

"Beca will always be important to me and I won't give up trying to win back her friendship. We gave it a shot—it felt like the right time to do that—but I've been ignoring a niggling feeling in my gut for months. She's not *made* for me, Ellie. Please trust me on that."

I want to, I really do, but as we ride through the Berwyn Mountains, skirting glittering lakes and waterfalls, I can't help but remember that *I'm* not made for him either.

22

WE'RE STANDING IN THE MIDDLE OF A TOWERING arched stone bridge that carries the Llangollen Canal across the River Dee, far in the valley below. I'm staring with incredulity as a barge glides right by us, followed by a couple of canoes full of people. I have never seen anything like this in my life: the Pontcysyllte Aqueduct is literally a stream in the sky.

"This was probably Taran's favorite place in the whole world," Ash confides, turning his back on the canal and sitting down.

He tugs off his boots and slides his feet between the railings that protect pedestrians from the long drop down to the river below. A couple of people walk past on the footpath behind us, but he casually pats the space beside him, so I sit down and do the same, letting my legs dangle off the side of the bridge. Just as well I don't suffer from vertigo.

"I reckon he would have ended up being a structural engineer if he'd lived," he adds. "He loved it up here, but he loved it down there even more." He nods at the river. "We used to go swimming and float on our backs, looking up at this giant structure."

"'Swim in more rivers,'" I say.

"Hey?"

"Taran's words, what he said to you just before he died. If he'd known how little time he had, he would have swum in more rivers."

"'Stayed up late more often to watch the stars . . . cherished the sound of the rain on the roof and the birdsong in the woods,'" Ash finishes softly, repeating what he told me all those years ago.

"Yes." My eyes prick with tears as I stare down at the wide green river stretched out below us in the valley. "I thought of those words when I was gearing up to leave Knap, along with what you said to me on the platform: 'Follow your own path. Life is too short not to do what you love. You and I know that better than most.'"

"I'm sorry for everything you've had to go through to get here, but I'm so proud of you for chasing your dreams," he says huskily, reaching across to squeeze my shoulder.

"It kills me that you can't do the same."

He lets me go, his hand falling back to his lap.

"What does Beca do for a career?" I ask.

He casts me a sideways glance, his brow furrowing as he returns his gaze to the river.

"She works in fashion PR, but does a lot of stuff remotely."

"I'm sorry you feel as though you've lost another friend."

He blows a heavy breath out through his lips. "I wish you'd been able to meet her under different circumstances."

"She said a similar thing."

"She did?"

"Yes, when she came to see me."

"I think you would have got on."

I consider this for a moment. "It doesn't sound like we have a whole lot in common."

"True. I mean, *she* wouldn't drink a piña colada out of a real pineapple or play pool in a weird bar or buy a dress off the rack at a tourist market," he says, his expression teasing. "But she has a wicked sense of humor and she's kind. I honestly don't know what I would have done without her all these years."

"You'll win back her friendship, Ash," I reassure him.

"I'm going to try," he replies solemnly.

This is our last stop of the day. Ash said it was on the way home, but I know he's just got it in his head that he needs to beat Evan to it.

WE GO BACK to the cabin soon afterward so I can get changed out of my bike gear before returning home. He drives me down to the farm track and there's a marked difference to his riding style when I'm not wearing proper protection. I felt safe out on the open road, but he's so cautious that I'm just as relaxed, if a little cold, with only a sweater, shorts, and his black leather jacket on.

He slows to a stop and puts his feet down. The sun is low in the sky, bathing the hedgerows in gold.

My arms are around his waist, my chest pressed to the broad expanse of his back. I'm reluctant to move.

Without saying a word, he reaches behind and gently lays his hand on my leg, his bare skin against mine giving me instant goose bumps.

I flatten my palms against the taut ridges of his abdomen because I want to feel his muscles contracting again, and I smile to myself when they do. His fingers move downward and tuck into the crease behind my knee, his thumb stroking the top. I tighten my grip on him and rest my forehead against his back, brushing my lips against his T-shirt before straightening up.

"Watch yourself on the exhaust," he reminds me as I climb off his Triumph Scrambler—I know the make of his bike now.

"Leave it on," he says as I start to remove his jacket. He climbs off the bike.

"What are you doing?" I ask.

"I'll walk you as far as the workshop," he replies.

We wander along the farm track in comfortable silence, past the rows and rows of timber piled up in the yard behind the sawmill. A lorry dropped off a whole bunch of logs yesterday, and soon they'll be processed and turned into beams and joists for houses. The sound of machinery carries on the wind while I'm working, as does the smell of freshly cut wood. It's nice. I like it. I like everything about this place, actually.

I glance across at Ash to see the sun shining on his face, highlighting the sharpness of his jaw, the shadows beneath his high cheekbones. When he meets my eyes, his are a clear light brown.

Pain lances my heart.

"Hey, what happened?" he asks with confusion and concern, halting at the look on my face.

I shake my head at him. "I don't know if I can do this."

"Give it a chance," he implores.

I shake my head again and quickly walk away, fighting back tears. Beca might not be made for him, but how can I be if I don't want the only life he can offer me? I don't fit in with the people who were at his parents' fortieth—I don't *want* to fit in with them. I'm a gardener, not a viscountess in the making, and I wouldn't have it any other way.

I've only just found my feet. I worked so hard to get where I am, went through so much with my parents. There's too much at stake if things sour between Ash and me. Not just my fragile mental state, because there's no doubt that I'd be completely fucked if I had to go through anything like Madrid again, but my whole job would be in jeopardy. How could I possibly continue to work at Berkeley Hall if I couldn't stand to be in Ash's vicinity? I couldn't. It's too much of a risk.

He jogs to catch up with me. The outbuildings are up ahead, blocking our view of the cottages.

"This is so complicated," I murmur.

"It doesn't have to be."

"We're from different worlds."

"Come on." He sounds exasperated. "It's not the Dark Ages."

"How could we possibly work?" I ask him. It's a reasonable question.

"We just will," he says, halting behind the furniture work-shop, which is as far as he can go without being seen.

"You're being idealistic." My tone is growing increasingly brittle.

He places his hands firmly on my biceps and stares down at me. "I'm not."

"Ash, you barely know me. Not really. I sure as hell don't know *you* as well as I thought I did."

"Rubbish," he snaps. "You know everything about me that matters. And if I don't know you as well as you want me to, then we'll fix that."

"Why? So we can fall head over heels in love with each other and have our hearts broken again? We have no future. We can't get married. We can't have children. Not just because I'm a gardener and you're the son of a viscount, but because I don't want this life and I would never want my children to be born into it either!"

He gapes at me as my voice rises to a crescendo, his face paling with shock. I feel as though my heart has been through the sawmill.

"We should stop this now before it's too late," I say in a low, tortured voice.

We're still staring at each other, so I see the exact moment that his expression clouds over.

That's my cue to leave. But only a split second after I begin to walk away, he cuffs my wrist with his hand and my own momentum has me hurtling right back into his arms.

"It's already too late," he says roughly, his eyes blazing.

And then he releases my wrist to take my face in his hands and I stare at his blackening pupils and know that he's right.

Our mouths crash together and he walks me backward until I hit the workshop wall. Sensation flames inside me, full-body shivers rolling up and down my spine as his tongue parts my lips and presses against mine. My blood is molten, caramelized, and I'm kissing him back just as deeply, just as fervently. His hips pin me to the wall, his jeans rough against my bare legs. His hands dive inside his leather jacket that I'm still wearing, gripping my waist, and mine are on his neck, his collar, his shoulders. His mouth breaks away from my lips to skate along my jaw and I'm staring at the sky, panting frantically and wanting him like I've never wanted anything or anyone. I'd have him right here, right now, if it wasn't for the sound of Celyn shouting to someone nearby.

I scramble to push Ash away, my body flooding with cold air as I cock my ear toward the cottages.

Harri shouts something back—they're just making plans for tonight.

I meet Ash's eyes. His chest is heaving. Reaching out, I hook my finger through his belt buckle, tugging him closer. He moves his hands to my waist and I rest my chin on his shoulder as we stand there a moment, trying to recover.

"Don't overthink this," he says in a low, firm voice.

I lift my head to look at him. "How do you know I overthink things?"

"I know *you*."

His pupils have relaxed to allow some of the light brown to come through, but his eyes are serious.

I nod at him and he curves his fingers around the nape of my neck, pressing a soft kiss to my lips before sliding his hands over my shoulders and slipping his jacket off my arms. He releases me and backs up.

"I'll text you."

I nod and watch him walk away, still trying to catch my breath.

23

STOP OVERTHINKING, ASH TEXTS ME THE FOLLOWING evening.

Is he a mind reader? He asked earlier if he could see me and I replied that I couldn't because Siân seemed in need of company. She was a little down this morning, but perked up when I suggested another *Glee* marathon. She never watched it when it first aired and has been hooked since Bethan's birthday.

But now I'm staring at the TV in a daze, unable to concentrate. Heartbreak is on the horizon and I'm catapulting toward it.

Everything I said to Ash last night was true: whatever this is between us cannot last. I *do* want a family one day, and the thought of my children having to deal with the pressure of being the twenty-second generation of Berkeleys is inconceivable.

Maybe it's because of what I went through as a teenager, but I'm not comfortable around posh people, and I hated feeling invisible at Ash's parents' party. I can't bear to imagine how some of those people would look down on me if I had to socialize with them, the comments they'd make after finding out that Ash left the beautiful Bex for a grubby gardener.

I do a full-body shudder at the thought. No. Whatever this is between Ash and me has a limited lifespan.

Unless he commits to gifting this property to a charity like the National Trust once he inherits it, but the thought of asking him to turn his back on his heritage makes my blood run cold. He would never forgive himself for letting down his friends and family—the past generations of Berkeleys, including his late brother, and the future generations he feels a responsibility toward. From the way he was talking, he wouldn't walk away from his duties under any circumstances.

We're between a rock and a hard place.

I don't know how to reply to his text message.

Hey, he texts again.

Hi, I write back.

I miss you.

His words don't melt my insides, they make me feel sick. I stare down at my phone, the sound of Lea Michele and Cory Monteith wailing on about holding on to this feeling in the background.

I have to go away tomorrow for three days, Ash texts again, giving up on waiting for my response. Conference with my father. I'll be back on Thursday.

OK. Hope it goes well.

Are you all right? he asks.

Confused.

Come over tonight?

The sudden rush of wanting is almost too much for me to bear.

I can't, I force myself to type back. But I'll see you soon.

I **SPEND THE** early part of the week overseeing the volunteers, clearing the foliage and deadheads of the big round purple alliums in the walled garden to make way for the annual plants that have been grown in the greenhouses over the winter. By Wednesday, I've moved on to helping Evan cut the box hedges in the courtyard and the topiary birds around Cedar Lawn and the lower terrace.

Although I have plenty of time to think about Ash and the impossible situation we've found ourselves in, my mind doesn't race at work as it does at home.

On Thursday evening, I arrive back at the cottage to see that about a dozen or so sawmill and workshop crew are in the courtyard of the outbuildings, sitting at bench tables in the sunshine, drinking beer.

They do this occasionally, but today I notice that Celyn is there too, as well as Dylan, his fellow ranger. They look to be in high spirits about something.

I hear a door slam behind me and turn to see Siân, her face red from crying, rush up the stairs.

"Siân?" I hurry after her, but she's already disappeared into her bedroom. "Siân? Can I come in?" I knock tentatively and then take a chance, opening the door. She's lying on her bed, sobbing. "Hey, what's wrong?" I ask with sympathy.

Her sobs begin to die down, but she keeps her face buried in the palms of her hands. Her voice is so muffled and shredded that I can barely make it out when she says: "My heart is broken."

"Who broke your heart?"

She rolls onto her back. She looks absolutely wrecked. I can see her swallowing, as though she can't get the words out past the lump in her throat. "Celyn and Catrin are engaged," she replies, and then she bursts into a fresh set of tears. "We had something going once and he was so keen. I didn't know how lucky I was, so I didn't cherish it. And now it's too late."

I lie on the bed beside her as she tells me all about how they met ten years ago when she was twenty and first came to work here, how they used to flirt and tease each other incessantly until one drunken night they took it to another level.

She reveals what I already know about Celyn's younger brother Taran dying of leukemia, and how their relationship suddenly felt heavy. She wasn't ready to settle down and get serious in her early twenties, so they ended it.

But there have been times over the years when they've hooked up, and even then she took him for granted. Then Catrin came on the scene a couple of years ago and he shut it all down.

When Siân's tears have dried up, I go downstairs to make her a cup of tea.

There's an old gray Audi allroad parked by the workshop now. My heart jumps at the sight of Ash getting out of the driver's side. He goes to give Celyn a big hug, greeting the others with back pats and handshakes.

They must be celebrating Celyn's engagement. Poor Siân.

Ash goes round to the back of the car and looks toward my cottage window before popping the boot and getting out a chunky green cooler. The lads all cheer as he carries it back to the table and opens it up to reveal their usual array of neon-colored cans of Tiny Rebel craft beer. They dive in.

I feel nervous as I pull out my phone and text him.

Welcome back.

He looks over his shoulder toward my cottage and smiles before facing forward.

Are you watching me?

Like a creepy little stalker.

His shoulders shake and I know that he's laughing.

I didn't know you had a car.

My old banger.

I don't think you can classify an Audi as an old banger.

I can. It's eighteen years old and plays up sometimes but I
love it.

Cute.

I didn't tell you in case you made me drive you around in that
instead.

Now I'm the one who's laughing.
Celyn got engaged to Catrin today, he says.

I heard.

How's Siân?

Does he know about them? He answers that question in his next text.

They once had a thing going. I wasn't sure if Siân was over it.

She could probably do with one of your annoyingly long emotional hugs right now.

He looks over his shoulder, smirking, and I suddenly miss him so much it hurts.

I'll come say hi to her once I've had a drink here, he replies.

LATER THAT NIGHT, after Ash has been and gone and Siân has headed upstairs to bed, I pull on my shoes and coat and slip out the back door.

The tiny, subtle stroke he gave my arm as he was leaving still lingers on my skin two hours later and I've given up trying to fight this. It will end in disaster—there's no way we're coming out of it unscathed—but maybe if we let this thing between us burn brightly enough, the flame will fizzle out.

Or maybe it will crash and burn in a fireball so brilliant that we'll never recover.

Either way, I'm in.

24

WHEN I SEE HOW DARK THE CABIN IS, I SWITCH OFF my flashlight and head for the clearing. It's a half-moon tonight and by the time I'm stepping out of the woods into long grass, my eyes have adjusted enough to the darkness to see that Ash is at the top of the hill.

"Ash," I call quietly.

"Hey!" He jumps to his feet with surprise and immediately bounds toward me. When he reaches me, he clasps my face with his hands, almost as though he can't believe I'm here.

"Hello," I say, amused by his reaction.

"I'm so happy to see you." He really does sound delighted.

"I'm happy to see you too," I reply with a smile, bracing my palms on his chest.

"Come. The grass is so wet."

He takes my hand and leads me over to the blanket. I feel the crinkle of plastic from the waterproof liner as I step onto it and then he sits down behind me, tugging me into the space between his legs and circling his arms around me from behind.

It feels like the most natural thing in the world to be completely wrapped up in him again.

"How was your conference?" I ask.

"Boring as fuck," he replies.

"What was it about?"

"Estate management. My father makes me go to them occasionally."

"What do you call your parents to their faces?"

He always refers to them as his mother and father, never his mum and dad.

"Mother and Father," he replies.

"No, really?" I ask with astonishment, craning my neck to look at him.

He chuckles and I feel the vibration move right through my body.

"I didn't used to," he says. "I used to call them Mama and Papa, but Celyn and Taran made fun of me, so I stopped."

"That's so mean!" I exclaim, trying not to laugh. "What did they call their parents?"

"Mam and Tad—that's Mum and Dad in Welsh. The thought of calling my parents something so informal seemed ludicrous. So, Mother and Father it is."

"What will you get your children to call you?"

He hesitates. And then he shrugs. "I don't know."

"Not Mam and Tad?"

"I don't know," he says again.

"You're straddling two worlds."

"Stop with the two-worlds shit," he warns playfully, pressing his cheek against mine as we stare at the sky.

I feel so jittery being this close to him.

"What did Taran look like?"

"He was about my height and build, with short, dark hair."

"Did he look like Celyn?"

"Like a giant? No. Taran was slighter, but who knows who he would have grown up to become. He was only nineteen when we lost him."

"I'm so sorry."

His hold on me strengthens.

"Are all those stars like our sun?" I ask after a while.

"Some are a hundred times bigger."

"Whoa. Do they have planets too?"

"Most of them, but it's hard to know how many."

"How do you even know they have planets in the first place?" I ask with confusion. Surely they're too far away to be able to see.

"Most are detected by monitoring the light given off over time and looking for dips in brightness that may indicate an orbiting planet. And sometimes a star will wobble as a result of a planet's gravity—usually a very large planet that's in close orbit. We're talking super-Jupiters."

"Jupiter's our biggest planet, right?" I remember that much from school.

"Yep. If Earth was the size of a grape, Jupiter would be the size of a basketball."

"It's incredible to think that there really are other worlds out there."

"Whether or not they can sustain life, though—who knows? Earth is pretty special."

"I remember you telling me that you liked space because it's so big and it made everything you were experiencing at home seem smaller by comparison."

"Yeah." His voice suddenly sounds subdued.

"Tell me about your bedroom in the Tudor wing," I request softly. "I'm sorry I shut you down last time."

He releases a barely audible sigh, but I can feel it leaving his chest.

"We used to have outdoor seating outside the Great Hall—tables for the café. My windows looked over them. When I was about five or six, I remember peering down at some kids in the courtyard—a brother and sister out with their mum and dad, having cake. The girl was about my age and her brother was probably a couple of years older, and they kept getting down from the table to play tag around the fountain. I liked the look of them, kind of wanted to go down and play with them myself, but then the boy looked up and saw me—I can still picture him so vividly. He pointed and squealed, 'There's a ghost!' And I remember his parents and sister looking up too, and his sister looked so scared. I just backed away into the shadows of my bedroom."

There's nothing funny about this story. I can hear in his voice that he's still disturbed by it.

I rub his arm, encouraging him to go on.

"The thing is, I felt kind of invisible, growing up. I used to wander the corridors and the staff would ignore me. I knew my mother loved me, but she was often out socializing or was distracted by other stuff that was going on, and I had a string of nannies and au pairs that I struggled to bond with. Hugo was the center of my father's attention, the only one worth devoting his time to. And Hugo had absolutely no interest in me whatsoever—he was seven years older and he idolized our father. He was like his shadow, following him around, copying the way he spoke to staff, ordering them to do what he wanted. That felt wrong to me, even when I was young. You think I'm entitled, but you should have met my brother." He sounds bleak.

"I don't think you're entitled, Ash," I say seriously, wanting to right that wrong too. I'm ashamed for trying to make him feel small.

He rubs his thumb across my shoulder to show me that I'm forgiven.

"That boy calling me a ghost completely did my head in. I began to wonder if, to some, I really was invisible. I stopped wanting to go in the gardens during visiting hours, just in case it happened again. Looking back, I can see that I became withdrawn, but my parents didn't notice. I stuck to leaving the house in the evenings, and one day I ventured into the woods by the lake and bumped into Taran." He releases a small laugh. "He shot me with his Nerf gun. It was the start of a beautiful friendship."

I smile and dip my head to kiss his hand.

"I don't know what would have happened to me, what sort of person I'd have become, if I hadn't had Taran—and Celyn, and all the other estate workers—in my life. They more than kept me grounded. They taught me how to be human."

My heart has expanded to breaking point. I turn my face toward him and brush my lips against his in the sweetest of kisses.

We pull back and stare at each other in the darkness for a long moment, and then we're moving, turning to lie down and gathering each other closer: hip to hip, chest to chest, and finally, mouth to mouth. It's gentle at first, full of love and longing. I'm trying to pour every ounce of care and compassion into this kiss.

And now we're going deeper, escalating to skin-shivering, blood-warming intensity. His hands push into the hair at the nape of my neck, my fingers press against his jaw, his body moves on top of mine and my legs come around him, drawing him in as close as I can get him. We gasp into each other's mouths as the need and want become impossible to resist.

"Do you have anything?" I ask breathlessly.

"Inside." His voice is a guttural growl. He's never sounded sexier.

A minute later, we haven't even made it past his front door when my back is against the wood, my legs wrapped around his waist, his hands supporting my weight as our mouths come together. He releases one hand to cup my face and his hips take up the slack to hold me in place as we give everything we've got to our kiss, making up for lost time.

He lifts me away from the door and opens it, carrying me through and snatching up his wallet from the hallstand. Then we're collapsing on the sofa and for a few delicious seconds the whole weight of his body bears down on me. He tries to push himself up to give me room to breathe, but I don't let him go far—I like the feeling of his heart thudding against mine.

The wood groans and creaks beneath us and he laughs against my neck.

"This sofa is so old. Let's go upstairs."

He has to wrench himself away from me because I do *not* want to move from this position.

But now he's kicking off his shoes, so I sit up and remove my own and he takes my hand to lead the way to his bedroom. I feel edgy but in the best possible way, my breathing erratic and choppy as I try not to lose my footing climbing the stairs.

It's dark in his room and he leaves the lights off as we kiss each other at the end of his bed. When his mouth moves to my jaw and then to my neck, I look up and see stars twinkling back at me. There's a giant window in the ceiling, I realize, and then I'm not thinking about the sky because he's drawing my T-shirt up over my head and I'm turning my attention to the buttons on the front of his shorts.

We're completely naked when we fall down on the bed, and the shock of feeling so much of his warm skin against mine makes me gasp out loud.

He slowly runs his hand all the way down my body from my throat to my waist, our lips still connected. I slide my palms along the ridges of his broad shoulders and down his back, pulling him closer, and the sensation of him pressing against me with no barriers between us makes me feel like I've been spun in a circle.

He breaks away to grab his wallet and for a dizzying few seconds I'm glad one of us is thinking clearly.

When he's ready, he returns to his position above me and stares down into my eyes. I can't see the light in them—it's far too dark—but I can tell that his expression is serious.

Reaching up, I brush my thumb over the straight line of his mouth and his lips part, his teeth capturing my thumb between them, his tongue stroking the pad as his hips slowly surge forward.

I cry out, overwhelmed by how much I'm feeling, not just physically but emotionally.

"Are you okay?" he asks roughly, stilling.

"Don't stop," I beg.

His eyes rest on mine as he sinks fully down. And then our mouths come together again and we begin to move, unhurriedly at first, and then more urgently as we lose ourselves in each other, just as we did all those years ago.

I WAKE UP at the crack of dawn, when daylight seeps through the giant skylight in the roof of Ash's bedroom. He's sleeping peacefully beside me and I feel a rush of joy as I realize that I can stay here like this, with him. It's my turn on the rota this weekend, so I have today—Friday—and Monday off. Siân will assume I'm having a lie-in, so she'll head to work without expecting to see me.

An enormous modern white telescope sits beneath the window—about ten times the size of the older-looking one downstairs. I stare at it with interest before my bladder gets the better of me and I climb out of the warm bed, grabbing Ash's hoodie to put on as I hurry downstairs in the chilly morning air.

When I come back from the bathroom, he's awake.

"Sorry there's no en suite," he says with a sleepy smile as I rush back under the covers and into his arms, my heart skipping at seeing him again. "One day I'll make a whole bunch of alterations to this place."

"One day?"

"When it's mine. My father won't let me touch it now. He doesn't know about that, though." He nods at the skylight. "I figured it was worth the risk."

"That's some telescope."

"He doesn't know about that either."

An idea comes to me and I turn to look at him. "Have you thought about doing stargazing evenings? You could host them, teach people about the stars. Ooh, maybe you could even have schools or Scout groups come in! You're so good at speaking to people who know next to nothing."

He looks thoughtful for a moment, and then his eyes cloud over. "Maybe. One day."

One day . . .

"Is it hard to work with your father?"

He gives me the smallest of nods, his jaw clenched, then he

reaches for a small battery-operated alarm clock and checks the time.

"Do you have to rush back?" he asks, a twinge of hope taking the edge off the darkness I saw on his face a moment ago.

"No."

His face breaks into a grin and I suddenly know exactly what we're doing this morning.

THE SUN HASN'T yet risen over the Berwyn Mountains and the dim light and cool morning air make the Pistyll Rhaeadr seem almost otherworldly as it tumbles over the edge of a cliff eighty meters up in the air and pours into the circular pool at our feet.

The walls around it are alive with bright green plants, long, trailing grass, and furry moss that makes me think of the Initiation Well in Sintra. There's even a natural rocky bridge a little way up that the water has carved over time. It's absolutely beautiful—and there's not another soul to be seen.

We climb right up to the edge of the water, and it's invigorating, a cold spray carrying in the morning breeze to kiss our faces.

"Have you ever swum here?" I ask Ash.

"Once," he replies, grinning. "It's *really* cold."

He crouches down by the crystal-clear pool, trailing his hands through the water before scooping some up to splash his face.

I kneel down on the smooth, flat rock beside him, wanting to do the same, but as soon as my fingers sink into the ice-cold depths, I sharply retract them.

He laughs and flicks a little water in my direction.

"Don't you dare," I warn, making him chuckle.

Behind him, the water continues on its journey, bubbling over rounded boulders on its way to the river down in the valley.

He straightens up and pulls me to my feet, taking my face in his hands. I lay my palms on his chest and we gaze at each other, our lips tilted into small smiles. At the edge of my vision, I can see a long strip of brilliant white, considerably higher than Niagara Falls, crashing down the vivid green rock face. The sound of the waterfall drowns out my shallow breathing as Ash bends down to claim my mouth in a long, slow kiss.

Afterward, we hike up a mountain track to watch the sun rise over the valley.

"Thank you for bringing me here."

We're sitting side by side on the gnarled root of an old tree, sheep nibbling at the short grass around us.

Ash tucks a lock of hair behind my ear and presses a kiss to my cheekbone before asking, "Where do you want to go next?"

"Wherever you want to take me."

"Bed?" he asks hopefully.

I think I smile the whole way back to his bike.

25

WHEN I'M NOT LOSING MYSELF IN ASH OVER THE FOL-
lowing days, I'm losing myself in gardening. We've been
weeding and deadheading, clearing areas of spent low-growing
perennials such as leafy *Symphytum* and white-green *Brunnera*,
turning the compost, and pulling cow parsley. The lawn has also
gone wild with the warmer weather and it's a full-time job just to
stay on top of mowing and trimming.

But Ash is never far from my mind. It's hard to escape to the
cabin without drawing attention, but Siân and Bethan went to
the cinema on Sunday night, and on my day off on Monday, he
took me to Portmeirion, a beautiful Italianate village on a private
peninsula overlooking the coast.

We wandered between the colorful buildings, stopping for
lunch at the café before returning to his car and parking in a re-
mote location to make the most of his fold-down seats.

We're burning brightly, but that's no surprise—everything is
all still so new.

I'm so caught up in thinking about Ash as I water the pots in

the greenhouses on Friday that I don't notice Philippa Berkeley
until she's right at the door.

"Ah!" she says. "Eleanor!"

I almost jump out of my skin.

"Good afternoon."

"Those should be going in about now, shouldn't they?" She
nods at the pots.

"We're putting them in next week," I reply, noticing again that
I've adopted my "proper"-sounding voice.

"I just came past the lilac circle. It's looking a bit worse for
wear."

"I'm afraid we've been short on volunteers this week. Deadheading is on the list of things to do."

"I see."

She seems to be waiting for something, and then I realize it's
quite possibly me.

"I'll do some deadheading now," I tell her, retrieving my pruning shears from my basket.

"Wonderful," she replies.

I follow her out of the greenhouse and almost jump out of my
skin for the second time that day when I see Ash making his way
through the walled garden.

"Ashton!" his mother calls.

Ash glances our way and does a double take. His eyes flare
slightly, but the way his mouth tilts at the edges tells me that he's
pleased to see me.

"What are you doing out here?" Lady Berkeley asks her son.

"Just taking a shortcut to the workshop."

He's got his Honorable Ashton Berkeley voice on, but it
doesn't freak me out the way it used to. In fact, I find it kind of hot
how curt he sounds, how . . . *commanding.*

I have a vision of him tying me to his bedposts and doing naughty things to me and then Lady Berkeley brings me back down to earth with a bump.

"Have you met our new gardener, Eleanor Knapley? She's here from RHS Garden Wisley in Surrey."

"Yes, I know."

"Of course—I've introduced you already."

"No, Mother," Ash says, and his eyes land on mine for the briefest of pauses before returning to his mother. "This is Ellie."

It takes me a second to realize what he's doing.

Philippa Berkeley looks at me.

"Ellie..." Her brow furrows as though she's trying to place me.

"Ellie," Ash repeats, with even more meaning.

Suddenly she does a double take that makes her look just like her son.

"Oh!" she says with shock. And then she says it again with significance: "Oh."

No. *No. NO!*

It's overcast today, but it may as well be forty degrees Celsius and climbing. My blood is on fire.

She looks at me directly, her gaze shrewd and penetrating as my heart races, and then her eyes move up to the bun perched on top of my head.

"Is this why you went so heavy on the red in the Georgian garden?" she asks, turning to address her son.

He nods slowly, his lips pressed into a straight line.

She glances at me. "The lupins in the King George Garden," she says brusquely. "Planted a few years ago. It's the only time Ashton has ever shown an interest in perennials."

Ash is responsible for Nan's rainbow of lupins? I'm too shocked by what he's done to let the fact land.

She looks at her son, her expression growing contemplative. "I presume this is why Rebecca left for London."

His eyes are gleaming with some sentiment as he gives his mother a single nod.

"I see." She flashes me another quick, disconcerted look and then addresses her son. "I think we'd better have a talk."

"I'll come and see you later," he promises somberly.

She doesn't make a move to leave, but neither does he. He just stands there, one meter away from me, as my heart pounds so violently I feel as though it's going to leap out of my chest.

It finally occurs to Philippa Berkeley that her son is going nowhere, so she decides to make her own exit, stalking away with a weary sigh.

Ash meets my gaze calmly.

"Oh, Ash, what have you done?" I whisper with horror.

"I didn't think our secret had to extend to my own family," he says reasonably.

"Of course it does!" I screech-whisper, looking around wildly to ensure no one's in earshot. It's the middle of June—the place is swarming with visitors.

"I understand how you might be embarrassed to be with me when it comes to your colleagues, but how can you be embarrassed about me around my own mother?"

He hasn't switched back to his Welsh accent, but I can still hear gentle Ash beneath his clipped tone, trying to make light of the situation.

"I'm not embarrassed of *you* around her. I'm embarrassed of *me*!" I wave my hands over my gardener's shorts and polo shirt. How is he not taking this seriously?

He gives me a sympathetic look and reaches out for me.

I lurch backward and quickly check to make sure no one has seen us.

"Ellie," he says.

I shake my head at him, anguished.

He grabs my hand and pulls me under the cover of the nearby laburnum arch. It happens too fast for me to think about resisting, but as soon as we're out of view, I spin on my heel to face him.

"What if she fires me?"

"She's not going to fire you." He sounds dismissive.

"I can't believe you would risk ruining this for me."

"She's not a *monster*." He sounds taken aback.

"What if she tells someone else?"

"I'll ask her not to."

"But now she thinks that I'm the other woman! *Ash*!" I'm distraught.

"She *does* want me to be happy, Ellie," he says equitably. "I know she liked Beca, but she'll like you too when she gets to know you."

"What's the point in her getting to know me? This is not going to last!"

He looks shocked, standing there on a carpet of yellow as the last of the laburnum blooms float down around him.

He shakes his head at me. "I can't believe you're talking about us ending when we've barely begun."

"Please stop making me say it: we have no future."

My eyes prick with tears as I turn and walk away.

"Ellie!" he calls after me in dismay.

"No!" I reply angrily. "I have to sweep up those dead flowers."

Another job that's suffering from a lack of volunteers.

246 • PAIGE TOON

At the sound of my raised voice, a couple of old-age pensioners look toward me. My face burns as I head to the Mess Room.

I'M SO UPSET with Ash that I don't even reply to his text messages that night, telling me that he's been to see his mother and sworn her to secrecy.

I'm sure she was happy to oblige, I think to myself darkly. She'd be too mortified to tell a single soul that her son is having a sordid affair with a gardener. She probably thinks we'll fizzle out anyway. I bet she hopes for it with all her heart.

I've been neglecting Siân—she's still emotional about Celyn—and I feel guilty for having turned down the invitation to join her and Bethan at the cinema, so on Saturday morning I suggest that she and I go into Wrexham for a long-overdue shopping trip.

Bethan, Harri, and Evan get wind of our plan and join us that evening for a pub session. Evan hasn't invited me on another day trip since I told him I'd already visited the aqueduct with "my friend Chloe." He seems to have gotten the message that I want things to stay platonic, but he's still being friendly and it's good to be able to kick back with him.

When I'm drunk and a little emotional, I go to the bathrooms and reply to another text from Ash asking me to come over that night. I say that I can't and tell him that I'll be busy the next day too.

He doesn't reply, and I spend the whole of Sunday stressing.

But on Sunday night, I get a message from him: Can you meet me at the house? Not the cabin.

I'm so relieved to hear from him after twenty-four hours of silence that I reply straightaway.

Why?

My parents are out for the evening. I'd like to show you around.

It hasn't escaped my notice that he still hasn't apologized.

What if someone sees us?

The only staff who live here have retired to their private quarters. There's no better time.

I wish I could resist, but my willpower is shot.

OK.

Come to the gatehouse. Can you be here in 10?

I send a thumbs-up emoji that directly contradicts how pissed off I still am at him. I make my feelings clear by taking a good fifteen minutes to get ready.

We're approaching the summer solstice, so it's still light and balmy when I leave the cottage at 8 p.m., telling Siân that I'm off to get some fresh air.

I walk down the track that runs adjacent to the walled garden and then cut across the field to reach the neat stretch of gravel in front of the hall.

I'm rarely around this side of the house—all the garden rooms that we're responsible for are at the back of the property—and now the sight of the mansion looming in the dusk takes my breath away. I look up at it as I approach, noticing how the windows differ in design from arched to rectangular, and how the walls of the eighteenth-century bays on either side of the gatehouse are rendered while the gatehouse is built from cream-colored stone.

I'm so caught up in the detail that I miss that the Honorable Ashton Berkeley is leaning against the frame of the giant arched gatehouse door, watching me.

He's wearing a black shirt tucked into light gray trousers, and his hair is falling into his eyes.

A shiver races down my spine. I'm beginning to realize how much I like Ash's many looks.

"Been waiting long?" I ask him dryly as I approach.

"A while," he replies, just as aridly.

His arms are folded across his chest, but he steps back to make room for me to enter, closing the heavy door behind me with a low whoosh and a thud.

I stand and stare at the inside of the gatehouse. It looks exactly the same as last time, but now everything feels different. What is the significance of the old tapestry hanging on the wall? Did one of his ancestors wear that shining armor into battle?

I ask Ash the questions and discover that the tapestry was commissioned by a family member in the mid-1600s and the armor was brought back from France in the early eighteenth century during one of the Berkeleys' first Grand Tours of Europe. Many of the artifacts in the rest of the house arrived the same way.

"Evan said that in olden days people in carriages used to drive straight through to the courtyard."

"They did."

"He also said that Henry VIII gifted your family this gatehouse."

"Not Henry VIII. Henry VII," he replies. "He was born in Wales—the first Tudor king. Has our resident Aussie been trying to give you history lessons? He could do with getting his facts straight."

"Stop being so touchy, Ash."

He sighs and looks away, peeved.

I walk over to the window.

"Are you going to forgive me?"

At the downhearted sound of his voice, I turn around. We stare at each other until his expression softens and then I mumble, "Yes."

He gives me a relieved smile.

"But I'm still annoyed at you," I point out, putting up my hand in protest as he reaches for me.

He ignores my attempt to stop him and tugs me into his arms, burying his face against my neck.

I stand there stiffly but can't resist melting into him after only about three seconds. The warmth of his skin has seeped straight into me.

"I'm sorry," he whispers after a while.

I draw back to meet his eyes. He's genuinely apologetic.

"I really didn't think anything bad would come of it. I had to tell someone. It's been killing me keeping it to myself and I couldn't bear to see you standing there while she boasted about your credentials. I wanted to tell her that you're not *her* Eleanor, you're *my* Ellie. And she'd better not take you for granted."

Heat stings the backs of my eyes. "I've been so upset," I admit.

"I know." He reaches out to caress my cheek. "I didn't mean to hurt you."

"This job is so important to me."

"I know."

"You don't. Not really. My parents made such a success of their business. I was lucky enough not to have to worry about money when I was younger, but I don't have that luxury now. My dad can't believe I left Knap to be a gardener. I bet my mum is laughing her head off at the thought of it. She'll be *desperate* for me to fail. Her idea of heaven would be me running back to her, begging for help. I will *never* ask for help. Not ever. My mum would probably turn me down if I did. I *cannot* lose this job. I have to make this work."

"You will *not* lose this job," he says seriously. "But I'm so fucking sorry for everything," he adds, his eyes gleaming. "I wish you'd talk to me more about what you've been through."

"I'd rather forget about it."

He looks a little hurt and I sigh.

"What did your mother say when you spoke to her?" I ask.

He swallows. "Not much. But she accepts it. She does care about my happiness, Ellie."

He seems convinced of this.

Me, I'm not so sure. It's not that I think his mother would want him to be miserable, but I'd put money on her hoping he'd settle with being a little less happy if it meant being more socially acceptable.

"Shall we continue with the tour?" he asks. "There are a hundred and seventy-four rooms in this house and we've only seen one."

"We'll be here all night!"

"Don't worry, I'll just show you the best rooms. There are other things I want to do with you later."

"I hope the very best room is your bedroom," I say with a smirk.

"Oh, it *definitely* is," he replies, making me laugh.

I only realize as we walk down a long corridor, between double doors that have been pinned back, that Ash is still talking like Ashton Berkeley. I hadn't even noticed.

It warms my heart to realize that I *do* know Ash—not just both sides of him but the whole person—and he's the same underneath, no matter how he sounds.

I'm in this deep.

He takes me through the former bedrooms, halls, staterooms, and the old kitchen with its giant stone hearth. Occasionally he tells me about antiquities that his ancestors brought back from one of their Grand Tours, an ancient Egyptian statue of a cat or a Ming vase from China.

He knows so much about the oil paintings hanging on the walls and the various ornaments within locked glass cabinets that it amazes me how he retains all the information. But I guess it's part of his job to know these things. He needs to understand his family's history so he can pass it on to his own heir one day.

The realization is sobering.

We near the end of the tour through the Tudor wing in Ash's childhood bedroom, which looks onto the courtyard, just as he described.

We stand shoulder to shoulder and stare at the fountain and, like me, I imagine he's thinking of the ordinary children who played down there and thought he was a ghost. A heaviness has come over us that I abruptly feel determined to lift.

"Okay, so now I've seen little Ashton's room, can I see grown-up Ash's big one?"

He casts me a sideways smile, his eyes sparkling with amusement.

We came up to the top floor of the Tudor wing via an intricately carved dark wooden staircase, but instead of going back down the same way, Ash takes me to a door that I hadn't even noticed because it's seamlessly disguised with the same William Morris wallpaper that's on the walls.

I remember Bethan talking about secret doors and experience a thrill at getting to go behind one.

We come out onto a landing where there's a narrow, less-embellished staircase and a door marked PRIVATE. Ash uses his key to unlock it.

These are the rooms his family relocated to a couple of decades ago, after vacating the Tudor wing for the benefit of visitors, but their current living quarters don't look all that different from the rest of the house. They're a little more cluttered maybe, but just as grand, with antique furniture, rugs, oil paintings, and collections of ornaments contained in glass cabinets.

"This is my mother's favorite room," he says as we walk into a large living room with a chintz-covered four-piece sofa. Three sets of butter-yellow curtains hang at intervals on the wall. "She does most of her socializing in here—too many afternoon teas to count. During the day, it's very bright with all the windows."

"I can't get my bearings. Does it face the fields at the front?"

We've taken so many twists and turns—it's like a rabbit warren.

"No, the hills to the west and the church."

"Ah, okay. We were down at the church today, having a tidy-up. Apparently, there's a wedding blessing here on Saturday."

He shrugs. "We have them occasionally. Not official ceremonies. The church is only open for tours these days, but it's worth the effort to host the odd blessing and wedding reception, even if it does mean closing early to visitors."

I feel a wave of respect for him at everything he's had to learn in order to be able to run this place one day. Stepping up on my tiptoes, I press my lips to his. His arms instantly come around my waist and he deepens our kiss until I feel breathless and wobbly, but then he abruptly slides his mouth away, staring with consternation past my right shoulder. He takes my hand and firmly tugs me just behind him, tucking our joined fingers close to our bodies so they're hidden. He's gone rigid.

An attractive middle-aged brunette walks into the room.

"Good evening, Master Berkeley," she says in a demure voice.

"Meredith," Ash replies curtly, glaring at her.

Her eyes do a quick sweep over me and her lips curve up slightly as she walks straight past us and goes out the door.

"Who was that?" I ask when she's gone. "You sounded so surly!"

"Housekeeper. She's the only member of staff I wish my parents would get rid of."

"Why?"

He stalks out of the room, taking me with him. His grip on my hand has tightened.

"Ash?" I press.

"I don't like her," he replies shortly. "And she knows it. She calls me Master Berkeley to annoy me. It's how the staff always addressed Hugo, so it makes me think of him."

"That's awful. Why would she wind you up like that?" I ask with concern as we walk along a corridor.

He shrugs and comes to a stop at a door. "This is my room." He leads me inside and switches on his overhead lights, pushing the door closed behind us.

It's a large, square room with antique dark wooden furniture, including a big four-poster bed in the middle.

How many people have slept in that bed? The thought leads

me to wonder how many times *Beca* has slept in that bed and my stomach drops.

I'm sure you'll console him . . .

Her words come back to me, along with a twinge of guilt. I'm guessing she feels worse than I do right now.

"This faces onto the fields," I state, sure of where we are in the house now.

"Yep." He backtracks to flick off the ceiling light and then goes to one of two sets of midnight-blue curtains, pulling them back to reveal an arched window with a white frame.

"Wow. That's a view and a half."

The sky is awash with color. The sun set only recently, and one star hangs near the horizon.

"Is that Jupiter?" I ask.

"No, Jupiter will rise over the hill by the cabin in a few hours. Will you come and camp out with me on Saturday night?" he asks out of the blue.

"Uh, sure."

"There's something I'd like you to see, if it's not too cloudy."

"What?"

"It's a surprise. Enough talking."

We're both smiling as our lips come together, and then I'm tugging him in the direction of the bed and soaking up the feeling of his warm, hard body as it settles over me. Running my hands along his slim waist, I pull his shirt out of his trousers and press my fingers to his flat stomach. As his hands lift up my T-shirt and his mouth moves from my lips to my neck and finally to one of my nipples, I gasp and arch my back.

"Okay, okay, enough foreplay." I sound delirious as I tackle his belt buckle and push his trousers partway down his legs before wriggling to lift up my skirt.

We're still half-dressed, but I'm impatient.

"I don't have any condoms," he realizes.

It's like I've stepped into a cold shower.

"Neither do I."

The disappointment is so immense that there's no way in hell we're not finding a workable solution.

"I've never slept with anyone without a condom before," I whisper.

"Neither have I."

I retreat to look at him. "Really?"

"I swear."

I was more surprised than doubting him.

His pupils are so dilated. It's sexy as hell.

Our mouths come together again.

"I'm not on birth control, though." My voice sounds garbled.

"*Fuuuuuck*," he moans against my neck.

"Pull out," I urge.

He hesitates. Then he lifts his head to look at me directly again. "Are you sure?"

I nod. "I'm sure."

We break apart only far enough to slide down our underwear, and then he repositions himself between my legs.

"Are you sure about this?" he checks again, his voice strained.

"Fuck, Ash, please, I want you so much right now."

He sinks down and I lift my hips up simultaneously. The noise I make when we're connected intimately, skin to skin, is feral. It's so intense, so mind-blowing. He's ruined sex for me with any other man forever. The thought of him stopping what he's doing is beyond the realm of possibility, but, argh . . .

"I really could get pregnant," I say against his mouth, warning him.

"If I get you pregnant, I'd have to marry you," he replies roughly, still moving. "I can't have an heir out of wedlock."

I laugh against his shoulder. "Don't joke about it."

Fuck. He *is* joking, isn't he?

Suddenly there's a knock at the door. We simultaneously freeze.

"Ashton?"

It's a man's voice.

Ash pulls out abruptly. "Don't come in!" he yells, reaching for the hem of my skirt and tugging it down to cover me up before scrambling off the bed and yanking up his trousers.

"Is that your father?" I recognize his voice.

Ash nods, his expression racked with tension and something else . . . Fear?

"I'm coming in," Peter Berkeley warns.

"Wait!" Ash shouts.

Heart pounding, I leap from the bed, searching around wildly for somewhere to hide.

I'm just stepping toward the wardrobe when I hear Ash say; "Don't you dare."

I look over my shoulder at him, surprised at how sharp his tone is.

He shakes his head at me, graver than I've ever seen him. "I'm not hiding you like a dirty little secret."

A second later, the door opens and his father strolls in. He flicks on the light, making me flinch for a second before I'm able to look at him properly. I've only seen him once since I started working here, and I thought he was fairly attractive, standing on the steps of the Regency wing, delivering his speech.

But now there's a cruel glint in his eyes and a nasty twist

to his mouth that a part of me recognizes as he slowly looks me up and down, his gaze moving languidly to the rumpled bed-cover.

There's absolutely no doubt about what we've been doing.

My face burns fiercely.

Ash is still buttoning up his shirt, looking absolutely livid.

"I told you not to come in," he says cuttingly.

"I gave you more than enough time," his father replies evenly, his eyes returning to mine.

I feel a skipping sensation beneath my rib cage and I'm shocked to realize that I'm scared. *He's just a man,* I try to tell myself. But the weight of his gaze feels like a dark echo and sends an icy finger of fear sliding down my spine.

"What are you doing here?" Ash asks, finally drawing his father's attention away from me. "I thought you were out tonight."

"I had other plans."

"I bet you did," Ash mutters darkly.

His father smirks at him. "Are you going to introduce us?"

Ash gives me a tortured look.

"I'm Ellie," I barely manage to get out, saving him the dilemma.

Lord Berkeley cocks his head to one side, eyeing me thoughtfully. His eyes widen suddenly and his mouth breaks out into a big smile.

"You're one of our *gardeners,*" he says with delight, his voice silken, making me shudder. He glances at Ash. "I didn't think you had it in you, son."

"Get out," Ash commands through gritted teeth.

"Oh, I will."

"Now!"

He takes his time walking to the door.

"As you were."

I can hear his low chuckle as he pushes the door shut behind him.

Ash stares at me, his face racked with misery.

"Get me out of here," I plead, my heart bolting, demanding escape.

Only once before have I felt this intimidated and frightened by another human being and I can't leave that house fast enough. The quickest way to exit is via the narrow staircase and an understated side door, and as soon as I'm outside in the fresh air, I want to run.

That man holds too much power over me and I don't doubt for a second that he'd wield it.

He evidently holds too much power over his son too.

Ash is mortified. "I'm so sorry." He sounds haunted as he hurries to keep up with me.

"Just let me go," I warn. I need some space.

"Ellie, please," he begs, pulling me to a stop by the walled garden.

I wrench my hand away and shake my head. "I didn't like that."

It's the understatement of the century.

"I know. I'm sorry."

"I didn't like it at all, Ash."

"I know," he whispers, pained. "I hate him." His face contorts with rage, then regret. "He was supposed to be out tonight. I would never have subjected you to that."

"Did he ever do that to you and Beca?" I ask with bewilderment. "Just walk in on you?"

He looks anguished as he shakes his head. "He left us alone."

"How did he even know I was in there?"

A shadow passes over his face. "Meredith, I imagine."

"Please let me go now," I plead, backing up a few steps. "I just want to go to bed."

I don't hear his footsteps the whole time I'm walking away.

26

YOUR JOB IS SAFE, I SWEAR, ASH TEXTS ME IN THE middle of the night.

I haven't been able to sleep. He also seems to be suffering from insomnia.

How can you be sure? I reply.

My phone begins to ring. I pause a moment before answering.

"How can you be sure?" I repeat my question aloud, sounding ragged.

"He has nothing to gain from firing you."

"He has nothing to gain from keeping me either."

I hate that I'm at his father's mercy.

He sighs. "This is going to sound twisted and I'm so sorry about that, but it's preferable to you having to worry about your job."

"Tell me."

"It amuses him that I'm having an affair with a member of staff."

His tone makes me feel queasy.

"Does he know who I am? That we met years ago?"

"No!" he exclaims. "He just thinks you're—"

"Your bit of rough," I interrupt him, a dark little part of me seeking to press his buttons again.

He falls silent. And then he says, coldly, "Do not ever refer to yourself like that again."

"I have to go."

"Wait!"

"No. I need a few days to get my head around this."

"Do *not* overthink."

I let out a miserable laugh. "Too late."

ASH CALLS ME in the afternoon at four forty-five, just as I'm arriving home from work. I barely slept last night and I'm shattered.

"I said a few days."

I feel guilty the moment the harsh words have left my mouth, but before I can soften my tone, he speaks.

"You'll get them. I'm on my way to London."

"Why?"

"Beca called me. She's very upset."

I feel as though he's dumped an anvil on my stomach.

"I'm going to see her, to try to sort it out," he explains.

He's dropping everything for her? Even me?

"Ellie? Are you there?"

I know I told him I needed space, but this feels like abandonment.

"Ellie?" he asks again.

"I don't know what to say."

"Please don't worry. I'll be back before the weekend. I just want to make sure she's all right. It's the first time she's reached out to me since we broke up."

"Okay," I reply shakily.

"I'd better go. This car is too old to handle putting you on speakerphone and I'm about to hit the motorway. I'll call you later tonight."

He doesn't.

THE NEXT DAY everything goes even further downhill. I walk into the Mess Room at break time and every single one of the gardeners—Evan, Harri, Bethan, *and* Owain—stop talking.

Bethan looks at me, her expression cagey. Harri and Owain avert their gazes and Evan shoves his hand through his hair, turning his back on me and draining his tea.

"What's going on?" I ask carefully.

"Is it true?" Bethan asks.

"Is what tr—"

She cuts me off. "You and Ash?"

My rib cage feels constricted. Harri tentatively lifts his gaze to watch my reaction. Owain keeps his averted.

I don't need to say a word. The look on my face answers her question.

"Wow," she says flatly.

"How did you find out?"

Evan lets out a humorless laugh and walks right past me, out the door. Owain releases a long, heavy sigh and follows him. Harri and Bethan are the only ones who remain, and neither of them looks happy.

"People talk," Bethan says tightly.

"Do you know that he's gone to London to see Beca?" Harri asks, and there's something mean about his tone, as though he wants to twist a knife.

"Yes."

"Well, good luck to you," Bethan says flippantly, unsmiling. "It's the first time Ash has got with a member of staff, apparently."

I feel so sick that I turn and leave, returning immediately to my cottage. There's no way I can finish the day's work.

This is my worst nightmare. And Ash is not here to support me.

People know about us, I text him, my fingers shaking so much that I have to retype the words three times before I can get it right.

I keep a close eye on my phone for the next few hours, but he still hasn't replied by the time Siân comes home at five thirty. I'm upstairs on my bed, feeling wobbly and weird, and she comes straight to my door.

"Yes," I call when she knocks.

She opens the door, her face ashen. "What the hell?"

"Please don't start," I reply unsteadily, sitting up on the bed.

"How on earth did it happen? Hugo had a reputation for sleeping with staff, but never Ash. I thought he was different."

"He *is* different!" I snap, but from her dubious expression, she thinks I'm delusional.

Ash should be here for this. He's the one who should be making it clear to everyone that this is not some sordid affair. I just want to get away, but nowhere is safe. Could I hide out in his cabin until he returns? Would anyone have a spare key? Celyn?

Siân follows me as I hurry downstairs and exit the cottage via the back door. There, on the lawn, is Celyn himself, along with Bethan, Harri, Evan, Dylan, and Jac, having a lovely big chinwag at my expense.

They all turn to look at me, their expressions wary.

"I've known him for *years!*" I cry. "We have *history!*"

"What history?" Siân asks, confused.

"We met when we were interrailing almost six years ago."

"Did you *come* here because of him?" Bethan asks with shock, and Evan's stare turns hard as he waits for my answer.

"Of course I didn't! I didn't even know his surname when we met! I literally saw him on the steps for the first time at his parents' anniversary party—it's why I freaked out and ran off," I tell Evan desperately.

"So you knew nothing about the family you were coming to work for," Harri says dubiously.

"Nothing!" I turn to Evan. "*You* approached *me*, remember? I didn't look for this job."

He sighs and nods, conceding that this is true.

"Wait," Celyn interrupts suddenly, taking a step closer. "You're *Ellie.*"

"Of course she's Ellie!" Bethan snaps.

"No." He looks at Siân.

She stares back at him, and then her eyes widen with some understanding and she gapes at me.

"You're Ellie," she whispers, because of course, she's worked here for a long, long time. How much does she know? "You're the one that got away."

27

B Y THE TIME ASH RETURNS FROM LONDON ON FRIDAY, my colleagues have more or less accepted that I'm not a gold-digger, but they're still wary about the present state of my relationship with Ash. I'm so hurt and upset with him that I can hardly bear to look at his face when he turns up at my back door.

There's no reason for us to hide now. I told him what had happened when he finally rang me back, but he ended our call abruptly because Beca had returned from wherever she'd been and he didn't want to upset her by being caught speaking to me.

I was breathless with hurt.

In our next rushed conversation, he confessed that his mother had confided in Beca's parents about us and that they, in turn, had told their daughter. Beca was beyond humiliated to hear that people were beginning to find out, and then Ash admitted to me that he'd cocked it up further by revealing that his father had walked in on us and now knows too.

Apparently, Beca was beside herself to hear that he'd brought me into the family home, into his bedroom, and into his bed.

That admission took some teasing out of him, but I got there eventually.

I don't think she ever in a million years expected him to introduce me to his parents, let alone take me to his private living quarters.

It is everything I feared, and it's made me certain beyond a shadow of a doubt that Beca let Ash go because she thought he'd see sense and come back to her.

And he still might, with or without a push.

"It's the Honorable Ashton Berkeley," Siân says as she opens the door to Ash, her tone not quite as teasing as the last time she announced his arrival with his full title.

I stay where I am, backed up against the kitchen counter. Ash stares at me jadedly as he enters. He's wearing gray shorts and a white T-shirt: casual Ash.

The wilted daisies inside my chest have lifted their heads at the sight of him, despite everything.

"Hey," he says.

He hasn't taken his eyes from mine, and I'm holding the eye contact, but I don't go to him.

Siân is watching us. He comes to stand in front of me.

"Ellie," he says quietly, running his fingertips along my arm.

He looks wretched. My throat begins to swell.

"Come here."

I don't fight it. He tucks me against his body, cradling my head against his neck, just holding me in the tiny kitchen while Siân stands by.

I don't care that we have a witness. I need to be close to him right now, even though I'm wounded. I know he'll make it up to me later. I know that I'll forgive him. I know that I can't walk away from this, even if I wanted to. I'm in it to crash and burn.

Eventually he releases me, but his arm remains around my shoulders as he turns to face Siân.

"So this is happening," he says casually, indicating the two of us.

Siân looks stunned. "So I see," she replies, her eyes moving back and forth. "That was some *cwtch*."

ASH STICKS AROUND for our Friday barbecue and I'm glad to have him there, even if the atmosphere among the workers is strained. I was worried about what people would think, and I'm still worried—the reaction of my colleagues earlier in the week tells me that favoritism is a concern for them. Whether Ash likes it or not, they disapprove. But he won't feel their disapproval in the same way that I will.

Siân and Bethan have been frosty all week and I know they're hurt that I not only failed to confide in them but actively lied—Siân especially, after she opened up to me about Celyn. I hope she'll forgive me eventually.

I just wish that Ash and I could have held on to our secret. It's all so real now, and not in a good way. I'll be watched like a hawk from here on in, judged by everyone to make sure I'm doing my job to the best of my abilities—and I'll probably *still* fall short of expectations.

"Will you come back to the cabin with me?" Ash asks as he's leaving.

I hesitate. I want to. I want to run away, but I know it will only make things worse if I don't stay and face the music for a bit longer.

"Tomorrow, then," he says when I shake my head. "I have to catch up on some business with my father in the morning, but I'll be home from three—or I can swing by and pick you up?"

"I'll walk up," I reply.

He nods and presses a kiss to my lips before saying goodbye.

I feel the weight of every single person's stare as he walks away.

THREE O'CLOCK THE next day cannot come soon enough, and I do feel a little buzzy as I pack an overnight bag. But I still have an underlying dread in the pit of my stomach. Ash hasn't filled me in on his time with Beca. He stayed with her for four nights—what did they talk about? What did they do? How did he comfort her? He deserted me when I needed him, so desperate was he to console his ex-girlfriend. He chose her over me, leaving me to fend for myself. I understand it, but how can I not be hurt by it? At the end of the day, the person who shares the most history with Ash is Beca. Of course he's going to want to protect her and put her first.

If only there had been more of a break between them splitting up and us getting together. It feels messy and complicated and I know the guilt must play on his mind.

I think about this all the way up to the cabin, but the sounds of the forest act as a balm, and then Ash opens his door to me with his warmest smile and engulfs me in a hug so heartfelt that the ache inside me is soothed a little further.

"I'm so sorry about everything," he murmurs. "I'm going to do my best to make it up to you."

I'd already guessed that he'd try.

"We're all set up," he says. "Do you need to use the bathroom before we go?"

"Go where? What's been set up?"

"The tent. We're camping, remember? Just out in the clearing," he adds hastily. "So you can come back to the cabin whenever you want."

I smile. "I'm good. Let's go."

There's a three-person tent at the top of the hill. In front of it are two camping chairs, one of which is holding the soft gray blanket I love so much. Ash has also brought a table outside, upon which is a campfire stove.

"Are we cooking out here too?"

"We're doing it all," he replies, and it's sweet, seeing him happy like this.

"Can I peek inside the tent?"

"Go for it. It's zipped up to keep the bugs out."

I peer through the window and the first thing I see is his giant white telescope.

"Are we stargazing?" I ask with excitement.

"Planet-gazing," he corrects me. "The weather forecast is supposed to be clear, so fingers crossed."

"What planets are we going to see?"

"All of them."

"All of them?"

"All of them in the sky at the same time."

"That's pretty cool."

"And the five main planets will appear in the same order that they spun out from the sun."

"That's *really* cool. What time is this happening?"

"Around three a.m."

"Ash!" I exclaim with a laugh. "Are we not sleeping tonight?"

"Not if I can help it."

I look inside the tent again. There are two sleeping bags, two pillows—and is that an inflatable double mattress?

"This isn't camping, this is glamping," I tease.

He chuckles. "I bought the mattress this morning. It's the least you deserve. Can I get you a drink? Cup of tea?"

"I think what I want most right now is to snuggle up with you in there."

He looks at me, his lips curving in a gentle smile. "Come on, then."

He unzips the tent and we crawl inside and lie on the bed. He slides his arm beneath my shoulders and brings me closer. I rest my cheek on his chest and try to soak up his warmth, wishing I didn't have so many misgivings.

"How was Beca?" I hope he can put my mind at ease about how the land lies with her, at least.

"Not the best." His voice already sounds heavier.

"She thought you were coming back to her, didn't she?"

"She knows I'm not."

He hasn't answered my question, but he may as well have.

"Do you think you'll ever be able to repair your friendship?"

I'd be lying if I said that I'd be fine with him being as close to Beca as they were before they became romantically involved. I hate that he's hurting, but clearly Beca still wants him and that puts me on a knife-edge.

"I hope so. It helped, going there. I think she needed proof that I still care about her."

My stomach pinches. How many more hoops will Ash jump through to prove to his friend that he cares? He's given me no reason to doubt his feelings for me, but I don't think I'll ever relax if Beca's back on the scene. What if he continues to put her first at my expense?

I feel uneasy as I ask, "Does your father know our history now?" Everyone else does.

"No."

"How do you know?"

"I'd know. I saw him this morning. He thinks this is just a fling."

That's exactly what it's supposed to be, but it feels blasphemous to think about our relationship like that now. I still have all the reservations I had before we went into this, and I know that those hurdles remain, but somehow I've managed to shut out my concerns in order to live recklessly. The thought of our love having a limited lifespan is too unbearable to contemplate.

"And he's okay with you having a fling with a gardener?" I ask.

"Yep."

I turn to look at him. His tone sounded flippant, but his jaw is clenched. He reaches back to fold his pillow over so it's easier to see my face.

"My father has had affairs all my life," he confides. "Their big anniversary celebration was fake as fuck."

My eyes widen. "How do you know he's had affairs?"

"Well, I walked in on him fucking Meredith when I was six."

My chest constricts at the sound of his casual misery.

"She still puts out for him whenever he wants it. That's why he won't get rid of her."

"But what about your mother?" I'm shocked.

"She tolerates his indiscretions. He's had plenty of others. I'm almost certain he's why I went through so many nannies and au pairs when I was younger. Although I'm pretty sure my last au pair quit because of Hugo."

"Jesus! Ash!" I'm reeling.

Siân said Hugo had a reputation for sleeping with staff. Ash told me that his brother was his father's mini-me. Was there an element of power play to their affairs? I feel sick at the thought.

"So, yeah, he won't care about you," he says wearily. "It kills me that he thinks I'm just like him. Like my brother. And I have to let him believe it because the alternative is that he might cause trouble for us. If he realizes it's serious . . ."

My blood runs cold as his voice trails off.

"What if your mother tells him?"

"She won't. They may be married, but it's not a marriage. There's no love between them. They have separate rooms, have done almost all my life. They're together out of duty, nothing more."

"Fucking duty," I mutter, snuggling back against his chest. "I can't believe you had to grow up with that."

"It's why I'm determined to marry for love."

His words should warm my blood, but they don't.

If I get you pregnant, I'd have to marry you. I can't have an heir out of wedlock.

My eyes go wide at the memory of Ash's words. I'd laughed, thinking he was joking, but there's a chance that he wasn't.

I'm too exhausted for overthinking right now. I just want to soak up his warmth.

We end up falling asleep in each other's arms, waking when the air has grown cooler.

"I need to make you dinner," Ash says, sitting up.

"I'm not that hungry."

"Well, I'm starving, so you can eat when you're ready."

"I like this blanket," I say when I'm snuggled up beneath it on a camping chair. "It's so warm."

"Taran's grandmother knitted it for him. He suffered from the cold before he died." His eyes brighten. "I like seeing you wrapped up in it. You look so at home."

Let the overthinking begin.

IN THE MIDDLE of the night, I stare through Ash's telescope at the planets fanning out across the sky. They're on the ecliptic, so they look as though they're more or less in a straight line.

The five brightest planets—Mercury, Venus, Mars, Jupiter, and Saturn—sit sequentially in their order from the sun, and between Mars and Jupiter hangs a thin crescent moon, representing Earth's position in the solar system.

The only outliers are the ice planets of green-tinged Uranus, which is sitting between Venus and the moon, and blue Neptune, which hangs in the sky between Jupiter and Saturn.

Saturn was the first planet to appear, rising just before midnight, and it took my breath away to see its rings through Ash's powerful telescope. Jupiter rose just after 1 a.m., shining twice as brightly as the brightest star in the sky. Next came Mars, with a distinct orangey-yellow hue, and at just after 3 a.m., Venus graced us with her presence to become the brightest member of the line-up. Finally, just a few minutes ago, tiny Mercury peeked above the horizon, an hour before the sunrise will wash all the planets from the sky.

The next time the five brightest planets will align sequentially like this won't be for almost twenty years, so I feel privileged to have witnessed it.

I also feel connected to the universe in a way that I never have before.

It blows my mind that the solar system was formed five and a half billion years ago out of a dense cloud of interstellar dust and gas, and that the spinning, swirling disk of material that was created when the dust cloud collapsed eventually became the planets that we see orbiting the sun today.

Ash explains that in another five billion years the sun will exhaust all the hydrogen fuel in its core, its outer edges will begin to inflate, and it will become a red giant, expanding millions of miles out into space. Mercury will be engulfed, as will Venus. Mars may hang on beyond the dying star, but our rivers and oceans will dry up and all life on Earth will be extinguished.

Ash is right: the enormity of space makes everything else feel small. Out there, new stars are being born and new worlds are being spun into existence.

But here on Earth, four and a half billion years after our sun was formed, five billion years before it will start to die, one girl sits on a hill in Wales, falling in love with a boy. And nothing can stop it from happening.

28

JUNE BLAZES INTO JULY AND THE TEMPERATURE SOARS. In the middle of the month, Wales experiences its hottest day on record.

But despite what the weather forecast says, the climate at work and at home remains frosty.

I've been spending most of my free time up at the cabin. It's more bearable in the woods.

"Have you been in touch with your dad since you started working here?" Ash asks one evening as I lie on the sofa, my head in his lap.

He's lazily stroking my hair and I don't want to move, even though the sagging seat cushion is doing my back in.

"No, only before I left, but my parents' PA texted me out of the blue yesterday to tell me that one of my sofa ranges has been featured in *ELLE Decoration* magazine."

It was actually nice to hear from Alison. She sent me a screenshot of the article.

"That's cool. Which one?"

"The Stella range."

"Oh, I like your Stella sofas. I saw them when I googled you. Hot pink and black, right?"

"That's right." I smile up at him.

"Why the hot pink? I had a feeling there was a story behind it."

"Color of her lipstick on some of our favorite nights out. The black is a nod to her winged eyeliner, and, of course, they're modern wingback sofas, so the design is a nod to it too."

"You're so talented. Your Lisbon range is my favorite. I love the curved tram shape of the canary yellow and the contrast with the light brown. Why *did* you use that color?"

I feel my cheeks warming as I lift up his T-shirt and press a kiss to his flat stomach.

"Are you trying to distract me?" he asks with amusement, tugging his T-shirt back down past my face and touching my jaw with his fingertips. "Why brown?"

"It's the color of the peach iced tea I was drinking on the rooftop of the hostel when we met."

"Oh, right!"

I bite my lip, looking up at his face. "It's also how I remembered the color of your eyes," I admit.

"Aw! Are you serious?" he asks with a cute laugh.

I'm laughing too as I reach up to touch his cheekbone. "I didn't do them justice."

He takes my fingers and kisses them, then picks up a lock of my hair. "I looked for this color everywhere. My mother was right. I did go heavy on the red in the Georgian garden."

"I still can't believe you re-created my grandmother's lupin rainbow."

"It's the only time I've ever been involved in a garden scheme. I hoped you'd see it one day. And now you have. And you will do again, and again, and again."

He's looking down at me with such adoration in his eyes. It's blinding.

"How would you feel if I bought the Lisbon range for up here?" he asks, glancing over at the threadbare armchair. "This furniture is in dire need of updating."

"You're not wrong," I agree, arching my back to relieve some of the tension.

"Would you mind?"

"No, I'm proud of Lisbon. It would work well up here." I look around his living room. "Shame I can't get you a discount."

He strokes his hand over my hair. "How much have you tried to reconcile with your parents?"

I avert my gaze. "I haven't, really. My dad and I tick along, touching base but never really talking, not about anything that matters. And my mum and I don't speak at all."

"Do you try calling her, ever?"

"No," I reply bluntly. "And she's never once tried calling me."

"Maybe she's too proud. She might need you to make the first step."

This conversation is making me tense.

"What if we went to see them in person?" he suggests. "I could come with you for moral support."

I recoil. "There's *no way* you're going anywhere near my parents."

He frowns. "Why not? You're not still embarrassed about me, are you?"

"Are you kidding? My parents would have kittens if they

found out I was seeing the son of a viscount. The number of times they shoved me in the direction of rich, well-connected boys at school," I say bitterly.

A memory comes back to me of our school play, the spring I'd turned fourteen, and the boy who was cast in the lead role.

I suddenly feel cold.

"Are you okay?" Ash asks with concern as I sit up, agitated.

"I don't want to talk about this anymore," I reply, swinging my legs off the sofa. "Do you want a cup of tea?" I call over my shoulder as I head into the kitchen.

I need something to take the edge off my internal chill.

He follows me as I fill the kettle and flick it on.

"Ellie."

If I answer him, I'll snap, so I don't.

"Hey," he says gently, placing his hands on my shoulders from behind.

For a split second, I feel trapped, but the feeling passes when I remember who I'm with and I twist in his arms, burying my face against his chest, letting his warmth surround me.

"It's okay," he whispers, cradling my head against him as I take several ragged breaths, twisting his T-shirt in my hands.

BUT IT'S NOT okay. The following week, Beca comes back to Wales.

Ash calls me on Monday to cancel our dinner plans because she's invited him over. He's determined to make amends where she's concerned, but it's hard to take a step back.

I decide that rather than risk letting him see how insecure I feel, I'll stay down at the cottage for a few days. I need to prove to myself that I'm still capable of standing on my own two feet, so I suggest giving him some space to catch up with Beca. I don't like how easily he agrees that it's a good idea.

The weather is unbearable and the heat and airless nights make it even harder to switch off my mind. My colleagues and I have taken to waking at five and finishing earlier, but it's too hot for most of our volunteers and we have to find jobs out of the sun for those who do come.

We've been strimming edges, deadheading, weeding, chopping back herbaceous plants, and planting annuals, plugging the gaps from earlier flowering bulbs like alliums, tulips, and daffodils. Everyone's cranky and sluggish and it's an effort to stay hydrated.

Ash asks me to sleep up at the cabin on Thursday night and I spend the whole day looking forward to it, but that afternoon, he texts to cancel.

I'm so sorry, I can't see you tonight after all. My mother has invited Beca and her parents over for dinner. I really have to be here.

I'm taken aback by the force of my disappointment. I don't know how to reply, so I don't.

He calls me early that evening. I'm still feeling on edge as I answer the phone.

"Hi."

"Hey, are you okay?" he asks, sounding wary.

"I'm all right," I reply.

"I'm sorry about tonight. Can we do something tomorrow instead?"

"Sure." A moment passes when neither of us says anything. "Where are you?" I ask at last.

"At the house, just waiting for the Bramptons to arrive."

"Do I have anything to worry about?"

I could kick myself for letting the question burst from my mouth.

"Of course not!" he exclaims. "They're old family friends. I'm just trying to smooth things over."

I'm so angry at myself. I *hate* feeling this needy. It's like I'm a teenager again, racked with insecurities.

"Ellie?"

"Honestly, it's fine. I hope you have fun." My voice sounds stronger, if a little cool.

"I'll text you later."

"Okay, bye."

I get off the phone and force myself to take several deep breaths, then I reach for *A Court of Mist and Fury*, the sequel to *A Court of Thorns and Roses*, which I finished rereading last week, finally making it through the last chapter.

Although it pained me to know that Stella's handwriting was missing from the front of the book, Ash was right, it did make me feel closer to her. Plus, it's been a good distraction while I've been here at the cottage.

I still feel an uncomfortable degree of separation from Siân, who hasn't suggested another *Glee* marathon since she found out about Ash. Things aren't right with Bethan either, and Evan and Harri are both still giving me a wide berth.

I haven't tried hard enough to repair any of these friendships. The thought of attempting to reconcile and getting rejected is just too much for my current fragile state. There's no doubt that what happened with my parents has had an impact on me. I suspect it will for the rest of my life.

I've considered continuing with the counseling sessions I had in the wake of Stella's death, but there's something about the notion of exploring my feelings and digging into my childhood that makes me feel unsettled.

Thumbing through the book until I find where I last was, I begin to read.

I'm so caught up in the story that I lose three hours to it. Stella would have been obsessed with this sequel. I loved *ACOTAR*, but the follow-up is even better.

Sometimes it's the little things that pain me the most when I think about what she missed out on due to her life being cut short. She died just months before *A Court of Mist and Fury* was published, and realizing this brings on a rush of emotion. There's no point in trying to stifle my grief tonight—it needs a release. I close up the book, curl into a ball, and let myself cry.

I end up falling asleep and forgetting to set my alarm, so I'm in a panic when I wake up and see that it's four forty-five and I only have fifteen minutes to get myself outside to the walled garden.

But by six o'clock I'm in the swing of it, chopping back bright pink geraniums, purple *Nepeta*, and the other herbaceous plants in East Court that will put on a second flush.

I'm just getting my bottle of water out of my basket when I see Beca coming in my direction.

My heart lurches unpleasantly. What is she doing here at this hour?

"Oh! Hello," she says, her eyes widening at the sight of me.

"Hi," I reply warily as she slows to a stop.

She's more classically beautiful than I remembered, with fine facial features and pale blond hair floating past her shoulders.

"You're here early," I say, my senses on high alert.

She looks awkward. "I stayed over." Her voice sounds husky as she adds, "Hit the tequila a bit hard."

I stare at her, reeling. She and Ash did tequila shots the night they first slept together.

How can I be doubting Ash? I'm even less secure in our relationship than I thought.

"I'd better go," she says, making a move to walk away. "Maybe see you sometime," she adds hesitantly.

"Yeah, maybe," I reply.

She carries on toward the car park.

My stomach is churning, but I force myself to work for another half an hour before breaking for tea early. I don't go to the Mess Room; I head straight to the cottage. I left in such a hurry earlier that I didn't even check my phone, but now I see there's a missed call from Ash—he rang at 10 p.m. but didn't leave a message—and a text he sent at just after midnight.

I read the text.

Hey, sorry it's late. Just to say that things went well tonight but Beca's pretty drunk so she's crashing in a guest room. All good though. Miss you. Speak in morning.

The flood of relief I feel is immense. I reply right away.

Only just read your text. I saw Beca leaving earlier. What time should I come over?

It's so frustrating that he has no reception up at the cabin. It could be hours before I hear back from him. Resentment begins to simmer at how on edge all this is making me feel. I decide to take my phone back to work and hate myself for it. There is no chance that I'll lose myself in gardening today.

But as soon as I arrive at Maple Garden, my phone buzzes with a message. My stomach falls when I realize it's from Ash. How does he have phone reception?

He's answering my question about what time to come over.

As soon as you finish work?

I reply immediately. Where are you?
It's a few moments before his response comes.

At the house, having breakfast with my mother.

I feel as though I've been scalded.

You and Beca both stayed there last night?

My phone begins to ring. My hands are shaking as I answer it, but I wait for Ash to speak first.

"Are you okay?"

"Not really," I reply.

"Where are you?"

"Maple Garden, behind the orangery."

"I'll be there in five minutes."

He hangs up.

I'm relieved I'm alone because I dread to think of anyone else seeing me.

Few perennials can compete with globe thistles for drought tolerance and our *Echinops* are thriving, even in the heat wave. I'm severing the stalks holding up a sea of round, spiky blue heads the size of golf balls when Ash appears around the corner of the orangery.

"Hey," he says, his expression full of trepidation as I get to my feet.

He looks hungover, and when he pulls me into a hug, I can smell alcohol on his breath.

I'm stiff in his arms, breaking away before he's ready to let me go.

"I swear to you there's nothing to worry about," he says fervently, gripping my biceps and staring me dead in the eyes. "I slept in my room, she stayed in a guest bed. I didn't even see her this morning."

"But it went well last night?" I ask nervily.

He nods, but seems reserved. "We got on, had a laugh, on a *purely platonic level*," he stresses.

"On your part, maybe."

He shakes his head, but doesn't try to convince me that his ex is not still romantically invested in him.

"Please be okay with this, Ellie. I don't want to lose her friendship."

I can't help wincing at this and he tugs me back into his arms.

"Trust me," he murmurs in my ear, holding me close. "I want *you*. It's *you*. It's only ever been *you*."

He presses his lips to my temple, my cheekbone, my jaw. I'm breathing shallowly as his mouth finds mine and then he's clasping my face in his hands and kissing me hard, telling me with his body that this is not fizzling out.

I give it back to him just as urgently, my heart beating fast inside my chest as though it knows how all things that burn brightly must fade with time.

And right now, I feel as though our time is slipping away.

Suddenly I don't care that he tastes of the tequila he drank with his ex last night, I just want him to consume me.

He walks me back against the orangery wall, presses me up against the warm cream stone, cups his hands under my thighs until my legs wrap around him, and then he rocks against me hard, not just once but again and again, and I feel as though I'm seeing stars as he makes love to me fully clothed.

CLAP.

We freeze, startled.

CLAP.

We slide our mouths apart.

CLAP.

We look in the direction of the sound and see his father coming toward us, his hands creating one last resounding CLAP as he comes to a stop.

My whole body goes rigid as his steel-gray eyes lock with mine.

"Do I need to give you lessons in discretion?" Peter Berkeley asks acridly, his gaze roving to his son as Ash, muscles taut with tension, carefully sets me down on my feet and straightens my top. "And you should be at work," he says to me.

He tuts, which is condescending enough, and then he begins to wag his finger, adding insult to injury.

"Father," Ash cuts in, backing up a few inches.

"Off you scoot," Peter Berkeley says, giving me a dismissive wave.

"Do *not* speak to her that way," Ash warns through gritted teeth, placing his hand on my hip.

The gesture is meant to be reassuring, but I push him away, unable to fight against my body's sudden strong repulsion at being touched.

Ash glances at me with confusion, his expression wretched.

"I hope you're not getting attached, Ashton," his father says drolly, regaining his son's attention. "I don't think Rebecca will stand for it."

"Rebecca and I are not together," Ash snaps, taking my hand and tugging me close to his side, ever so slightly behind him.

This time I let him touch me, but I'm as stiff as a board.

Peter Berkeley's eyes dart between us. "Oh dear," he says, and I can see his mind recalibrating. "This won't do."

"Ellie, you should go," Ash says, his voice strained.

But I'm glued to the spot, unable to move.

He's just a man, I try to tell myself as my heart pounds hard and fast.

But it didn't help before and it doesn't help now.

"Ellie," Ash prompts sharply.

Peter Berkeley laughs as I jolt to attention.

"I'll come and find you later," Ash promises.

I feel his father's eyes on me as I quickly hurry away.

ASH FINDS ME in the walled garden, plucking off the brilliantly colored daisylike flower heads of *Argyranthemum* as though they've personally insulted me. The adrenaline pumping through my body is making me work at breakneck speed. I'm in full sunshine and the SPF 50 I plastered on earlier will be wearing thin, but the heat is a distraction.

I feel dazed, confused, out on a limb. I feel fucked.

Ash pulls me into the shade of the apple orchard and takes me in his arms. He's cool, not hot and sweaty like I am. I'm guessing he's come from the house.

"I spoke to my father," he says. "I told him in no uncertain terms that Beca and I are over, that you and I are together, and he's just got to accept it. I explained about Lisbon."

I tense up and try to pull away, but he holds me tighter.

"There was no other way. I had to try to appeal to him somehow."

This is the beginning of the end. I feel it in my bones.

A FEW DAYS later, I'm up at the cabin, waiting for Ash with a spare key he gave me, when he returns, distraught. He looks shocked to find me napping on his bed, and not at all happy—I think he wanted time to recover.

"What happened?" I ask, scrambling to my feet.

He shakes his head, his eyes bright with tears.

"Is anyone hurt?"

"Everyone's fine," he assures me. "It's okay, I'll sort it out."

"Ash. I need you to tell me what's wrong. I can't trust you if you keep things from me."

He sits down on the edge of the bed, looking utterly trauma-tized as he meets my eyes. I sink down beside him.

"He's threatening to sell the land. The cottages and sawmill."

"Oh, Ash," I murmur, a wave of nausea sweeping through me.

"Owain and Gwen have lived at number one for thirty years. We've supported our workers for over a century, provided jobs and housing for generations. The sawmill and workshop are a family business, the sort of family business I would have given anything to be a part of. It's what I'm most proud of and he wants to throw it all away."

He's on the verge of breaking down.

"Does he need the money?"

"Things are tight, but we could make other cutbacks, or he

could parcel off a different piece of land. He's doing it to get to me. He says he'll put this place on the market too."

"Why would he want to hurt you so much? He's your father!"

The look on his face is tearing me apart.

He lets out the saddest of laughs. "He claimed to be doing it for my benefit. He said he has to do something to make me see sense."

"See sense about what?"

"You. Beca." His voice has become a monotone.

"What about Beca?" I can hardly stand to ask.

"He said if I give you up and marry her, he'll sign over the sawmill and cottages to me now. Along with this place."

There's a vise around my throat, tightening, suffocating.

"I won't do it," Ash says vehemently. "I won't give you up. But though it kills me to say it," and now his eyes are bright with agony, "I think you should look for another job."

29

EUROPE IS BURNING. WILDFIRES ARE TEARING THROUGH France, Spain, and Portugal, and smoke from the latter can be seen in Lisbon and smelled hundreds of miles away in Madrid.

At Berkeley Hall our lawn is crisp and brown and the fields are yellow. I arrived in paradise in May, but now, in August, there's an end-of-the-world feel about the place.

Our garden beds are hanging on, though, and some of our plants are thriving. While everyone else has to deal with garden-hose bans, we draw water from the lake and irrigate at dawn, trying to be mindful of visitors who aren't so lucky.

I've applied for three new jobs and I've interviewed for two. I tried to keep them to a one-hour driving distance, but when I saw that the National Trust had an assistant head gardener position going at Hidcote Manor Garden in Gloucestershire, in the North Cotswolds, I couldn't resist giving it a shot.

Ash has retreated into himself, so racked with guilt over his father's threats that he's driven himself sick with worry. I've been carrying a horrible sense of dread in my stomach too, my heart pounding at the thought of running into Peter Berkeley again.

An estate agent came to view the cottages a few days ago and word has spread among my colleagues. Every time I walk into a room, people stop talking.

And while I've been quaking in my boots, Beca has been Ash's pillar of strength. Yesterday I arrived at the cabin to see a car parked in the woods, and when I approached the front door, I could hear Ash laughing.

He stopped when I knocked, of course, and Beca left immediately, looking uncomfortable, but I could see how much lighter he seemed, the way the heaviness had lifted from him, if only for a short while.

It's hard to console each other when we're both consumed with the dark cloud looming over us. We haven't had sex in three days, and the last time we did, I could tell Ash had other things on his mind. We can no longer lose ourselves in each other. We're too caught up in the outside world.

IN THE MIDDLE of August, Owain comes to see me, bringing news that has felt imminent.

"I'm sorry," he says gruffly as he sits across from me at my kitchen table. "I've been told we have to make cutbacks and I need to lose one of my crew. It's likely to be a case of last one in, first one out, so it'll be nothing personal if you're the one to go."

Of *course* it's personal. Ash mentioned that he'd been looking into making cutbacks, but I know he was determined that no staff would lose their jobs.

This is not his doing. I bet he has no idea, but it's obvious what's happening here.

I stare down at the letter Owain has just given me. The rest of the day's mail is on the table, but only the envelope with the oak leaf and acorn emblem has been opened. It feels so twisted that one of my proudest moments is coinciding with one of my lowest.

"It's a good voluntary redundancy package if you choose to take it," Owain says. "Saves the faff of official proceedings." He sounds a little brighter as he nods at the piece of paper in my hands. "Best I've seen, actually. That lump sum should see you right until you find another position. But it's dependent on you agreeing to accept redundancy without delay."

Effective immediately. I'm being paid off. Peter Berkeley wants me out of here and his power is absolute.

But I have one way of keeping some semblance of control over my own fate.

"I've actually found another job," I reply, nodding at the envelope on the table.

"At the National Trust?" Owain asks with amazement, recognizing the logo.

I nod.

"Oh, this is wonderful!" he says with relief. "You'll be able to use the redundancy package to set yourself up in a new place before you start!"

"Will you give me a reference?"

"Of course I will!"

I have to see Ash.

ASH IS SITTING on the sofa with his head in his hands. "I'm not ready for this."

"I've emailed to accept, and booked myself into a B and B

until I find somewhere to live near work. I leave tomorrow," I tell him robotically.

He lifts his head to look at me, shell-shocked. "How could you do that without speaking to me first?"

"There's no other choice!" I snap, softening my tone as I add, "I can't stay here."

"You could. I'd support you—"

"Ash." I cut him off sharply.

He stares at me. "Then I'll come with you."

"Stop it," I say wearily, running my hand through my hair.

I'm sitting on the armchair just across from him, but I feel a million miles away. I've been taking these small steps to distance myself and I'm so tired. I don't have the strength to fight for what I want anymore.

"This is where you belong," I say. "It's ingrained in you. You know it."

"I don't want it. My father can go fuck himself."

"You sound delusional." I let out a long breath.

"He'll die one day," he states. "When he's gone, I can do what I want."

"But he will have already sold off the sawmill, cottages, and this cabin," I point out. "If I leave quietly, maybe it'll be enough to convince him not to do that."

I don't know how my eyes remain dry. Perhaps reality hasn't sunk in yet.

Ash's expression is haunted. "There must be another way," he says.

And then he gets up and stalks out the front door.

I follow him in time to see him climbing onto his bike. "Where are you going?"

"To see my father."

"I CAN'T BELIEVE you're leaving," Siân says, stunned. "Just like that."

She came back to the cottage at lunchtime and found me packing.

"There's no point in delaying the inevitable."

"What about Ash?"

"Don't talk to me about Ash," I say.

"But I thought you loved him. He gave up Beca for you."

Siân has always spoken her mind, but I can't handle her accusatory tone today.

"Can you please leave?" I raise my voice.

She exits my room without another word.

I WALK TO the cabin via the farm track to wait for Ash. I have no idea why I haven't broken down yet—there's a numbness that has spread the length of my torso, and my limbs feel strange, as though they're not fully connected to the rest of my body. My head feels foggy, hazy. It's like I'm not entirely here.

But somehow, I'm moving forward, putting one foot in front of the other, knowing what needs to be done.

Beca's car and Ash's motorbike are parked up outside the cabin. I realize that they're both inside, and yet I don't feel a thing.

As I'm approaching the door, I hear the sound of Beca's voice coming through the window.

"It's okay. It's okay. Shh. It's going to be okay."

She's sitting with Ash on the sofa and they have their backs to me. Her arms are looped around his shaking upper body, her chin resting on his shoulder. I realize he's sobbing and I feel a jarring motion inside my chest, but the sensation is muted and I'm too dazed to react.

"It's for the best, Ash," Beca says. "You know it deep down. She doesn't want this life. She's told you so many times. You have to listen to her, respect her wishes. You have to let her go."

He lets out a yelp and my foot jerks toward the door just as he turns and buries his face against her neck, his arms coming around her shoulders.

"Shh, it's okay," she coos, kissing his temple. "It's okay, Ash. Aw, baby."

Her voice has grown thick with emotion, and I watch as her own shoulders begin to shake as he sobs against her skin. They're clutching each other tightly and she's cradling his head with her hand, her fingers half buried in his dark gold hair.

I feel anesthetized as I back away.

Suddenly the thought of spending one more minute here, in the Berkeleys' vicinity, is inconceivable.

If I leave now, I could be in Evesham by tonight—the journey will take three and a half hours and I know there was availability at the B and B I've booked.

I call a taxi on my way back to the cottage, as soon as my phone picks up reception.

Siân has returned to the kitchen for the afternoon shift and Bethan, Harri, Evan, and Owain are all still at work. There's noise coming from the workshop—men shouting over the sound of machinery—but no one sees me as I walk round the back of the building, return to the cottage, and take my bags out the front door.

I stand there in the late-afternoon sunshine, listening to the sounds of bees buzzing around the climbing roses, children playing in the walled garden, the low hum of cars coming and going to and from the car park, and I feel empty.

ASH CALLS ME when I'm on the train. I think about not answering, but he'll only call again. And suddenly the hopelessness of us is unbearable.

"Where are you?" His voice sounds raw.

"I've left," I reply dully.

"You've *what*?" he asks with shock.

"I had to go."

"You've *left*?"

I'm staring out the window, looking, not seeing, unable to find the right words.

Because there aren't any.

"What the *fuck*?" He's baffled, wounded, angry.

"It's for the best," I murmur, resorting to Beca's words, seeing as I can't find my own.

"But you—you—" Now he's the one who's speechless. "I can't believe you'd just go," he says, stunned. "That you'd leave me when I need you most."

This comment pierces through the numbness for the briefest, brightest of seconds. And then my head detaches from my heart and delivers the words I need to say to make it stop.

"After what you and your family have put me through? I'm done. It's over. Give Beca a call, I'm sure she'll console you. I never want to see any of you ever again."

I end the call and a trembling begins in my hands and moves to my chest and suddenly I'm shaking so violently that I feel as though my body is about to shut down.

With the greatest will in the world, I harness my emotions and wrestle them under control, tamping them down, down, down, until they're buried deep under six feet of soil.

———

I MOVE THROUGH the week in a daze, buying a cheap car for commuting to and from my new job, hunting out somewhere to live and eventually settling on a tiny apartment in Evesham, about twenty-five minutes from Hidcote. My new boss, Lottie, is pleased to hear that I can start work earlier than expected, but it takes every ounce of strength I have left to put my best foot forward and make a good first impression.

After all these years, I'm finally living on my own, but the solitude is both a blessing and a curse, giving me too much time to think.

When thoughts of Ash surface, I choke them to death so I can get through another day.

But at night, my mind is left unbound and my nightmares are maddening, unhinged, causing me to wake in a cold sweat with a pounding heart.

Eventually the walls holding back the dam of emotions begin to crack, and when they finally break apart in a deafening roar, I go to another place entirely. I have never felt more alone.

I don't hear from Ash, and I don't reach out to him either. But one night, when I've been drinking too much and I'm raw with pain and longing, I look him up online. The headline that greets me chills me to my bones.

The Honorable Ashton Berkeley and
the Honorable Rebecca Brampton Announce Their Engagement

I'm too shocked and breathless to cry. I've only been gone a few weeks.

But it's what I need to accept that I must close the book on our final chapter.

Over the next few months, stone by stone, I build back those walls, wrestle my mind under control, even at night, and begin to make Evesham my home. I find solace within the stunning Arts and Crafts–inspired gardens of Hidcote, and after another quiet Christmas on my own, I decide to take control of my loneliness and make it a choice, rather than something that has happened to me.

Swapping out my smartphone for a cheap Nokia that I'll use only for emergencies, I pledge to living a simpler life. I listen to the radio and read more books. I give up social media and watching the news. I commit to moving onward and upward and embracing the chance I've been given.

Eventually I begin to feel better. I still avoid thinking about Ash and the way I left—I'm not sure I'll ever find peace where he and Berkeley Hall are concerned, but that's a problem for another day, and maybe even another counselor. Whether or not he was coerced into marrying Beca to save the sawmill, cottages, and cabin, or whether he chose to marry his best friend of his own accord, I don't know. And at the end of the day, it really doesn't matter. He's where he needs to be, doing his own thing. And I'm here, doing mine.

PART
THREE

30

'M IN ONE OF THE RED BORDERS, DEADHEADING FIERY
red dahlias—"Bishop of Auckland" and "Grenadier." It's the last
Friday in September and my little robin friend is back again. Yesterday he hung around as I was weeding in Mrs. Winthrop's Garden and taking cuttings of the blue and yellow salvias. The day
before, I saw him when I was hedge-cutting on the Long Walk and
collecting seeds from the blue globe thistles growing in the Old
Garden. And now he's perching on the giant leaf of a red banana
plant, chirping.

Maybe it's not the same bird, but I like to think it is.

I'm smiling as I pick up my basket.

I love working at Hidcote. It's in a hamlet in the North Cots-
wolds, nestled among rolling hills, and it has the most beautiful
Grade I–listed garden, the first garden-only property that the
Trust acquired.

The garden rooms here are formed off a central axis that runs
east to west and north to south, and each has a different character. Near the house, they're smaller and very formal, but as they

expand outward, they morph into more natural areas that blend in with the surrounding countryside.

The property is tiny compared to Berkeley Hall, but I feel so much safer here. It's such a relief being employed by an organization that I respect, trust, and believe in rather than finding myself at the mercy of a single powerful individual. I still can't think about Peter Berkeley without feeling physically sick.

But now my future feels full of possibility. I don't plan on leaving Hidcote anytime soon, but it's exciting to think about the opportunities I might have to work at other properties in the future.

I'm finishing work a bit earlier than usual today as in the morning I'm off on holiday for a week in Southwold. I've already packed and I'm looking forward to a seaside break in Suffolk, even if there's a part of me that will miss the gardens here.

"I'll be back in a week," I tell the little robin. "Will you wait for me?"

I talk to birds now. No madness in my family.

I pop by the office to say goodbye to Lottie and collect my things. She's been reviewing the planting for next year—looking at the balance of texture, height, and color of the foliage and flowers. I've learned so much from her.

Right now, she's sitting at the desk, staring at her laptop screen, catching up on some admin.

"Isn't Berkeley Hall the place you worked at?" she asks casually, glancing over her shoulder at me as I pick up my tote bag.

My chest violently constricts.

"Yes?"

She returns her attention to the screen. "A head gardener position has come up there."

I frown at her. "What are you reading?"

"Work email."

"From the National Trust?"

She nods and I slowly put down my bag.

"Why is the NT featuring gardening positions at Berkeley Hall?" I ask carefully. "It's privately owned."

"No, we acquired it earlier this year," she corrects me.

"What?"

I feel as though the blood has drained from my body as I read over her shoulder.

I can't believe what I'm seeing.

IT'S BEEN JUST over two years since I left Berkeley Hall and it took me a good long while to recover. But this year, thanks to a lot of counseling that I finally stopped shying away from, I've begun to feel like my old self again.

I was traumatized by what happened—the lack of control I'd had over my job, the power Ash's father had wielded over both Ash and me, the falling-out with my colleagues, the way Ash turned to Beca, time and time again. Coupled with the pressure of finding somewhere to live and starting a new job, I felt as though I was cracking up.

I'd thought I was prepared for losing Ash. I wasn't. Looking back now, it's obvious that I had some sort of breakdown.

My counselor has helped me to work through not just what happened at Berkeley Hall, but everything in the years that led up to it. I'm still reeling from what we uncovered in our sessions, but my journey makes more sense now.

A couple of months ago, I wrote my parents a letter. Really, it was my mum I most wanted to say my piece to. I was nervous at the thought of her reading my words, or worse, not reading them, but to my surprise she texted within a couple of days to ask to speak.

I can still remember the timbre of her voice, the unnerving hesitation before "I'm sorry" left her lips.

I know how much it cost her to say those two words, but they lifted a weight. I carry hope now for a future where we might have some sort of relationship.

Thinking of Ash is still so painful, but I haven't ruled out the possibility of one day trying to find closure with him too. Presently, though, the thought of him being married to Beca makes me feel as fragile as cracked glass, so for now I need to leave him in my past.

But with this news of Berkeley Hall's acquisition, I won't sleep until I find out exactly how this happened. Did Peter Berkeley die?

I make it only as far as my little blue Renault ZOE in the car park before I'm typing **Viscount Peter Berkeley** into the search engine of the new iPhone I got a few months ago so I could listen to audiobooks on my commute to work. I'm still on a hiatus from social media after I went onto Instagram one time and couldn't resist checking out Evan's profile. He'd obviously left Berkeley Hall, but I felt so raw at seeing his face and being taken back to that time, I deleted the app.

The results for Viscount Peter Berkeley turn up contact information, a Wikipedia entry, and . . . an obituary:

Viscount (Peter) Berkeley has died, aged sixty-five.

The article waxes lyrical about his important work, his varying interests, and the history of his family, so I skim over the words, feeling ill at the sight of his smug face and steel-gray eyes, until I reach the bottom.

The heir to his viscountcy is his only remaining son, Ashton.

I quickly scroll back up to the top to check the date and I'm shaken to discover that Peter Berkeley died in the middle of January, five months after I'd left Berkeley Hall.

Did Ash try to reach me? Did *anyone*? This was around the time I'd changed my phone, but my number should still have worked. I'm disturbed by the way my stomach has become taut with tension.

I'm trembling as I type **the Honorable Ashton Berkeley** into the search engine before deleting it and typing **Viscount Ashton Berkeley** instead.

Very little comes up about him, but I do find the news of the house sale to the National Trust, as well as the mention of his engagement to Rebecca. There appears to be no coverage of their wedding.

The hope that floods my chest at this scares me. I'm not thinking straight as I open my contacts and curse out loud at the reminder that I only transferred over the details that I wanted at the time.

Back to the internet: I start with Siân, finding her on LinkedIn. I'm surprised to read that she's left Berkeley Hall and now works near Cardiff at Dyffryn Gardens, which is run by the National Trust.

Using the same standard configuration for all NT staff members, I type out an email.

Subject: Hello stranger!
Siân! How are you? I hope you don't mind me emailing you out of the blue—it's been a long time, sorry—but I've only just heard about the acquisition of Berkeley Hall. Do you know anything about it? I'd love to talk to you. If you could give me a call, I'd really appreciate it.

I sign off with my name and number and then start the ignition, turning my attention to driving home.

My phone rings with a number I don't recognize soon after I've arrived back at my apartment.

I've just been reading what I can about Beca. She seems to be living in London and working for a fashion PR company, and her Instagram page shows images of her on holiday in Crete, draped over a hot man with an eagle tattoo on one arm.

The sight of her with someone other than Ash makes my pulse race with frightening speed, but I don't dare hope, not until I know for sure what's going on. I haven't found any more news about Ash.

I answer the phone. "Hello?"

"Ellie!"

"Siân!"

"It's so good to hear from you!"

Some of the tension in my body begins to ease at the sound of her warm voice.

"Thank you for calling me," I say.

"I was so happy to see your name in my inbox. I've thought about emailing you so many times, but I never quite managed it. It all became so weird at the end."

"I know," I agree.

"But enough about the shit old days. How are you?"

"I'm well, thanks. I'm still at Hidcote—I love it. I see you're at Dyffryn?"

"Yeah, can't believe I made the change after so long at Berkeley, but I haven't looked back. Celyn and Catrin tied the knot last summer, I don't know if you know that?"

"I haven't stayed in touch with anyone," I admit.

"I hear from Bethan from time to time. Harri left too, after they split up, but she's seeing Jac now."

"Really?"

"Yeah, I know! I always thought he was such a lad, but they live together at number two."

"You mean at the workers' cottages? They weren't sold?"

"What planet have you been living on? No, I don't know what all that was about, but Lord Berkeley seemed to lose interest in the idea after you left. Or maybe the sale was ticking along in the background, but then he had his stroke and was incapacitated—"

"Peter Berkeley had a stroke?"

"Two, in the end. The second one took him out."

Am I cruel to feel no sympathy?

"What happened to Ash?"

"Well, obviously he inherited because he sold the place, but Lady Berkeley is still at the house. Ash did a deal with the NT so she could carry on living there."

My insides are a writhing tangle of nerves. "I couldn't find anything about his wedding to Beca."

"Wedding?"

"I saw an engagement notice online."

"Fake news! God knows where that came from."

I'm barely able to concentrate on what she's saying. My head is buzzing, my pulse tripping.

Is it possible that Ash is out there somewhere with no ties to anyone or anything?

Hope blooms bright, lighting my insides, and the daisies inside my chest cavity lift their heads and reach for the sun.

"Do you know where Ash is?" I interrupt Siân to ask outright.

"I'm afraid not, but Celyn might. Do you have his number?"

"No. Could I have it? Does he still live at number five?"

"As far as I know, but I made it a point not to ask. Let me find his contact details."

Celyn doesn't answer, but it doesn't matter. I can try again once I'm on the road.

Just before I leave, I open the Airbnb app, find my booking in Southwold, and press the button to cancel, not even flinching at the penalty I'll be paying for the late cancelation.

I dread to think what would have happened if I'd heard this news earlier in the week—I suspect I might well have walked out on the best job I've ever had.

I need to be in Wales right now, looking for answers.

Finding Ash.

I'm terrified.

31

I'T'S AFTER EIGHT WHEN I ARRIVE AT BERKELEY HALL, BUT I'm in time to see the sunset coloring the vast building orange. My chest feels tight at the sight of Ash's family home, the setting for some of the highest and lowest moments of my life. But it is still so beautiful.

Light reflects off the myriad tiny panes of glass in the gatehouse, diamonds of gold that seem to flicker on the aged mottled glass as I drive along the public road adjacent to the family's rarely used private driveway.

Instead of carrying on toward the car park, I pull to a stop by the dirt track that leads to the cottages. There's a wooden gate across the opening that wasn't there when I worked here. It has a sign marked PRIVATE fixed to it.

I'm a little confused. Siân said that Lord Berkeley didn't sell off the cottages or workshops. Did Ash? It doesn't look as though they're NT-owned.

It occurs to me that the public car park might be closed at

this hour, so I take a chance and open the gate, driving through and shutting it again.

I come out past the walled garden to the row of five terraced cottages. They look exactly the same as when I left them, and I'm so sure I'll inhale the fragrant scent of roses as I climb out of the car that I'm a little taken aback to smell barbecued meat instead.

And then I'm smiling, even through my nerves, as I walk around the back of the cottages and see that Friday night's barbecue is in full swing.

I spy Bethan's high brown ponytail just as she jumps up from her chair to go inside, and then she sees me and her mouth drops open.

"Ellie?" she squeals as I step over the lavender border.

She races toward me and, okay, I'm guessing she's drunk and merry, but I couldn't hope for a better reaction.

I open my arms to welcome her.

"What are you doing here?" she asks as the others in the deck chair circle look over to see what's causing the commotion.

I do a quick scan for Celyn, but only recognize Jac and Dylan among the half dozen faces.

"I thought I'd come back and see you all," I reply.

"Oh my God! Are you applying for the head gardener position?"

"What? No!" I exclaim as Jac and Dylan get to their feet to greet me.

Bethan introduces me to the others, all young guys, all workshop crew. She makes a point of telling me who lives where.

"Where are Owain and Gwen?" I ask with a frown.

They'd lived at number one for thirty-odd years.

"They retired recently, but they haven't gone far, only to Chirk."

"What about Celyn and Catrin?"

"Oh, they're up at the ranger's cabin now."

My chest contracts. "Do you know where Ash is?"

She calls over to Jac. "Where does Ash live now?"

Jac shrugs. "Somewhere near Powys, isn't it?"

He looks at Dylan, who nods and shrugs, taking a sip of his beer.

"Do you have an address for him?"

They both shake their heads. "We don't see much of him these days. He's a bit off-grid."

"Do you have a number?"

"No. Celyn might," Dylan replies. "The phone reception's nonexistent up at the cabin, though, so he might not answer."

"Want a drink?" Bethan asks hopefully.

I hate saying no to her, especially as my repeated prioritizing of Ash over our friendship was partly what drove a wedge between us, but I've come here to find answers that I won't get if I'm deep into a bottle of prosecco.

"Another time? I really need to go and see Celyn."

I DRIVE UP to the cabin, hoping that the summer tires on my little electric car will be able to handle the perpetually muddy farm track. I feel as though half a dozen birds have taken up residence in my stomach. If Celyn's not here, my next point of contact is Philippa Berkeley. Will she tell me anything? Will she even answer the door?

The sight of smoke trailing from the chimney is a welcome one.

Catrin and I have to manage a hug around a rather large bump—she's eight months pregnant.

"Can you believe the size of this monster?" she asks as she ushers me inside. "That'll teach me for marrying a giant."

I'm taken aback at the sight of the Lisbon sofa in canary yellow and the peach-iced-tea-brown armchair. I hadn't realized that Ash had placed the order before I left. I bet he regretted it.

"Oh, *helô*!" Celyn says with surprise, coming out of the kitchen, where he seems to be cooking up a storm. He still has a big black beard and he has to duck under the doorframe so he doesn't bang his head.

"Hi. I'm sorry to drop in unannounced, but—"

"You're looking for Ash."

His eyes are kind, knowing. I nod.

"I wish I could tell you how to get in touch with him."

All of the birds in my stomach drop to the ground.

"We only see Ash when Ash wants to be seen. And I'm afraid that isn't often," he says.

"He doesn't have a phone?"

"Not as far as I know. Not that it would do us much good anyway. We still need to put in a landline."

"Like, yesterday," Catrin says, rolling her eyes at me. "Come and sit down." She pats the yellow sofa.

"Do you have any idea where he is?" I ask as I perch.

"He bought a piece of land in Powys, near the border, but I don't have an address. He hasn't invited any of us down there."

"What happened? Who owns this cabin now?" I look around the interior. Ash's books about space have been removed from the bookshelves, but the old brass telescope still sits by the window.

"Ash does. He sold the house and gardens to the National Trust, but retained the workshops, cottages, and land. Wanted to make sure none of it could ever be sold off to developers."

I am feeling *so* many things.

"Why have you come back now?" Catrin asks.

"I just found out about the acquisition. I thought he'd married Beca," I admit.

Celyn frowns and shakes his head. Then he seems to realize something. "Oh. Did you see the newspaper article?"

"I saw something about their engagement online."

"The story was planted by his father, according to Ash, though he never admitted to it. I think he thought that if he wanted it to happen enough, it would. But his plan backfired."

"How?"

"Ash left. Just got on his bike and went to Europe. We didn't see him for months."

Ash left Berkeley Hall only weeks after I did? If he was willing to walk away from his family and all this, why didn't he come to find me?

"He came back after his father died," Catrin reveals.

"Can you tell me anything else?" I ask desperately.

"No, but his mother might be able to."

THE PUBLIC CAR park is closed to visitors and a green barrier is down across the entrance. I notice a National Trust office that wasn't there before, with a new entranceway to the house and gardens. Over the top of a beech hedge is what looks to be the beginnings of a children's adventure playground.

Pride swells inside me. I can't believe Ash did it. It can't have been easy to give five hundred years of his family's heritage. How did he come to make that decision? The regret I feel at not being here to help him face whatever he's been going through makes me feel as though I've stepped into quicksand.

But I have to keep my chin up. I still need answers.

In the end I park on the verge by the walled garden and walk to the hall. The sun set a while ago and the sky is a deep navy blue, but there's enough light to see the house looming above me as I approach, and once I reach the gatehouse, I can see that there is no doorbell.

Suddenly I remember the understated side entrance Ash and I used after his father walked in on us. I feel a wave of nausea at the memory as I walk on past the western bay of the house, my footsteps on the gravel sounding overly loud.

A small security light comes on as I approach the private entrance to the family's living quarters, and I'm relieved to see that there's an intercom with a built-in camera fixed to the wall. But then I remember who I've come to see and my anxieties rise once more.

I press the button and wait, folding my arms across my chest.

"Hello?" A tinny voice comes out of the speaker.

"Hi, I'm here to see Lady Berkeley."

"Who shall I say is calling?"

"Eleanor Knapley."

"Please wait."

What if she refuses to see me? There's every chance she will. I still have Beca as an option, but I'll have to create an Instagram account and the thought of contacting her makes me want to crawl out of my own skin.

I will, though. I'll do anything.

The door opens and a young woman in her early twenties appears, dressed in a black dress with the Berkeley crest embroidered in white on her right breast.

"Come in, please."

Relief cascades over me as I follow her in and up the narrow staircase to the family's private door. She deposits me in the grand living room that Ash once told me was his mother's favorite place to socialize.

"Please wait," the housekeeper says. "Lady Berkeley will be here in a minute."

I don't sit down. I'm too agitated remembering what happened the last time I was here. But then I look toward the windows and try to think of the view, the Berwyn Mountains off in the distance.

"Eleanor Knapley."

At the voice of Philippa Berkeley, I whip round and breathe in sharply.

She looks like a different woman. She's wearing no makeup and she's drawn, gaunt. Her dress is loose-fitting, but I can see how thin her arms are, and when she walks toward me, her hip bones jut against the pale gray fabric.

"Please, take a seat."

She indicates one of her sofas and sits down opposite. We're divided by a low wooden coffee table.

"I didn't think I'd see you again," she says.

She doesn't sound bitter or haughty or angry.

She sounds tired.

"I didn't think you'd see me again either," I reply, adopting a similar tone.

"May I ask what's brought you here?"

"I'm trying to find Ash."

"Oh." She sighs. "I hoped you might be bringing me news of Ashton yourself. The last I heard, he'd gone back to Europe," she adds.

This blow almost fells me. I've psyched myself up and I'm running on adrenaline, but if I've come all this way and he's not even in the UK . . .

PAIGE TOON

"You're not in touch with him?"

"Rarely, and only on his terms. He's still angry at me."

"Why?"

She meets my eyes. "I would have thought that's obvious."

"Because your husband announced a fake engagement?"

She shifts, looking flustered and defensive. "I had nothing to do with that. But Ashton still blames me for not standing up to his father over his threats to sell the land. He got his revenge on me in the end, though." She looks around the room with a distinct air of self-pity.

"I'm sorry for your loss," I find it in my heart to say.

"I'm not," she replies sharply. "But I am sorry in other ways." She meets my eyes and I see a twinge of regret buried there. "He was so sure you were the great love of his life. He was very upset when you left."

"I need to find him."

"If he's not abroad, he'll be at his place in the woods."

"The ranger's cabin?"

"No, no." She shakes her head dismissively. "On the outskirts of Knighton. He went there for the dark skies. I believe there's an observatory somewhere nearby. If he's in Wales, he'll no doubt turn up there at some point. He can never stay away from the stars for long."

IT'S PAST TEN by the time I leave Berkeley Hall, and I'm starting to spiral. Knighton is forty miles south of here, about an hour and ten minutes away, according to my iPhone's GPS, but the address I input is for the Spaceguard Centre—I discovered it when I did a Google search of the area around Knighton.

The most significant natural danger to life on Earth comes from aster-

oids and comets, the information on the website reads. *The Spaceguard Centre is a working observatory, and the main source of information
about near Earth objects in the UK.*

There's a tour in the morning, but I'm going to head there tonight on the off chance that Ash might still be in Wales, watching
the stars.

My car is running low on electricity by the time I roll into
Knighton and I really need to find somewhere to plug in and
charge up, but I can't bear to face another delay. I drive up into the
hills, following signs for the Spaceguard Centre and keeping a
close lookout for a large rounded shape in the darkness. Eventually I come to a wooden gate and pull to a stop, and there, at the
end of a dirt track, is the green dome of an observatory. Out of the
dark, two headlights appear, and now they're coming toward me.
I hurriedly reverse out of the way and exit the car in time to see a
gray-haired man in glasses and a black fleece climb out of his ve-
hicle.

"Excuse me!" I call as he opens the gate. "I'm looking for Ash."

He might not even know who Ash is, but I want to sound like
a friend, and hopefully I'll get a friendly answer.

"I haven't seen him in a couple of days," the man replies.

My heart leaps and soars. Does that mean he's in the country?

"Do you know when he'll next be here? Or where I can find
him tonight?" I ask.

"He comes in sporadically and he lives somewhere over there."
He points down the hill.

"I don't suppose you know where exactly?"

"Only that it's in the woods. Can't be far. When he comes, he
comes on foot."

"Okay, thank you."

He gets back into his car and drives through the gate. I close

318 • PAIGE TOON

it behind him and he calls out a thank you before disappearing down the track.

I stand in the cool night air, looking down into the valley at a dark patch of woodland in the distance. Could Ash be somewhere among those trees? Are we staring up at the same sky, the same moon, at this very moment?

I walk to the edge of the field to try to get a better look, but I don't have a flashlight and all I can see with the light on my phone is a barbed-wire fence.

Climbing back into my car, I take a look at Google Maps and try to work out if there are any roads leading into the woods down in the valley. There aren't, but the map might not show dirt tracks.

Folding my arms over the steering wheel, I rest my forehead against them and release a long, shaky breath. Then I straighten up, download the Instagram app, set up a brand-new profile, and send Beca a DM, hoping it won't get lost in the wilderness of her hidden messages.

I'm trying to locate Ash. Please can you help?

Even if she can, I think my quest to find Ash might have to wait until morning.

32

WELL BEFORE DAWN, I GIVE UP ON THE HOPE OF snatching even one more minute of sleep. My body aches from trying to squeeze my five-foot-nine-inch frame into my tiny car, and it was cold in the night too—I had to unpack half my suitcase in the boot to try to find my hoodie and tracksuit bottoms. The extra layers still weren't enough, so I dragged on a few more.

My car battery is running low, so I didn't dare risk a drive back into town last night. Depending on what I can see when it's light enough, I'm thinking that the best way to find Ash might be to try to follow his footsteps from here. But first I check Instagram to see if Beca has replied. She hasn't. Hardly surprising, considering the hour I tried to contact her and the hour it is now. Chances are it'll go into her hidden requests and she won't even see it.

I'm not expecting to find *literal* footsteps, so when dawn breaks to show several sets of large boot prints trodden into the soft earth right by the barbed-wire fence, hope surges in my stomach.

I quickly take off most of my extra layers so I look less like someone wearing a novelty sumo-wrestler costume and more like the Ellie that Ash might remember, and then I pull on the only pair of trainers I was expecting to use for my now-abandoned holiday in Suffolk.

Ash's footprints—if they *are* Ash's footprints—are quickly swallowed up in the long grass, but the grass has been flattened into a long, straight line that points at the woods in the distance. It's possible that an animal created the track, but it's also possible that Ash did and it's my best hope of finding him, so I set off at a brisk pace, trying to ignore the fact that my trainers are soaked through after only a few meters.

It's downhill all the way, with the occasional very slippery slope. I sincerely hope that I won't have to climb back up here wet and weary and still none the wiser as to Ash's whereabouts.

I reach the woods after about twenty minutes, and apart from scaring some sheep who ran from me bleating in terror, the journey has been uneventful. Birdsong rings out from above and I look up and see birds—hundreds of them—in the treetops. They're so noisy I barely hear a regular, low thudding over their rattles, squawks, and trills.

Pausing for a moment, I try to work out what the noise is—and where it's coming from. I detect the sound of running water too and wonder if there's a stream or a river nearby.

In the lightening sky, I can make out the faintest of tracks at my feet, so I continue onward on high alert, scanning the trees in every direction.

The deeper into the woods I go, the thicker the vegetation becomes. If it weren't for the uplifting birdsong and the sound of tumbling water, I might feel as though the forest was closing in on me.

The cabin I eventually come across is so hidden behind dense foliage that I almost don't see it, but the regular, low thudding has led me here, and now, suddenly, it's stopped.

I want to call out, but what if it's not Ash out here? What if it's another man? A stranger in the woods?

There's a gap in the foliage, so I step carefully through it, wincing at a burgeoning blister on my left heel. When I reach the back of the cabin, I tentatively creep around the perimeter, my heart in my throat at what I might find.

Please, please, please . . .

There's a crunch of footsteps, the sound of rustling followed by another thud, louder this time, and then a knock. As I peek around the edge of the cabin, my stomach cartwheels at the sight of a half-naked, very broad man standing with his back to me, an axe in his hand.

It takes me a second to realize it's Ash.

My heart hangs motionless in my chest for a beat as he brings his muscled arms up and over his head and swings the axe down, slicing it clean through a log that's sitting grain up on a thick tree stump—and then it begins to *thump.*

He throws both pieces of firewood onto a nearby pile—they land with a knock—and then he grabs another log and repeats the process, his back muscles rippling with the motion.

I'm struck frozen, speechless. I always loved his leanly muscled frame, but I can't tear my eyes away from his lumberjack impression. And then I realize that it's not an impression, it's real. I'm very likely standing next to a cabin he built with his bare hands, judging by the clearing dotted with tree stumps up ahead.

He lays his axe down on the stump and stretches his bent arms over his head, flexing his neck. I hear a crack and then another crack as he releases the tension in his joints. A pair of weathered khaki shorts sit low on his hips and his skin is golden brown.

He rakes his hand through his shaggy hair—longer than it was the last time I saw him and closer in length to when we met interrailing—and reaches for a water bottle. As he tilts his head back and drinks, I notice another detail about his changed appearance: he has a thick, dark gold beard. He finishes drinking and puts the bottle down before picking up his axe and reaching for another log from the pile.

"Ash."

His name has come out of my mouth of its own volition.

He freezes, still bent at the waist.

I force myself to step out from behind the cabin, my pulse sprinting.

"Ash," I say again.

And then he slowly straightens up, still with his back to me. He's like a statue carved from marble by an old master.

"It's me. Ellie."

My heart keeps stuttering. I'm so on edge, so full of hope and longing. I've found him. He's here. It's Ash.

I watch as his chest visibly expands and contracts, listen as his lungs release a long, heavy breath, and just as I'm wondering if he might have lost his ability to hear, he turns around.

The man staring back at me is not the man I remember. His expression is hard, cold. There is not an ounce of love in his eyes, not a smidgeon of gentleness.

He's regarding me with hatred.

"What the fuck are you doing here?" he asks.

33

MY HEART TRIPS, STUMBLES, AND FALLS OFF A CLIFF.

"I . . . I . . ."

I actually can't speak.

"How did you find me?" he growls.

"With difficulty," I reply.

"Because I've done my damnedest to ensure people don't."

His muscled torso is glistening with sweat and damp hair falls down across his forehead and cheekbones.

This Ash is *feral*. But still sexy as hell.

"I've been determined."

"Why?" For just a flicker of a second his mask slips, but then he puts it back on again. "You know what? Fuck it. I don't care. You can go back the way you came."

He stalks toward his cabin, goes inside, and slams the door shut.

I don't move an inch. I'm too stunned.

I'm also flushed to the point of needing fireproofing. I didn't know I could be attracted to rude men.

But, of course, I'm only attracted to Ash.

Despite the not-so-warm welcome, I'm suddenly giddy that he's here. I *definitely* saw his hard exterior crack a little. He can give up on the idea of me leaving; I'm going nowhere.

Did he sound different? I don't think his accent was as broadly Welsh, but nor was it posh English—it was some sort of amalgamation of the two. Ash 3:0.

My insides are buzzing as I turn around to study his cabin. It's small and single-story with a pitched roof and clad with wood painted black. On the left are four large picture windows that have been fitted so closely together that they read as one big window, and on the right is a matte-black door.

Turning slightly, I spy what appears to be a shed, also black, and looking a bit farther, I see solar panels in the clearing.

Suddenly the door to the cabin opens and Ash storms out, carrying a towel and fresh clothes.

"You're trespassing on private property," he warns.

"Got any handcuffs?" I ask, holding my wrists out to him.

My adrenaline has spiked again.

His eyes narrow momentarily and then he shakes his head and stalks off, muttering under his breath.

The sound of running water grows louder as I follow him out of the woods onto a circular patch of long grass hugged on one side by a medium-sized river.

He dumps his clothes by the shore on a handmade bench formed from three logs, then bends down and unlaces his boots, peeling off his socks before unbuttoning his shorts.

I glance up at the ominous-looking clouds in the sky—it is definitely not the right weather for a swim—and then the sound of splashing water yanks my attention back to the river.

Ash is in up to his waist, his hair wet and slicked back from his head.

I watch as he starts to scrub at his hair with soap, lathering it up into a foam.

"Coconut wax from the Body Shop will really have its work cut out if you shampoo your hair with soap," I point out, trying to get a reaction, preferably an amused one. "It's very dehydrating," I add, a little delirious.

He turns his back on me, soaping up his body.

The buzz I feel at finding him after the enormous high of discovering that he not only didn't marry Beca buts sold Berkeley Hall to the National Trust outshines every other emotion. The wild-goose chase I've been on has also been full of highs and lows, but, just for the briefest of moments, a sickening apprehension kills off my dizzying lightheadedness and I suddenly feel dark.

Does the Ash I knew exist anymore? What if I've lost him for good?

The thought is so unfathomable that with the greatest will I quash it, steeling myself to break through his shell.

I drop my tote bag to the ground and start to take off my shoes. They were white earlier; now they're a filthy, muddy, sodden mess.

I almost lose my balance as I'm tugging the damp fabric away from my swollen feet, and then I'm carefully treading over the slippery rounded stones on the shore until I'm standing several inches deep in the water. My body has a delayed reaction to the temperature.

"How can you *swim* in this?" I force myself to stay put, hoping the cold will soothe my mushrooming blisters, but Ash ignores me as he sinks fully beneath the water, a trail of wispy foam floating away from the place where I last saw his head.

He reemerges and flicks his hair back, then swims to the bank and climbs out, inch by inch, foot by foot, until—okay, so he's naked.

I look the other way, my cheeks burning. As he dresses, the dark feeling swallows me whole. He's acting as though I don't even exist.

He's on his way again before I remember that I'm barefoot.

"Wait, hang on." I quickly turn around to climb out of the water, but my head begins to spin.

Whoa.

I put my hands out, but there's nothing to hang on to and I suddenly feel queasy, my vision turning red and then blackening. I've fainted once before and I know what it feels like—there's nothing I can do to stop it from happening again.

The shock of the cold jolts me back to full consciousness, but I've fallen to my side into deeper water and it's so disorienting, I panic. I can't keep my head fully out of the flow. I'm gasping, spluttering up liquid ice, trying to find my footing on the rocky riverbed, and then there's a loud splash and two strong hands are lifting me up from behind and dragging me out of the river.

Ash lays me down on the grass.

"Are you hurt?" he asks urgently as he checks me over.

I'm soaking wet from head to toe and shivering uncontrollably. That was so fucking scary, I felt like I was drowning.

"Are you okay?" he demands, placing one hand on my cheek.

Still shaking, I weakly cover his hand with mine as I nod.

He jerks his hand away and stands, backing up two paces before turning and dropping into a crouching position, holding his head in his hands.

I'm still too shocked to speak and my teeth are chattering violently.

"Fuck!" I hear Ash shout at the ground. He bolts upright and turns around to face me again. "Can you stand?" His tone has grown sharp again.

I try to sit. I don't know what's wrong with me—exhaustion, shock, the stress of trying to find him, his unwelcoming reception—whatever it is, I feel weak, as though I have no control over my body.

He bends down and helps me to my feet, but the second he tries to let me go, I wobble and he steadies me again.

Maybe he thinks I'm putting it on to get attention—I'm not.

"I just need to sit awhile," I tell him feebly, but before I can sink back down again, he swings me up into his arms and carries me like a baby back into the woods.

I can't even find the strength to loop my arms around his neck, but he's warm and it helps subdue my shivering.

He takes me straight to his cabin, kicking the door back as he maneuvers us through the narrow opening. It smells of log fires and coffee in here—that's all I'm capable of noticing until I find myself in a small wood-paneled bathroom that still carries the scent of the pine it was crafted from. There's a white enamel toilet and a matching hand basin, plus a towel rail with a dove-gray towel hanging on it, and in one corner an unenclosed shower. Ash places me down just outside it and turns on the tap. Water comes spilling out of the large round showerhead onto his hand.

"It's not that warm, but it's warmer than the river," he mutters after a moment. "Can you manage to get undressed?" He meets my gaze briefly before looking away again.

All the light has gone from his eyes.

Where are you, Ash?

I nod and step forward into the shower, fully clothed. I'm wet anyway.

He's still standing behind me, I can sense him. I place my hand against the wall so I don't faint again.

"I'll get you a towel and some dry clothes," he says roughly.

A moment later, I hear the sound of the door clicking shut.

The water is *a lot* warmer than the river. If it was any warmer, it would probably feel too hot after the cold I've just endured.

With difficulty I take off my wet clothes. Noticing some soap on a shelf, I use it to get myself clean before shutting off the water and cracking open the door to find a towel and a pile of clothes on the floor outside the bathroom.

If it weren't for the Y-front design, I'd think that Ash owned a pair of gray yoga pants, but they're surprisingly not too baggy. I pull the oversized long-sleeved black T-shirt over my head, forgoing my wet bra and knickers. He's given me a pair of thick green socks, so I pull those on too and, leaving my hair wrapped up in the towel, exit the bathroom.

There's another room opposite and through the open door I can see an almost wall-to-wall double bed covered with a dusky-green bedspread. The top of the mattress lines up with the bottom of a big picture window facing the woods, and the whole space is flooded with natural light.

I carry on and come out into a small open-plan kitchen and living space. On my left is a stainless-steel sink sunk into a chunky wooden L-shaped counter, charcoal-gray cupboards, and an electric oven with four hobs, upon one of which sits a kettle. Another, smaller, window looks out onto the same aspect as the bedroom.

On my immediate right is a square table with two bench seats built into the walls perpendicular to each other, then there's a woodstove, already lit with a roaring fire, and farther along, two creamy-yellow leather butterfly chairs. They're designer—Bonet, Kurchan, and Ferrari Hardoy—and they sit on a thick gray rug facing a wooden coffee table and the four large windows that I saw from the outside.

The walls are filled with bookshelves and many of the spines are familiar to me from two years ago.

The place is simple, clean, and uncluttered and so much more stylish than the ranger's cabin.

There are no other rooms and I'm at a bit of a loss as to where Ash is.

I'm still feeling cold and shaky, so I go and kneel on the rug in front of the fire. Over on the hob, the kettle begins to boil. I'm about to get up to turn it off when Ash comes in through the door and kicks off his unlaced boots. He doesn't meet my eyes as he goes to the hob, but he looks harassed. His hair is still damp, as is his green T-shirt, which he was wearing when he dragged me out of the river.

"I'm sorry," I say.

I've sobered up after my earlier high.

He acts as though he hasn't heard.

I watch miserably as he gets two dark blue mugs down from a shelf and opens a small fridge under the counter, bringing out some milk. He throws tea bags into the mugs, pours in water, and then slices some bread.

"Toast?" he asks, still facing away from me.

He can't even bring himself to look at me. I think of his small, steady smile, his warm, fixed eye contact, and an overwhelming sadness bears down on me.

"Yes, please," I reply quietly.

I suspect it won't help if I cry. He wanted me gone the second he saw me.

I haven't had time to process any of this—I've been on auto-pilot since I heard about the acquisition—but suddenly it all feels surreal. Why did I think I could just waltz back into Ash's life after two years of radio silence?

He brings over two blue metal camping mugs with silver rims and drags the coffee table toward me before putting them down. He doesn't want to risk touching me again.

He returns to the kitchen and comes back with buttered toast on two aluminum plates, placing one next to my mug. Then he goes and sits on one of the chairs, facing the windows.

I stare at his broad shoulders as he hunches over, eating his food, drinking his tea, and feel sick to my stomach.

It's an effort to force down the first few mouthfuls of toast, but pretty soon my stomach realizes how famished it is and sends a message to my brain that it does want food. The last time I ate was yesterday lunchtime and I ran out of water on my way to Knighton, so it's no wonder I fainted.

Ash and I drink our tea and polish off both pieces of toast without saying a single word to each other. My earlier bravado has well and truly disappeared, along with my giddiness.

Placing my mug next to the plate, I take my hair out of the towel and run my fingers through it, trying to detangle it without a comb, then I change position and sit with my arms looped around my knees, staring at the fire.

"How did you find me here?" Ash breaks the silence so suddenly I jolt.

I look over at him, but he's still sitting on his chair, hunched over, and from this angle I can see that he's staring down at the mug in his hands.

"I walked from the Spaceguard Centre. Saw your footprints by the fence," I reply.

"How did you know they were my footprints?"

There's an edge to his questions, but he no longer sounds as though he hates me.

"There was a man leaving when I arrived last night. He told me you lived this way, said you usually walked. When I saw the footprints this morning, I figured they might lead me to you." My vision blurs.

"What time did you arrive?" He sounds confused.

"It was getting on for midnight. It was late by the time I left Berkeley Hall."

He looks over his shoulder at me, his brow furrowing as he sees me drag my fingers beneath my eyes. "Why were you there?"

"I was looking for you."

He stares at me, his jaw clenched. "Why now?" he asks after a few seconds.

"I heard about the acquisition yesterday afternoon."

He stares at me for a moment longer. "You didn't hear before?"

I shake my head. "My boss read about a head gardener position on a work email. She mentioned it. I still work at Hidcote."

He's staring at me, not warmly, not the way he used to, but at least he's not treating me as though I don't exist.

And then, suddenly, the eye contact is gone. His body position hasn't changed—he's still hunched over, forearms resting on his knees—but the upright position of his head implies that he's staring out of the windows. What is he thinking?

"So you discovered it yesterday afternoon and drove to Berkeley Hall last night."

"Yes. I spoke to Siân, Bethan, Jac, Dylan, Celyn, Catrin . . ." It's hard to find the energy to say all those names. "And finally, your mother."

He gets up abruptly and turns his chair around, his face a picture of disbelief as he sits down again.

"You went to see my *mother*?"

I nod. "She told me there was an observatory near where you lived in Knighton."

"What else did my mother say?"

"That you were still angry at her." The shadows beneath his cheekbones flicker. "She also said that she was sorry."

"What for?"

I shrug. "I'm not entirely sure, to be honest. All I cared about was what she had to tell me about you. I was terrified that you might have gone back to Europe."

His mouth is still set in a straight line, but I can't help noticing that his eyes are slightly less vacant.

"Is your car still parked up at Spaceguard?" he asks as he puts his empty mug on the coffee table.

I nod. "It's low on battery."

He frowns. "Not sure where around here you'll be able to charge it."

"Do you have electricity?" I glance over at his hob.

"Not enough for a car. Only solar power."

"Is that what heats the shower?"

He shakes his head. "It's wood-fired. If I'd known you were coming, I'd have thrown more logs on."

Hope ignites in my stomach. That sounded friendlier.

"Why did you come?" he asks harshly, his expression hardening.

I shake my head at him, my eyes brightening with tears that I can no longer control. "I only found out yesterday that you didn't marry Beca."

He recoils, shocked.

"I saw the story your father planted. I thought it was real."

"But I *told you* that I wouldn't marry her," he states irately.

"I thought you might to save the workshop, the cottages, the cabin. And it's not as though you didn't love her. You did."

"As a *friend*!" He rises angrily to his feet. "I took you at your word, why didn't you take me at mine?" He's pacing and looking agitated.

"What word?" I ask with confusion as he rakes his hand through his hair with frustration.

"That you never wanted to see me again!" he practically yells.

"I'm hotheaded, Ash! I was a wreck when I said that!"

"No. You meant it," he says menacingly. And then, slowly and deliberately, he spits out the question: "*Why are you here?*"

I should have told him two years ago.

"Because I love you."

And then he stills, his eyes on mine as fresh tears roll down my cheeks.

"No, you don't," he replies quietly, distrustfully.

I nod. "I do."

He sinks slowly back into his chair, his eyes fixed on mine. And then he drops his head into his hands.

"I can't do this again. I can't do it," he murmurs in a low, tormented voice.

"Ash," I plead.

He lifts his head. "You broke my heart," he says seriously. "Again. Except this time it was intentional."

"Do you think I wanted to?" I'm getting heated myself now. "Do you think I wasn't broken too? I was shattered when I left you!"

"Exactly! YOU left ME!" he yells, springing to his feet and pacing again. "I wanted to come with you!"

"How could you? You had responsibilities . . . Ties to the house—"

"I sold the fucking house!" he all but shouts over me. "Revoked my title, spat on five hundred years of history, and I just—" He stops speaking abruptly and looks so tired all of a sudden, so lost. "I just . . . I needed you and you weren't there. And I'm not sure I can get over it."

I want to go to him, but he turns and walks out the door without another word.

34

AFTER TEN MINUTES, WHEN ASH STILL HASN'T RETURNED, I get up and take our plates and mugs to the sink, washing and drying them and looking around for where to put them away.

I remember that he got the mugs down from a shelf and see that there's space for plates too. Are these the only plates and mugs he has? Everything is so organized; he has no more or less than he needs.

I use the facilities in his bathroom and when I come out again he's standing in the middle of his living room, looking freaked out.

"What's wrong?" I ask.

"Nothing." He shakes his head before admitting, "I thought you'd gone."

"Where did *you* go?" I ask.

"Nowhere. I just needed some air."

Suddenly the heavens open. I look up at the ceiling as rain pounds down.

"Oh shit, I need to get my bag," I remember. I left it by the river.

Ash holds out his hand to stop me from passing him and nods at the table.

My bag is sitting there, and in front of the fire I find my trainers. They're a whole lot cleaner than they were before.

"It was the best I could do," he says.

"Thank you." I'm touched. "I hope you're not drying them so you can send me on my way again."

He huffs. I'm not sure you could call it a laugh.

"Can I hang my clothes up somewhere?"

"Use the towel rail in the bathroom. They'll dry soon enough."

There's an edginess behind my rib cage, a ghost of the giddiness that's returning as I go to the bathroom. I'm here, with Ash, and he has no ties to a house or a title that I couldn't bear to burden children with. *And* he's single. I think.

"You don't have a girlfriend, do you?" I ask cautiously as I come out of the bathroom.

He gives me a weird look. "Where do you think I might be hiding one?"

"In your shed? What else have you got in there?"

"My car."

"So you could drive me up to Spaceguard?" I ask, perking up.

He shakes his head. "It's out of commission. Why do you want to go to Spaceguard?"

"I have dry clothes in my suitcase."

"You brought a suitcase?" He looks bemused.

"I'm supposed to be at an Airbnb in Suffolk right now."

He stares at me. "For how long?"

"A week."

"You don't have to be at work for the next week?"

I shake my head.

"Where are you staying instead?"

I shrug. "I haven't managed to book anything yet."

He looks disconcerted as he goes over to the burner and puts another log on the fire, then he walks toward me, his eyes on mine.

My heart thumps harder as he comes to a stop. What's he doing?

He nods past me pointedly.

Oh. I'm in his way. I step to one side, blushing, and he walks into his bedroom.

I feel awkward as I make my way over to his second butterfly chair and sit down, facing the window. The rain is really coming down. Could I hike back up to my car and get some more clothes? The thunder cracks the sky apart and I stop debating. I'm not going anywhere for a while.

Behind me comes the sound of Ash's footsteps.

"Do you still have your bike?" I ask over my shoulder as his soft gray knitted blanket lands on my lap, together with his answer.

"Yes."

"Oh my God, I've missed this blanket!" I gush, dragging it over my lap.

He doesn't react, just sits down in the other chair and nonchalantly leans back, resting his ankle on his other knee and propping up his chin with his palm. He stares broodingly out of the window at the rain.

"Are these your leggings?" I ask curiously, pulling down the blanket to show him my Y-fronted pants.

A tiny glimmer of a smirk lifts the edge of his mouth before it's gone again.

"They're long johns. They're warm. *You* try sleeping out here through a cold winter."

"Okay, thank you, maybe I will," I reply glibly.

"Ellie," he chastises gruffly, his eyes sliding to mine. "You know this isn't going to work."

"Oi. That's my line," I jest, even though my stomach has dropped.

"Haven't you noticed?" He looks around his cabin. "We still don't fit."

"Why don't we fit?"

"You want to be a loner in the woods?" he asks dryly.

"I don't know," I reply with a shrug. "Maybe."

He narrows his eyes at me.

"At least it's just you and me here," I add. "No one else to interfere or fuck it up."

"Just us," he says. "We'd still fuck it up."

"Not necessarily."

He moodily returns his gaze to the view outside the windows.

I do the same, and soon the warmth of the fire coupled with the coziness of his blanket and the sound of the rain makes my chest feel heavy.

I adjust my position, wishing desperately that we could go back in time, before things went south, and that I could lie on his crappy sofa, my head in his lap, while he strokes my hair.

His eyes cut to mine. I stare back at him, my half-closed eyes opening fully.

He jerks his chin in the direction of his bedroom. "Go and have a lie-down."

I do feel very, very sleepy, but I'm reluctant to leave him, so I stay where I am.

A couple of minutes later, my head lolls and I jerk awake to find him watching me. There's a light in his eyes, an amusement. It gives me a fizzy feeling as I snuggle deeper beneath the blanket.

The next thing I know, I'm in his arms again, blanket and all, and he's carrying me into his bedroom. My heart warms and opens as I reach up to touch his beard.

He frowns and lays me down carefully on his bed.

"Just rest awhile," he commands, flipping the other half of the duvet over me and backing up into a standing position.

I'm too tired to argue.

35

WHEN I COME TO, THE RAIN HAS SLOWED TO A GEN-
tle drumming. I roll onto my back and stare up at the
ceiling.

No wonder this room is so light—it has two big skylights. I
lift my head and smile. There, on a high raised platform accessed
by a wooden ladder, is his big white telescope. My heart floods
with love.

Sitting up fully, I notice my suitcase on the floor. What? How
did he get that?

I climb out of bed and open it up, riffling through the contents until I find jeans, a T-shirt, a sweater, and fresh underwear. I
get dressed quickly and come out of the bedroom to the smell of
frying bacon.

"Hey," I say.

Ash is at the hob. He gives me a quick once-over before returning his attention to what he's doing.

"How did you get my suitcase?"

"I found your car key in your bag. Didn't think you'd mind.

Took it to a charging station before driving it back down here. Figured you could do with some clothes that fit."

"That's amazing, thank you. I really appreciate it."

I kind of liked wearing *his* clothes, but there's no doubting I look better in mine.

"It was like a jumble sale in your boot," he gripes.

"I was cold in the middle of the night. I was just dragging on what I could find. Didn't exactly have a chance to repack neatly. Thank you for bringing my car back."

"Should make your getaway easier."

I frown at him. "I'm not going anywhere. Not unless you pick me up and—actually, forget I said that. I don't want to give you any ideas."

He's perfectly capable of picking me up and putting me wherever he wants to. Ash 3:0 is built like a Marvel superhero.

And there it is: his lips curving upward at the corners.

"Aha!" I shout, pointing at his face.

"What?"

"I just saw a smile under that beard!"

"That wasn't a smile, it was a smirk."

"Whatever. I'll take it."

He returns to flipping bacon.

"Are you hungry?" he asks in a low murmur.

"Famished. What can I do?"

"Sit down. There's not really room for two in this kitchen."

"Rubbish." I get up and slip into the space between the right-hand side of his body and the counter, reaching up to the shelf to bring down his two aluminum plates. "It's almost as though you knew I was coming. Two plates. Two mugs. Have you got two sets of cutlery too?"

I've woken up perky.

"I like to have a spare set. That's all I need."

"We might have to nip to the shops and get a couple more sets then."

He sighs. "What are you doing, Ellie?"

I turn around to face him. "I'm making myself at home. Hope that's okay."

"Not really, no."

"Do you want me to leave?" I ask. "Honestly?"

He meets my eyes. "Better now than later."

"How about you give me a week?"

"What's the point in that?"

"You might fall in love with me and ask me to stay forever."

I'm trying to sound bright and flippant, but the shakiness in my voice betrays my anxiety.

His eyes flare wide, and then he puts down his spatula, switches off the hob, and takes a couple of steps toward the windows, dragging his hand over his face.

"I'm sorry," I say somberly as he scratches his jaw. "I don't mean to make light of this. I just want to spend some time with you."

It's exactly what he said to me when I started working at Berkeley Hall.

He turns around and studies me for a moment and I wonder if he's remembering the same thing.

"Lunch is getting cold," he says wearily, returning to the kitchen.

"Shall I slice some bread?"

"There are fresh rolls in that bag." He nods at a white paper bag that wasn't there earlier.

"Have you been shopping?"

"Made the most of your car. Knife's there." He nods at a knife block.

We eat our bacon sandwiches at the table, sitting on the built-in bench seats. I bring my knee up and twist to face him.

"I saw your telescope in the bedroom."

"Bit hard to miss."

"You still love the stars?"

"Always."

"Do you work at the Spaceguard Centre?"

"No, I volunteer and use the observatory occasionally."

"Do you think you'll ever go back and do your master's?"

He lifts his shoulders and looks down at his plate.

His answers are coming much more slowly than my questions. I'm guessing he's out of practice with carrying on a conversation.

Will I ever get the old Ash back? I wonder with a pang. *What if he's a different person now, set in stone?*

WE TAKE THINGS easy that afternoon. I'm acutely aware that I'm in a space that Ash has never had to share, so I don't harass him with questions and in turn he barely speaks to me. We sit in silence and listen to the rain, watching it fall in sheets outside the windows. When I grab a book out of my suitcase, he takes one down from his shelf and we read side by side in the butterfly chairs.

It's nice, peaceful. It's restorative.

"Are you planning on finding somewhere to stay tonight?" he asks when it starts growing dark.

"Will you let me stay here?" I ask tentatively. "I can sleep on . . ." I look around the room. "The floor?"

The corner of his mouth twitches. I stare at him with anticipation, my insides lifting . . . And then he drops his gaze and shakes his head.

My stomach swoops. I'm not sure how many more of these mini-rejections I'm going to be able to bounce back from.

"You can stay," he surprises me by saying.

And I'm up again, soaring toward the treetops.

"Really?" I ask hopefully.

He nods, letting his eyes rest on mine for a beat. "Sleep in the bed, just . . . let's . . . let's just not—"

"Okay." I cut him off before I die of embarrassment.

Ash clears out one of two deep built-in drawers under the end of his bed for me so I can unpack and then he takes my empty bag to deposit in the garage. His tiny home definitely can't accommodate a bulky suitcase.

We call it a night after a light meal, with Ash asking me to get ready first. I don't know if it's a tactic to remove me from his space, but half an hour passes without him even so much as using the bathroom. I'm not tired after my earlier nap, so I switch on a reading lamp fixed to the wall and continue with my book.

Eventually I see him walk past into the bathroom and the surreal feeling comes over me again. I suddenly feel uneasy as I place my book down on the shelf behind the bed and shut off the light.

Have I made a mistake coming here? I'm isolated out in the woods with a man who has changed and moved on. What makes me think I can integrate myself into this new life that he's forged for himself? What if it's impossible?

He's right: I was the one to leave. And he never called. He believed me when I told him that I never wanted to see him again.

I hear the bathroom door open and a moment later Ash comes into the room.

My breathing has grown shallow. I'm facing the wall, but I hear him flip back the cover on his side of the bed, and then I feel the mattress compress as he crawls into place, drawing the duvet over himself.

He looks different. He smells different. Who is this man I'm sharing a bed with? And can I truly still love him if I don't know who he is?

I lie awake long after his own breathing begins to settle.

36

I STIR AROUND DAWN AND SHORTLY AFTERWARD, ASH does too. We lie side by side in bed, both wide awake, neither of us speaking.

Then, without warning, he flings his side of the cover back and slides out of bed, feet first. As he leaves the room, I notice that he's wearing a dark gray T-shirt and black boxer shorts.

He uses the bathroom and heads into the kitchen. I hear him filling the kettle.

Fuck, this is so weird.

I remind myself that I *am* still attracted to him. And I like the way he smells, even if it's different. It's just soap. They're just muscles. It's just hair.

I remember what Ash said to me when I was trying to make sense of his interchangeable accents. I thought he was like two different people and he corrected me: *Not two people. One. This is me, Ellie. You met me. You know me.*

This Ash might act, look, and smell different, but he's still Ash. I've simply got to get to know this new version of him.

I sit up, just as he comes back into the room with two mugs of tea.

"Thank you," I say, accepting one.

He eyes his side of the bed, seeming to hesitate.

"Let me hold that for you," I offer, reaching forward to take his mug.

I'm not sure he felt comfortable coming back to bed.

He lets me take his mug and returns to stretch out beside me, propping up his pillow.

We sit there in silence, sipping our tea.

"If you have a hot shower, why did you swim in the river?" I ask, puzzled.

"I think it's kind of obvious I needed to cool off," he replies gruffly.

I throw him a smile. "Where do you do your washing?"

"Sometimes in the river. Sometimes at a launderette." He glances at me to gauge my reaction.

"It's like we've gone back in time," I reply with amusement.

"This life is not for everyone."

"It's your dream, though, right? To be a hermit in the woods? Off-grid?"

"And your worst nightmare."

"Not at all. What makes you say that?" I ask with a frown.

"Come on," he mutters.

"All I need is a hot tub."

"Ellie, please be serious."

"I am. I've become kind of reclusive myself, you know."

He turns his face toward me, his expression dubious.

"I'm not on social media, I don't watch the news, my best friends are audiobooks—I only recently replaced my Nokia with an iPhone so I could listen to books and music on my drive to work. I like my colleagues, but we hardly ever socialize outside of work."

I'd love to know what's going through his mind, but he averts his gaze and finishes his tea, climbing back out of bed.

"I'll go throw on some logs to heat the shower."

"Shall I make us breakfast?" I call after him.

He pokes his head back around the doorframe. "How about a walk first?"

"Okay."

"ARE THOSE THE only other shoes you have with you?" he asks a few minutes later when I join him.

He's standing just outside the front door, wearing his big black boots.

"I thought I was spending a week in an upmarket seaside town. I wanted to look nice."

He eyes my high-heeled ankle boots circumspectly. "You're going to get them muddy," he warns.

I shrug. "Mud comes off. At least they're not white," I say, thinking ruefully of my trainers, which are still too wet to wear.

My Renault ZOE is parked behind his shed, and now I can see that there's a dirt track beyond it.

"So your car and bike are in the shed. Anything else?"

"Only a few things in boxes that I didn't want to throw out."

"What, like family heirlooms?"

He shakes his head as we walk in the direction of the track.

"I didn't keep anything for myself."

"Nothing for your children?"

"My mother can pass on what she likes. *If* I have kids," he adds tonelessly.

"Do you want them?"

"Maybe. One day. But I couldn't raise a family out here. It's too isolated."

"Nah, it's just a bit too small. You'd have to build an extension."

He throws me a wry look.

"Did you fell all those trees?" I nod toward the clearing we're walking alongside.

He snorts out a laugh. I'm taking it as a solid no.

"How else did you get the wood for the cabin?"

"I own a sawmill, Ellie. How do you think?"

"Oh." My face heats up as I giggle.

I may have just made myself look stupid, but the sound of his amusement gives me such a rush.

A thought occurs to me. "So people *do* know where you are."

"How do you figure that?"

"You must've had the wood delivered . . ."

"No, I brought it myself."

"Ah. Sneaky."

He snorts again.

The air feels so fresh. It smells of rainfall, wet grass, and damp earth. My favorite kinds of smells.

"Man, those birds are loud," I say, looking up at the treetops. "What are they?"

"Starlings." He pauses. "Have you ever seen a murmuration?"

"A what?"

"I'll show you later."

I smile to myself. With every moment we spend together, he's starting to feel a bit more familiar.

———

WE RETURN TO the cabin after a while because my blisters are beginning to burn. Ash says he thinks he has a box of bandages in his garage, so I hover by the door while he looks through a plastic container at the back. His bike is parked up at the front and I feel a pang of longing as I stare at it.

"I'm guessing you got rid of my bike gear."

He glances over at me, mid-rummaging. "Why, you feel like going for a ride?"

I look at him hopefully. "I'd love to."

He shakes his head, finally locating what he's looking for. "I only kept what I needed," he says as he makes his way back out of the garage and hands me a box.

"Thanks."

I sit on a log outside the cabin and pull off my boots and socks, applying bandages to my rubbed-raw skin. I have two blisters now and they really bloody hurt.

"Is there a shoe shop anywhere nearby?" I call through the door.

Ash walks over and leans against the doorframe, a mug of coffee in his hands. He's wearing black jeans and a blue-checked flannel shirt over a white T-shirt.

Yep, definitely still attracted to him.

"Not in Knighton. Why? You thinking of getting some walking shoes?"

"I could do with something to wear for the week." I left my outdoor boots at home, assuming trainers would be fine for beachside strolls.

"You might find some in Kington, but I'm not sure any will be open today." It's Sunday.

"Kington? Knighton? That's confusing."

"Knighton is the nearest town, but Kington is bigger. It's across the English border, about twenty minutes away. You could always order some to come next-day delivery."

"You get mail delivered here?" I ask with surprise.

"No. I have a post office box in Kington. I'll give you the address."

He disappears inside.

I get up and look at the few meters between where I'm standing and the door. Could I make a jump for it? Save me putting my boots back on?

I take one giant stride, trying to land on my tiptoes, and then another, just as he reappears at the door. I crash straight into the hard wall that is his chest.

"What the hell are you doing?" he asks with amusement, steadying me with his hands.

"Trying not to get my feet dirty," I mumble, my face flushing as I meet his eyes.

He looks down. "Yeah, that did not work."

I glance at his right hand—his grip feels different to his left—and see that he's holding an iPhone.

"You have an *iPhone*?"

"Why are you shocked?" he asks, his hands fixing me in place as he takes a step backward, putting distance between us again.

"I thought you were a hermit in the woods."

"Hermits like music too, you know. At least, this one does."

"Does anyone have your number?" I ask as I follow him inside, brushing off my feet and subsequently cringing at the state of my hands.

"I'm on a WhatsApp group with some amateur astronomers."

"No one else?" I ask as I wash my hands at the sink.

"Who are you thinking of?"

"Beca?" I glance over my shoulder at him.

He instantly looks weary. "She's got my post office box address in Kington. We've exchanged birthday and Christmas cards, but we haven't spoken in nearly a year."

"Why not?" I ask nervously.

He sighs and nods at the butterfly chairs.

I notice a second mug of steaming coffee on the table and pick it up with a thanks before taking a seat, facing him.

He releases another long, heavy breath and meets my eyes. "She tried really, really hard to convince me not to sell," he confides.

"But you did anyway."

"Yep."

"And she wasn't happy?"

"No."

"I contacted her on Instagram," I admit.

"Did you?" He's taken aback.

"Late Friday night. I haven't checked to see if she's replied."

"If she has, she wouldn't be able to tell you much—only my postal address. I don't pick up my mail very often."

I stare down at my coffee. "I saw her that day, the day I left. I came up to the cabin to say goodbye and you were in each other's arms on the sofa."

I lift my eyes to see him cocking his head to one side with confusion.

"We weren't doing anything wrong. I was upset. She was comforting me."

"I know. I heard. She told you to let me go, pointed out I didn't want that life and you should respect my decision."

"All of which was true. Doesn't mean I listened to her. I came down to the cottage to try to talk to you. I couldn't believe you'd already gone."

"I couldn't stay," I reply dully.

He shakes his head and looks away, his jaw muscles tense.

"Sometimes I wonder how things might've panned out if you'd come to Berkeley Hall six months earlier," he says.

"Before you and Beca got together?"

"Yeah."

"I probably still would have struggled with your friendship," I admit.

"How?"

"You suspected she had feelings for you when you were interrailing—you told me about it on the beach. I would have been on edge every time you put her first, knowing that she wanted you and that one day you might realize you wanted her too."

"No one ever held a candle up to you," he states gently but firmly.

My heart squeezes at his words, but the vise around it tightens. "You prioritized her over me time and time again."

He frowns. "I was just trying—"

"I know you wanted to repair your friendship. I know it was important to you. I understood it then and I understand it now. But it was *hard* for me, Ash. I felt like I was drowning and you weren't there for me."

Compassion clouds his eyes and he sits forward in his seat, giving me his full attention. I'm leaning back in mine, my legs crossed.

"I'm sorry," he says quietly. "I was going through so much myself."

"And I know you didn't feel like I was there for you either."

"It was a stressful time," he agrees, reaching out to brush the back of his hand tenderly across the side of my knee.

I uncross my legs and place my foot on the corner of his chair.

"I don't know if you remember much about that day, but I'd gone to see my father," he says. "He told me a piece of family history that he had previously kept to himself," he adds ominously.

I'm all ears.

He reclines in his chair again. "My mother always said that our house had driven my grandfather into the ground. I didn't think she meant literally. My father told me that his father committed suicide."

I breathe in sharply.

"He overdosed on tablets and drank himself to death. My father was twelve."

"Shit. I'm so sorry." I move my foot closer to his leg so we're touching.

"There's more." He covers my foot with his hand. "His grandfather got into gambling debt and hanged himself."

"Oh, *Ash*."

"It was all hushed up, of course," he continues with a sigh. "A stroke might've taken my father out in the end, but he wasn't healthy. He drank too much, his blood pressure was sky-high. He told me that he needed to fuck other women to *relax* himself." His tone has grown bitter, but his thumb has started making slow circles across the top of my foot. "Hugo was the same, but he also got his relief by being reckless."

"Was his death definitely an accident?" I ask cautiously.

He nods. "My brother was too narcissistic to take his own life. But the point is, the pressure was too much for them. *All* of them. My father thought that by telling me about my grandfather and

WHAT IF I NEVER GET OVER YOU · 355

great-grandfather, it would stiffen my resolve and I'd get on and do my duty, and he was right. But not in the way he was expecting."

His tone has softened a little. He curves his hand around the back of my ankle and lifts my foot to lay it in his lap. My insides feel jittery, but I rest my head back on my chair, watching him, waiting for him to go on.

"I didn't sell the house because I couldn't handle the pressure, or because I wanted the money. I wasn't weak or desperate like my mother and the society press made out. But even if I knew I could've handled the responsibility myself, why the hell would I want to pass on that legacy to my kids?" He shakes his head and meets my eyes. "Somebody had to say enough was enough."

My heart is so full of love for him right now.

"Wow," I murmur, lifting my head. "That must have taken so much courage."

He maintains our eye contact.

"I wish I'd been there for you through all of that."

"I wish you had been too," he says. "Anyway." His tone changes, grows a little lighter. "You don't have to worry about Beca anymore. Her interest in me went along with my title."

"Bullshit."

He raises an eyebrow at me.

"You don't just fall out of love with someone because they're no longer a viscount," I say. "Especially when that someone is you."

He lets out a small laugh before his expression grows serious and he tries to explain. "Beca grew up in a big house with a title of her own—that was the lifestyle she felt comfortable with. This sort of thing would have scared the shit out of her." He waves his hand at our surroundings. "When I needed to escape to the cabin or out on the bike, she'd get spooked. She felt as though she didn't really

356 · PAIGE TOON

know me. And honestly? She didn't." He sighs. "I'm not saying she doesn't still care about me, but her feelings are a hundred percent platonic. My title, and all the responsibilities that came with it, was the part of me that Beca understood. Without it, I'm no longer someone she could see herself growing old with."

"Does any part of you regret it?"

"What, selling the house?" he asks.

"Yes, and revoking your title."

He shakes his head. "It's a relief to know that the house is in safe hands. The National Trust will look after it and that makes me proud."

I love hearing him talk like this. "What about your title?" I ask. "Why did you do that, by the way? Was it something you had to do when you sold the house?"

"No, it was a choice. I didn't need it, didn't want it."

"What if your kids do?"

"Then I won't have done a very good job at parenting."

I grin at him.

His eyes crinkle.

I lean forward and touch my hand to his bristles. "I can't see your smile unless you show me your teeth."

He throws his head back and laughs. The sound makes me feel so lightheaded.

"I can shave if you like," he offers.

"I'll take you however you come," I reply.

37

BY THE TIME WE GET AROUND TO EATING, BREAKFAST has become brunch. Ash is at the hob, making an omelet; I'm to his right, slicing bread for toast.

I arm-bump him, pretending to jostle for space. He nudges me in return, firmly, so my other side is squished against the counter.

"Argh, Ash!"

The sound of his low chuckle as he drops his arm makes me feel so light, it's as though I've swallowed a helium balloon.

I turn to face him, leaning my back against the counter.

"See? There *is* room for two in this kitchen," I say with a cheeky grin.

His responding smile is not as broad as I was expecting.

And when we're at the table, tucking into our food, Ash's mood takes a downturn. He's finished his meal and is sitting with his elbow on the table, his body turned away from me, staring broodingly across the room.

Eventually I can stand it no longer. I put down my knife and fork and push my plate to one side, reaching over to squeeze his arm. His muscles tighten beneath my palm.

"What's happened?" I ask. "You've retreated back into your shell."

He sighs and shakes his head. Then he gets up and takes our plates to the sink, proceeding to wash them.

"Ash?" I get out from behind the table and walk a few paces toward him.

"Why are we doing this?" He turns around to face me, shaking off his wet hands. "I have nothing to offer you."

"You have *everything* to offer me," I reply fervently.

"My car has been sitting in that shed for six months because I can't afford to replace the turbo. Everything I kept for myself, I spent on this place." He drops his gaze to the floor. "I barely have enough to get by."

I frown. "I don't care what you have, I'm more than capable of looking after myself. But what happened to the rest of the money from the house sale?" I'm confused. It must have amounted to millions.

"I put some in a trust fund for the workers—they'll never have to pay rent on the cottages or the cabin—and I gave a chunk to my mother to see her get by comfortably. The rest I donated to the National Trust."

I stare at him, reeling. He shifts on his feet self-consciously.

My eyes well up and I walk straight into his chest. His body is hard and unmoving as I slip my arms around his waist and rest my cheek on his shoulder. But after only a few seconds, his hands come around my back and his body softens against mine.

"I'm so proud of you," I whisper.

I feel him draw in a long, shaky breath and exhale just as jaggedly.

LATE THAT AFTERNOON, we walk out to the edge of the forest with a blanket, two camping mugs, and a bottle of wine. Ash says that he wants to show me something, and I have no idea what.

Once we're seated on our blanket, he opens the bottle and pours some wine into my mug, followed by his own. We knock them together and take a sip.

I smile up at the sky. "It's beautiful here."

"So peaceful."

"Apart from the birds." They're still making a racket in the trees.

He chuckles. "I find that sound peaceful too."

"You're basically living the life Taran wished he'd had more time for—swimming in rivers, watching the stars, listening to birdsong and the rain."

He nods, looking contemplative.

"Sounds like a pretty nice existence," I say.

"It can get lonely."

I turn to look at him. He briefly meets my eyes before averting his gaze and raising his mug to his mouth.

"Maybe I could help with that," I dare to suggest.

His mug hitches against his bottom lip. He lowers it again and turns to face me, hooking one arm around his knee.

"Just theoretically, how could this work? *Theoretically*," he stresses, motioning between us.

"I could commute—"

"Two hours there and back?"

"You know how far it is to Hidcote from here?"

He nods meaningfully.

"I was going to say that I could commute until I find something closer."

I love my job, but I love Ash more. And I really can picture myself living out here in the woods, surrounded by nature.

To be honest, I could picture myself living with Ash wherever he is. Even in the hustle and bustle of a big city, I'd want to be at his side. I feel as though we've been given another chance. I'm ready for this now in a way that I wasn't before.

"What about the head gardener position at Berkeley Hall?" he asks.

My eyebrows jump up. "You'd *want* me working there?"

"Why not?"

"It wouldn't freak you out?"

"Would it freak *you* out?" he asks.

"I don't know. I mean, maybe not. I did love it there at first, and I'd feel a lot happier being employed by the NT than by your parents."

I wouldn't want to tread on Bethan's toes, but she seemed excited when she thought I was there to apply for the position. And I'd definitely be considered. The NT is very supportive of young gardeners coming up through the ranks, and it might help that I have previous experience of working there.

"But wouldn't it feel weird for you, knowing that I was a gardener there again?"

He thinks about this for a moment. "No. Maybe if I felt more conflicted about selling the place, but I'm always glad to go there and have a beer with the guys."

"You still do that?"

"Every so often."

"What about seeing your mother?"

He shakes his head. "She's still so angry at me."

"She said you were angry at *her*."

"No. I've let it go. But she'll never forgive me for selling the house."

"What did you agree with the acquisition team to enable her to stay there?"

"She's the last generation of Berkeleys who will live at Berkeley Hall. When she has passed, the living quarters will be subsumed into the rest of the house."

"So you haven't actually changed the way she has to live her life."

"No. Doesn't mean she doesn't lay on a massive guilt trip every time I see her, though. She's upset that I've denied my children and their children and their children their rights to the house. She doesn't think I get it now, but she's sure I will once I have a family of my own."

I might be with his mother on this one. It's a concern for me too. Has the enormity of what he's done truly sunk in?

"I'm sure she'll change the record eventually," I try to reassure him. "She really hoped I was bringing news of you."

"Shows how out of touch she is," he says sardonically.

"I'm sure she misses you."

"What's the status of your relationship with *your* parents?" he asks.

"That's a much bigger conversation," I reply. "I *will* fill you in," I promise seriously. "I know I've been reluctant to talk about them in the past, but I've been seeing a counselor and I feel quite positive. I have so much to tell you, but not now."

"Okay," he replies with an accepting nod. And then he grabs my wrist and looks toward the treetops.

Hundreds—no, *thousands*—of starlings are taking flight.

"Is this what you meant by a murmuration?" I ask with amazement.

It's so *noisy*!

He nods. "It's named after the sound all their wings make." He has to raise his voice to be heard.

I watch with wonder as the birds gather like a giant black cloud above our heads, swooping and swirling into spheres, planes, and waves, a moving picture across the clear blue sky.

The noise levels fade the farther away they fly.

"It's one of the most beautiful things I've ever seen. God, Ash, you're so lucky living here."

"I'm not at all convinced you'd love it full-time," he replies with trepidation.

"Give me the week. I already feel pretty sure that this lifestyle would suit me to a T, but after a week maybe you'll trust that I can handle it too. You might even fall a little bit in love with me," I tease with a smile, showing him my finger and thumb hovering a centimeter apart.

"I'm already in love with you, Ellie," he replies gently.

38

GOING TO BED WITH HIM THAT NIGHT FEELS DIFFER-ent. We've both committed to taking things slowly, so there's no chance of us reconnecting physically, but I feel as though I'm lying next to Ash tonight—*my* Ash. He's no longer a stranger to me.

I'm facing his way when he climbs into bed and this time we mirror each other's body positions, our heads on our pillows, staring into each other's eyes. I've noticed he can look at me again now for extended periods of time. It's everything.

He reaches out and lays his hand between us. I follow his lead and do the same. Our palms fit together like they were made for each other.

"Good night," he whispers.

"Good night," I reply with a smile.

We fall asleep like that.

THE NEXT DAY, I receive an email telling me that the boots I or-dered yesterday have been successfully delivered. When I come out

364 • PAIGE TOON

of the bathroom after showering, I find my bike helmet and armored gear laid out on the bed.

"You said you'd given it away!" I exclaim.

Ash pokes his head around the doorframe from the direction of the kitchen. "No, I said I only kept what I needed."

"You needed my bike gear?"

He shrugs. "When you left, I took you at your word. Doesn't mean I didn't also sometimes dream that you'd come back."

I frown. "But if you knew there was a chance of that happening, why didn't you reach out to me yourself? And why were you so hateful toward me when I *did* come on Saturday?"

He sighs and walks toward me. I back up so he can sit down at the end of the bed and then I take a seat next to him.

"By that point, I'd convinced myself that I genuinely never wanted to see you again, fully talked myself into hating you."

Pain lances my heart. "You did seem to detest me."

"It was better than the alternative."

"Which was?"

"Giving up."

HIS WORDS STAY with me all day. They plague me as we ride to Kington to pick up my boots. It's hard to connect to the journey, to enjoy being his passenger again, the rush of air, the freedom. Even as we cross back over the English border into Cymru—the Welsh name for Wales—I can't shed the darkness. There's still so much he doesn't understand.

When he suggests that we go out for dinner, I agree, thinking that this conversation might best be had in a public setting where I can't crumble.

I'm not just worried about my reaction. I'm worried about his.

When we're seated opposite each other at the pub after ordering, I take a ragged breath, bracing myself. "I need to tell you something."

"What is it?" he asks warily, his previously relaxed posture growing tense.

"The counseling I've been doing this year . . . I've been looking back at my childhood, trying to get to grips with the way I was raised, unpicking the past and making sense of things."

His brows draw together and he reaches across the table and takes my hand.

"I know I gave you no chance to talk me out of leaving that day—"

"You didn't have a choice," he interrupts. "My father had fucked you over with your job."

"That's true. But you must have felt so hurt and abandoned. You were going through a lot too."

He swallows, giving me the slightest nod.

"My need to escape was overwhelmingly powerful. I was *terrified* of your father." His grip on my hand tightens. "I used to know someone just like him. They were uncannily similar, from the way they spoke to the way they talked, even down to the way they smiled."

I take a shuddering breath, steeling myself. Ash is beginning to look freaked out, but I try not to let his expression put me off saying what needs to be said.

"When I was thirteen, my parents pulled me out of the normal school I'd attended for two years with Stella and put me in private school. I hated it. I was so out of my comfort zone. I didn't fit in and I missed Stella, but if I expressed any pain, my parents, especially my mum, came down on me like a ton of bricks."

Ash squeezes my hand again, concerned.

"The thing is, they didn't put me into private school for my own benefit," I continue. "They did it for theirs. They used me to make connections with wealthy clients. It's how they built their business." I swallow. "But I was a fish out of water. My mum made me join clubs and audition for plays, even though the thought of being up on a stage in front of strangers made me break out in a cold sweat. I didn't get a part in either the Christmas play or the spring one, but we all went as a family to watch them anyway so that Mum and Dad could mingle with other parents. My mum had done her research before the spring play—she knew that the boy starring in it had a father who was a newspaper editor and a mother who worked at a style magazine. He was also one of the many kids who had not bothered to show up to the excruciating fourteenth-birthday party my parents threw for me. When Mum realized after the play that she had another opportunity to make a connection, she insisted that I go up to congratulate him on his performance." My breathing feels constricted even now. "But when this boy saw me coming, he point-blank ignored me. My parents swooped in with a charm offensive on his mum and dad, and he got told off for not being more polite. It was *mortifying*. But as we were leaving—" I break off to swallow. My throat feels so dry. "His father shook my hand. But he didn't just shake it, he ran his thumb over my wrist and pressed down. It sounds like nothing."

I reach for my drink and take a sip, trying to swallow the bile creeping up my throat. Ash's expression has become very apprehensive.

"But he did it with meaning, and the look in his eyes . . ." I take another shaky breath. "My parents felt like they'd nailed it because he and his wife commissioned them to design a bespoke sofa range. A couple of weeks later, we were invited to go to their house for dinner, to talk about a color palette and inspiration for the range and to see the space where the sofas would sit. I didn't want to go. I had a bad feeling about that father, but when I confided in my mum that he creeped me out, she told me not to be ridiculous. She insisted that I join them. I kept feeling his eyes on me, and he kept asking me questions, trying to come off as polite and interested. My mum in particular lapped it up. I wanted to leave, but the night wore on and on. Their son disappeared upstairs to his room, making it clear I wasn't welcome, so I had to stay at the table with the adults. I don't know if you remember me telling you that when they drink, my mum gets meaner and my dad gets louder?"

Ash nods. He's looking gravely concerned.

"Well, my mum started making belittling comments about my dad and me, and Dad was getting louder and louder, and it was embarrassing. I just wanted a hole in the ground to swallow me up. Eventually I escaped to the toilet, and when I came out, the father was there."

Ash shakes his head slowly. I can almost hear his voice in my head: *No. No. No.*

"He pretended to bump into me, but it wasn't an accident. He pressed me up against the wall outside the bathroom and I could feel him rubbing his erection against my back. I felt frozen in place, completely overpowered. Then he just walked away." It makes me want to throw up, thinking back to that night. "That's all he did. He never touched me again, never so much as looked my way, never asked another question, made me feel like I was nothing. It doesn't sound like much, but, fuck, it messed with my head."

"Jesus fucking Christ," Ash murmurs, his eyes filling. "Did you tell your parents?"

I nod. "I told my mum. She said I was being melodramatic and was so dismissive that I couldn't bear to bring it up again, let alone confide in my dad and have him reject me too. They wanted that man for a client. It didn't fit with their narrative, him clearly being a fucking pedophile, but God, I felt so alone." I shake my head, emotion welling up inside me. "I didn't even tell Stella. Or my grandparents. Maybe I just didn't want to worry them, but it's always been there, needling away at me under my skin."

Ash draws in a sharp breath. It's hard to look him in the eye.

"Your father reminded me of that dad from school. I felt incredibly vulnerable around him, horrifically under his control." I can still hear his silken voice, still see his penetrating steel-gray gaze. "No one could protect me from him." I meet Ash's eyes across the table. "Not even you."

He looks destroyed.

I release his hand and stand up. "I need to go to the bathroom."

"Ellie?" he asks with panic.

"I'm okay. Just give me a sec."

Running my hands under cold water, I press them to my cheeks, staring at my haunted expression in the mirror. When I return to the table, our food has arrived.

Ash stares at me as I sit down. "I'm so sorry," he whispers, distraught.

"It's okay. I've been working through it all with a counselor, but I thought it might help you to understand why I was so desperate to leave the day your father ripped my job out from under my feet. It was too much. I had to get out of there. But the thought of you hating me for leaving like that—"

"I have *never* hated you," Ash states fiercely. "Not really. My walls have been up, but I loved you then and I love you now. Please forgive me for not protecting you from him. I wish I'd been stronger."

I press my hand to his. "I don't blame you. I couldn't be prouder of you for making the decisions you have. I love you so much. I just want to move forward with you now."

"I want the same thing."

IT'S DARK WHEN we arrive back at the cabin, and the starlings are asleep. There's a full moon tonight, so we don't need to turn on our phone lights to see the way, and it's intimate, this darkness, this quiet. I feel as though we're the only two people in the world.

Inside the cabin, Ash starts a fire while I light the candles in the glass lanterns around the house. The walls flicker with a golden glow as we sit down opposite each other, gazing at one another in silence.

"What do you want to do tomorrow?" he asks.

"What do you suggest?"

"I wondered if you might like to go to Raglan Castle. We could take a ride, maybe bring a picnic, see some sights like we used to do."

"I'd love that." I tuck my hair behind my ears, wondering if what I'll say next will ruin the moment, but I can't keep things from him. "Beca replied to my Instagram message. I saw it as we were leaving the pub."

His eyebrows jump up. "What did she say?"

"*Why has it taken you so long?*"

He huffs out a laugh and I smile at him.

"She also gave me your postal address and directed me to the Spaceguard Centre, so I would have found you eventually."

"I'm glad you found me at the *beginning* of your week away."

"I can't believe I've only got a few more days left," I reply. "How would you feel if I handed in my notice tomorrow and applied to Berkeley Hall?"

His eyes glimmer. "Shouldn't you wait until you find out if you've got the job before handing in your notice?"

"I've barely socialized in two years, Ash. I've got plenty in my savings account to get by until I find another position. It's going to be hard enough being away from you while I work out my notice."

He shakes his head at me, slowly, tenderly. "I could come with you back to Evesham if you want?"

My heart leaps. "You'd leave the *woods*? For *me*?"

My voice sounds so breathless and the questions come across as so silly that we both burst out laughing.

He's still grinning when he places his hand over his heart. "Still gets to me." *My sniggle.*

I slide out of my chair and go to him.

"Hey," he says with a low laugh as I try to curl up on his lap. "I don't think these chairs are built for two people."

"Then take me to bed," I demand softly, touching his cheek.

He hesitates. And then he stands up, with me still in his arms, and walks into his bedroom, laying me down. This time he doesn't back up, doesn't retreat, he stays with me.

It's darker in here without the light of the fire, but the lantern behind us has been lit and the windows above our heads are navy blue, not midnight black. I reach up and trace his brows, his lips.

"I love you." My voice is filled with emotion.

He smooths away my hair and lays his hand gently on my throat. "I love you too."

As our lips meet, my blood comes alive. He may look and feel different, but the way he kisses is the same: all-consuming, sure and deep. I bring my legs around him to draw him closer in a move that is familiar to us both. When his body connects with mine, we let out hot moans into each other's mouths, and then he breaks the kiss.

"Do you have anything?" he asks, breathing heavily.

"No." Oh fuck. Not this again.

He returns his lips to mine.

"Are you smiling?" I ask, taken aback as our teeth knock together. "I take it this means you do?"

"No."

"How is this a good thing?" I ask with alarm, pulling back so I can see his happy face flickering in the lantern light.

"I'm just glad you didn't pack condoms to go on your seaside holiday."

"Oh." I laugh. "No. You're the last person I slept with."

"Same," he replies with a grin, adding, "Look at that smile," when I can't stop beaming.

I bury my face in his neck and he squeals.

"Oh my God, you are still so ticklish!" I exclaim, cracking up. "You sound like a little girl."

He silences me by grinding his hips against mine.

"Okay, yes, you're very much a man," I concede breathlessly, reaching down to unbutton his jeans.

"Are we doing this?" he asks.

"Please, I want you. It's not the right time of the month for me to get pregnant."

"And if you do?"

"I'd have to marry you. I can't have an heir out of wedlock."

He laughs against my mouth.

We drag off the rest of our clothing, and then we stop laughing, because as soon as our bare skin connects, I am just sensation and heat.

My scalp tingles as we stare deeply into each other's eyes. And then he sinks into me, and I'm wrapped up in love, wrapped up in hope, wrapped up in Ash.

It's the way I want to live for the rest of my life.

PART
FOUR

39

"I CAN'T SLEEP," ASH WHISPERS INTO THE DARKNESS.

I've been lying on my side, my face turned toward the sky, staring through the huge skylight at the full moon, but now I look toward Ash and see his eyes glinting back at me.

"Are you excited?" I ask, and his teeth catch the moonlight as he smiles and nods. "Me too," I tell him.

He lifts his head from the pillow and leans across to press a kiss to my lips, slipping his hand inside my pajama top to rest on the soft curve of my belly as he does so.

"Don't wake them," I chide, teasing.

"I still haven't felt them kicking," he replies wistfully.

"You will," I promise.

Every time our babies remind me of their presence, he seems to be somewhere else.

I touch my hand to his clean-shaven jaw. He looks like Ashton Berkeley these days, but he still sounds like Ash 3:0. Sometimes his Welsh accent rings through more strongly than his English— and I love it when that happens.

Ash has been busy this year, trying to get this place ready for our arrival. Celyn and Catrin relocated to cottage number one last autumn, soon after their baby, Rhys, was born. They missed the social aspect of living among the other workers, so Ash took over the ranger's cabin again and set about renovating it, keen to bring it in line with the stylish interior of his tiny dark-skies cabin near Knighton.

At first there wasn't any rush to do the work and he enjoyed spending his days up here toiling away while I did the same in the gardens at Berkeley Hall—we'd both return to off-grid living in the evenings. But when, back in January, we found out I was pregnant, we realized our long motorcycle journeys had a limited lifespan.

As of two nights ago, this cabin became our primary home, but we plan to escape to our tiny cabin on weekends and Ash will build an extension there too in a year or so. We want our children to grow up connected to nature, and I dream of them dipping their feet in the river, running through the grass in the rain, and watching the starlings take flight in the autumn. I couldn't imagine a happier childhood for our little ones.

I didn't fall pregnant that first week in Ash's cabin. Our not-quite accident happened two and a half months later; we'd been playing a game of chicken with each other for weeks. We actually got quite competitive, seeing how far we could go before one of us called time—on a few too many occasions neither of us did—but then we did once admit to each other over a game of pool in Lisbon that we were competitive when it came to playing games.

I know that I will always look back on those early days in the woods with fondness—the books we read, the stars we watched, the games of cards we each won and lost.

Ash persuaded me to go wild swimming in the river with him before the weather got too cold, and for weeks we walked out to the edge of the forest to watch the starling murmurations in the sky.

We kept each other warm when winter came, and made the most of his telescope to study the planets on the long clear nights.

When we found out I was pregnant, we both cried tears of joy. To discover at our twelve-week scan that we were expecting twins took a little more getting used to, but now we couldn't be happier or more excited to meet our children.

"Is it even worth trying to get back to sleep?" I ask.

"Probably not. We can sleep later, after we've consummated our nuptials," he replies playfully.

"Twice in one day?" I ask innocently, dipping my fingertips beneath the waistband of his boxers.

"Oh yeah?" he asks in a low voice, catching my hand as he turns toward me.

"Got to kill the time somehow."

He draws me as close as my bump will allow, catching my mouth in the sweetest of kisses.

His hand is on my waist when it happens.

Ash and I both gasp, but his is louder as he moves his hand to my belly to feel our son or daughter slowly change position.

"Oh my God," he murmurs, his eyes wide with wonder. He leans down and presses his lips to my stomach. "Daddy loves you, Taran and Stella," he whispers.

This man has my heart, and it is *bursting* with love.

As soon as we heard that we were expecting a boy and a girl, Ash and I knew instinctively that we'd name our children after our childhood best friends.

Stella was my star, and my daughter will be too. Both our children will have names inspired by nature, because Taran, of course, means "thunder" in Welsh.

Even the excitement of our babies' movements doesn't stop us from wanting to lose ourselves in each other, and now the moon has drifted out of sight of the window and Ash has gone back to sleep. I trace his features with my eyes, luxuriating in this quiet moment and reflecting on my luck, on our happiness. Later this morning I will marry the love of my life.

We want this moment, while it's still just the two of us, to be able to stare into each other's eyes uninterrupted and say our vows.

I reach over and pick up my ring from the bedside table, a circle of perfect daisies, made out of white gold.

Philippa gave this to me when Ash broke the news of our engagement—it belonged to her mother. She said there was no pressure to wear it, but I couldn't love it more.

I've grown surprisingly close to Philippa—or Philly, as she insists I call her now. She's superexcited to become a grandmother, although sometimes she gets caught up in worrying about everything Ash has sacrificed. She still believes that one day he'll come to regret denying his children their heritage, and I have to admit that I'm also disposed to overthinking when it comes to this subject.

Sometimes I'll imagine our daughter sitting out on the hilltop by the cabin and staring down at the grand mansion in the sun with its golden gatehouse that was gifted to her family by a king. I'll imagine her running barefoot in the woods as a young girl and slipping her feet into high heels as a grown woman. Will she ever wish that she could have grown up living a grander life as the daughter of a viscount and viscountess? Will she wish she could have gotten married in the beautiful gardens that she will never be able to call her own?

I'll imagine our son tearing down the corridors of his grandmother's residence, his footsteps reverberating like his name, thunder, against the walls. I'll think of him walking at ten, loping at thirteen. How old will he be when he can no longer enter those corridors and claim any right to them? Will he be at peace with it when his grandmother is no longer there to call on? When he realizes that his father gave up his ancestral home?

Will he think of his own children and what they might have had, and *their* children, and the children who might come after? Will he resent his father for taking all that away from them?

When I find myself spiraling like this, I think of the words Taran said to Ash days before he died. And I remind myself that we *do* swim in rivers, we *do* watch the stars, listen to birdsong and the sound of the rain. We live *good* lives, do *good* things, and appreciate every moment.

So I try not to think about tomorrow. I try not to think about twelve years' time or fifty or a hundred. I try not to think about five hundred years of the past, or five hundred years into the future. I try not to think about what the world will be like in a thousand years, or a million, or five billion, when the earth is ash and dust and life is a long-lost memory near a dying star in the vast universe. I gather my loved ones close, my boy of thunder, my brightest star, my strong, steady Ash, and I cherish today.

SONGS THAT INSPIRED THE WRITING OF *WHAT IF I NEVER GET OVER YOU*

"Lisbon"
Wolf Alice

"Happy Place"
SAINT PHNX

"Smalltown Boy"
Bronski Beat

"Creep"
Radiohead

"Total Eclipse of the Heart"
Bonnie Tyler

"Bitter Sweet Symphony"
The Verve

"When You Were Mine"
Cyndi Lauper

"Common People"
Pulp

"Twice"
Catfish and the Bottlemen

"You're Somebody Else"
Flora Cash

"Constellations"
(piano version)
Jade LeMac

"I Remember Everything"
Zach Bryan (featuring Kacey
Musgraves)

"Let Me Hurt"
Emily Rowed

"Lipstick on the Glass"
Wolf Alice

"**Deep End**"
Holly Humberstone

"**Something in the Orange**"
Zach Bryan

"**Astronomy**"
Conan Gray

"**Starlings**"
Shed Seven

"**Breakdown**"
Norman Vladimir

"**After Rain**"
Dermot Kennedy

ACKNOWLEDGMENTS

THANKS TO *YOU* FOR CHOOSING TO READ *THIS* BOOK—
I know you had lots of other amazing options, so I'm very
grateful. My favorite part of being an author is writing, but my
second favorite part is meeting readers at signings and chatting
with you on social media. Please come and say hi and give me a
follow if you haven't already on TikTok, Instagram, Facebook,
and X @PaigeToonAuthor, and if you sign up to The Hidden Paige
at paigetoon.com, I'll email you with news of signings and extra
content, including an upcoming deleted scene from the epilogue
of *What if I Never Get Over You.* I hope to meet lots of you this year!

When I'm writing, I live in my own little world and experience
so many emotions along with my characters. I feel deeply connected to my story, but the moment I deliver it to my publishers, it
no longer belongs only to me. What could be a painful moment of
letting go is instead an exciting and joyful experience, thanks
mostly to the following people: my superstar editors, Emily Grif-
fin and Tara Singh Carlson, and Venetia Butterfield, who has also
been a huge part of my publishing journey since I first signed with

Penguin Random House. Working with you all to create the best version of my story possible is an absolute dream come true—thank you!

I also feel very lucky that I get to work with this lovely and talented bunch: Claire Simmonds, who is currently covering Emily's maternity leave—I'm so happy to be working with you again!—and the rest of the team at Century/Penguin UK, including Hannah Bailey, Charlotte Bush, Claire Bush, Briana Bywater, Phoenix Curland, Anna Curvis, Emma Grey Gelder, Emily Harvey, Rebecca Ikin, Laurie Ip Fung Chun, Rachel Kennedy, Jess Muscio, Jason Smith, Jade Unwin, Selina Walker, and Caroline Johnson. Ditto the wonderful team at Putnam/Penguin USA, including Ivan Held, Lindsay Sagnette, Brennin Cummings, Molly Donovan, Ashley Hewlett, Aranya Jain, Ashley McClay, Jazmin Miller, Lorie Pagnozzi, Sofie Parker, Shina Patel, Alexis Welby, Claire Winecoff, and Chandra Wohleber.

Thanks also to Monique Corless, Amelia Evans, and the PRH foreign rights team, as well as my publishers from around the world, who bring my stories to new readers. I always translate foreign posts into English so I can read them, so wherever you are in the world, if you're a book reviewer, thank you so much for shouting about my books and please do tag me in any future posts @PaigeToonAuthor!

I really went to town on my acknowledgments for my last book, *Seven Summers*, so I won't list a gazillion names again, but I am so very thankful to my fellow authors for all their support.

Thank you to Lottie Allen, the head gardener at National Trust property Hidcote. I know nothing about gardening and I would have felt completely overwhelmed by the research I would have needed to do if you hadn't been at the end of an email—I'm very grateful for the help you gave in abundance.

Also from the National Trust, thanks to Alison Dalby from the press office and Jo Cooke, Head of Governance, for helping me to understand how acquisitions work.

Thanks also to Claire Thorpe and Katrina Hill from the Royal Horticultural Society.

Thank you to Jay Tate from the Spaceguard Centre in Knighton, Wales. If you're ever in the area, do check out Jay's tours—they're fascinating! Thanks also to Rachel Cavanagh from the British Antarctic Survey for the information on space weather.

Thanks to Jane, Katherine R., Colette, Femke, Katherine S., and Bex for reading this novel early enough to help catch mistakes and typos, and for your general kindness and support.

And thank you to the reader who, at one of my signings, told me a story that later inspired Ellie's texts to Stella—I wish I'd made a note of your name at the time, but if you see this, please do get in touch so I can say thanks properly!

Finally, thanks to my family: my parents, Jen and Vern Schuppan; my parents-in-law, Helga and Ian Toon; my children, Indy and Idha; and especially my husband, Greg, who helps so much behind the scenes with everything from research to plotlines and wider strategy. I may write the books, but you're as much a part of my publishing team as anyone else and I really appreciate you.

"This book wrecked me in the best possible way."
—Carley Fortune

Liv and Finn meet six summers ago working in a bar on the rugged Cornish coastline, their futures full of promise. When a night of passion ends in devastating tragedy, they are bound together inextricably. But Finn's life is in LA with his band, and Liv's is in Cornwall with her family—so they make a promise. Finn will return every year, and if they are single, they will spend the summer together.

This summer Liv crosses paths with Tom—a mysterious new arrival in her hometown. As the wildflowers and heather come into bloom, they find themselves falling for each other. For the first time, Liv can imagine a world where her heart isn't broken every autumn. Now she must make an impossible choice. And when she discovers the shocking reason that Tom has left home, Liv will need to trust her heart even more. . . .

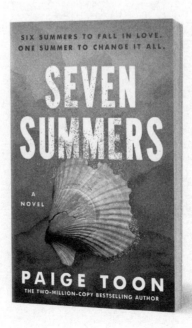

1

THIS SUMMER

PERFUME EMANATES FROM THE PURPLE AND WHITE wildflowers growing on the grassy banks, and the morning air is crisp and still as I set off to Seaglass, the restaurant-cum-bar on the beach where I work. On either side of me, the hills seem to climb higher and higher as the road cuts down through the valley, and in the far distance, the Atlantic Ocean comes into view, a deep blue where it hits the horizon. I follow the curve of the road past whitewashed cottages, the pub, and the Surf Life-Saving Club before Trevaunance Cove appears in full. The tide is halfway in and the curling, clear aquamarine waves are lapping gently against the creamy-white sand.

Summer has landed and Cornwall is radiant. I feel the hope of it in my bones, as though I might finally be ready to step out of the cold shadow that has lingered over me lately.

My new hair is helping too. I've worn my dark hair long ever since I can remember, but yesterday I went to the hairdresser and told her to do whatever she wanted.

Now it swings in waves just shy of my shoulders and I *love* it. I feel like a whole new person, which is exactly what I need.

My thoughts turn to Finn and my mood takes a nosedive, but

then a breeze catches my hair and blows it back off my face, almost as though Mother Nature herself is reminding me that it's time for a fresh start.

As I head up the external staircase to Seaglass, my attention is caught by something unusual down on the beach below. The stream that leads to the ocean has carved myriad tracks out of the sand and someone has dug a number of the rivulets deeper by several inches so that now they look like tree branches forking outward from a trunk.

I pause so I can better study the art etched into the sand. The tree is leafless, which makes me think of winter. I wonder if it's winter in the artist's imagination too. What tools did he or she use to create the work? As a sculptor, I'm interested.

A wave collapses onto the shore and licks over the highest branches. It won't be long before the tide wipes the canvas clean, and I hate the thought of something so beautiful being stolen away before others have had time to appreciate it.

An idea comes to me and I take out my phone and click off a few shots, posting the best of them to Seaglass's Instagram page, along with the caption **How about a little sand art with your brunch?**

I'm an artist, not a wordsmith, so that will have to do.

Checking my email, I see that I have a new message from Tom Thornton:

Hi Liv,
Just dropping you a line on the off chance that the
cottage will be available earlier than 4—I'm already in
Cornwall.
Thanks,
Tom

I sigh. My guests are always trying to secure earlier check-ins. I type back:

Hi Tom,
You're welcome to park your car on the drive, but I haven't had time to clean the place yet, as my last guests have only just left. I'm at work, so I doubt it will be ready before 4.
Cheers,
Liv

I feel guilty when I see that he sent the message two hours ago. The rules are clear on the website, but I'm so grateful that he booked the cottage for the whole month of June after a last-minute cancellation that I'm thinking maybe I should make an exception for him. I was stressed about how I would fill four weeks outside of the school holidays and then this Tom guy swooped in and saved the day.

I decide to duck out at some point this morning and get the place ready early. I owe him that.

The familiar scent of stale beer and sea-damp mustiness washes over me as I enter Seaglass. I'm the first to arrive, but our chefs, bar staff, and waitstaff won't be far behind. We run food out of the kitchen and restaurant upstairs, the lower-ground floor is the cellar, and this middle level is all about the chilled bar vibe. On the left are French doors that open onto a balcony and face straight out to sea. And on the right is a dark-wood-paneled bar that takes up about half the length of the wall, with space for a winding open staircase and the bathrooms at the far end. A little along from the main door, perpendicular to the bar, is a performance stage.

My stomach pinches as I stare at this small raised platform, and for a moment I'm back in the past and Finn is at the mic, his lips cocked in a half smile, his gaze tangled up with mine.

Will he come back this summer?

Enough.

Behind me, the door clangs open, making me jump. I turn around, expecting to see staff, and instead find a stranger: a tall, broad man carrying a large black rucksack, his hands jammed into the pockets of a dark gray hoodie with the hood pulled up over his head.

"Sorry, we're not open yet," I call.

He comes to an abrupt stop, looking thoroughly fed up. "What time do you open?" he asks shortly.

"Ten a.m."

It's only a quarter past nine.

He mutters under his breath as he turns on his heel and walks straight out again, leaving the door wide open.

Rude!

I go over to shut the door and glance down at the beach in time to see another wave crash onto the sand, erasing a whole section of tree. Despite my determination to stay upbeat today, I can't help but feel a little melancholic as I get on with opening up.

THERE'S NO CAR parked on the drive when I return to Beach Cottage, the aptly named house that has been my home since the age of thirteen. A few years ago, I had it converted into two separate apartments, but from the outside it looks like a two-story cottage. It's built of gray stone with a central door and four symmetrical windows with pale blue frames. Peeking above the high wall enclosing the property are the spiky heads of three fat palm trees. Along the front runs a bubbling stream, which is hugged by a waist-high stone wall with so much lush moss and foliage packed into its cracks and crevices that it looks half alive. Two bridges, only a meter and a half long, allow access to the driveway and my front door.

I cross the tiny bridge to the main door and let myself into the hall before unlocking the downstairs apartment. My previous guests didn't have children and Tom is coming on his own, so there's little to do in the bunk room and its adjoining bathroom.

Wandering through to the cozy living room, I look around, smiling at the perfectly plumped sofa cushions. The open-plan kitchen and dining area at the back of the cottage are equally spotless. If only all guests were this thoughtful.

Satisfied that I'll have the place ready in no time, I tap out a quick email to Tom, letting him know that he can let himself in at midday. Hopefully, the news will make him happy.

THE NEXT MORNING, when I get out of bed, I go straight to the window and pull back the curtains. *Still* no car on the drive! Did this Tom guy even check in? I haven't seen or heard him and he didn't reply to my email.

An hour later, all thoughts of my wayward houseguest are forgotten as I stand on the balcony outside Seaglass and stare in stationary silence at the *two* trees now etched into the beach.

The first, on the left, stretches outward from the stream in the same style as yesterday's, a span of leafless, elegant branches.

The second has been sketched directly onto the sand in the center of the beach, a tall, slim, spire-shaped conifer that makes me think of the Italian cypress trees I once saw lining the paths of the Boboli Gardens in Florence.

The memory makes me feel hollow.

I find myself being drawn down to the beach and, up close, I notice how the edges of the cypress feather in a way that looks realistic. I think they might have been created with a rake, but the tree that is emerging from the stream seems to have been scored into the sand with a sharper object. I'd wondered if it had been imagined in winter, but next to the tall, strong cypress, it appears starved of life.

I'm desperate to know what my fellow artist was thinking and feeling when they created these pieces. Did the work come from a place of joy or sadness or from somewhere else entirely?

There's an ache in my chest as I walk the length of the cypress and stand staring out to sea and thinking about Florence, a place that once held so much hope for me.

I'd only just left university when I attended the Florence Academy of Art six years ago and I still felt very much like a student playing at being an artist. But during my four weeks there, as I made cold clay come to life under my hands each day, the future felt wide-open and full of possibilities. I was so excited about the next stage of my life: moving to London and getting a job in a studio.

Then it all came crashing down.

I may not have made it to London or back to Italy as I'd once dreamed, but I *am* a professional sculptor now. It doesn't matter that I'm not sculpting full-time—I like working at Seaglass during the summer months.

I smile at the sea and the ache in my chest recedes.

Returning to the balcony, I take a few pics and post one to Instagram with the words: **More exquisite sand art gracing our shores this morning . . . We'd love to know who our mystery artist is!**

SATURDAYS ARE MY busiest day, what with opening up for brunch, followed by several hours of cleaning and prepping the three other holiday cottages I manage before returning to Seaglass for the evening shift. Before rush hour kicks in, I take a quick look at the post and discover that it's already closing in on fifty likes. I scroll through the comments, hoping for answers but finding none.

One of my oldest friends, Rach, has commented.

Which one's your favorite? she asks.

I reply without thinking: **They move me equally, but in different ways.**

Somehow they both speak of loss, even as one thrives while the other falters.

She must be online because she replies within seconds: **Wonder if there will be more tomorrow...**

I tap out: **If you're reading this, mystery artist, we'd like a whole forest, please!**

At least I remembered to use "we" for that one, instead of "I." It's supposed to sound as though a team of us are bantering away with our customers, when actually it's just my solitary twenty-eight-year-old self.

I'm run off my feet until closing time at midnight, so when my alarm goes off at seven the next morning, I whack the SNOOZE button and almost fall back asleep.

But my desire to catch the sand artist in action supersedes my exhaustion and I pull myself from bed, hoping that I've timed it right. Low tide was a whole hour and two minutes later today, so there's every chance he or she will still be at work.

When I arrive at the cove, however, I'm once again too late, but my reverence smothers any disappointment I might have felt.

A winding pathway has been carved into the beach, wide where it begins at the boat ramp and narrowing to a single wiggly line where it reaches the shore. On either side of the path are pine trees drawn roughly with sharp, serrated edges. In the forefront they're tall and majestic, but they become smaller and more roughly sketched as the path tapers away.

Suddenly I want to be *in* the picture, walking along that magical pathway leading through an enchanted forest and experiencing it firsthand.

On impulse, I head down the boat ramp and step onto the sand. I follow the curving path, smiling as it shrinks away in perfectly sketched perspective. Soon I feel as if I'm the size of a giant and eventually I have to put one foot directly in front of the other, walking the last section with my arms stretched wide as though balancing on a tightrope. Joy rises up inside my chest and I can't contain the feeling, so I spin in a circle, my arms still outstretched.

The smile is still on my face as I make my way back along the winding path toward Seaglass. And then I look up and do a double take. There's a man sitting on a bench up on the cliffs, half hidden behind gorse bushes bursting with brilliant yellow flowers. I stumble and trip, managing to right myself, and when I look up again, he's gone.

ON MONDAY MORNING, I arrive at the beach to find that it's still a blank canvas.

Am I here in time to catch the artist or have they moved to another cove?

In case it's the former, I slip up the stairs to Seaglass, figuring

I'll stay hidden for a while and wait. And that's when I see it: the life-size drawing on the sand that I'd missed.

It's a simple outline of a girl wearing a knee-length summer dress, similar to the one I had on yesterday, with its hem trailing off to one side, caught in an imaginary breeze. Her wavy hair comes almost to her shoulders and her arms are spread wide in a gesture of joy.

A shiver runs down my backbone.

I walk tentatively to the railing and look up at the cliffs.

He's there once again, the man on the bench. Is he the sand artist? Was he watching me yesterday?

I hurry down the external staircase and run up the road, veering left onto the coast path. Gorse scratches my legs with each imprecise step as I climb the narrow, rocky track, my mind racing.

No one who draws that beautifully could possibly be a psychopath, I tell myself.

My compulsion to meet this artist overrides any concern for my own safety.

I know exactly where the bench is because I've sat there many times, watching the tide roll in or surfers riding the waves. My heart is in my mouth as the path opens out onto moorland with far-reaching views, and then I'm looking down at an empty bench, chest heaving, trying to catch my breath.

Where has he gone?

I continue on until the steep path levels out, and *there*! Off in the distance, striding along toward Trevellas Cove, is . . .

A tall, broad man in a dark gray hoodie.

I cast my mind back to Friday morning and the man who was none too pleased when I told him we weren't open yet. I can't

398 • PAIGE TOON

remember his face. He's about to crest the brow of the hill when the word flies out of my mouth of its own volition.

"HEY!"

He looks over his shoulder at me and comes to an abrupt stop, turning around to face me. He's too far away for me to be able to make out any of his facial features, but I wave my hands over my head, requesting that he wait as I step up my pace.

I've only gone a few meters when he turns around again and strides away.

"HEY!" I shout again. "WAIT!"

But either he doesn't hear me or he chooses not to listen because a moment later he's vanished from sight.

I feel an unusual mixture of emotions as I make my way back home. I'm elated and frustrated, excited yet disquieted.

It's the most I've felt in a long time.

I'M STILL FEELING all these things an hour later when I'm heading out for the brunch shift. I'm on my way down the stairs to my private entrance when I hear the main front door of Beach Cottage unlocking.

I'm finally going to meet the mysterious Tom.

I heard him pottering around yesterday afternoon, but he's generally been as quiet as a mouse and he never did park a car on the drive. I've been too distracted to give him much thought.

I open up the door, plastering on my warmest, brightest, most welcoming smile, and come face-to-face with a tall, broad man in a dark gray hoodie.

I breathe in sharply, my eyes widening.

At a guess, he's in his early thirties, and up close he's even taller and broader—he practically fills the small hallway. His hood

SEVEN SUMMERS · 399

has been pushed back to reveal short, dark blond hair, a strong brow, and a square jaw graced with heavy stubble. His eyes are the color of maple syrup held up to a light, shot through with shards of golden brown.

"You," I whisper as his expression transforms from shocked recognition into a look of weary resignation.

"Ah, fuck," he mutters.

2

SIX SUMMERS AGO

MY FEET HIT THE ASPHALT IN TIME WITH THE BASS AS gravity and momentum send me charging down the hill. I'm on a mission: it's Friday night, I'm home at last, and I can't wait to see my friends.

Amy told me that Dan's band is in residence at Seaglass, and from the sounds of it, tonight's set is already under way.

It's amazing to think that I was in Florence this morning and a month before that I was graduating from my BA Hons in Sculpture at the Edinburgh College of Art. For four years, I trod cobbled streets between historic buildings and fell asleep to the hustle and bustle of a busy, vibrant city. And now here I am in St. Agnes, where the only sounds filling the air are coming from the crashing waves, the sea breeze cooling my sun-scorched skin, and the band playing at Seaglass.

Bounding up the external stairs in time to a frenetic drum crescendo, I round the corner to find a packed balcony, cigarette and vape smoke rolling like sea mist across bobbing heads.

A squeal rings out and the crowd parts around Rach as she bulldozes her way toward me. A moment later, we're in each other's arms.

"Where have you been?" she yells right in my face as the song comes to an end and the band launches into another.

"There was traffic coming back from the airport and then my parents wanted me to have a family dinner—I haven't even had time for a shower!"

"You look fine! Come on, you've got catching up to do!"

She yanks me through the nearest set of French doors and makes a beeline for the bar. Her hand is gritty with sand and she looks as though she's come straight from the beach. Knowing Rach, she probably has. Her auburn hair is pulled into a low ponytail and the strands falling loose around her neck are damp from the sea air. I recognize the halter-neck tie of her army-green tankini protruding from her oversize white T-shirt and her trademark baggy board shorts. Classic Rach attire.

I thought I'd gone for casual in jeans and a black top, but my friend takes the description to another level.

"I've never seen it this busy!" I exclaim as she squeezes herself into an impossibly tiny gap at the bar.

"I think Dan invited half of Cornwall. Loads of people from school are here."

I glance toward the band and my eyes alight on Dan Cole, the broad, blond lead guitarist who was the most popular boy in our class at secondary school. Amy used to have a crush on him, but he had a steady girlfriend until his first year at uni, and from what I've heard, he's been sowing his wild oats ever since.

The bassist, Tarek, and the drummer, Chris, were also in our year, as was the band's frontman, Kieran, but he's missing. My eyes snag on the new guy.

His dark, disheveled hair is falling forward into downcast eyes and his slim hips are jutting off to the side as he cradles the mic between his hands, his lips pressed to the metal.

His voice is good: low and deep, but still musical.

"Who's *that*?" I ask.

"You remember Finn, he was in our art class."

"No way."

The Finn we went to school with was really shy. He always wore beanie hats that he'd pull down so low you could barely see his eyes. I don't remember him being part of Dan's crowd back then. I don't remember him being part of anyone's crowd. From what I recall, he was a bit of a loner.

This Finn is next-level hot in black jeans and a loose black chunky-knit jumper that's riddled with holes—very carelessly sexy rock star.

Suddenly he hollers the lyrics *"I'm lonely,"* followed by a beat of silence from the band that ripples through the crowd. His sharp intake of breath can be heard over the microphone as he launches into the next line and the guitar riff repeats.

The hairs on the back of my neck have stood up . . .

© Greg Toon 2022

ABOUT THE AUTHOR

Paige Toon grew up between England, Australia, and the United States and has been writing emotional love stories since 2007. She has published seventeen novels, a three-part spin-off series for young adults, and a collection of short stories. Her books have sold over two million copies worldwide. She lives in Cambridgeshire, England, with her husband and their two children.

Visit Paige Toon Online

paigetoon.com

 @PaigeToonAuthor

 @PaigeToonAuthor

 @PaigeToonAuthor

 @PaigeToonAuthor

PAIGE TOON

**"Nobody writes angst and
joy and hope like Paige Toon."**
—Christina Lauren, author of *The Unhoneymooners*

**"Paige Toon is the queen
of heartrending love stories."**
—Sophie Cousens, author of *Just Haven't Met You Yet*

"Toon's writing is emotional and riveting."
—Jill Santopolo, author of *The Light We Lost*

For a complete list of titles and to sign up for
our newsletter, scan the QR code.

or visit
prh.com/paigetoon